Return of the Romans
Fascism comes to America

By Gene Skellig

Edited by R. Williams

Guest Editor: Ted Clarke

Cover by Jack Tzekov

DISCLAIMER

This is a work of fiction. The characters and events portrayed in this book are fictitious. Any resemblance to real world events or persons living or dead is purely coincidental or used fictitiously. There is content of a sexual nature and depictions of violence which may not be suitable for young readers. The exploration of contentious philosophical issues including climate change, religion, political philosophy, and human rights may be provocative for some readers. The author has made every attempt to ensure that while the reader may be exposed to concepts which may contradict the reader's beliefs, the reader's values and biases should not be insulted. Rather, the author hopes to engage the reader in meaningful contemplation of these deeply personal and meaningful topics.

ISBN: 0-9878645-2-1
ISBN-13: 978-0-9878645-2-9
e-Book: 978-0-9878645-3-6

DEDICATION

This book is dedicated to the 1994 group of students, along with Langara professors "Bruce" and "Don", who I had the great pleasure of studying under during the Art History & Philosophy European Field School. Starting in Rome and ending in London, this was a "Grand Tour" experience. Impressions made then, and years of reflection afterword, have led me to the conclusion that such an exposure is absolutely essential in order to adequately grasp how the world has come to be as we find it today.

Special thanks to our bearded benefactor of Guinness, Ted P, may he rest in peace. And yes, Million, the Judas Trees in Ostia do smell like cake!

Future releases:

Return of the Romans Vol II – Battle for America
Return of the Romans Vol III – The New Worlds
Return of the Romans Vol IV – Perilous Contact
Return of the Romans Vol V – Return to Capricornus

NATALICIVM

21 APRIL 2767 AVC (2014 A.D.)

In small tribute to all that the Romans have contributed to western civilization, *Return of the Romans* was published on this auspicious day, just in time to celebrate the festival of Parilia and the birthday of Rome – 21 April. This year, that is also Easter Monday.

While we gather in Rome to march from Circus Maximus to the Flavian Amphitheatre, we can hear the footfalls of leather sandals as Romans of the past, and Romaphiles of the present, fill the city with the familiar sound of Romans on the march. When the parade is over, and we return to our farms and homes to tend to our families, our herds, and our enterprises, we carry the same burdens and responsibilities as the Romans of antiquity. And yet, with all of the advancements in knowledge, science and technology, in the world as it is in our time, we are wilfully oblivious to the dangers that lie ahead. *Enjoy the party.*

ACKNOWLEDGEMENTS

This book could not have been completed without the research assistance provided by a large number of people. In no specific order, I would like to acknowledge and thank members of an international on-line community of Romaphiles that includes Roman military enthusiasts, battle re-enactors, Latin scholars, historians, students of Classical Studies and others who graciously and patiently contributed suggestions, corrections and encouragement as this challenging project progressed over the past two years.

Enormous gratitude and appreciation go to my wife and our four-ring-circus of children, who provide inspiration and support for my efforts to improve as an author. Much sympathy and gratitude for my editor, Rand, for his effort to elevate the quality of this project. A special note of thanks to my "anvil chorus" of beta readers: Jonathan Ruano (PhD History), R.J. Sutherland (MA Classical Studies), Ira, Catherine, Mark-Anthony, Vaughn, Terry, Alex, Josee 'Mama-Jo' Lachaine (and her wolf pack: Draven, Ethan, Patrick, Logan and Jamie) — all of whom read the manuscript at various stages and provided feedback on areas that needed more work, cutting, or other improvements.

Despite the contributions made by these and other supporters, there will no doubt be some errors.

If you find glaring errors please take a moment to send an email to support@fleacircusbooks.com or using the "contact the publisher": www.returnoftheromans.com, www.ROTSPQR.com and, if reasonably possible, the error will be corrected in a subsequent edition of the novel. Accordingly, the publisher bears sole responsibility for any linguistic or historical inaccuracies and is entirely responsible for the content of this novel.

CONTENTS

FABVLA { STORY }

PREFACE

Return of the Romans will introduce you to a variety of Latin terms, Roman names, Roman history, Roman military terminology and Celtic mythology.

Much of this terminology is explained contextually during the story; however you may want to open up a web browser and search additional details to enhance your reading pleasure. While this is by no means a scholarly work, and a great deal of artistic license has been taken, many historical figures, facts and events intersect with the story. For those with an interest in classical studies, creative anachronism, Latin, Roman or Celtic history – my apologies in advance for what you may see as errors. Please remember, this is a work of fiction, and enjoy the adventure.

Have you ever gone away from some place only to return there several years later and notice how much has changed? Well that is one aspect of this novel that you may enjoy experiencing. You may come to the conclusion that two thousand years really is not such a long time in the grand scheme of things.

Before going on to read *Return of the Romans*, take a moment to put away the modern distractions of your life. Imagine a time when all that a man possessed could be carried on his back, when life was simple, contingent on those with power, and very short. Imagine a time when the world was full of the unknown....

PERSONAE POTISSIMVS - Key Characters

ROMANI - The Romans

Tribune **Marcus** Horatius **Avitus**, COH VIII / LEG II
Immune Lucius **Antoninus Commodus**, COH VIII / LEG II
Centurion Aulus Villius **Tappulus**, Praefectus Castrorum
Legatus Quintus Julius **Agricola**, Son of G. Agricolos
Tribunus Laticlavius **Kaeso** Petillius **Cerialis**
Vibius Quintus **Metellus**, Rhetorician, mentor of Tacitus
Marcus **Fabius Quintilianus filius**, Philosopher
Centurion Spurius **Sallustius Crispus**, Primus Pilus
Tribune Gratianus, Governor of Planeta Metallorum,
Legatus LEG XXVII
Emperor Domitian (81 - 96 A.D.), Third of Flavian line
Consul Sabinus, Co-consul with Domitian in 82 A.D.

The Celtis of Hibernia (Éire)

High **King Findmal** mac Cassan
Queen **Laelie** mac Cassan
Maura mac Cassan (sister to king F.m.C.)
Queen **Achall** Noichrathach / Lady Achal
Avita **Neasa** - wife of Marcus Avitus
Niamh Noichrathach (daughter of Achal)
Daffid Og Briogan - Merchant, advisor
Allanon   - Druid

Contemporary Americans

Eduardo Cuervo and twin brother **Nestor Cuervo**
Ruth Daley, PhD candidate, Celtic Studies
President Russell Carnegie **Ross**

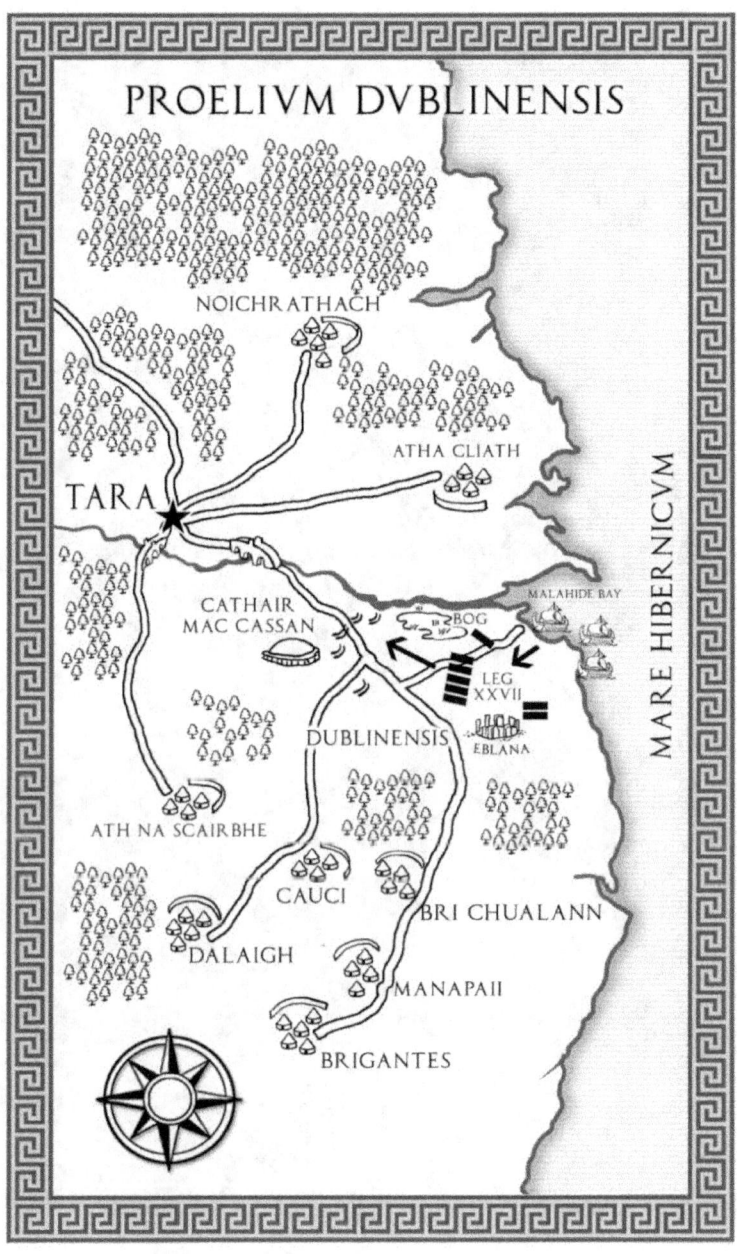

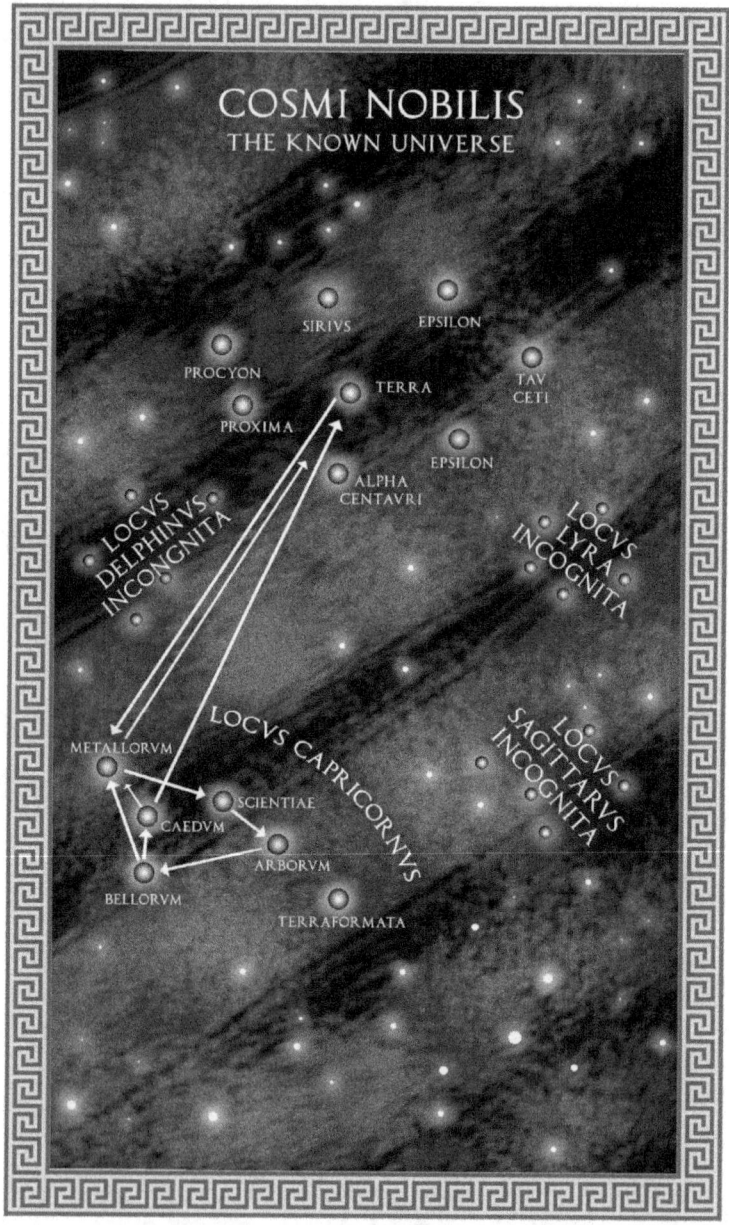

GENS SIPHONAPTERIST
{ MONSTER FLEA }

GENS OCTOPODA

GENS DUPLI-TRI

Gene Skellig

PART ONE

I

ADVENTOR EX ROMA
{ Roman Visitor }

Lugo, Spain, year AD 1975 *(2728 AUC)*

Despite the longing in his ancient bones for the young woman he would not see for another forty years, Marcus Avitus tried to enjoy the voyage across the Atlantic. It was not a cruise, and he did not have a passport, or any other documentation for that matter. After spending three years in Spain, all he had was the small bag of silver and gold coins that Kaeso Petillius Cerialis had given him, some very basic English skills to go with his unusually accented Spanish, and a clear sense of purpose.

The deck of the aging Greek cargo ship, *ANE Zakynthos III*, felt as solid as concrete under his feet while slicing through the gentle one-meter swells. As he stood beside the ship's railing, looking out over the unusually calm waters of the North Atlantic, he thought back to a different time and place, and a much smaller wooden vessel. He thought of the crossing of *Oceanus Hibernicus*, the Irish Sea, by the men of *Legio II Augusta*, the Second Legion, along with elements of *Legio XX Valeria Victrix*, the Twentieth Legion. The men were assembled together to form *Legio XXVII Hibernicus Victrix Domitianus*. Marcus recalled vividly the battle that had taken place soon after landing in *Éire*, and the astonishing sequence of events that began on that fateful day.

Thinking about Ireland, still called *Hibernia* in Marcus' mind, his thoughts turned to Princess Neasa, his none-too-gentle Hibernian wife. From Neasa's perspective, Marcus knew, they had only been separated for a matter of a few weeks, but for Marcus Horatius Avitus, Tribune and commander of *COHORT VIII, LEGIO II AVGVSTA,* it had already been five years since their parting.

1

After landing in Spain with his fellow Roman, Lucius Antoninus Commodus, Marcus had fought the urge to move aggressively. So much was at stake and the risks were simply astronomical. Besides, there was plenty of time.

Marcus and Antoninus had decided to make their landfall in Spain, a place they had known as *Hispania* so many centuries in the past, before moving on with their individual tasks. Both men were familiar with the lay of the land. Marcus himself was born and raised in Lugo, in the northwest of Spain. Antoninus had spent some time at the garrison outside of Lugo, on the way to his assignment with Legio II Augusta at the castra at Isca Silurium, near present day Newport, in south Wales.

That had been nineteen centuries earlier. So much had changed since: the terrain in which Lugo was situated was the same, but the foliage was less lush, the soil more arid; the roads were wonderful, smooth and well organized. Unusual self-powered auto-carriages that had frightened the two men at first, until they came to accept that the beasts were made by men and controlled by whoever was holding onto the hand-wheel. Their heads spun at the noise and chaos all around them.

But what had changed the most was the people. They were enormous! Most of the adult men they passed on the street were at least five to ten *digiti*, fingers, taller than Marcus and Antoninus, many as much as a *pes*, foot, taller! The next major difference were how strangely they dressed, how little they interacted with each other and how hurried and stressed they seemed to be.

Their first attempts to communicate in Spanish had been dismal failures, with the local merchants looking at them as if they were crazy when they had asked where they could find a "money-changer." After being treated like they were stupid, the two men had decided to get as far away from Lugo as they could, so as not to reveal their true identity and origin. Most likely, rather than to believe them, people would have considered them to be crazy.

They eventually found an isolated and sparsely populated village, Cervantes, where they befriended an old man who they had overheard muttering in Latin. After striking up a conversation with the reclusive old codger, they learned that he was eager to have some company, and that he had once been a Catholic monk.

At first Marcus and Antoninus were shocked to meet an openly Christian person, what with Christianity banned, along with Druidism, in Hispania in their time.

Sensing that the two travelers wanted a place to stay, he invited them to stay with him at his small, dilapidated apple orchard, in exchange for a contribution of labor. He was glad to have someone to talk to after years of living alone. For their part, the men were happy to barter their work in exchange for room and board, and not to have to use money, as the two Roman soldiers did not yet fully grasp the nuances of modern-day commerce.

The old man communicated with the men in Latin, and helped them modernize their Spanish so that it could be understood by Spanish speakers of the twentieth century. Although curious and somewhat suspicious about their backgrounds, he never pried into their personal lives. Soon his initial doubts gave way to trust as he got to know the men, putting them to work reviving his neglected orchard. He found the men to be skilled with hand tools, and possessing a formidable work ethic.

Marcus Avitus and Antoninus Commodus soon learned from the old man that a new system was being used to mark years, and that the current year was called "1975" and no reference was even made to the current ruler of the Roman Empire. So much had changed since what the old man called the "1st Century" – their time. When they later learned that Rome had fallen some fifteen hundred years before, they were as surprised as they had been when they had learned that man could fly.

Having discovered that they were now the only Romans remaining on earth, they were that much more careful not to reveal their identities, or their mission.

Marcus Avitus and Antoninus Commodus soon took to calling themselves simply "Marcus" and "Tony", and were careful to speak to each other only in contemporary Spanish.

After three months, when they were more confident in their language skills, they began returning to the provincial capital,

Lugo, where they eventually exchanged a few gold coins for a fistful of paper money.

They were astonished at the quantity and quality of goods the seemingly worthless paper money could buy, and thought that the money changer had made an error. Of course, the coin dealer had actually paid them far less than the actual worth of the gold *aureus* and silver *denarius* coins, which he recognized as being from the period just prior to Emperor Nero. The dealer offered twelve thousand pesetas in exchange for the four aurei and sixteen denarii the men offered for sale.

When he had excitedly asked where the men had found the coins, and if they had any more to sell, Marcus saw the crazed look of greed in the man's eyes. He told the dealer that the coins were the last of his father's coin collection, and that he would not have sold them if he were not in such dire need of the currency used in Spain "these days."

Rubbing his thumb over the elephant minted on the face of one of the denarius, the dealer suspected that Marcus was lying. However, as the valuable coins were untraceable and easily sold for four times what he had paid, he left it at that and counted himself lucky.

While living at the old man's farm in Cervantes, Marcus and Tony used their money very carefully. To repay the kindness of the old man, and for the learning experience involved, they had gone into town to buy nails, wire and hoses which were needed for repairs to the small orchard. They took great pride in bringing the orchard back to life. It was a relatively simple task of labor, and one which they understood, in sharp contrast to the headaches they encountered with each new piece of information they tried to digest about the many ways in which the world, and mankind, had changed.

These purchases also gave them the opportunity to browse through the hardware store, where they discovered countless amazing inventions which they had never seen before. Most of the time they had no idea of the purpose of the strange gadgets, but they learned quickly.

After the old man realized how little the men knew about the world of the nineteen-seventies, he came to the conclusion that the men were from some strange Italian monastery, perhaps of the Franciscan Order, where the men had been isolated from the modern world and where they had spoken an archaic form of Latin.

The old man was surprised to learn that the men knew nothing about plumbing, electricity, or anything modern. The way the men spoke about 'auto-motive carriages' made him think that they were from some place where they still used horses and carts. When they expressed curiosity about a piece of machinery or a tool they found on his farm, what it was used for or how it functioned, the old man always was happy to provide an explanation.

The way that the men expressed delight in learning how a toilet worked, and the 'amazing' pressurized water system used in the orchard, gave the old man an idea. One day he accompanied Marcus and Tony to the regional library in Lugo, where he helped them to register for their very own library cards.

Marcus and Tony spent the next six months devouring books they borrowed from the library, which they read and discussed back home at the farm in Cervantes.

After a year with the old man, the men had come to understand how much the world had changed since the First Century AD, when they had served in Britannia, and the Twentieth Century they found themselves transplanted into.

But when the old man had taken ill and members of his extended family began coming around more frequently, Marcus and Tony became uncomfortable.

It was the way the old man's family looked at them, like adversaries, that made them feel unwelcome. Tony suggested that the old man's family were like vultures, waiting for him to die, and that they saw Marcus and Tony as threats to their inheritance.

So Marcus and Tony bid the old man farewell, thanked him for his kindness over the past year, and left him to the clutches of his family.

Knowing that the two young men would now be adrift in a world that they clearly did not belong to, the old man had insisted that they take with them one of the kittens that his cat had recently had.

As much as the men knew that it would be something of a burden, Antoninus reached out to accept the little grey kitten. He had been the one who sat up with the mother cat to comfort her while she had her litter, and had named each and every one of the kittens. All perfectly grey, the remaining kittens of the rare breed of Russian Blue, would easily find homes.

With Archimedes, the little *canutus catulus*, grey kitten, to keep them company, Marcus and Antoninus then spent the next six months living in a rooming house in Lugo. Compared to Cervantes, the noise and bustle of the larger city was intimidating, and Tony and Marcus frequently returned to the small town for short visits. They felt a sense of attachment to the smaller community.

The provincial capital city, Lugo had a population of close to 100,000 people. For Marcus, who had seen the city when it was being converted from Roman military camp into a proper, fortified Roman town, the changes were drastic. The Lugo he recalled had less than 10,000 residents, including the garrison of soldiers, and a collection of craftsmen, artisans, whores and farmers who had made their way to Lugo to earn money working on the bridge that the Romans were building over the river Minho.

Marcus was glad to see that the bridge had been completed, and that the wall his fellow soldiers had built had been enlarged and reinforced in the years since. As Marcus recalled, in the 1st Century, the original wall had been less than two meters high and had only a few towers. At some point in the 2nd and 3rd Centuries, it had been expanded to fully enclose Lugo, and had been built up to a height of almost fifteen meters. That Rome had continued to be strong for a few centuries after their time had been reassuring to the two men, who still had difficulty accepting that Rome had come to an end. *At least for now,* Marcus corrected himself.

Once established in the rooming house, they hired an English tutor they had found through a bulletin-board at the local community center. The English teacher believed that the men were from a distant part of Spain, and was pleased to find that they had a solid foundation in Latin which helped with their study of the English language.

He was particularly impressed with their work ethic, which was refreshing after the lazy, half-hearted effort of his other students.

After almost a year of focused effort with the tutor and consuming as much of the main library as they could, Marcus and Tony decided that it was time to go their separate ways, to focus on their assigned missions, until they would be reunited when their missions were complete.

That would not be for decades.

With over forty more years to wait before the legion would arrive, Marcus and Tony, young men in their mid-twenties, each sought employment so that they would not deplete their limited supply of gold and silver.

Of course, the two men had quite different missions, with Tony focusing on technology while Marcus had been assigned to study social and political structures.

It was not surprising that Legatus Agricola had chosen the two men, given that they both hailed from the Second Legion, which had endowed the men with the mental capacity to better absorb information than their friends from the Twentieth. The men of the Second were far better equipped to adapt to the changes in society and technology than the rugged warriors of the Twentieth.

The Second Legion, unique to all active legions of the Roman Empire in the 1st Century, had been raised by Emperor Vespasian out of Roman naval marines. Originally part of the *Fleet of Ravenna*, which had been created by Gaius Julius Caesar himself, the fleet had been used with great effect and attained immortal glory under the command of Imperator Caesar Augustus, Gaius Octavius, and

Admiral Marcus Vipsanius Agrippa in defeating Mark Antony in the final war of the Roman Republic at the battle of Actium – ultimately leading to the suicides of Mark Antony and then Cleopatra, and to the Roman domination of the Mediterranean. This ended the turmoil of the civil war, and led to the restoration of at least the outward appearance of a free Republic – with some powers returned to the Roman Senate and magistrates. It ushered in a lengthy period of peace and stability across the Roman Empire, the *Pax Romana*.

With Rome in control of the Mediterranean, and the land battles in Germania and Britannia requiring additional resources, Vespasian was free to use the maritime soldiers of Legio II to strengthen his forces in Germania. This resulted in great victories in Germania Inferior, most notably in putting down the Batavian Rebellion. Vespasian then went to Rome and became emperor, while command of Legio II was passed to Quintus Petillius Cerialis, who was ordered to take the Second to Britannia to assist Legatus Agricola and the Legio XX in fighting the Celts of *Caledonia*, Scotland.

By the time Marcus was with the Second, in Hispania and then in Britannia under *Legatus Legionus* Cerialis, the Second Legion was a land army. But it still retained the character and traditions from the time when the it was tied to naval warfare.

The men of the Second understood geography in terms of celestial navigation, and they preferred to move their supplies by ship and barge whenever possible. They also counted a disproportionate number of craftsmen amongst their ranks, who knew shipbuilding, carpentry, engineering and other skills which many other legions were not as adept at.

The naval pedigree and engineering competency of the Second had been instrumental in the ultimate success of the composite legion, Legio XXVII *Hibernicus Dominitius*, in overcoming their unexpected new adversary after *Proelium Dublinensis*, the Battle of Dublinensis.

The battle had been fought at a place the Hibernians called 'Dubh Linn', the 'black pool,' near present day Dublin. This event had put Marcus and Tony on the path that had taken them to

Spain of the 1970's. So it is not surprising that, at least in the case of Marcus Avitus, finding employment as a crewman aboard a merchant ship was a fitting way to see the world and to catch up on almost two thousand years of change, while keeping a low profile.

And so it was on this last crossing of the Atlantic after two years as a merchant marine, on a ship bound for New York City, that Marcus looked to the darkening sky and watched for the constellation Pyxis to rise low in the sky to the south-east.

Marcus had first learned of constellation Pyxis, the mariner's compass, as a smaller part of a much larger constellation, *Argo Navis*. As a boy in Hispania, in splendid darkness in the hills outside of Lugo, he could make out all four parts of Argo Navis: the keel, the stern, the compass, and the sail.

He would stare at the stars for hours and imagine all of the adventures of Jason and the Argonauts, the mythological hero who was represented in the stars of the Agro Navis constellation.

Planeta Metallorum and the other planetae he had seen on his own odyssey in the cosmos were in the completely opposite direction. But Marcus always sought out Pyxis first, as it was easiest to find. Then he would draw an imaginary line from Pyxis, to himself, and then extend it in the opposite direction, low on the horizon, and cast his mind towards *Locus Capricornus*. That was where his heart lay, along with his wife, his child and all of his comrades. This connection to his boyhood, to his distant past, to the present, and to his longed-for future made the constellations Argo Navis and Capricornus that much more important as his personal compass, his north and his south poles.

That Argo Navis had been abandoned by history and was no longer officially recognized as a constellation was a poignant reminder that his comrades and their exploits in Hibernia had also been stricken from the historical record, in this case by Emperor Domitian, as if it had never happened.

The past is gone, but the future is ours, Marcus thought, as he stared longingly toward Locus Capricornus.

Gene Skellig

II

HIBERNIA INSVLA IVERNORVM
{ Ireland, Celtic Island }

Laelie's unwanted marriage to King Findmal mac Cassan had made her wealthy, and this had pleased her father to no end. Her popularity among the other clanns had helped her engineer Findmal's election at Tara to be High King of the Dubh Lin region. That had increased her own influence, and given her the opportunity to travel and build relationships with other clanns. This brought her a great deal of satisfaction, even if none was found in King Findmal's bedchambers – Laelie simply did not love the old man. *Perhaps in his glory days, but not now. He is simply too old*, she thought.

Today, Queen Laelie was particularly dissatisfied. She and all of the female warriors under her command were being held back from the coming battle with the Romans.

What bothered her most was that best young students would not have a chance to demonstrate the fighting arts they had learned under her tutelage.

Women from nearby Clann Dalaigh and some of the other clanns were being allowed to fight along with their men, and yet the High King had ordered that none of the women from Clann mac Cassan were permitted to fight.

True, she had been given command of the defensive forces, to protect the *Cathair* mac Cassan fortress, and the surrounding village, from any Roman incursion. Laelie and her female warriors were given high praise as the last line of defense, but that rang hollow to her. Laelie knew in her heart that the Romans could be defeated, just as her Celtic kin had done so many times in Caledonia and Britannia.

The only reason she could think of for her husband keeping all of Clann mac Cassan's women in a defensive role was that he had lost confidence. *He thinks we are going to lose the battle.*

Laelie knew who to blame for her husband's lack of confidence. It was that meddling druid, Allanon, who sowed the seeds of defeatism. Allanon was a great advocate of peace and trade with the Romans. Laelie suspected that he had personal aspirations about the trappings of wealth and influence with the Roman nobility, and this made her doubt Allanon's loyalties.

The interfering Druid had been going from roundhouse to roundhouse every night since the Romans began to arrive at Malahide Bay eight days before. The invaders had immediately begun to lay out a large military camp on the Dubh Linn lowlands. The token negotiations between King Findmal's emissary and the Roman advance party had quickly broken down, followed without pause by the full deployment of the Roman main force over the last several days.

Reports from King Findmal's spies established that the Roman force was an unusual composite legion, commanded by a young noble. From the way that foolish girls who strayed too close to the Roman camp were treated, and the casual way the Roman sentries murdered any men who came too close, it was clear that confrontation was inevitable. The Romans were not here to negotiate. They were here to conquer all of Éire.

Laelie's students told her how Allanon had told a story about the great Roman general, the dictator Gaius Julius Caesar, and how a few lifetimes ago he had given the last army of Celts in Gallia one opportunity to abandon their fortress and surrender, or they would all be killed – to the very last of the women and children. According to Allanon, the Gallic king had let his pride corrupt his judgment, and he had not surrendered. He had squandered the chance to save his people, as allowing them to become Roman slaves would have been far better than for their people to be exterminated. Caesar built a fortress wall all the way around the Gallic fortress, and starved them for over a year. When the Gallic king finally asked to let the women and children out, Caesar had refused. After a desperate attempt to fight their way out, all of tribe, down to the smallest child, was cut to pieces. The women were brutally raped and mutilated before their children's eyes.

The Romans were destined, Allanon had told anyone who would listen, to defeat the nine clanns who had joined King Findmall's small army. Their attempt to block the Roman advance to the sacred hills of Tara, where the High Kings of Éire are elected, was futile. Once in control of Tara, the Romans would enslave all of Éire. Only those who did not oppose the Romans – those who willingly served their new masters – would be rewarded.

It had taken Laelie's best efforts to dispel the lies of the impossible exploits of the Romans and their legendary Julius Caesar, and to counteract the poisonous influence of the Druid Allanon. Thankfully, her husband had promised to restrain the Druid, and to 'find some better use of the man's lying tongue'.

Laelie's best students knew how little regard their queen had for Allanon. So his treachery had only inspired a battle lust. Queen Laelie was proud of her young cousin, Neasa, and even the elderly noble woman, Queen Achal, wife of King Fedlem Noichrathach from the north, for scoffing at Allanon's mischief. The women were steadfast, even eager, to prove Allanon wrong about the invincibility of the Romans. They decided that the best way to do so was to castrate as many Romans as they could, and shove the testicles into the priest's face.

But for these brave Clann mac Cassan women to be ordered to rear-guard duty while the women of the other clanns, especially the bitches from Clann Cauci, was an insult to all Clann mac Cassan women. *Not bitches*, Laelie chided herself. *They were my enemies in the last war we had with Cauci, but that was settled at Ath-na-scairbhe, the town of the difficult river crossing, and now they are here with us to fight a common enemy. I must soften my heart to these noble women, we can always fight again after we destroy the Romans*, Laelie concluded to herself.

Following the advice of the well-travelled trader, Daffid Og Briogan, a trusted advisor to King Findmal, Laelie planned how best to achieve her ambition. It would take all day to put her king into, in her opinion, the 'right state of thinking'. Queen Laelie knew that she might have only this one last opportunity to change his mind.

That morning, Laelie took particular care to brush her long hair, wash herself well, and dress in a pretty slip that she knew Findmal liked. Then she stayed close to him, without interfering, as he greeted visiting nobles from the arriving clanns. She played the role of the quiet, supportive woman, helping her king be an effective leader of men. But it was all part of her larger strategy, to seduce Findmal into underestimating her, into seeing her as merely a support for himself as leader, rather than as a leader in her own right.

At the end of the day, as Findmal and Laelie retired to their bedchambers, Laelie helped Findmal to undress. Her soft touch on his naked body began to have the desired effect.

She waited until he had settled naked in bed next to her before she began, so that he would be less inclined to abruptly end the conversation and leave her, as was his way when she pressed him too hard.

"*Rí túaithe*," Laelie began, using the ancient honorific to show her respect. "I have been giving a lot of thought to how I will deploy the women for the defense of our cathair, and the village. I think I will need more than the two hundred women you have given me," she began.

"There is no prospect of that, woman," he replied, as he stroked her naked leg, under the deer-hide bedcover, "We need every warrior for the battle."

"So which battle plan did you decide upon? Drawing the Romans up to the ridgeline above Dubh Linn and hitting their left flank from the southern forest at Eblana? – or plunging through their center to try to decapitate their commander?" she asked, genuinely interested in the strategic plan.

"Oh, that was a difficult decision. We spent hours going over Daffid Og Briogan's reports. Did you know that the Romans have sent almost an entire legion? They seem to all have arrived now, as their ships are no longer going back and forth to their bases in Britannia. All of their ships are tied up in Malahide Bay now. They even have a number of horses, for their general's personal guard, their officers, and nobles. Perhaps not a full *turma*, squadron of thirty cavalry, but a very capable reserve force nonetheless."

"So what is the number now? Are there more than thirty groups of tens of eights?" she asked, struggling with the complex numbers, but imagining thirty groups, each with ten pairs of hands, each finger representing a *contubernium*, "tent group", of eight soldiers each – the basic fighting group of a Roman cohort.

Laelie and other nobles of Éire had a basic grasp of Latin due to their frequent interactions with Roman provisioners and traders during peace-time, but the Irish did not understand written Latin, nor mathematics. They also had no direct experience of doing battle against large Roman military formations. When they had fought the Romans in the past, it was always fast-moving raids along the west coast of Britannia Major, and always at a time and place of their choosing. They had never fought Romans on the island of Éire, but they always knew that the day would come when the Romans would punish them for their persistent harassing attacks in Britannia.

High King Findmal and the other kings of the nine principal clanns of Tara had agreed to come together to fight the Romans when the time came. But they knew little about the Roman military's principles of organization, command structure, and other details. To some of them, when their advisors attempted to explain the structure of a standard Roman legion, it all seemed extraordinarily complex and ridiculous. However, with conflict now an imminent reality, understanding the Romans now was of critical importance, and more so with each passing night as the Roman encampment swelled to a size that seemed impossible to comprehend. *How can so many men, with so much metal and other wealth, come to be in one place at one time?*

Daffid Og Briogan, a trader of jewelry and metal implements, was the most widely-travelled of King Findmal's advisors. He knew more about the Romans than anyone else, and hoped that his knowledge could help save his people from annihilation. He spent countless hours providing instruction to the king on the

Romans and their language. He used small pebbles to represent soldiers, grouping them into the various units which a Roman legion was based upon, to illustrate their tactics and movements.

Laelie, who listened in whenever she could, was still somewhat confused regarding the details of how the Roman military operated. It seemed to her that there were far too many titles. She also had difficulty appreciating the importance of how Roman soldiers were trained to fight as a unit rather than fight according to their individual talents. She could not believe the stories that Roman soldiers were absolutely silent in the hours leading up to the commencement of battle. Thinking about it, she decided that it would be unnerving to see a massive formation of Romans lined up in perfect order and in absolute silence.

She did not yet have a sufficient understanding of what it would be like to fight against an entire Roman legion, so she turned her focus to reducing it down to smaller components. Queen Laelie was fairly certain that she understood the idea of a *contubernium*, the smallest grouping, which was eight soldiers who typically shared a tent. So whenever she looked at the growing Roman camp down at the Dubh Linn lowland, she saw each of the brown tents as representing eight men who lived and fought together, and that helped her appreciate the daunting task that she and her husband were up against, in preparing to fight such a powerful enemy.

To explain the number of soldiers that they were to face, Daffid Og laid out pine cones on a table, one for each finger on his hand. He then had King mac Cassan, Laelie and others understand that each pine cone counted for an eight man contubernia. The Celts, not having any form of mathematics other than counting fingers and groupings of very small numbers, had no concept of multiplication. But they could grasp the notion that if there is a pine cone for each finger on a man's two hands, and that each tent group had eight men, then one of these groupings, each of ten fingers representing a tent-goup, would be a *centuria*. This single unit, a century, was clearly a great many fighting men – about as many warriors as a medium-sized clann could muster. This was a number of men that they could understand.

It seemed important for Daffid Og to make people understand that this grouping, a *century* of men, was commanded by a *centurion*, and that his uniform and headdress would be different than the legionaries in the century.

Killing a centurion, Laelie understood, *brings great honor.*

The next size formation, a *cohort*, was roughly equivalent to King Findmal's own fighting force. Comprised of six eighty-man centuries, and visibly illustrated by Daffid Og holding up six fingers now representing a century each, Laelie and others could understand that a cohort was a very large grouping, with 480 men.

Laelie soon grew comfortable with the concept of '100' being ten groupings of ten fingers. She soon began to look at things in terms of hundred-counts, when comparing the size of clanns arriving to join forces with the mac Cassan warriors. She even understood that the Latin word 'century' meant 100, *but a century in a legion was two handfuls short of a hundred-count,* she reflected, even though she was not yet able to count to eighty in Latin.

Also paying close attention, King Findmal was the first to understand that the grouping of six centuries, almost five hundred-counts, constitutes a full cohort, and that these could in turn be combined on an even larger scale.

"These cohorts: if each of my fingers is a cohort, and I have two hands full of cohorts, so ten cohorts" he held up his ten fingers. "This many cohorts, that is a legion?" Findmal asked.

"Yes, my King. And there will be a flag, with LEGIO XX" or "LEGIO II", as I have seen at the Roman encampment.

"And each of these cohorts will have a red flag, with these strange symbols, so we know who they are?" Laelie asked, keeping up with the discussion.

"Yes, my Queen. The Romans need to use these flags and other symbols on long poles, so that their men can find their leaders, and put themselves in the right place."

"Why don't they just speak to each other, and tell each other where to stand?" she asked.

"Because when you have so many men, animals, blowing horns, and other sources of noise in such close proximity, it is too difficult to hear each other. Using these flags as a way to communicate or to organize the soldiers makes it easy for them to assemble into these turtle-shaped formations, they call *testudo*, and other groupings directed by the officers," Daffid Og replied.

"And those cohorts you told us about will have flags too. Flags with "COH" on them?" King Findmal asked, tracing the Roman letters on a table with the charcoal at the end of a burnt stick from the fireplace.

Findmal was eager to comprehend the Roman military formations because he had heard how effective they were. He was impressed with Daffid Og's explanation of how, in some of their formations, Roman legionaries took turns at the front line, fought intensely for a few moments, and then retired to the rear of the formation to rest. On the other side, such as in battles with his Celtic cousins in *Caledonia* and *Britannia*, the men at the front fought until they tired and were killed, or until they killed every Roman in front of them. Because of this lack of cooperation many Celtic warriors had to wait a few rows back from the fighting, until those at the front were worn down, exhausted, and ultimately killed before the fresh men could begin to fight at all.

Understandably, in this type of battle, it was typically the Romans who won the day. As their formations ground through the tired lines of Celtic warriors, the Romans seemed capable of fighting all day long if necessary.

I have to find a way to allow our warriors to take turns fighting, like the Romans do, but that would be difficult to organize. The men would have to all understand what each other was doing, when it was time to replace each other, and where to go when not fighting at the front line, King Findmal reflected, with a new respect for the power of how disciplined and organized the Romans were, and why they spent so much time *disciplina*, drilling in their units.

And then King Findmal suddenly asked. "Daffid Og, a moment ago you said that you have seen the flags of two different legions. Does that mean that there two full-sized Legions here? It cannot possibly be that many men."

Daffid Og thought about it for a moment. "You are right, my King. Very wise. I will go and look some more, but clearly there are men here from two different legions. I think that Legio XX is their main force, maybe five cohorts, each with six centuries. There are perhaps three cohorts from Legio II. So there are eight cohorts," he held up his hands, showing eight fingers, and then wiggling the two bent fingers. "A full legion is made up of *ten cohorts*, so the force we are facing is a little bit less than a full legion," Daffid Og concluded.

"Is that normal for the Romans? It is like what we have assembled here, with warriors from nine different clans?"

"No, my King, it is not. Romans normally fight as one coherent unit, under one name, and always under the golden eagle banner of their emperor in Rome, Emperor Domitian."

"So if we try to capture these cohort flags, and kill the leaders, these *centurions* and other commanders – those *tribunes* you told us about, who are dressed differently than the *legionaries* – that can make it more difficult for them to stay organized?" he asked.

"Yes, my King, that is something we should try to do."

"And if we capture this golden eagle, it will hurt their great king in Rome, this King Domitian?"

"Yes, it would be a great annoyance to him."

"I would like to annoy him, and make him take notice of us."

"My King. Emperor Domitian is far more powerful than you. He commands as many Legions as you have fingers and toes. You, even with the warriors of the nine great clanns of Tara assembled, control less than half of one legion. And hey have *metal*; each and every one of their legionaries has a sword, a Roman short-sword."

"Roman warriors are themselves wealthy men?"

"No, my King, it is the Emperor who is wealthy. He is so wealthy that he can equip his army so that each man has a *gladius* short sword, and other weapons. True, his soldiers must repay him for their own personal armor and weapons, but they are well paid, professional soldiers. Not conscripts. And when they have served Rome for twenty five years, they are given pensions – paid money for the rest of their lives. That is part of why they are so good at warfare.

"And the territories he controls, his empire, it would make all of your lands – from the hills of *Tara* to the crossing at *Ath-na-scairbhe* – no more than a pimple on a man's body. We are that insignificant to Emperor Domitian."

After a pause, when King Findmal digested the insult, he smiled.

"And yet he wants to burst this pimple. Why?"

"Because when we Hibernians, as they call us in Latin, raid his trading posts in Britannia, we distract Twentieth Legion in Britannia from their wars against our Caledonian cousins. They want us quelled, all of Hibernia no longer a source of distraction for his legion at Deva, so they can conquer all of Britannia.

"So if we can defeat his army, we help our cousins? And if we can take his golden eagle and shove it up the Roman general's arse, then we would be defeating the greatest of all kings, this Emperor Domitian?" King Findmal concluded rhetorically.

Relieved that the insult had not been taken personally, Daffid Og also smiled, "My King, when you do that, you will be immortalized in song and story for all time."

"Can we make some imitations of these flags, with "COH" and other markings, to show our people?" asked Queen Laelie interjected, inspired by King Findmal's ambitious goals.

"Yes, that is a good idea. And we can also get an artisan to draw one of these turtle formations, so we can explain how they rest their soldiers during a battle. Maybe some of our captains can find ways to pull these formations apart." Daffid Og said, and then added: "That gives me an idea. If we…." Daffid Og went on to discuss a strategy with King Findmal which could interfere with the Roman way of fighting even more than focusing on killing their officers, their centurions and tribunes.

Days later, in bed with her king, Laelie continued to work on him, trying to get him to give her a free hand and permitting her women warriors to fight in the coming battle.

Now, with a better grasp of the Roman numbering system, counting in tens and hundreds, even thousands, they discussed the current state of the two armies. The mathematical concepts made such talk feel more sophisticated to Laelie, and much more interesting than counting fingers and pine-cones like little children.

"Would you believe it, they have as many as fifty hundred-counts here, a full legio!" Laelie said.

"That is a lot more than we have, even with all nine clanns with us. What do we have now, eight, nine hundred-counts?"

"More, my King. Daffid Og told me that yet another group from the south, from Cauci, Bri Chualann and smaller hamlets from the Manapaii and Brigantes territories will be joining us tomorrow, adding four hundred-count and two hand-counts. So with their four-hundreds and two-tens, we have twelve-hundreds and six tens."

"How many are women, not including your two-hundred count?"

"Oh, I never bothered to tally, as they are deploying their woman alongside their men. But I guess there are about an equal number, no, a bit less than equal, with my small force not counted."

"So for every one of us there are four Romans?" the King asked.

"Yes, about what you and the other kings thought would be the final number. Is that why you all decided to go against their left flank? – and not to try to cut through their center?"

"Yes. At the center, we would be throwing our lives into Roman steel. And our attempts to teach the warriors about how to fight cooperatively, to take turns as the Romans do, have been unsuccessful. We tried to rehearse it with the best of our warriors, but we just do not know how to fight like that.

"Maybe that's why the Romans are always practicing and training, in groups. So we decided that our best plan is to draw them up onto the ridge above the Dubh Linn lowlands, to stretch them out, and then to hit their left flank from the forest to the south, from the Eblana ruins." he said, as he adjusted his pillow to lay comfortably next to Laelie.

"That would be fitting, as that area is inhabited by the ghosts of our ancestors. Maybe they will help us, with their haunting squeals at night." mused Laelie, before returning to more serious thoughts. "Which clann is the blade that enters their ribs, then?"

"Clann Dalaigh, Clann Cauci and Clann Bri Chualann. Five hundred-counts, more or less. As long as we have surprise in our hands."

Laelie thought about it for a while, and then had an insight that excited her, and changed the direction of the discussion.

"What do we know of the Roman formation now? Are they still mostly from Legio XX, with less from Legio II?"

"Why do you ask?"

"Because I remember something Daffid Og said, that their general, Agricola the Younger, he is the son of the actual commander of Legio XX, operating out of the Roman castra at Deva, north of the Devonian territory, in Britannia."

"So?"

"Well, if he has the same low opinion of Legio II, making them work like slaves to build their stone castra fortress, fortifications, roads and so on, then maybe he will be using them as expendable dogs, to test our front."

"Daffid Og and I did not consider this, which units the Romans will send. They could just as well send the First Cohort from Legion XX, who are very tough. They defeated our cousins in Britannia, after all."

"Yes, but Legion II was not in that battle, right?"

"What is your point, lass?" he said, putting his hand under her bedclothes and then softly guiding a finger from the center of her chest, feathering it across the ridges of her defined abdomen and toward her taut navel.

Deliberately ignoring his wayward hands, Queen Laelie continued.

"But this is important, and before the battle we can watch for signs of which centuries are preparing for battle with more purpose than the others, to identify who will be the shock-troops. Once we know that, we can adjust our battle plan. Those 'COH', 'LEGIO XX' and 'LEGIO II' flags will tell us all we need to know, now that Daffid Og has told our captains how to interpret them."

"Why? We know what the Romans will do. They always do the same thing, at least from what they have been doing in Britannia and Caledonia. So why is it relevant which cohort from which legion is in front?"

"Because Legio II are *people of the sea*. Without them, Legio XX could not have sailed across Muir Éireann from Britannia to Éire."

"I think I know where you are going, my Queen."

"So the key here is not to kill the commander, but to destroy Legio II and the ships. That will strand the remainder of Legio XX and also cut off any hope of resupply."

"But if we commit forces to carve the stomachs of Legio II, we will have nothing left. Legio XX will be able to defeat us. And if you are right about what Agricola the Younger thinks of Legio II, then he will be willing to sacrifice them for the larger victory. There will be nothing to stop him from seizing all of the Dubh Linn area, all the way to the sacred hills of Tara. After that, he can control all of Éire."

"Not at all, great High King."

King Findmal noticed the more respectful tone, and the way his hot-and-cold wife was now pulling his hand onto her breasts, welcoming his curious touch.

As mac Cassan began to suckle Laelie's breasts, she continued talking, not pushing him away as she often would. Now gently placing a hand between her legs, Findmal continued talking, feeling certain that he was in control. "I think that Agricola the Younger is not stupid. Once he sees that the cohorts of Legio II are the target, and they are facing a larger force, he will send in his reserve forces to augment the Second Legion.

"This changes the face of the battle, from a frontal assault," she said, as she abruptly pushed her husband's probing hand away from her most private place, and placed it back on her breast, "to a defensive battle," Laelie concluded.

Following her logic, the king added, "And we will have the initiative. They will change to the turtle formation, and will draw their centuries closer to each other. Then we can use a smaller force to keep the turtles from fighting us in the open. We then let them march their turtles onward towards our side of the ridge..."

King Findmal was very excited as he thought it through, no longer just pretending to listen as a way to get on top of his Queen. "So rather than send in Clann Dalaigh, Clann Cauci and Clann Bri Chualann as the blade into their ribs, we send them a smaller force of the fastest of these men, and as many as possible on any horses we can spare – our own cavalry – completely around the Roman left flank and beyond to their rear, and go after the ships. Then Agricola the Younger must choose between dividing his forces to protect the ships while having already reinforced the leading cohorts with his reserve cohorts, or throwing everything he has into the front, towards our main position on the ridge.

"So all we need to do is have plans for what we will do in each of those two cases. If he puts all of his forces into the front, we let Dalaigh, Cauci and Bri Chualann destroy the ships and then we use another force to go after Agricola's command tents and retinue, and cut up their balls," she said, leaving the bait out there for her king to swallow.

"But I don't have another formation to send after the Roman right flank. And how could they reach the Roman command tents? That side is the great Dubh Linn bogland, completely impassable," the king went on, now oblivious to the fact that Laelie had gently moved the king's hand back to her lap, invitingly.

"Daffid Og has told me that his scouts watched as the Romans lost a handful of men exploring their side of the bog," he continued.

"Well, you could use my force of women. And I know a way to turn the bog into an advantage…"

She told him her plan, and how many more women she wanted from the main force. The king thought about it for a while, not realizing how well he had been outmaneuvered by his warrior wife. He was inspired by both the exciting possibilities his new strategy brought to mind and the sexual energy that Laelie was giving off as she writhed under the experienced, though rarely welcomed, touch of his finger on her clitoris.

"That could work," he said, moving up to penetrate Laelie.

"So what is your decision, my King?" she asked, slightly out of breath after her climax. She opened her legs, allowing him to enter her.

"You and your girls can have Agricola's balls," he said, as he put his own into action.

The sex had been satisfying and vigorous, as King Findmal and Queen Laelie were both as excited by the blood lust that was rising in them as they were in their anticipation of the coming battle. After they were done the sexual energy subsided, but not the battle lust. They both simply got up and dressed, to carry on with the preparations for war.

For Queen Laelie, that meant gathering with her captains in the roundhouse reserved only for women. As she got started, she was pleased to encounter Queen Achal Noichrathach, queen of the clann north of Tara, who had just arrived. High King Findmal had already told King Noichrathach that the two queens would be leading a special force, and that Findmal wanted Queen Achal to contribute her one fifty-count of female warriors to the special force. He had ordered that they immediately leave their encampment with the Noichrathach men in the forest west of Dubh Linn, and find spaces in the roundhouses and hovels around Cathair mac Cassan.

To King Findmal, this was a political decision as much as a strategic one, as he and King Noichrathach had been working on an alliance that could see High King mac Cassan become the next Grand High King of all Éire – not just of the nine kingdoms of the Tara region – and also elevate the prestige of King Noichrathach in the process.

With the women of the two clanns playing such a pivotal role in the defeat of the Roman invaders, the two clanns would cement their alliance in blood and glory. In saving Éire, they would also gain the support of most of the one hundred and forty kings of Éire, at the council of High Kings in Tara, in four months' time.

With the other warriors receiving their orders in the forest, the women from Clann mac Cassan welcomed the women of Clann Noichrathach into their midst in the roundhouse, and together settled down for Queen Laelie's speech.

As the women warriors quieted, Queen Laelie began by addressing her counterpart from the north.

"Achal, Queen of the Noichrathach, welcome. Is this little Niamh? Your golden-haired daughter! How she has grown!"

"This is indeed my little golden flower. She has now eighteen seasons and has even warmed her hands in the blood of battle," said Queen Achal Fedelm Noichrathach.

"Brave Niamh, in which battle had you your first kill?"

"A battle with Skraeligs from the rocklands of Baile-an-Skaellig."

"I have heard of them. Some say they are an ancient tribe with magical powers. Is it true?" asked Queen Laelie.

"Not true according to my eyes. They are just people, who try to appear mystical. But the man I killed…"

"Man? Well done, lass!" interrupted Laelie.

"Thank you, Queen Laelie. Anyhow, the man was only a man. I ducked under his wild sheleighly swing and spun around – like this," she demonstrated a low whirl, coming around at the queen with a three-pointed *gae bolga*, deer-antler weapon, thrusting it part-way towards the gueen's belly faster than even Laelie could react. "And once I had my belly ripper in his gut, he was not so frightening. As he lay dying, I climbed atop him and looked into his eyes. They went out the same as a doe or any other animal. There was nothing magical in him at all."

Impressed by the skills of the young warrior, and aware of her mother's advancing years, Queen Laelie followed her intuition.

"Elder sister, would you do me the honor of naming me as your blood sister, and second mother to Niamh? I wish to mentor her alongside my husband's young sister, Princess Maura mac Cassan," Laelie indicated Maura with a nod of her head. Maura smiled, happy to be acknowledged so graciously. Laelie continued. "And perhaps let Niamh mentor us, in the killing ways of the Noichrathach?"

Accepting the proposal would bring King Noichrathach great prestige, strengthening the budding alliance with High King mac Cassan, so Queen Achal quickly agreed.

She also knew that it meant that she herself would have to play less of a leadership role in the coming battle, as tradition dictates that under such an arrangement there should only be one leader, one mentor, for the shared daughter.

"Niamh is now your daughter, sister. Teach her as you would teach your own. And I, as your elder sister, ask you to lead her in battle, so that she will look to you and not to me."

"As it must be, my sister," said Queen Laelie, happy to have settled the matter. Having the elderly Queen Achal hold back from what would be a strenuous, running battle was a relief. *The proud old woman must be approaching fifty seasons by now*, thought Laelie. "One more thing, sister Queen."

"Yes, sister?"

"Will you take charge of my older, slower women in the battle? Lead them as our second wave. There will be plenty of Romans left for you to kill, and I want someone I can trust to lead them to the battle, at their own pace. Your presence will give them courage. And when we are victorious, it will be with the help of all of our female warriors, young and old. We will share in the honor of looting their corpses, collecting finer clothing and steel weapons, and then burning their many corpses with honor, together."

"Agreed, and thank you for the honor, sister Queen."

Her spirit lifted by the close cooperation she and the elderly Queen Achal had established, Queen Laelie turned her attention to the assembled women, some of whom had overheard the negotiations between the two queens and were excited about the deepening ties with the powerful clann to the north.

As always, Queen Laelie used her time to greatest effect by first recounting a glorious story or legend and then identifying some of the most promising leaders in her ranks. Then having acquired their undivided attention, she proceeded to explain the battle plan and the task assignments for her warriors.

"Sisters," she began, "on the morrow we will go to war with the brown-skinned ones from the east. We will warm our hands in the blood of Romans!"

The women cheered.

"And even if you have heard the rumors that there are four Romans to every one of us, we have a battle plan that will bring us a victory for the ages. But before I tell you the plan, and send you off with your sisters to prepare, I will tell you the story of *Siol, the Seed of Tormod.*"

Some of the more mature Noichrathachi warriors listened politely to the story they had heard many times before while the many younger warriors among of Clann mac Cassan listened intently to the legend for the first time.

"You all know about *Cu Chulainn*, the hero of the cattle raid of cooley? Some call him the Hound of Culann. But how many of you know about his adventure on the Isle of Skye? Well, this is the story of the Siol Tormoid, Seed of Tormod," she began.

As she spun the story eloquently, Queen Laelie demonstrated how well she had learned the oratorical art from Daffid Og Briogan. She told the story of Cu Chulainn so well, in fact, that she captured the imagination of even the oldest of the warriors, Queen Achal of the Noichrathach.

And as Laelie brought the story around to her objective, the teaching point she wanted them to consider, her voice was the only sound in the round house.

"Cu Chulainn was not yet magnificent at this point, as he had not yet completed his training with Scathach. His teacher, Scathach, was a formidable warrior and master of all the warrior arts. Celtic warriors came to her from Alba, in Caledonia, and as far away as Gallia to be taught her magical ways. She had instructed men for centuries, but Cu Chulainn was her best student – for a male that is," Laelie said, drawing out a roar of laughter from the women but also a few frowns from some of the younger women.

"You may wonder how Scathach, a mortal, could teach for centuries. Well, she was one of the lucky ones who had been taken along with Oisin and Naimh of the Golden Hair to Tir na nOg – the land of the ever-young. And each time she returned to the world she was no older than the day she had left. So she only aged while on the world, training her warriors." All of the women knew about Tir na nOg, the land where people were sometimes taken by the faeries, where they did not age and where they would have magical powers.

"It was on the Isle of Skye that Scathach taught Cu Chulainn his famous 'salmon leap' technique, taught him some of the very same warrior techniques that I have taught you, and gave him his magical armor and weapons. Now I am no Scathach, but you each have your own *gae bolga* 'belly ripper' sticks, and some of you have fashioned your own *gath bolag* 'spear of light'. And just like Cu Chulainn, girls, we will use our gath bolags to kill hundreds of Romans as we close with them, and then when we get in close, we will use our gae bolga's to rip out their innards," she said, bringing the female warriors into a battle frenzy.

"Now, I want you all to feel your *riastrad*, your battle rage, which was the most powerful weapon that Scathach ever gave Cu Chulainn – even more powerful than his invisible shield and his thunderbolts – it was his battle rage that terrified his enemies. It was his battle rage that let him kill the three hundred-count of Medb's Army of Connacht, when he turned himself inside-out so that he could use his bones as knives and wrap his veins and other organs around the necks of his enemies and strangle them to death!

You will each kill five Romans, perhaps not by turning yourselves inside out like Cu Chulainn, but you will use every weapon you have: your *gae bolgas*, your *gath bolags*, your fingers, your teeth, your feet, even your forehead – and tear off the testicles of any Roman standing over you, rip off the head of any Roman in front of you, bite the fingers off any Roman who tries to close his hands on your throat, and push sticks into the eyes of any Roman who even looks at one of your sisters!"

The women warriors were fully in blood lust now, so it was time to bring them back down and begin the battle briefing.

"And here is how we are going to do it," she began, with a more measured tone.

She paused and listened as the women around her continued to breathe heavily, blood pumping with adrenaline.

"The hardest part for you, my warriors, will be standing still, ready to kill as you are right now. But stand still you will, beside me, beside Queen Achal of the Noichrathach and the other queens of Tara," she said, nodding her head at the queens who had joined ranks with her clann, "for we are the *sucellus*, hammer, that will deliver the final blow."

Laelie then moved to the dirt floor in the middle of the round house, and took out her *claiomh*, sword. As she brandished it, the other warriors looked on in envy. Most had weapons made from antlers and other hard bones tied tightly to sticks. Some had skull-crushing hammers fashioned from stones, sinew and wooden handles. A few had only simple knives made from shards of obsidian. Some had bronze implements, but those could not hold an edge and were far inferior to Roman steel. Very few, mostly her lieutenants and captains, had weapons made from any hard metal whatsoever.

She dragged her sword over the dirt, tracing out the ridgelines that formed the gently rising valley up to the fortress, Cathair mac Cassan, from Dubh Linn, and the ridgeline that led southward, to the ancient ruins of Eblana and onward to the harbor at Malahide Bay..Finally, she traced the forested area inland, where the men of the assembled clanns of Tara were gathering and then stuck her sword into the ground to represent hills of Tara, farther inland to the West.

"This 'LEG XX'," said Laelie, as she traced in the dirt on the floor of the roundhouse, "is the symbol you will see on a banner carried by the lead elements of their main force." She looked up to see Princess Maura unfurl the crude imitation of the Roman battle standard. "Thank you, sister. Remember that banner, it will tell you where the enemy's center is," Laelie continued, pretending she did not see the bruises and welts on Princess Maura's face. *Looks like she found a way to get herself into trouble. I wonder where her lady in waiting is? She should be here, attending to the princess...*

"There will be as many as two hundred-count of these men. They are slow, and heavily armored. Each of them carries what is called a *gladius*, a short sword, like my sword, only shorter and fatter. They also have daggers, long poles, throwing bolas and shields. Ask your sisters about these weapons, and how to fight them, but they are not what I want to focus on right now.

"This lead force will be drawn up towards the ridgeline, attacking our main force. Clann Brigantes and Clann Manapii along with some of the Caucis, Dalaighs and Bri Chualanns, these brave men and their women alongside them, they will bear the brunt of the attack. And, when the High King gives the order, we will send additional forces – the best of the Dalaighs, Caucis and Bri Chualanns – to attack the ribs of these 'Legio II' soldiers. This will look like we have committed the last of our forces to destroy Legio II.

"Now this is critical," she continued, more quietly so that they would listen intently. "We want the Romans to believe that the destruction of Legio II is our battle objective. So the nine clanns will make as much noise as possible, and throw everything they have at the Romans. We know that the Romans will respond by putting their shields together to make a *testudo*, what will look to us like a summer fishing shelter of *currachs*, shaped like this." She sketched out a turtle-shaped box in the dirt with a knife from her belt – once again displaying her wealth, in that she had an actual steel knife, rather than a sharpened bone or shard of obsidian.

"They do this to protect themselves, yet they will keep driving forward aggressively. Romans never back off. So the nine clanns will begin to give way. At this point the Romans will commit reserves from Legio XX, their main force of about twenty hundred-count," said Lailie.

They women looked confused, so Laelie tried to simplify: "Their main force, not including their reserves, is more than all of the warriors of the nine clanns camped at the forest. Their reserves are half again that many."

That was a number the women could understand, and more people than they had ever seen gathered together in one place.

"These extra reserves will push their assault through the warriors of our nine clanns. And this is the moment we must wait for," she continued, allowing her excitement to rise.

"When the Romans are committed, we will send some riders on horses and the fastest on foot of the Dalaigh, Cauci and Bri Chualann clans. They will move quickly toward the shoreline, to destroy the Roman fleet of ships. The Romans will see this, and then they must send troops from their final reserves, the more agile and responsive troops of Legio II, to protect their ships. They may also send their only cavalry and their commander's personal guards as a last resort.

"If they do not do this, then they will throw these Legio II reserves into the main battle with the nine clanns, at the highlands above Dubh Linn lowland. Either way, the Romans will believe that we are fully engaged, so they will smell victory and will be fully engaged themselves.

"And we women will have to stand still all morning while this happens. We will be scattered in small bunches around the roundhouses and forage-grounds. The Roman scouts will watch us, and report that we are weak women and do not represent any kind of a threat.

"And then, finally, after having to stand by while our brothers and sisters die in the main battle, we will spring into action." Laelie paused as she assessed the expression of her warriors.

They were patient, calmed by the serious talk of the battle plan, but now eager to hear what their mission would be.

"After the main battle begins, those of you who I have selected, and shall be led by our sister Niamh, daughter of Queen Achal," said Laelie, nodding respectfully to her sister-queen, "will sneak up close to the Roman scouts on our side of the valley. When you hear the beautiful sound of the *buinne* of King Findmal at the main battle area, its sound will drown out the unpleasant noise of the Roman *cornicenae* battle trumpeters, that is your signal to *move*."

The assembled women were so worked up at this point that they almost began to move, but sat still, listening with adrenalin flowing through their veins.

"From the various places you will have been dispersed, looking meek and uninvolved in the battle, you will pick up your *sciathi*, your wicker shields, and your *adharca* and other weapons, and you will...."

She went on to explain how the sciathi shields would be used.

When they grasped what this would do for the small force of women warriors, and the harm it would do to the Romans, they felt honored to be given such an important task.

"And that is why I previously asked you to weave so many sciathi. Now you know why they must be strong, light, and wide."

Before they understood their purpose, many had thought the shields completely useless. With no layers of hide or thick wood, the wicker shields would be useless against arrows and Roman short-swords.

The women looked down at the intricately-woven shields the mac Cassan women had been told to make: the loopy willow branches arranged in concentric circles and snake-like curves, the shields fashioned with the distinctive craftsmanship and art form of the women of Tara.

The newly arrived women from other clanns were envious, as they had not been told to craft their own sciathi. And then a young warrior, Neasa, the cousin of Queen Laelie, handed the best of her three sciathi to one of the Noichrathach girls from the north, smiling lovingly at the young girl, who was no more than fifteen winters old.

Reaching out reverently to accept the gift, the young girl looked around nervously, trying to determine if she could really accept such a wonderful gift. She patted her hand against her deerskin slip looking for something to give in return, and encountered one of the two *gae bolga* on her belt. She handed the deer antler weapon to Neasa, meekly, as though the carefully crafted three-pointed weapon was a worthless offering.

The delight on Neasa's face, to have a legendary Noichrathian adharca, antler weapon, of her very own, was sincere.

Observing the exchange, Queen Laelie and Queen Achal shared a contented look. The two largest clanns in the region, once staunch rivals for the eastern approaches to the hills of Tara, now had a firm alliance. *They will fight well together*, Laelie knew.

"These shields are our secret device, against an enemy equipped with awesome weaponry. With these sciathi you will then be inside their perimeter and joined by the fastest of your sisters. Together you will fly upon them like Cu Chulainn, and slaughter each and every one of their final picket of sentries."

"The rest of us women – slower, yes, but strong, fierce, and with all of our battle fury – we will be only a few strides behind you…"

Some of the women still seemed confused, particularly those who came down with Queen Ebdani from the northwest inlands on the far side of Tara, as they were not familiar with the Dubh Linn lowlands where the Romans had encamped. They had never encountered Romans, not even the small trade missions that took place up and down the coast. They had never seen the wondrous fabrics and colorful flags of the *centurial signum*, the battle-standard poles which each century rallies around when assembling into battle formations; they had not seen the *imaginifer*, holding the golden eagle standard of Emperor Domitian – claiming the ground as part of the Roman Empire; and they had not seen the wondrous sight of the bright red and white fabric of the Roman general's colorful tent, nor the smaller, colorful tents of his various tribunes, advisors and other nobles.

Laelie left it to others to explain the details of the Roman camp, trusting them to step forward as leaders, building strong bonds with the newly-arrived women.

"You and I, girls, along with our sisters from other great clanns, we will be suddenly inside their midst and leaping onto their backs to cut into the throats of their leaders. I will personally cut off the testicles of this Agricola the Younger, and we will throw the bodies of his entourage into a heap. Then, when they are all dead, we can honor them as vanquished enemies, as warriors worthy of respect. We will light a sacred funeral pyre which will burn for many days!"

With her *ban fejnnidh*, band of warriors, now once again at a fever pitch, Laelie gave her sister-in-law, Princess Maura mac Cassan, her trusted second in command, a nod indicating that she should take charge. *Her bruises maker her look more credible,* Laelie observed. She then retrieved her sword and walked around the room to clasp hands with each and every one of her lieutenants and captains before leaving.

Meanwhile, an elderly woman of at least sixty seasons began singing a variation of a well-known warrior's song that the Tara region's clanns knew well. The women of Clann Noichrathach, Dalaigh, Cauci, Bri Chualann, Ebdani and the other great clanns surrounding Dubh Linn all joined in, unified in their battle preparation.

Not far off, in the camps where the men of Clann Cauci, Clann Dalaigh, Clann Bri Chualann, Clann Atha Cliath and Clann Ath-na-Scairbhe and the others were preparing for the coming battle, the confidence and strength of the women warriors wafted in the early morning air, and gave the men in the forest a boost of strength.

Allanon, the High Druid of Tara and resident of Cathair mac Cassan had not been seen in any of the camps recently. He had been sent by King Findmal on a fool's errand, to visit the Roman General Agricola's tent, ostensibly to sue for peace.

What Allanon did not know was that the plans he had overheard King Findmal discuss with his advisor Daffid Og Briogan and the assembled kings of the nine clanns of Tara were not the plans that King Findmal and Queen Laelie would formulate later that night. Therefore, Allanon's secret intention to betray his people – for the a suitable reward – was destined to fail.

III

LEGIONES XX ATQVE II AD HIBERNIVM PRODEVNT
{Legion XX and Legion II sail for Ireland}

Year AD 82 / 835 *AB URBE CONDITA*

The invasion of Hibernia was launched in the year of the consulship of Domitianus and Sabinus, what is now described as the year 82 *Anno Domini Nostri Iesu Christi*, AD, the year of our Lord Jesus Christ. If counting years since the founding of Rome in 753 BC, Before Christ, it would be expressed as 835 *Ab Urbe Condita*, AUC. For Marcus Horatius Avitus, Tribune of the Eighth Cohort of the Second Legion, the crossing of *Oceanus Hibernicus* was a rare and welcome opportunity to be at sea.

He had been at sea a year prior, when he and the men of COH VIII of Legio II departed from Lugo, Hispania, to travel across the *Oceanus Britannicus*, the English Channel, to Britannia. The time in Lugo had been very pleasant; the men of the Second Legion enjoyed the wine and women of their main base, in sharp contrast to the bitter cold and hardships they had faced while fighting in Germania. But that campaign, under the late Emperor Vespasian – when he was still a general – was now well behind them; their wounds largely healed and their lost men replaced by fresh young legionaries, citizen-soldiers of Rome.

Surprisingly, from Marcus Avitus's perspective, formations of *auxilia* were also being sent to Britannia. Comprising essentially the same types of units as regular cohorts of a standard Roman legion, auxilia were less prestigious, lesser equipped, and less reliable than true Roman legionaries, as auxilia were raised from *peregrinia*, non-citizens, drawn from the occupied territories of the empire. As a result, auxilia were expendable shock-troops, normally used only in emergencies or major campaigns, where they would be used to test enemy defenses before committing the more valuable Roman legionaries.

That told Tribune Marcus Avitus that the campaign in Britannia was at a crucial stage. *That means that Emperor Domitian in Rome will be following this campaign closely. And that means that political decisions would be interfering with military tactics, a recipe for disaster...*

Marcus had learned that a massive army was being deployed to Britannia, to give *Legatus Augusti pro Praetore* – governor and commander of Roman forces in Britannia, Legatus Gnaeus Julius Agricola – the forces necessary to defeat the Celts in Britannia once and for all. Legatus Agricola was a very successful general, but the Twentieth Legion simply was not large enough to quell all of Roman-occupied Britannia while taking the fight to the Celts in Caledonia, in the far north.

For Governor Agricola, the problem was the constant harassment from the left flank, where Celts from the mysterious island of *Hibernia, Éire*, would raid Roman forts and trade posts along the west coast of Britannia Major. This forced Agricola to garrison sizeable forces in the west, reducing the size of units he could deploy against the Caledonians.

Rome was an empire built on expansion fueled by military success, and does not tolerate stagnation well. As a result, after their success in Germania, Legio II and a variety of auxilia were dispatched by Emperor Domitian to bolster Legatus Agricola's forces in Britannia.

With two over-strength legions at his disposal, Governor Agricola now had options.

Now, six months later, Tribune Avitus and his men, the Eighth Cohort of the Second Legion, COH VIII/II, were about to set foot in Hibernia as part of a rare, composite legion.

But orders had been issued that the unit must not be openly referred to as a legion. Rather, until victory was achieved, it was to be referred to simply as a force.

It was politics, of course. And Marcus Avitus understood Roman military politics as well as any other tribune.

It was all about grooming Governor Gnaeus Julius Agricola's son, Quintus Julius Agricola – *Agricola the Younger* – to be a rising star in the Roman military. This was to be achieved by allowing him to command an entirely new and victorious legion as *Legatus Legionus*. The plan, rumor had it, was that after he was successful in conquering the local Hibernian kings in the Dubh Linn area – the very approaches to the hillsides of Tara – Governor Gnaeus Agricola Britannicus would authorize the formal designation of the new legion as LEGIO XXVII Hibernicus Victrix Domitianus, under the command of his son, Quintus Julius Agricola, who would therefore become governor of a new province and elevated to the title *Legatus Augusti pro praetor Hibernicus Victrix*, commander of the Roman legion stationed in Hibernia in the service of Emperor Domitian. He would then go on to a string of victories to conquer the entire island province, and be Governor of Hibernia, ruler of the lands and people of Éire.

But before this great pathway to military success and the senatorial appointment that would inevitably follow, Quintus Julius Agricola first had to achieve this small victory at Dubh Linn on his own. With a retinue of the best available philosophers, strategists, technicians and all manner of advisors, Governor Agricola had given his son, Q. Julius Agricola, all the ingredients for success.

Governor Agricola's only qualm was his son's lack of experience, a commodity that would be purchased with blood. *Blood of the Hibernians*, Legatus Gnaeus Agricola hoped.

Young Legatus, Quintus Julius Agricola established his camp just south of the boglands east of King Findmal's *oppidum*, major village, and immediately began working on his battle plan. The oppidum was situated on the opposite side of a forested ridge that looked down over the bogland, the Dubh Linn lowlands, to Malahide Bay, where the Roman fleet was anchored.

Agricola was interrupted from his planning, as a Tribune entered the General's command tent.

"Legatus!"

"What is it, Tribune Avitus?"

"We've just lost four men."

"How? Has King Findmal attacked us somehere?"

"No, Legatus. It's the bog."

"What happened?"

"I can verify when Centurion Tappulus is finished getting re-dressed, but it appears that the bog is impassable. Tappulus had sent some men to probe the bog, looking for a way across it to the forest north of the camp. But the first two men quicly got into trouble."

"They got stuck?"

"Yes, After just a few strides, they two men became mired in the spongy mud."

"Sounds more embarrassing than dangerous. What happned next?"

"Tappulus was right there. He tried to pull them out himself, but got stuck in with them. Then two of my immunes tied a rope around him, and had a horse drag him out. I saw that part, you should have heard Aulus swearing. I guess the bog held on fiercly, and the horse pulled with great force. Maybe Tappulus was stretched a few digiti."

Laughing, Agricola imagined the muscular centurion being dragged through the mud, cursing.

"And then?"

"The first two men had disappeared into the mud. So two others went in after them, holding ropes. They got a hold of one of the first men's hands, but could not get him to the surface, and could not tie a rope around him. Then these two men got sucked under. When Tappulus had the immunes try to pull the soldiers out, he slapped one of the horses asses too hard, and the horse bolted," said Tribune Avitus.

"Bolted? With the rope attached?"

"Sadly, yes. The third soldier was cut in two. We were all so shocked by what we saw that we did not hear the screams of a fourth man, at another part of the bog, who had also become stuck. We were able to get the second rescuer out, by pulling on his rope ourselves, without using a horse. He swallowed a lot of sphagnum, but, but by the time we got him out the fifth man had disappeared from sight. All we found of him was his *sacullus*, pouch," said Marcus Avitus.

"So the bog is impassable, all around?"

"Yes, Legatus. You could march an entire legion into that bog and not as single man would make to the other side. It is a death trap," Marcus Avitus concluded.

Legatus Agricola received the report as useful information about the local terrain, and considered having paid for it with the lives of four men as being a fair trade. *Good thing we did not lose Aulus, though,* he reflected. Having the bog on his right meant that he could concentrate his forces in other directions, to the front and to the left.

Over the next four days, as the Romans and Hibernians prepared their forces for the coming battle, a steady routine of small raids and stealthy nighttime probes provided young Agricola and his advisors with all of the battlefield intelligence they required. They formed their battle plan, applying standard Roman military doctrine for a powerful frontal assault on the Hibernian lines at the forested ridge overlooking the Dubh Linn lowlands.

The battle plan was to send the Second Cohort of Legio XX along with four centuries of Legio II and two centuries of auxilia against King Findmal's main force. They were to deploy the main killing force, COII I of Legio XX, under the command of Primus Pilus Spurius Crispus. The objective was to punch through whichever part of the Hibernian line seemed most vulnerable, and press on all the way to King Findmal's oppidum, and victory.

Legatus Agricola had great confidence in Spurius Crispus. As centurion of the double-strength First Cohort of Governor Agricola's original Legio XX, Spurius Crispus was a seasoned veteran. From the moment that the First Cohort was assigned to him, Agricola the Younger had been impressed with the centurion's grasp of the strategic role that his men, the punching fist of the legion, were to be used for. Crispus could be counted on to do whatever it took to achieve victory, no matter how difficult.

Putting aside planning the role for his reserves, his personal two contubernia of seasoned warriors, Agricola turned his attention to the enemy. The Hibernians were expected to hold their reserves in the forest and to attack the Roman left flank in the vicinity of some ancient ruins. Roman military doctrine, drilled into him by his father's very best advisors, was clear in his mind and was not to be disregarded.

Agricola knew that if doctrine was not followed it could lead to confusion on the battlefield. The complex management within each cohort, with men taking their turn at the front, hacking at the enemy line with great intensity for only a short time before ducking back to rotate to the rear of the echelon while the next legionary steps into line with fresh vigor – against a now tiring enemy front rank – required predictable movements of each and every legionary within the eighty-man centuries which made up each of the ten cohorts. This method of fighting, if applied with precision and control, produced a well-coordinated and highly efficient killing machine. This was the Roman genius, the tried and true way to defeat such undisciplined armies as the Hibernian Celts.

As long as everyone knows their job, and orders were issued in a timely fashion, the thousand or more Celts would be cut to pieces, with no more than a few tens of legionaries and perhaps a hundred auxilia falling to the insane Celts.

But the young, inexperienced commander, Quintus Julius Agricola, knew from the accounts of his father's campaigns against the Caledonians that if the number of Celts is greater than anticipated, or if their leader has any tactical tricks up his sleeve, then Agricola will have to respond instantly, sending reinforcements to the flanks of the main force, or risk losing the initiative.

According to their battle plan, the worst case scenario would be if the Hibernians gave ground too fast, and drew the Second Cohort of Legio II too far inland. This would stretch the resupply lines of fresh centuries to the front and opened up too much space between the front lines and the reserve formation,

COH I, which was to remain stationary until the opportune time to press whichever advantage became apparent.

Agricola reflected on it: *I will have to progressively reposition COH I to keep it in range of COH II and the rest of the battle line, but that will put a vast open space between our rear element, my command position, and the bulk of my forces. That leaves me vulnerable if they have cavalry or some other fast-moving force to swing around my left flank. But they do not have such a force...* he thought, working through possible scenarios for the hundredth time, always coming to the same conclusion.

Legatus Agricola was satisfied that the tactics and logistics of the coming battle were well prepared. Despite his lack of experience commanding an entire legion, he was confident that he would soon have his first major victory, and the title *Legatus Legionus XXVII Hibernicus Victrix.*

He looked forward to having Vibius Metellus, the mentor of Tacitus himself, write out the dispatch to send back to the Roman base at Deva, in Britannica: *Tara is now in Roman hands! The talented artisans formerly of Legio II are working on a fortress while the hard-charging soldiers of Legio XX are hunting down and destroying the lesser kings and tribal leaders and their pitiful, fleeing Celtic warriors,* he thought to himself, relishing how he expected the Hibernian campaign to unfold. Next, additional centuries from his father's forces in Britannia would be sent to reinforce Legio XXVII in Hibernia, to round out the occupation force. This would allow his loyal second in command, Tribunus Laticlavius Kaeso Petillius Cerialis, to command his own subordinate, under-strength legion, while Agricola the Younger, the new Governor of Hibernia, would share the wealth by portioning out the best landholdings to his officers and others in his retinue, beginning the transformation, through Roman administration, of the Hibernian back-world into what would become known as Hibernicus Romanus – Roman Éire.

"Vibius Metellus, I hope you are taking good notes, as you will soon be as busy archiving this campaign just as your student, Gaius Tacitus, has been archiving that of my father in Britannia!" said Agricola.

"Rest assured, Legatus, I have already worn out three of my best quills since we landed here!" said Metellus.

"Did you write much about the rough voyage we had crossing Oceanus Hibernicus?"

"Oh yes, to be certain, it was a wild ride and worthy of careful record. But I omitted the part about Fabius Quintilianus getting sea sick. No point in embarrassing the poor man. How is he, by the way?"

"He has completely recovered. All he needed was one night of debauchery with some Celtic whore he found, and a day of rest. Now he's fit as a fiddle. I sent him up along with Kaeso Cerialis to get a taste of battle with the First of the Twentieth."

"Won't that be dangerous for him?" asked Vibius Metellus, the more trusted of the two philosophers in Agricola's retinue.

"Not very. The Celts don't have archers or weapons with any sort of range. All they have are sharpened sticks, clubs and hand-thrown rocks. So long as Fabius Quintilianus stays behind the front century, he will be able to smell fresh blood without contributing any of his own."

"Will you let me go up and take a look, maybe later in the battle?" asked Vibius Metellus.

"Of course, Vibius. You'll come out there with me once we see what the Hibernians are doing. I'll personally lead our small number of cavalry to cut the legs out from under their reserve force, and you will ride behind me."

"That sounds very daring, Legatus. Shouldn't we wait until the battle is over? After all, you are too important to lose."

"*Cūlus*, Metellus! I thought you were made of stronger stuff. Or is all of your bold talk of courage and adventure only so much wasted breath?"

"Not at all, Legatus, my elocutions are about your courage and your glory, not my own."

"Ah, so now we have it! You want to be close to glory and conquest, and that's why you came with me on this enterprise, but you don't have the stomach for it yourself? Well, I'll change that. By the end of the day, you will have killed a man – or a woman if I can arrange it! – Centurion!" Agricola commanded, drawing the immediate response, "Legatus!" from the Tribune originally from COH VIII of Legion II, who had been standing outside the tent, waiting for orders.

"Tribune Avitus, you know my new philosopher here, Vibius Metellus? He has joined us from my father's retinue, and needs to get some blood on his hands today. You will keep a contubernium around our precious rhetorician, and when the opportunity presents itself, you will personally ensure that he kills a Hibernian whore. Slice her up a bit first so that she is not much of a threat, but let her have one of those sharp sticks those crazy female warriors use, just to make it real for Vibius Metellus. Get his hands bloodied, kill his first Hibernian *Lupa*, she wolf!"

"As you command, Legatus", said Tribune Avitus, stepping out to make arrangements while Vibius Metellus and Agricola continued talking in the command tent.

"Legatus, have you ever fought a woman of Éire-Land? Metellus asked, curious, as he thought about what it would be like to kill someone. *Killing a man is one thing, but killing a woman must be much more difficult, at least for a good man, not a brute. Maybe it would be better to ask Tribune Avitus to arrange for me to kill a man, instead of a woman,"* thought Metellus.

"Éire-Land? or did you say 'Ireland?' Is that what these Celts call Hibernia?"

"No, Legatus, not 'Ireland' – that sounds far too Germanic! Are you inventing a new name for the Island of Éire? Better to just call it 'Éire', 'Ivernia,' or Hibernia, and you will be understood by the Hibernians. Your invention, 'Ireland," will never catch on, Legatus," the rhetorician laughed. "Although, come to think of it, it does work in a way..."

"Not *my* invention, Vibius! It first came out of your mouth, so you shall record yourself as the one who first referred to Hibernia as *Ireland!*" commanded Agricola, half-jokingly.

"As you wish, Legatus. I will record our conversation in my next tablet, when I chronicle the coming Battle of Dubh Linn, and the first great victory of Legion XXVII Victrix Hibernicus," said Metellus.

"Make it so, philosopher," Agricola said, as he got up to investigate the sounds he heard coming into his tent from outside. He knew that the time had come for him to show himself to his men, for them to be inspired by seeing that their general was with them as they went into battle.

With the help of his personal attendant, a Greek slave that had been the property of his family for years, he ensured that his battle armor was fitted just right, and then headed for the exit.

"Well, if I am going into battle, maybe I should also put on some armor," said Metellus, walking behind Legatus Agricola.

With a nod of the Legatus's head, one of Agricola's armorers rushed out to find suitable armor for the philosopher-turned-soldier.

Less than an hour later, amid the din of soldiers preparing to move into line, the sun rising over Malahide Bay, Vibius Metellus was dressed in ill-fitting leather battle armor. Despite the best efforts of the two armorers who dressed him, he did not look like a Roman warrior. But in the company of all the magnificently fit and confident tribunes, centurions, immunes and others he encountered outside of Legatus Agricola's command tent, Vibius certainly felt like one.

The tightness and stiffness of the leather armor made him feel less vulnerable. However, in the back of his mind he was terrified of having a sharpened stick or other primitive weapon thrust into his ribs by a screaming, insane Celtic woman warrior.

Metellus stayed close to Tribune Marcus Avitus.

Not long after Metellus had been dressed, he was standing in the command tent once again with Agricola, who had returned from his final inspection of the battle preparations. Metellus did not realize that he was insulting his former student by not removing his helmet, but he corrected himself when Kaeso Cerialis, Agricola's second in command, entered the tent and promptly removed his own headdress.

Cerialis gave Metellus an amused look, and then turned his attention to Agricola.

"Legatus – "

"Come on, Kaeso, we are friends. In private, you must call me Quintus as you always have."

"As you wish, but after. Not now. This is our first campaign, and your father put *you* in command. You can call me General when I take my own legion to clear out the Hibernian province of Connaught – and choose my own landholdings. But for now, I serve as your Tribune."

"Very well, Tribunus Laticlavius, what is it?" Agricola asked, with sincere respect for his lifelong friend. "Why are you back from assembled cohorts?"

"The Hibernians are up to something."

"Really? Could it be that they have spies all around us, their unwashed stench still wrapped around the cocks of some of us?" he said, causing Cerialis to blush. It was known throughout the camp that Cerialis had spent considerable time with a young Celtic woman he had captured on their first day in Ireland.

"Quite, General. Anyhow, their scouts are paying very close attention to the Second of the Twentieth, the First of the Second, and most of the cohorts of our primary reserve."

"And what does this tell you?"

"It tells me that maybe they are not such ignorant savages as we thought."

"We?"

"Well, I know what you said, about them having communications with their kin in Britannia Major and Caledonia, and that maybe they know our battle procedures, but there is something more here. We may have underestimated their commander."

"Go on," Agricola said, trying to sound like a real general, never surprised.

"I mean, maybe we didn't bring a large enough force. Maybe we should pull the cohorts back, garrison here for a few more weeks, perhaps do some skirmishing around on their flanks."

"I am with you there, Kaeso. There are still far too many unknowns. Taking a little more time would be prudent in that regard. However, I was forced to reject the idea of taking more time to gather intelligence on the enemy, because that would give King Findmal more time to build up his army. Every night more men from the Dalaighs, Manapii and other nearby clanns are drawn to him. Why, we even have reports that many of the other so-called kings are sending troops down from Ulaidh, in the far north, as well. They are like moths coming to the flame, and we are the light. So if we don't move fast, we risk losing the initiative altogether."

"I understand, and agree, but still, I feel we should be cautious."

"Do you want to change the battle plan? We don't have much time to issue new orders, you know. So what do you want to change?"

"Well, I think we should create a tertiary reserve – cut away one of the better cohorts, or at least a century or two each from the Twentieth and the Second, and put them under the command of say, Tribune Avitus from the Eighth of the Second. That way, we could throw them at any flanking move by the Hibernians and still have the primary reserve to press their weak line, as per the battle plan. That would give us flexibility to respond to King Findmal without giving up the initiative."

"That's a good idea. Too bad we don't have the normal size of cavalry. Two or three contubernia are simply not enough to be used to great effect, other than to harry the enemy once we break them and they begin to flee.

"How does my father expect me to conquer all of Hibernia on foot? At least Findmal's force will also be on foot. No, we'll use my two contubernia of mounted guards as the final reserve, and keep extra pickets along the left flank to watch for surprises from those ruins. But I'll tell you what, you can move most of the pickets from our right flank, along those deadly boglands, up to Tribune Avitus's position. Give them to him and tell him that he can deploy them as he deems fit along the left flank of the Ninth of the Second. Tribune Avitus can use them as a small dagger to cut deeply into any vulnerabilities that show themselves, particularly if the Hibernians over-commit. Or he can use them to bolster any failing auxilia centuria. After all, they will be taking the brunt of the Hibernian assault. Does that give you enough flexibility, Kaeso?"

"Yes, Legatus! That will be easy to manage. I'll have a clear line of sight over to Marcus Avitus's axis of advance!" said Cerialis, who suddenly looked a bit hurried.

"You need to get up there, Tribune. Is there anything else?"

"No, General, that is all. May I be dismissed to my duties?"

"Yes. Oh, wait; make sure you keep a close eye on Marcus Quintilianus. Tell him that I'm taking Vibius Metellus up with me later, to kill his first Hibernian woman, so the gauntlet has been laid – which of our two philosophers is more than mere talk of glory! If Quintilianus does not get one, then I will see to it that you won't be laid again for a month! You are dismissed, Tribunus."

As Cerialis slapped his fist on his chest and then extended it outwards, palm down, in the Roman salute, and backed out of General Agricola's tent, he was not entirely sure if his friend was joking or not.

He was certain of one thing: His best friend was in every way a general, despite his youth and lack of battlefield experience. *All of that is about to change.*

Gene Skellig

IV

SENATVS POPVLVSQVE ROMANVS
{ SPQR – Senate and People of Rome }

"Emperor Domitian will be here shortly, brothers, so let's make a decision!" said Senator Gaius Crispus, leader of the group of senators who had been lingering in the Senate Chambers when the courier had arrived with a message from Britannica.

They had been unable to force the low-ranking *tabellarius*, courier carrying the dispatch, to let them examine the message from Legatus Augustus Pro Praetore Britannicus, Governor Agricola, in Britannia. The communication from Governor Agricola to Emperor Domitian was comprised of two wax tablets which closed like a book, and was tied closed with a string, and sealed with Legatus Agricola's personal stamp.

The urgent communiqué could not be opened by anybody other than the emperor, so Senator Gaius Crispus shifted his efforts to trying to place some of his spies as close to the emperor as possible at the time and place he was most likely to receive, read, and react to the long awaited report on the expeditionary probe, if not invasion, of Hibernia. For Senator Gaius Crispus, any news of his son, Centurion Spurius Crispus, would be secondary to the political value of whatever information could be gleaned from the communiqué.

As the bewildered tabellarius tried to avoid speaking to any of the senators, many of them began to tease the slave for his Greek heritage. Other senators were more kind, and understood that the Greeks made some of the best slaves, as they were typically more well educated, able to read and write, which had its uses.

"It does not matter what the news is; we have to decide if now is the time to end the Flavian Dynasty for once and for all," he said, quietly to his fellow plotters.

"And as I have said, until he is weakened by a major defeat or some other problem, he is simply too strong. Even if we succeed, as we did with his brother Titus last year, we won't live to celebrate this time. Domitian is too popular with the *plebeians*, the public at large. His reform of the gold market, with the new gold coins, has done wonders for the economy; those weekly events at the Flavian Amphitheatre are drawing in tourists from throughout the empire – along with their gold – and the increased shipments of grain and other commodities from Egypt, Achaea and other provinces continues to make the citizens happy and prosperous," said Consul Gaius Catilinus, whose powerful family held the greatest influence in the senate.

But influence in the Roman Senate no longer held the importance it had when the republic still answered to the senate. Ever since the first emperor, Augusts, took power the Ssnate had become merely an administrative court, and in terms of real power, an empty shell.

Ever since Emperor Domitian had declared himself the new Augustus, perpetual censor, and by demanding to be addressed as *Dominus et Deus*, Master and God, the emasculation of the Roman Senate had been complete.

And they resented it deeply.

They had assassinated Domitian's brother, Emperor Titus, for less. At least under Titus there had been a modicum of senatorial control and limits to the power of the emperor. But now, under Domitian, they were faced with a tyrant, the likes of which Rome had not seen since the days of Julius Caesar, some 122 years before.

For his part, Emperor Domitian detested the corruption and idle sloth of the senators. He also hated that the senators, almost to a man, all had full heads of hair.

Despite his power and the success he was having in his first year since accession to power after his brother's murder, the emperor was very insecure. It was not the constant threat of betrayal or assassination that he faced from the one hundred of the most powerful men in the Roman Empire, that was a political reality he was comfortable with having been raised within the powerful and politically incisive Flavian family. It was his *baldness* that he was most insecure about.

When he spoke to the senators he could feel their eyes on his bald head; when he walked the marble halls from his private chambers just off from the Senate Chamber, he could hear their whispers and snickers about his baldness.

Emperor Domitian wanted to abolish the senate. However, without a senate, he could not see any possible way to actually administer the sprawling Roman Empire, which extended from North Africa to Germania and from Mesopotamia to Britannia.

The administration of such a massive empire, which required constant inputs of commodities, slaves and wealth from the conquered territories to support the lavish life of nobles and plebeians of Rome, was accomplished through a chain of command that was highly effective. At the top were the magistratus, who proposed legislation; next were the censor, praetor, curule aedile and quaestor. Any of these magistrates could obstruct or veto any action being taken by a magistrate of lower ranking. At the bottom of this power structure were those elected to high office, the plebeian tribunes and plebeian aediles, who had administrative roles but no power to veto or obstruct anything directed by the small number of magistrates who, until their powers were largely stripped away by Emperor Domitian, were the powerful elite of Rome.

They hungered for a restoration of the old order, the Republic of Rome, and sought any shred of news that could help end the dictatorship of Emperor Domitian.

What the senators did not know was that Domitian had had the message intercepted by a contubernium of his most loyal Praetorian Guards, so that the contents of the message could be copied and provided to Domitian in advance of the message's 'arrival' in Rome. So the tabellarius was brining word to Rome which Emperor Domitian already knew all about.

The way he played it was to pretend that he was sharing the long-awaited news with the Roman Senate, with no foreknowledge. To make it more realistic, he tried to look eager to know if there was to be good news of General Agricola's campaign against the Celts in Caledonia. As though another military victory would be great news, and put off the chatter of assassination that Domitian's spies continually reported of the group of senators that were scheming against him, and making fun of his follically-deficient scalp.

Even before he had secretly learned what the news would be, he had already decided to send Consul Sabinus to Britannia to take command of Legio XX from Agricola and to send Senator Catilinus to take command of Legio II and to move the Second Legion to Hibernia.

Dispatching Catilinus to such an awful, cold, wet and pitiful island will be suitable punishment for his role in assassinating my brother Titus, he thought with satisfaction.

As the emperor entered the Senate Chamber, the group of conspiratorial senators quickly switched gears into sycophantic mode, lavishing false praise and affection on the man they detested.

"*Dominus et Deus*, how wonderful to share this great moment with you. What can you tell of the news from Britannia?"

"Nothing at all, my dear friend Sallustius Crispus, for I have not had it read to me yet," said Domitian.

"Not read yet? Why for the Gods have you not?"

"I wanted to share it with the fully assembled senate!"

The blood fell from Senator Crispus's face. That the Emperor was calling for a full session could only mean one thing: the days of peaceful politicking and carefully scheming against the emperor were about to come to an abrupt end. Senator Crispus knew that he was number one on the emperor's list of enemies to be dealt with, or perhaps a close second to Consul Sabinus. That all depended on whether Emperor Domitian suspected co-consul Sabinus of playing a role in the assassination of Domitian's elder brother, Titus, after only one year as emperor.

Putting on a brave face as his so-called friends visibly distanced themselves from him, Senator Crispus took his place in the front row, directly across from where Emperor Domitian had settled.

As the late-arriving senators rushed in to take their places and pairs of sentries took up positions at the exits, a silence descended on the chamber as if the room itself was preparing for what was to come next.

Many of the senators were uncomfortable to see so many sentries, even if they appeared to be unarmed, as per Roman law.

At the slight nod of the emperor's head, Consul Sabinus began speaking at just the time when the courier from Britannia was being formally presented to Emperor Domitian.

Senator Catilinus rose to make the formal introduction.

"Senators, it is our high honor to be present with our beloved Emperor, *Dominus et Deus* Domitian on the occasion of his receiving a report from our heroic General, our brother, Senator Gnaeus Agricola, Governor of Britannica and commander of Legio II Augusta and Legio XX Valeria Victrix."

The terrified tabellarius, courier, stood where he had been parked, in the center of the chamber, unsure of what to do next. The slave was accustomed to running flat out from one terminus to another, taking messages, tablets and packages with no idea of what they contained, nor who they would ultimately reach. On this day, however, he had been given a heavy set of tablets and escorted by Praetorian Guards, from the terminus at the Porta Aurelian on the west side of Rome, and escorted all the way to the Senate Chamber.

"With your permission, *Dominus et Deus*, may I break the seal?" asked Consul Sabinus.

"Proceed, and ensure that the rabellarius reads with a strong voice. Some of the senators are old men for whom it is a strain to listen," said Domitian, taking a shot at some of the elder senators, aged men well into their sixties.

As the young messenger broke the seal, Consul Sabinus whispered quietly to the courier: "Relax, tabellarius, you will do fine. Just read slowly and clearly, and pause after every paragraph. Look directly to me for when to pause, or go on."

Even more terrified, but grateful to Consul Sabinus for the guidance, the courier waited for the nod. He was so tense that he felt like he was about to faint. *At least I lived long enough to have a son,* he thought to himself.

Sabinus nodded, and the tabellarius began to speak. He looked only at the wax tablets, now open like a two-page book in his hands.

Senator Crispus listened for the words that would determine his fate. Good news from the front could mean exile for him personally; bad news, his salvation. But given the long series of successes that General Agricola had achieved in Britannia, Senator Crispus was not optimistic.

"My beloved Emperor, there has been a problem in Britannia."

The courier swallowed, trying to get some moisture into his parched throat. His first words had sounded like they came out of a dying old man. Judging by the pained expression on the face of Consul Sabinus, the tabellarius knew that he would have to do better. He waited, as Consul Sabinus watched the emperor, then the consul nodded for the *Tabellarius,* to continue.

Swallow, relax, and take a breath, he thought, as he read the next line.

"In order to neutralize the annoyance from the Celts on my western flank, and as we had discussed on my last visit to Rome, I had dispatched a composite legion, with elements from Legio XX, Legio II, and some peregrini cohorts of auxilia from Lugo. The objective was to defeat King Findmal, the ruler of an oppidum, just inland from Malahide Bay. The location controls the approaches from the Dubh Linn lowlands to a place sacred to Hibernians, known as 'Tara.'"

The tabellarius paused and, on a nod from Consul Sabinus, he continued. Had he looked he would have seen that the emperor and all of the senators had the same look of intense concern on their faces. All of them knew where Hibernia was, and the strategic importance of neutralizing the Celtic threat on

Governor Agricola's left flank before completing the conquest of northern Britannia, but none of them had known that Domitian and Agricola had secretly agreed to launch the incursion into Ireland.

This is important news, Crispus thought.

"Tara is the Hibernian equivalent of the Seat of Rome, where the most powerful Hibernian kings compete for support from the lesser kings, to determine who might rule their province. Hibernia itself is of little value; it can barely support its wretched inhabitants. They live in a disorganized, inefficient manner fraught with wars, famine and unproductive intrigue – much worse than you face, *Dominus et Deus*, from the scheming senators of Rome."

Nobody laughed at Agricola's humor at their expense. He was far away and could afford to take risks which none would consider taking here in Rome.

The tabellarius continued to read Agricola's dispatch: "My intent was to install a garrison there, and to then reinforce it with additional cohorts from my forces in Britannia."

Intent 'was', thought Senator Crispus, hoping against hope that this meant that Agricola had run into difficulties.

"To command this composite legion, I sent my son, Quintus Julius, along with Kaeso Cerialis – son of Senator Quintus Cerialis. They even have Centurion Spurius Crispus along to keep an eye on them. But they have not returned."

Many looked to see how Senator Crispus took the news. The man looked as if all life had been drained from his face.

The courier looked away from Consul Sabinus too soon, and resumed speaking without first receiving a nod.

"Also missing -" he began.

"What happened to them?" demanded the emperor.

Knowing that he had spoken too soon, the courier shut up and held his breath.

"Go on, tabellarius, read on!" ordered Consul Sabinus.

"Also missing is the son of Senator Marcus Fabius Quintilianus, along with legionaries from cohorts One, Eight, and Ten of the Second Legion, cohorts One and Ten from the Twentieth Legion, and a century of Hispanic Auxilia."

Pause, swallow.

"Continue!"

"All-told, five hundred and fifty seven men, comprised of three hundred and forty citizens of Rome, two hundred and ten peregrini, and seven tribunes including the three sons of the Senate and two philosophers."

Quick look at the consul, breathe, continue.

"Something happened just before the battle began, at a place the Celts called Dubh Linn, which we have charted as Dublinensis on the enclosed tabula, map. But the battle did not take place. Something inexplicable happened. The listed units and persons have simply vanished. Sub-unit commanders nearest the lead elements all reported the same, impossible story – that monsters from the sky descended from black clouds."

The courier stopped for a moment, and dared to look up. The words coming out of his own mouth were so unbelievable that he simply had to see what effect they were having on the emperor.

In that short look at Emperor Domitian, the lowly slave saw a fearful, pained expression on the face of the man feared as a living god.

This is terrible news, and I am the one delivering it...

The courier suspected that Domitian and Agricola were close friends, and that the three sons of nobility were well known, up-and-coming young commanders from the most powerful families of Roman nobility. But it was the mysterious circumstance of their disappearance that had really put everybody off-balance.

Nothing like this has ever happened before, he believed, so he was as curious as everybody else as to what he would read next.

"While I have no reason to doubt the integrity of my officers, I find it impossible to believe what they all have reported. Yet there is a consistency of evidence that leads me to believe that those who returned from the expeditionary invasion of Hibernia truly believe what they are reporting. What they testify to is either an act of the Gods, perhaps of Mercury or Mars, stealing the legion away, or it was some terrible trick of dark magic played on us by the Hibernian Celts."

The courier kept reading on, without looking up again.

"Not knowing what to do, the sub-unit commanders withdrew to their ships and returned to our garrisons at Isca Silurium and Deva in Britannia Major. They brought with them a number of prisoners, who we have since interrogated.

"The Celtic prisoners all say that along with our missing soldiers, most of the Clann mac Cassan women from Cathair mac Cassan, and a few nobles, were also taken.

"The Hibernians all say that these people have been taken away to a mystical place they call "Tir na nOg", and that they will never return.

"We will continue to investigate, however I will not send troops to Hibernia ever again. We will continue to trade with them and take the occasional prisoner to torture for intelligence on our missing soldiers, however any future thoughts of conquering this mystical island must be considered to be *non-compos mentis*, insane.

"Hibernia is now *terra infestus inconcessusque*, a dangerous and forbidden place. In order to snuff out the fearful effect this disaster would have on the Second and Twentieth Legions, I have executed most of the surviving commanders and decimated their formations. The Hispanic Auxilia and other legionaries have been redeployed to Caledonia, and will remain in outposts there until they are completely expended. I recommend that you do not share this information with the senate, or let word of it spread within the empire. It would promote superstition and erode morale.

"With love and terrible yearning for your wise council, your brother and servant, Gaius Julius Agricola"

"*Desino*, end of report," crackled the tabellarius, his throat now very dry.

Slaves washed the blood off the floor of the Senate Chamber where the tabellarius has stood when he had finished reading the communiqué from Agricola, the spot where he had been executed immediately by one of Domitian's guards.

It had all been orchestrated, of course, and the murder of the slave courier had been all theatre. The intent, clearly achieved, was to put great fear into the minds of the senators, that they had been privy to such a terrible secret that, in defense of the stability of the Roman Empire, Emperor Domitian would go so far as to murder in order to suppress what they had all heard.

With only the sound of slaves twisting rags, the bloodied water dripping into pails to break the silence, the Consul Sabinus and the other senators sat waiting for the emperor's next move.

After having watched the courier and all ten sentries subsequently murdered by Domitian's Praetorian Guards, who had been absent until immediately after the report had been read, the senators had been required to sit and wonder whether the emperor would let them live or not.

On the advice of his co-consul, Domitian had let them sit and suffer. Consul Sabinus had whispered that letting the senators live could prove useful.

It was the longest period of silence that had ever taken place in a sitting Roman Senate.

Satisfied that his enemies were now greatly disadvantaged, and therefore unlikely to murder him as they had done Titus, the emperor rose to address the senators.

Appearing to be speaking extemporaneously, when he was actually delivering a well-rehearsed speech, Emperor Domitian took full advantage of the situation he had engineered. He knew that he had them by the balls, and wanted to press his advantage.

"Brothers, it is with a heavy heart that I must now act," he began, unable to resist the chance to twist the knife just a little more.

"You all heard what our brother Agricola has reported. It is indeed unfortunate that, out of my love for you all, I chose to share this message with you without first having it read to me in private. And you know that he is right. This information must be suppressed, for the sake of Rome.

"But I will not harm you. That would violate your rights under our laws, and betray my love for each and every one of you. You are too important, and Rome needs you. You are the wise, experienced leaders who keep our economy working. While I may be the head, heart and the bones of Rome, you are the skin that holds everything together.

"So I shall make a decree, which shall not be recorded in the tabula. None who speak of what took place in Hibernia shall be permitted to live. Any who does speak of it shall forfeit the lives of their families and be declared cursed, expunged from the history of Rome and consigned to Abyssus."

Senator Crispus looked around at his fellow senators, one at a time, and saw the same beaten, terrified look on their faces as he wore on his own.

Sheer genius, he thought to himself. *He owns us now, all of us. None of us will make a move against him, ever! The emperor does not even need any pretext, he can kill any of us at any time and none of us will even make a peep. All he has to do is suggest that we spoke of the Hibernian disaster – or simply be accused of doing so! He has us by the short and curlies.*

While it took him fourteen years longer to see the end of the reign of Emperor Domitian, Senator Crispus never heard another senator speak of the events that had taken place in Hibernia. Even the two senators who had been in Britannia Major were silent: Senator Quintilianus the Elder, who retold so many of the great adventures of Governor Agricola in Britannia, and, Senator Publius Tacitus, the great chronicler of Roman history, never wrote of or spoke of the incident. It was successfully – along with Senator Crispus's son and those of other nobles – stricken from the annals of history, as though it had never happened.

It was as if the young men had never existed.

V

HISTORIA PVERORVM
{ Bedtime Story }

For the third night in a row, ten year old Horatius Avitus Connal cried himself to sleep, or at least tried to. When his mother Neasa heard him whimpering, she climbed up into the pod assigned to Marcus Horatius Avitus's family, and drew her hand across the illuminating-strip to increase the light so she could get a clear look at her son's face.

"What is it, Connal?" she asked, tenderly, using his Irish name rather than his Roman name. Even after ten years among the Romans, first living on Planeta Metallorum and now travelling in the starship once again, she still preferred to speak in *gaeilge arsa*, the archaic Irish language.

Neasa's aunt, Queen Laelie, had been quick to recognize the need for her people to adopt the Latin language, which was taught to them by the rhetoricians Fabius Quintilianus and Vibius Metellus. Of the Hibernian nobles, Queen Laelie had progressed the most, along with the *Filidh*, poet, Morcant the Widluios, the trader Daffid Og Briogan and the strange Druid Allanon. The nobles had worked tirelessly from the outset. Most had some previous exposure in Latin before the events at Dubh Linn, and had by now all mastered Latin. They then began conducting teaching assemblies in a few of the vacant animal-pods, organizing the Hibernians into groupings of people who were at common stages in their learning, in what the Romans called *circulus latinus*, the Latin circle.

Laelie encouraged all of the noblewomen to work extra hard. Despite her solid grasp of basic Latin, Princess Neasa, Laelie's cousin, had plateaued in her learning. Without her husband to help her, she struggled with the complexities and nuances of the

Roman language, but she found the art of writing and the act of reading aloud to children to be wonderful activities. There was nothing like that in gaelge arsa, as the archaic Irish language was an entirely oral tradition.

Princess Neasa had thrown herself into learning the language after she and Marcus had recovered from their first encounter and had found themselves in love. But she found it extremely difficult to translate the ancient stories – her personal source of wisdom, and a form of guidance from her ancestors – into the Roman language.

Her son Connal, on the other hand, was perfectly fluent in both and could handle simultaneous translations, bridging the gap between the Irish and the Romans even at such a young age. And he knew enough to speak only in gaeilge arsa when dealing with intimate mother-son issues.

"Papa! I want Papa!" he sobbed, yearning for the father he had never met, as Neasa stroked his back tenderly.

"I know, little wolf, but he can't be with us now. You know all about his important mission to Terra. But I know how you feel. I miss him as much as you do."

"But Mama, how long will he be away?"

Her heart broke, both for her son and for herself. She could not bring herself to tell him the truth. At ten years of age, he was simply not old enough to comprehend the strange reality they were caught up in, nor what 'normal life' would be like. For him, travelling vast distances through the stars to an uncertain reception on his parent's home planet seemed quite normal. What felt wrong for the young boy was being apart from his father for so long.

Coming to grips with their new way of living was difficult for Neasa, even after ten years since the Battle of Dubh Linn, and all the progress that the Romans and Irish had accomplished in terms of learning about the universe, the alien technology, and each other.

Wanting to shake her son out of his sadness, she decided to switch his attention subtly, in the hope that she could put his imagination onto a more productive path, one that would help him find more strength than any child should ever require.

She decided to begin his warrior training there and then. With Connal only tene years old, that was at least two years earlier she would have ever dreamed of doing back at Cathair mac Cassan.

She cast her mind back to where she should begin, as she had seen her cousin, Queen Laelie, commence the training with so many of the clann's youngest female warriors. It had to begin with developing the child's physical fitness, which was well in hand. The boy was sinewy, quick, and strong. More strenuous training could be coordinated with some of her husband's friends from the Eighth Cohort, as they had taken young Avitus Connal in as one of their own.

Next would be the development of his understanding of politics, of strategy, and of the complex web of alliances – in both Ireland and the Roman Empire – that had led to her encounter with Marcus Horatius Avitus.

"Tonight I will start your training as a warrior – as a wolf cub. And each night, at bed-time, I will tell you more. This will be in addition to your lessons for your Roman studies," she began.

Connal wiped the tears from his eyes and sat up to listen.

"Tonight I will tell you about the preparations for battle, the days before I met your father.

"My late uncle, King Findmal, was a master raider. Our clann's ships raided up and down the sunset coast of Britannia at will, stealing sheep, cattle and steel from the Roman outposts from *Erainn* and *Laigin* to *Deisi* and even as far north as *Dal Riata*. This was far more profitable than raiding other clanns of Tara, and having peace with our closest neighbors allowed us to trade Roman steel implements for cattle, find husbands for our women and negotiate political support.

This was how my uncle was able to gain the influence necessary to grow in power. At first he had been merely *túaithe*, king of his own family, the mac Cassan clann and a simple roundhouse atop a mound. But as his wealth and influence grew, and he had the allegiance of some of the nine clans of Tara, he became *ruiri*, Great King. Then, with the Romans preparing to invade the land of Éire, he gained the support of the nine kings of Tara and became *rí túaithe*, High King of Tara. Had we defeated the Romans at Dubh Linn, he would have had the prestige and wealth, from all the Roman steel and other treasures we would have collected from the battlefield. Findmal he would have been elected Grand High King of all Éire, ruler of a united Éire and master of all two hundred *túaithe*, lesser kings."

Young Connal was keenly interested in stories of Ireland, and was very quick to understand the main point.

"So it was by making peace and friends with his neighbors that grand-uncle mac Cassan got important?"

"Yes, very good, Connal."

"So it's just like in the teachings of Jesus Christ, 'love thy neighbor'?" he asked.

By the shocked and angry look on his mother's face, Connal understood that he had done something wrong, and began to cry.

I should not have told the secret. They told me I should never tell the secret Christian lessons to anybody, not even Mama, he thought.

Working through her anger quickly, Neasa decided to take it up with Laelie and Agricola, and not let on to her son that Christians within their ranks were once again violating the decree, from Agricola and Queen Laelie, that the teachings and legends of Jesus Christ must not be tolerated, that they were poisonous. She carried on with her lesson, putting her anger aside.

"From the crest of our Cathair on the hill with our clannsmen, Aunt Laelie and Uncle Findmal and I loved to look out over the Bay of Malahide. That way we were always the first to see what had changed in the daily comings and goings of ships each morning. Most of the ships were our own raiders, or currachs of Irish clanns from up and down the coast.

In the months before the battle of Dubh Linn, a merchant ship from our cousins, Clann Coraint in southern Britannia, brought reports of a Roman army preparing to send an entire legion to land at Malahide. The Romans were planning to lay waste to our clann and then march up to the Hill of Tara to seize our sacred *Lia Fail*, the Stone of Destiny.

From there, the heart of Éire, the Romans could garrison their legion and dominate the four provinces of Ireland, conquering the four *rí túaithe*, provincial High Kings, one after another and then subjugate all two hundred *rí túaithe* lesser kings, and make slaves of all of Éire.

"So my wise uncle, High King Findmal, sent word to his brother, King Fiche mac Cassan, King of the Monaig Clann to send word to the others of the nine kings of Tara, the Dalaighs, the Bri Chualanns, the Caucis, the Brigantes, the Noichrathachi and the others, to send all of their warriors to Dubh Linn, to fight as one. This was in sharp contrast to the cattle-raids and other small wars that the kings of Éire typically engaged in. So in a sense, young wolf, the threat of annihilation by the Romans was what brought us together as a people."

"Just like having the Tuathii as enemies brought the Romans and Irish together?" asked Connal, with an insight far in advance of his ten years.

Reflecting for a moment, and impressed with her son's maturity, she simply smiled, and nodded, before continuing.

"When the Romans began to arrive, the warriors from the nine great clanns quickly joined with us, so that our number grew at about the same pace as the Roman camp grew. For us, it was like a grand festival; something larger than had ever been done before. And here is the important thing to think about: why do you suppose they would travel such great distances to join a fight with such great warriors as your father and his Roman brothers?" Neasa asked, pleased to see how intent little Connal was listening.

"To help save Éire?" he guessed.

"Yes, that was the larger purpose, to be sure. But such high ideas are the world of scholars and nobles. What do you suppose was in the minds of the men and women warriors? I will give you a hint. What did I spear your father with, in our battle, before the Tuathii intervened to save the Romans from utter defeat?"

"That's easy, Mama! That gae bolag, deer antler, right there, on the wall over where you and papa sleep!"

"And what do all the other Irish warriors use in battle?"

"Shillelagh clubs, pointed sticks, wattles, spears, clubs, rocks, bones and antlers," he said with pride.

"And what do the Romans use?"

"Steel *gladius*, short swords, *Pugio* daggers, lances – and even the edges of their shield! And Momma, philosopher Fabius Quintilianus showed me a drawing of some *manuballista* and *arcuballistas* that can hurl a stone as large as a man's head to destroy anything it lands on!"

"That's right. The Romans have many powerful weapons. What else did they carry, on their bodies, into battle?"

Thinking hard, trying to solve the riddle, Connal began to understand. "They wore *cassis* helmets, *catafracta* suits of chain mail, *gladius major* swords, *spatha* broadswords and *scutum* shields," Connal said excitedly, and then went on another tangent. "Mama, did you know that some of papa's friends even carried *plumbata* and *speculum* darts – Centurion Flavius showed me some! Oh, and archers with *arcus* and *sagitta* bow and arrow, or *funditors* with their *lapis lings* and *fustibalus* cudgel-throwers!"

"Well done, you have listed almost the entire inventory of treasures…"

"Mama, these are weapons, not treasures," he corrected her.

"No. They are treasures. And do you know why?"

He thought about it. His mother was a wise princess, a noblewoman and one of the leaders of the Irish people. She was also highly respected by her father's people, but he could not understand what she was talking about. Treasure was gold and precious stones, as his Roman teachers had explained in their stories of the great riches the Roman Legions brought back to Rome, and put on display in the Pantheon.

Sometimes the Irish are a little bit crazy, Connal thought. *To them, a good three-pointed antler or a well-buttered Shillelagh club was a great weapon. Just because they didn't know how to make metal weapons,* he thought. "That's it, Mama! The metal! The metal was the treasure!"

Extremely proud of her little boy for making the connection, Princess Neasa rewarded him with hugs and tickles.

"And so ends your first important lesson. What motivates warriors to seek the glory of battle is not the high-minded goals of the leaders, nor to protect their villages, but to kill the enemy and take prizes from them after the battle. It is as simple as that! As a future leader, my smart little wolf club, you need to understand this, so that you can inspire your warriors to be brave, even eager, to battle against superior forces who may have superior weapons. If you do that, as High King Findmal and the nine clanns did before at the battle of Dubh Linn., you can defeat with a much smaller force, a great army such as your father's Roman Legion."

"But Mama, papa's friends say that you would have lost the battle if the Tuatha De Danann, the Tuathii, had not gathered up your warriors and Papa's army, and taken you all together to Tir na nOg," he protested.

"Little wolf, I am so pleased that you understand our mythology, but I think you should not call Planeta Metallorum Tir na nOg."

"But it is where the Tuatha de Danann took us, so it must be Tir na nOg."

"Who is telling you this?"

"Filidh Morcant the Widluios, and he says that we should be thankful to the Tuathii for taking us to their sacred homeland."

Princess Neasa was not impressed. The Irish people had been ordered to stop perpetuating the fantasy that the Tuathii are the mystical Tuatha de Danann of legend. Such foolish ideas would have her people embrace slavery. Far better to emulate the Romans and their long term strategy to lull the Tuathii into a false sense of security, never forgetting that the Tuathii are not gods, they are simply the enemy.

But she could not tell her son any of this. She made a mental note to discuss the fate of the Christians hiding within their people and their teachings of Jesus Christ and the pagan myths being propagated by the Filidh Morcant the Widluios. Perhaps

Vibius Metellus was right, and any form of religion is a cancer that should be excised.

"I think it is best if you stay away from the Christians and the Filidh. Some of their ideas are not compatible with the way things really are."

"Yes, Mama. I thought it all sounded a bit strange, but I liked the stories they told. However I like the way Vibius Metellus explained it. He said that legends are shadows of reality cast on a wall in the setting sun. They are not a good way to navigate. Far better to look at the stars themselves, and not be afraid of shadows."

"You are going to be a wise leader for both of our peoples," she said, tucking her son back into bed. "And now it is time to go to sleep. If you are quick, and fall asleep as fast as a bird flies across the sky, you may find yourself dreaming of some great battle, with all of the Irish and Roman weapons at your disposal."

Smiling at the prospect of an adventure in his sleep, and no longer pining to be reunited with his father, Avitus Connal settled into bed, eager to fall asleep.

He dreamed of an ancient battle, where his parents met, at a mystical place called *Eire*, Ireland.

VI

NAVIS E STELLIS

{Alien Ships From Heaven}

A cold, wet fog had rolled in over the harbor overnight, but was dissipating quickly as the Roman camp began to come to life.

Rising after only a few hours' sleep, Centurion Tappulus walked through the camp. He wanted to observe the mood of the men who had arrived in Hibernia from Legio XX's castra at Deva and Legio II's base, Isca Silurium, as they busied themselves with maintaining their battle armor, weapons and clothing.

While there was some consistency from one man to the next, there was also a great deal of variation, as Romans did not adhere to a uniform standard of dress. As long as it was serviceable, a *miles gregarious*, common foot-soldier, could wear pretty much anything he chose. Often, men wore a mix of old, nearly worn out components along with newer pieces. The men of Legio II, however, had a great deal of pride in their appearance, and fostered an unwritten code that each man must at least dye his woolen *tunica*, tunic, and *braccae* trousers – the basic garments common to all of the men – with bright red dye.

For those in leadership positions, from the most junior commanders up to centurion, and tribune all the way up to second in command, there were increasingly expensive and meaningful additional protection. For centurions and tribunes, it all came together into a highly effective system which provided considerable protection without impeding range of motion: Over the tunica, and held tightly to their bodies, were tough leather and metal *lorica*. *Lorica hamata*, chain mail, to protect the chest and legs; *lorica manica*, to protect the arms; layers of *lorica squamata*

71

as scales over the shoulders and joints; and large pieces of *lorica segmentata*, segmented armor, to cover the back and belly. To hold all of these pieces together, strong leather straps and sinew were threaded through holes and tied off in just the right way to give the man the ideal combination of flexibility and mobility while providing protective coverage.

Over one shoulder was a *baldric*, onto which weapons and other articles were tied. Around the waist, was a heavy belt, one of the few standardized items in a Roman legion.

Once they had completed replacing old leather straps, the men packed up their hand tools and private belongings into their satchels and turned their attention to sharpening their short swords. The primary weapon of Roman legionaries, each man carried a gladius, plus two or three other weapons, small and large, such as a Thracian *sica*, short sword or dagger, a smaller *pugio* stabbing weapon, and larger weapons, such as a two meter long *pilum*, javelin, or a *cestus*, a leather battle-glove adorned with steel spikes making a man's fist itself into a killing weapon.

For fighting formations, such as the turtle-shaped *testudo*, shield array, each man contributed their large, rectangular, semi-cylindrical *scutum* body shield resulting in a densely packed formation of overlapping shields. The *testudo* protected the sides, front, top and rear of each 80-man century of legionaries from projectiles and edged weapons. The tactic was normally used when pushing through a well-defended line or when ambushed or confronted by a superior force. It took out of the equation the effectiveness of archers and other stand-off weapons and brought the fighting down to the one or two meter range, taking away the numerical or tactical advantage that the enemy might otherwise have enjoyed.

After completing his rounds, Praefectus Castrorum Tappulus stood by the fire with other primus priori, centurions leading first-line centuries, to warm himself and gauge their mood.

The men were confident and ready, and everything seemed in order. Centurion Tappulus could sense this, because they were speaking of unimportant things, not arguing about problems.

All is good, he reflected, as he listened to the thread of the conversation.

"This *peta*, peat, is wonderful fuel," argued Centurion Spurius Crispus. As centurion from the First Century of the First Cohort, Legio XX, he was the highest ranked centurion, *Primus Pilus,* and soon eligible for Camp Prefect, a role held by his comrade Aulus Tappulus. This was not a great concern as the two men had worked out their personal issues during a night of drinking and arguing when they had first met at Legio XX's base, Castra Deva, in Britannia Major. They had fought side by side in the Ordovician campaign, and their commonality of experience forged a close bond that engendered trust.

Besides, Centurion Crispus had thought, *Aulus is close to retirement, I'll get my turn at being Praefectus Castrorum, so I may as well enjoy focusing on the First of the Twentieth and not have to worry about sucking up to the tribunes and our new legatus.*

"But what exactly is it? It burns, but it is not wood," asked Centurion Marcus Avitus, from the Eight of the Second, one of the new men who had arrived from Isca Silurium, home of the Second Legion in Britannia. Having been stationed at Silurium with the Second Legion, in the extreme southwest of Britannia, Centurion Avitus had not yet encountered the strange source of campfire fuel.

"It is dried-out *sphagnum,* moss. These lands are full of soggy wetlands, where the grasses grow on top and then sink into the bog each year when they die. The bogs are many *pes,* feet, in depth. What the Celts do is cut a drainage trench to drain a section of bog, and then carve out long slices of this muck. You see that pile over there?" Centurion Flavus, from the Tenth of the Twentieth, pointed at a dome shaped mound made up of slices of peat, looking like loaves of bread. "That is a pile of peat slabs, drying out. Once all the water is dried out, it becomes a very dense chunk of dried-out peat, ready to burn," Centurion Flavus said.

"But why do they not just burn wood?"

"I'm not sure, but I think it has to do with the fact that they don't have a lot of steel implements. Cutting a tree is a lot more work than slicing up slabs of wet bog, and they appear to have boglands in abundance around here. And from what I hear, forests are highly valued, something the local clanns come to blows over, but these peat bogs are abundantly available, if you have the courage to enter them."

"Courage?"

"They are actually quite dangerous. Stay away from them. Even the Celts only cut peat around the periphery of a bog. A man can quickly sink into it and die."

"Interesting," said the curious Avitus, throwing another slab of dried peat onto the fire. "They burn slowly, and with great heat. So why do the tribunes require so much firewood for their tents?"

"The senior officers do not like the smell. They feel that peat is too plebian for their noble blood, I suppose," Spurius Crispus offered.

As the group of senior centurions laughed, some of them looked up at the collection of tents on the hill, where candle-light cast a silhouette of two men, likely Legatus Agricola and his second in command, Tribune Cerialis.

He would not admit it to his Tribunus Laticlavius, Kaeso Petillius Cerialis, but the young Legatus, Quintus Julius Agricola was afraid.

He was not afraid to die, nor that he would be unworthy to command the composite legion his father had given him for the conquest of Hibernia. He was certain that he had been given enough of an advantage in terms of both numerical superiority and technological sophistication. The strongest unit given to him was the prestigious First Cohort from Legio XX.

Legatus Quintus Agricola was equally confident in the use of the *testudo* to punch through the Celtic center. If required, he was ready to change to other tactics, such as using some of the unusual 'crew-served' weapons being assembled by the carpenters and engineers of Cohort III of Legio II. For Agricola, whose only experience had been with the Twentieth Legion, the range of specialties of the Second Legion was unusual, and he was certain that he would find a use for the strange units that recently arrived from Hispania.

With an army of over four thousand at his disposal, just two cohorts short of forming an unofficial new legion, Legio XXVII, the young legatus was supremely confident that he had sufficient forces to conquer the tiny, albeit fierce, Hibernian force of poorly-equipped, undisciplined, malnourished and very dirty men and their she-wolves.

What he was afraid of was not doing it as swiftly and efficiently as he had promised to his father and the other nobles at his father's castra, base, at Devaback in Britannia.

He knew now, after experiencing the challenging logistics of transporting an entire army across *Oceanus Hibernicus*, the Irish Sea, and assembling them safely on the lowlands leading up into the forest at Dubh Linn, that it was one thing to put tokens onto a map and make large sweeping motions to show how he would prosecute the invasion. It was another thing altogether to execute the plan.

He now realized that each small step along the way required detailed planning, starting with the coming battle against the surprisingly well-informed High King Findmal and the other Celtic chieftains that were coming to his aid.

The many lessons that he and Cerialis had endured from the philosopher Vibius Metellus and the other advisors from his father's court now seemed to be far more useful than he had thought previously.

Before today, he had thought that battle drills and the study of military history was where he would draw what he needed for inspiration on the battlefield. Now, however, he understood that the battle would be won or lost in the detailed preparations, the careful evaluation of terrain, logistics, weather and other factors. The actual order of battle and disposition of enemy forces, on the other hand, now seemed to be the less challenging aspect of command. *Besides*, he thought, *so much will change once the battle begins.*

And after the battle is won, rather than sweeping up to Tara and quickly conquering the most powerful chieftains, Quintus. Agricola knew that he would be wise to establish a series of fortified outposts along the way, as Emperor Vespasian had done in his campaign against the twenty *oppida*, hill forts, in *Noviomagus Reginourm*, in the south of Britannica.

He also thought about the way that his father, as legatus of Legio XX, had applied the same caution, pausing to construct fortresses along the way as he steadily advanced after his initial invasion of *Caledonia*, fighting the insane breed of Celts called Scotia, in the north of Britannia.

As his servants dressed him in his battle armor, Agricola the Younger brought his focus to the matter at hand: to send larger groups of scouts farther into the forest along the ridgeline approach to Dubh Linn, to see how King Findmal responds.

Will he go for the ships of Legio II, or will he throw his reserves against the testudia of Cohort I from Legio XX? he thought, as he headed out of his tent.

"Gods be pleased! Our young commander has finally awakened. The battle is already over, Legatus; you have overslept again and missed everything!"

"Very funny, Cerialis. Give me your reports."

"As you command, Legatus," said Agricola's second-in-command.

"The men are formed up and ready to go. We have the cavalry and other reserve formations briefed for the contingencies we discussed last night, and little has changed."

"Little? Explain"

"Well, Centurion Tappulus believes that the Hibernian Chieftain is up to something."

"King. The man we are going to defeat today is a king," corrected Legatus Agricola.

"Come on, everybody and his dog is a king on this water-logged bog of an island," said Cerialis.

"You know what Vibius Metellus says about how respecting your enemies is essential for a leader, and where is our philosopher, anyhow?" asked Agricola.

"He's in the mess tent, arguing with Fabius Quintilianus about what you call the offspring of an Irish whore who was given a load of good Roman *semena*."

"In the mess tent? I did not see them on my early rounds this morning. And by the way, did you try the food today?"

"No, but I heard someone say *nemo potuit tangere: merda fuit*."

"I heard that too, that 'nobody could touch it because it was shit'. But I tried it, and it was only slightly off. I think that the men are unable to eat because they fear having their balls chewed off by the she-wolves," said Agricola.

Cerialis smiled mischievously.

"And you're not afraid of the she-wolves?"

"No, Legatus."

"And why not? Come on, out with it."

"*Graffito fututa sum hic*"

"You got laid here? When? How?"

"We captured two she-wolves scouting our right flank."

"And what did you get from them, other than their virginities?"

"One we killed outright. She told us nothing, and nobody wanted her. The other was very attractive. We all fucked and then tortured her, making her watch as we cut the first one to pieces and stuck her head on a pole to display to the enemy scouts."

"Kaeso, you know what the policy is, regarding sex in the camp. That's why we did not bring any whores with us. It creates all sorts of discipline problems. What the hell were you thinking?" demanded Agricola, visibly angry. As an inexperienced young general with his first major command, Agricola wanted everything to go smoothly, as much to impress his father as to become a good general in his own right.

"I had good reason, Legatus."

"Explain."

"We got good intelligences out of the second one, but I think the information she gave up came too easily, just as she did."

"What?"

"Do you see any scars on my face?"

77

"No. Why is that important?"

"Because unless she wanted to become my new wife, she gave herself to me too easily. She should have put up a better fight. It was almost as if she had been sent to fuck me, and fill my head with lies and my heart with confusion."

"She did not succeed?"

"She succeeded in passing her story, but I don't pay it much heed."

"What was her story?"

"That by the end of the day tomorrow we will all be dead. There will not be a single Roman left alive on Hibernia."

"Did she tell you the tactic that is supposed to defeat us? Or were you too busy to ask?"

"She said that we were cursed and that magical faeries would protect her people. And if that's not enough, she said that we would have to swim for our lives, as we would be without boats. But she seemed to regret that last comment."

"So you think she was sent in an attempt to deceive us?"

"Yes, definitely. So we returned the favor."

"You sent her back, alive?"

"Yup. Not very much alive, but enough to survive. After the boys from the First of the Twentieth tortured her for a while, they tied her up outside my tent. I then pretended to have a very loud argument with Tribune Marcus Avitus, you know, the young tribune from Legio II, commanding the Eighth Cohort?"

"Yes. A trustworthy and competent young officer, for a *gens hispania galaecia*, a Spaniard. So what was the planted message?"

"We argued about how long it would take for Cohort Three from Legio Twenty to march around King Findmal's left flank and take their mud huts while the First of the Twentieth keeps them busy in the valley up into Dubh Linn."

"But the Third of the Twentieth is still back at the Castra Deva in Britannia"

"Exactly."

"So what, you argued in Celtic? – I know the Spaniard Tribune Avitus is from *Lucus Augusti*, Lugo, in Galician Hispania, so he mightt speak some of the Celtic language, but how could you pull that off? You don't speak a word of Celtic, do you?"

"No, Legatus, I don't," smiled Cerialis. "We spoke Latin."

"So how did you expect her to understand your little deception?"

"Oh, she speaks Latin."

"How do you now that?"

"Because when I was done fucking her a few hours earlier, she called me an old man."

"Really? What did she say, exactly?"

"Well, I was laying back on my bed, satisfied like the drunken satyr that I am, and she looked at me from where she was on the floor and laughed at me. She said: '*seni supino colei culum tegunt*.'"

Legatus Agricola laughed uproariously and then asked: "Well, do they?"

"What."

"Do your 'old man's balls' cover your asshole when you lay down?"

The two men laughed about it as they walked towards the perfectly aligned cohorts, but then suddenly General Agricola stopped in his tracks.

"Wait a minute! How could she speak Latin? The only people who know how to talk civilized are their nobility."

"That's right, Legatus."

"So who was she?"

"I think she's the sister by marriage of Queen Laelie."

"You piss in my water, Cerialis! If you're right, we're going to have a fight on our hands today, even if the small-time king is fooled by your deception and holds back his reserve forces. You can't fuck a man's younger sister like and expect to get away with it!"

"I know. I probably should have kept her for the hostage value, rather than try to use her as a pawn. But it does reduce the old man's options to only two. He'll come after us up the center – if he makes it personal – and then he'll have to cover *his* anus with *his* testicles as we penetrate into his lines up on that ridge."

Impressed with the logic, Agricola looked at his best friend with new respect. "So that means he won't go after our ships down in Malahide Bay? Well done, Cerialis. We'll know soon enough."

The troops were off and watching with pride as the first two *testudae* of the First of the Twentieth began taking blows from the wildly chaotic forces of King Findmal. Legatus Quintus Agricola rode back to his command tent to await the scouting reports that would tell him which way the Irish were going to move.

It did not take long before his reports began to build a clear picture. Either the king had not taken the bait, or his sister had not understood what she had overheard, because the Irish king had indeed made the most incisive move possible.

It was what a Roman commander would have done, cut off the invader's logistical tail by going after the ships.

He waited as long as he dared, to make sure it was not a feint, and then sent the bulk of his reserves back to Malahide Bay. He had no choice.

It bothered him that he had lost the initiative so quickly, so he decided to take a risk and try to tilt the table back in his own direction by throwing his final reserves into the drive for Dubh Linn, to push through and then drive onwards to King Findmal's hamlet, Cathair mac Cassan.

Just as he rode out towards the front, to see how things were unfolding, he saw two things simultaneously.

First, he sighted a large number of small people sweeping across the bog and closing in on his rear formation, going directly towards his personal guards, the small reserve of cavalry, and specialty units of the Second Legion, who were clustered around his command tent.

So that's what he had up his sleeve, a cohort-sized pack of she-wolves meant to make a fast thrust for the throat, Legatus Agricola realized with respect. *Good thing I'm not there! I sure hope that Marcus Avitus can handle them,* he thought, as he turned his attention skyward.

He had sensed a darkening of the skies, and assumed it was just a change in the weather. Hibernia was legendary for its bouts of heavy rain alternating with glorious sunshine.

But what he saw next made him fall off of his horse, throwing his personal guard detail and his ever-present advisers and companions into chaos and near panic.

"Sol Invictus!" cried one of the more spiritual among Legatus Agricola's retinue, as a giant object suddenly obscured the sun.

VII

PROELIVM DVBLINENSIS
{ Battle of Dubh Linn }

He saw his young wife square off against a metal-clad Roman with a bright red brush sticking out of a shiny brass helmet. *That's a tribune she's killing*, King Findmal mac Cassan realized with pride as he watched Queen Laelie spin around and dive under the thrust of the tribune's short sword. From his vantage point at the ridgeline, to the side of the main battle area, Findmal was able to look down on the grassy lowlands where the Roman rearguard, command tent, and reserves were located. Despite the dust being generated by the larger contest closer to him, he was carefully watching Laelie's attack on the Roman right flank, hoping for victory as much as he worried for his queen.

It looked as though Laelie got the Roman in the belly with her antler weapon. But then he saw the Roman make a broad slash across her chest. The Roman tribune and Queen Laelie fell to the ground together. Strangely, the fighting began to die down as the Irish attackers and the Roman defenders became aware of two large objects descending from the sky.

Farther up the valley, initially oblivious to what was taking place to their rear, the lead Roman cohorts and the Celtic men continued the battle.

Satisfied that the battle was going well, Primus Pilus, Centurion Crispus saw a large shadow pass across the battlefield. He turned around instinctively. With horror, he saw his general surrounded by Celtic women warriors, who were moving in for the kill like a pack of blood thirsty she-wolves.

He still had not looked up to the heavens, as he reacted swiftly to the deteriorating tactical situation. He personally led as many men as he could, rushing back towards the command tent. But as he got closer, he realized that the fighting had stopped.

The women warriors backed away from the battle into small groups, with their backs to each other, forming protective circles. Crouching close to the ground, they looking at each other in panicked confusion. The Romans, more disciplined and organized, pulled back from the Celtic women and formed themselves into a smaller version of a *testudo* formation, close to where Laelie had fallen with the Roman tribune.

As if from a gap between clouds on a sunny day, a broad beam of bright light shot down from one of the ships. Soon other beams emanated from other parts of the egg-shaped vessel, until a broad yellow curtain carved out a large rectangular area.

Not far away, to King Findmal it looked as though the terrible wall that surrounded the battlefield around the Roman commander's tent seemed to be moving inwards, tightening like a fishing net, only this was one from which there was no escape.

He could see through the curtain, however what could be seen was indistinct, except for those people closest to the curtain.

The curtain had become entirely enclosed just after one group of Romans, led by a brush-hatted officer, had rushed back towards their general. Now, they shared his fate inside the curtain. A second group of men, only a few paces behind, had run headlong into the curtain. To Findmal's surprise, the men had vanished in a bright flash of golden light – except for the upper torso, head and arms of one man who had tried to pull up and stop himself, but had been a stride too late. The man's legs had penetrated the curtain, and had disappeared in a flash, as if converted from material into light. His torso and upper body, not having contacted the wall, fell backwards, cleaved off from the now non-existent lower half of his body. Of the other men who had perished in a flash, nothing remained – not even smoke, clothing, or weapons. There was not even any blood.

Findmal watched in horror as the wall continued to close in, to where his wife had fallen. He was sure she was mortally wounded, or dead, but to lose her body to such an unknown and seemingly evil force would add even more misery to his terror.

Running to get closer, to help his wife in any way that he could, he closed the distance quickly, passing motionless legionaries who had stopped fighting to watch in awe.

As he neared the wall, he slowed, panting and out of breath. He watched helplessly as a Roman soldier, caught inside of the enclosure, stumbling from a wound and unable to stay ahead of the advancing curtain, leaned towards the wall with his shield in an attempt to protect himself and the tribune who had fallen with Laelie. *The shield did not disappear in bright yellow light!* Findmal realized. It simply collided with the slowly moving wall, and was pushed inexorably closer to the wounded officer, pushing the survivors along like a spade scraping weeds along the surface of the ground.

By this time King Findmal was just a few paces from the ever-closing wrap, and could see to the inside of the enclosed area. He saw two large egg-shaped vessels, much larger than the two flying above, had settled on the ground.

He tried an experiment. He picked up a stone and threw it at the wall.

The stone disappeared in a small yellow burst, and was obliterated.

The wall does not destroy what it encounters on one side, but destroys whatever it encounters on the other, he realized.

He looked up, to see how high the wall rose.

It seemed to bend and gather itself the higher it went, like the fabric that surrounded his bedchambers to cut the biting draft.

And then he realized that *the strange terrible wall is somehow falling like a cascade of water from the stern of the vessel floating in the clouds!* The one in the sky looked much the same as the two very much larger ships that had landed on the ground.

Looking at the ships, he saw large oval portions of the sides opening and lowering down onto the ground, revealing that there were chambers and passages inside these incredible orbs from the sky.

The wall had closed in on his wife, and it began to roll her along the ground. *She is rolling away from the wall. She lives!*

The Roman officer had been picked up by some of his legionnaires, and was being dragged by the arms between two of his men.

By the way his head rolled up and down, the man was lifeless, or nearly so.

Well done, my queen, you killed your opponent! But where are they taking his body?

It seemed as though the soldiers were all moving as far away from the curtain of enclosing walls as fast as they could. And so were his people.

Tt the ever-closing curtain-wall seemed to be forcing all of the combatants towards the two ships. He had begun to think of them as ships, even though they were far larger than even the largest merchant ship he had seen at anchor in Malahide Bay.

It looked to King Findmal to be much like the way his people herded sheep and goats – only with dogs, not the mysterious moving curtain – into a pen for the slaughter.

A few of the Romans seemed to realize that they were running out of options, so they tested the sides of the strange ships with their spears and swords. Finding them solid, they then began to explore the openings in the sides of the ships.

Before they had worked up the courage to venture inside of their own will, they began to be forced in by the pressing wall of human flesh as the curtain walls closed in around the two ships, forcing the now shoulder-to-shoulder mass of what must be two hundred-counts of people inside each of the vessels.

And then the strangest thing happened.

Light appeared inside the bowels of the vessels, illuminating them as if to welcome the people inside. It seemed to break their hesitation, and the people began moving in, willingly, it appeared.

King Findmal sat on the grass next to the corpse of one of his women warriors for a long time after the vessels lifted off of the ground and joined others that had been floating in the sky.

The curtain walls had disappeared with them, and the small armada of three small and two large egg-shaped vessels became smaller and smaller, as if rising up to the heavens.

And then they were gone.

Eventually King Findmal got up and walked slowly back to where he and his brother had been destroying the first two turtles of the Roman force.

The battle had ceased, of course, when the fighting men had finally become aware of the strange events taking place down in the valley. When it was over, the remaining Romans had fled along the edge of the forest, making their way to Malahide Bay and the safety of their ships. No doubt they would be back in Britannia as fast as humanly possible. They had abandoned their battle standards, weapons, and any sense of order.

The valley was full of corpses, but from the fact that only Irish warriors were moving about between the fallen, it was clear that at least this part of the battle had gone according to plan.

He watched in silence as an old woman he did not recognize and a few of the older boys and girls from his own clann, killed wounded Romans. Others followed behind, undressing the bodies and gathering their weapons and uniforms into small piles – the booty of war.

He should have been excited to see that his clann, along with that of his brother and his friends from the Cauci, Brigantes and Manapii clanns, had achieved such a great victory. He should have been pleased with the treasure of metal, leather and other materials they had gained from the Romans, and the prestige that this should have given him. But his heart was heavy for the loss of the remarkable women he had never fully understood – the woman who had kept his balls in a Dubh Linn jar, and yet, the woman he loved with all that he was.

He had lost his young queen to some strange, magical power that was greater than himself, and even greater than the Roman emperor, Domitian.

Later, as he and the leaders of the other clanns argued about what had happened, he was silent. Barely listening, all he could do was watch from the ridgeline above Dubh Linn as the remainder of the Roman force, mostly cohorts of the Twentieth Legion, boarded their ships in Malahide Bay.

Clearly the Romans were mystified and demoralized by the disappearance of their command element and what sounded like the heart and soul of their XX and II Legions, and had decided to return to Britannia and not press on with their invasion of Hibernia.

There was only one explanation, he rationalized. The legends were true, and the Tuatha De Danann people had returned to gather the most noble people, his queen and her warriors, and, strangely, the command elements of the Roman force, and taken them to the mystical land of Tir na nOg.

He had thought that such legends were only stories to entertain children, but he had no better explanation.

It did put his heart at ease to know that Laelie was in a better place now. But it was also a place that he knew she would never return from.

For his fellow chieftain, King Techmar, who had landed in Malahide Bay just in advance of the Romans, joining forces with King Findmal and his brother, King Fiacha mac Cassan and the other local kings, this was a golden opportunity to set things right and undo the terrible wrong that had befallen their women lost to the Tir na nOg. Drunk with their victory and the spoils of war, and thirsting for vengeance against someone – anyone – for the loss of their women, Findmal's cousin, King Fiacha mac Cassan, along with the other chieftains quickly agreed to support Techmar.

All told, their assembled force now stood at over six hundred-counts of men despite the heavy losses incurred by the abduction of Findmal's queen and her women warriors, and the women warriors of King Techmar and the others.

They marched unopposed for two days, reaching Tara on the third day. From there, the sacred seat of power for all the Irish kings, King Techmar with the full support of King Fiacha mac Cassan and the half-hearted support of the grieving King Findmal, King Techmar went on to defeat the treacherous King Elim mac Conrach of Ulaidh at the battle of Achal. King Techmar was declared Grand High King of all Éire , just as his father had been before the betrayal of Elim mac Conrach had usurped him during the Mag Mucrama wars.

Soon after, the nobility of all Éire , including all two hundred chieftain kings, gathered at *Croc na Teamhrach*, the Hill of Tara, to swear allegiance to Grand High King Techmar, "The Legitimate", and his descendants.

It was not as though King Findmal was so quick to forget about Queen Laelie that he had thrown in with King Techmar and the dream of unifying all of Éire under one king. It was more that having come within a whisker of losing everything to the Romans, Findmal and the other kings wanted Éire to be free. The only way to be free, with an increasingly large Roman presence just across the waters in Britannia, was to be strong. As a bundle of a great many sticks is stronger than one, or two, or even nine. *Freedom requires power*, Findmal had decided.

King Findmal would never get over the loss of his queen, and her abduction to the mystical land of Tir na nOg. But with none of the faeries and mystical beings around to hold accountable, all he had to focus his rage upon were the Romans in Britannia.

He spent the rest of his life harassing the Romans up and down the west coast of Britannia, always with an eye to the heavens, looking for some sign of where his lost queen had gone.

The Romans came to fear the Hibernian raiders, who appeared without warning in their fleets of currach boats, causing General Agricola the Elder and his Twentieth and Second Legions no end of trouble.

In a largely successful effort to head off a disastrous erosion of morale, Gnaeus Julius Agricola, governor of Roman Britannia, had acted swiftly to silence the survivors from the disaster in Hibernia.

After dealing with the officers, legionnaires and others who had heard the stories, General Agricola the Elder set about writing the report to inform Emperor Domitian of the disaster, and his recommendations.

Rome would never again attempt to invade Éire, protected as it was by strange and terrible forces.

To even speak of the defeat of the composite legion that his son, Quintus Julius Agricola, had commanded; or the disappearance of the other young nobles who had accompanied his son on the ill-fated campaign, or the missing core elements of the Twentieth and Second Legions, this was punishable by death.

The Hibernian defeat of the Romans at the battle of Dubh Linn at Malahide Bay would not appear in the chronicles of Gaius Cornelius Tacitus – nor would the disappearance of Publius Cornelius Tacitus' own mentor, Vibius Metellus, ever be recorded. *It was as if it had never happened.*

The disaster would be stripped from the annals of history. From that moment on, it was as though General Quintus Julius Agricola had never had a son, and it was the same for the other nobles involved.

VIII

ITER EX PATRIA
{ Journey from homeland }

Fascinating, thought Aulus Tappulus, centurion from the Eight Cohort of Legio II as he stepped along, inside the belly of the monster.

For some reason, which Centurion Tappulus did not give much thought to, he did not feel any fear. *If the monster wanted them dead, it surely would have killed them by now*, he thought.

He was the first to enter, leading the way, with the legionaries from COH VIII following their Pilus Prior as much out of fear as obedience. For his part, the further inside Centurion Tappulus walked the more relaxed and at ease he felt. It was very strange. Moments earlier, he had been in a desperate battle, fighting for his life and that of his general. That battle now seemed a distant memory. He was no longer full of rage and blood lust, and when he looked at some of the Hibernian women also venturing inside, along the wall opposite the one he followed, he did not feel hatred. *Whatever this is, they are in it just as we are*, Centurion Tappulus thought as he continued deeper inside, fear and uncertainty overridden by a powerful and inexplicable intuition that he was safer inside the beast than outside.

Centurion Tappulus had not made any rational analysis of the situation that now confronted him; he simply knew that there were no other options than to explore the place that he, along with a crowd of Romans and Hibernians alike, had been herded into.

The darkness was soon replaced by a dim light provided by some unknown form of craftsmanship, where a uniform series of long, flameless sources of light had been placed at intervals along the tops of the walls. The walls were perhaps twice again the height of a man, and made of a perfectly smooth, consistent material which was colored a yellowish white, giving the long hall an illumination as bright as the afternoon sun. In his mind, perhaps due to the curving floor and passage, and what he had seen from the outside before entering, he began to think of the strange edifice as some kind of a flying ship of some unknown origin.

He looked back in the direction he had come and saw that all of the people who followed him – Hibernians and Romans alike, numbering into the hundreds it appeared - all seemed to have been calmed and drawn inside, much as he had been. There was a mix of abating fear and curiosity on the faces of the Celtic women.

One in particular caught his attention. When he looked at her, she did not shy away or glare at him with hatred. She smiled at him. For an instant, Tappulus stared at the woman, transfixed by her display of self-confidence – a trait he found highly attractive.

For Genovefa, one of Queen Laelie's captains, the handsome Roman had caught her eye. He was a muscular man, and was clearly some sort of leader. She liked the cautious way he led his men down the corridor. *If some terrible fate lays ahead of us, better he and his men face it than my girls*, she thought, while putting away the other things she found herself feeling for the man. *This is no time to fantasize.*

On the faces of the men, those Tappulus recognized from the Eighth of the Second, curiosity; those of cohorts of the Twentieth, on the other hand, confusion and hesitation.

That there would be a different reaction amongst the men of Legion II compared to those of Legion XX made sense to Centurion Tappulus: the Second Legion had a maritime background, after all, and maintained a history of traditions and skills which fostered experimentation and exploration.

All his twenty years of service had been in the Second Legion, right up to the re-assignment to the new legion under Agricola the Younger. It was a radical change.

In the past, hailing from the Second meant that Centurion Tappulus and the men of the Eighth Cohort in particular, had been given every undesirable job imaginable. All of the prestige and battle honors went to Legatus Gnaeus Agricola's original legion in Britannia, the Twentieth. And as shit rolls downhill, the less desirable maintenance and construction work was relegated to the newcomers to Britannia, the Second, and yet the Second Legion itself had perhaps the most unusual pedigree in all of the Roman Empire.

The Second Legion was originally part of the Roman navy. It was used to great effect by Octavian at the Battle of Actium and then policed the mediterrainian for decades. Eventually Roman naval dominance of the Mediterranian resulted in these men becoming idle at just the time that additional legions were needed for the conquest of Gallia and Germania. As a result, these under-utilized naval personnel were formed into *Legio II Augusta*. They participated in the final conquest of Hispania and had also been dispatched to Germania after the destruction of the Seventeenth, Eighteenth and Nineteenth Legions at Teutoburg Forest. Now entirely used for land-warfare, the Second was one of the best legions in the history of Rome. However, even when relegated to building stone walls, bridges and castra fortresses, as at Lugo, Hispania, and at various locations in Gallia, the Second never completely lost its seafaring origins.

They were taken along by then-legatus and future Emperor Vespasian in the Roman invasion of Britannia. Now, twelve years later, the shipbuilding and engineering prowess of the Second was generally devoted to constructing fortifications at each successive encampment as Legatus Legionus Gnaeus Agricola, steadily expanded Roman territory to the north, into Caledonia, and to the continued improvements to Legio XX's main castra garrison, Deva, in western Britannia.

They took great pride in constructing barracks, rock-lined fences, stone ovens and high wooden sentry towers, as well as managing local slaves in the digging of wells and the building of temporary corduroy roads and other crude improvements to new Roman outposts, crafted from local materials. Legion II was a proud fighting legion, but by virtue of having the reputation as the best soldiers to apply to such tasks, they were the de-facto custodians of just about every unusual trade, technology or craft within the Roman forces serving in Britannia, or even the entire empire for that matter, and they were the only legion with any skills in nautical tasks and astrological navigation.

And that suited Centurion Tappulus just fine. He enjoyed the technical challenges that his Eighth Cohort were assigned, despite the lack of respect they seemed to get from the land-locked Twentieth.

His men were the veterans of countless battles, however the bulk of their time had been spent leaning their shoulders into stone and timber, and using their hand-tools with craftsmanship that bordered on artisanship. Local slaves, of course, were used for the simpler work, when beasts of burden were in short supply. But for the more highly skilled work, such as throwing up a fortification in lands still under active dispute, such as in the hotly contested highlands of Caledonia, it was necessary to use soldiers from Legio II themselves, who could fight for, design, build and defend an outpost – all in a day's work.

As with any Roman legion, the Octavian Cohort, COH VIII, was given no special designation. Comprised simply of competent veterans, they did not have the added burden of the younger, less experienced troops as was the case for the Secondus, Quartus, Septimus and Nonus – COH's II, IV, VII and IX. While this made Tappulus's job as their centurion that much easier, it also came with the added responsibility as *Praefectus Castrorum*, the camp Prefect, for the entire legion. This meant that he would delegate some of his centurion duties to the *tesserarii* – leaders of each individual century within the cohort – and cultivated a high degree of mutual support among his men. This put him in a position to trust that his COH VIII would function as expected in battle or on major projects while he, as Primus Pilus and third in command of the legion, could remain abreast of tactical and political considerations by spending a great deal of time in the presence of the young new legatus, Agricola the Younger, son of General Agricola himself.

Despite having some very experienced legionaries from both legions, there were problems. The unusual combination of elements of the two different legions that formed Emperor Domitian's new legion for the conquest of Hibernia, Legio XXVII Hibernicus Domitianus, produced simmering rivalries.

Some of the men had felt that it was a bad omen for the emperor to give his name to the composite legion before it had set foot in Hibernia, while others argued that by hollowing out core elements from the Twentieth and the Second, to form an incomplete Twenty-Seventh Legion would leave Governor Agricola without a single, effective, fully formed legion in Britannia, only two partial legions.

The emperor's strategy, however, was to gain a foothold in Hibernia, announce his great victory to much excitement, and then able to raise the required funds to finance the required additional cohorts and supplies to make all three legions whole.

Back in garrison at the legionary castrae at Deva and Isca Silurum, the home bases for both the Twentieth and Second Legions, these conflicting perspectives had erupted into dirty tricks and occasional brawls between the two proud legions, but Centurion Tappulus was confident that after their first major battle in Hibernia, the men would sing victory songs together and begin to form the bonds and identity of their new legion.

Once they had taken Hibernian wives and began to settle into life in their new territory, as the resident legion of Hibernia, these bonds would become permanent.

Or at least that had been the plan.

But as he accepted the new reality that he was confronted with, that he and his men – along with a few Celtic men and a large number of the Irish she-wolves that had flown into the Roman rear echelon like a pack of rabid dogs – were now being herded into the belly of a ship of some kind. So his responsibilities as Praefectus Castrorum continued, in a new context.

He looked at his men reassuringly, as if to tell them that everything was going to be all right.

That was what he felt in his heart as he resumed his exploration of ship. It was still his responsibility to see to the well-being of the men – his own men, those of other cohorts, and perhaps even the well-being of the she-wolves who had been captured along with Legio XXVII Hibernicus Domitianus.

He could hear the shouted commands from tribunes and *pilus posterior* centurions, officers like himself, commanding the *principales* to get their men under control. He could hear the principales, the non-commissioned officers, calming the highly specialized *immunes,* the regular *miles gregarius* foot soldiers, and perhaps the most terrified of the soldiers, the untrained *milites* recruits to overcome their fear and to move along into the belly of the ship with a semblance of order and courage.

As the legionaries began to calm, and discipline returned, the Hibernian warriors seemed to calm as well.

Centurion Tappulus saw that the many women warriors and a small number of male Celts were gathering together, maintaining their distancefrom legionaries as the two groups of combatants were forced inside the strange ship.

Being from the Second Legion, with their naval pedigree, it was not unusual that Tappulus would look at this strange beast in naval terms.

It seemed to be a ship of some kind, albeit descending out of the skies rather than plying the waters.

The only other possible comparison he could make was to that of the catacomb tunnels, storage rooms, and halls buried under Rome's latest engineering marvel, the *Flavian Amphitheatre*, what would ultimately come to be known as the *Colosseum*.

As he made his way down the corridor, he counted his paces to form an internal map of the catacombs he was exploring.

He had entered the ship near one end, which he thought of as the anus, through a doorway slightly to the left side. After thirty paces, he encountered a much longer corridor, forking to the left and to the right. To the left, he could hear sounds and, lost in the distant curve of the corridor, could see only the shadows of other Romans and Hibernians. He assumed that others had been herded into the ship through other portals he had seen opening when the ship had settled on the ground.

As the men calmed and observed their surroundings, they began whispering comments to each other. Centurion Tappulus did not join them, and remained a few paces ahead, but he was pleased to hear some of them drawing the same conclusions he had, as though his own thoughts were part of a larger consensus of understanding. *They are from the Second, no doubt*, he thought as he explored the long corridor. It took him in a long curve leading to the right and downward, toward what he estimated to be the central spine of the ship. He saw some daylight and people coming in through portals at the far end, the nose of the ship, perhaps the distance of a good javelin throw farther along. That would make the ship about as long as his favorite building in Rome, the Pantheon, only this ship did not have an ocular hole at the top and seemed to be shaped more like an enormous egg than the Pantheon's domed wheel shape.

Sensing that what lay ahead, towards the nose of the ship, was much like what he had passed after entering at the anus, he stopped and turned his attention to the details along the side wall to his right. Reaching out to touch it, he found it perfectly smooth, like a well-crafted piece of metal. He tried to scratch the material with his short sword; *it is metal, only much harder and stronger than the steel of my gladius. Whoever made this ship must be enormously wealthy. They must know much more about metallurgy than any Roman*, he thought.

Then he reached up to put the tips of his fingers on the lower edge of one of the light-giving objects. Long and strip-like, they were not hot to the touch, which surprised him. Tappulus expected the source of light to be hot, like candles, or reflective mirrors used to send signals from one hilltop to another. *All sources of light I have ever known are always hot, or at least warm, yet these light strips are as cool as the metal walls.*

And then he saw something that really shocked him. He saw something alive, yet so absolutely out of place as to make him stop and stare. There, running along the top corner of the wall, and stretching as far as the eye could see, was a tree root, about as thick as a man's leg.

There were smaller roots branching off from the main root, at regular intervals of about ten paces. In some places, there were roots coming up out of the floors and reaching up to those along the high corners of the corridor. In other cases, roots made smooth turns at right angles, disappearing up into the ceiling.

As he tried to investigate where one of the roots led into the ceiling, he was astonished to see that the hole that the root had disappeared into seemed to have been cut with crude implements, as the size of the hole was irregular and jagged, and did not appear to have the same perfect craftsmanship that he had observed of the walls and light strips.

He then followed one of the smaller root-branches, and traced it until it disappeared into the wall. He realized that the branches seemed to disappear into the walls on both sides of the corridor.

He put his hand on one of the root branches.

In that moment, as the salty sweat of his fingertip made physical contact with the root on the wall, Centurion Tappulus's life changed forever.

Still terrified at the sudden appearance of the Tuatha De Danann, the mystical, shape-shifting people who occasionally come to Éire to take away some lucky people to Tir na nOg, Princess Neasa recognized that she was the ranking mac Cassan warrior amongst her group. She passed the word that the other Celtic warriors should follow her into the mystical ship, and that they should stop killing the Romans – for now. As she led them deeper into the ship, she kept an eye out for Queen Laelie, Princess Maura, or any other nobles of her clann, but saw none. *Perhaps they entered that other egg*, Neasa thought.

Allanon, the Druid priest that had followed King Findmal's female warriors into battle, had been very helpful in reassuring the Irish that no harm would come to them from *the ancient ones*.

All of the people of Éire knew the legend of the Tuatha De Danann, but none had been seen in Éire for many generations. Most actually believed that the stories were just legends to entertain and mystify the youth. So even if it appeared that the ancient ones meant them no harm, and that they would be taken to the otherworldly lands of Tír na nOg where they would live forever in happiness, the Celtic warriors of Éire were still afraid.

On her ship, they all looked to Princess Neasa for guidance, and she felt their fearing, wondering eyes locked onto her.

She took a deep breath, raised her shoulders to exude a confidence she did not really feel, and took in her surroundings with a similarly cautious and analytical mindset as her Roman counterpart, a few man-strides ahead.

As she watched the Roman, whom she realized was a centurion, Neasa saw his behavior change the moment his hand made contact with the large tree root on the wall of the corridor.

It was the look on his face which she first noticed. His look had changed from a concerned, intent and confused to one of absolute equanimity.

It was as if his mind had been transported to a happier time and place, or he had learned something that made him forget his worries and enjoy a moment of happiness. But he also seemed transfixed, frozen in thought.

It only lasted a moment, but that was long enough for Laelie to conclude that something important happens when you touch one of the roots.

She waited to see what would happen next, as did the Roman and Irish warriors who now populated the corridor.

Moments later, out of the corner of her eye, she noticed a change in the light, as if the corridor had become darker yet some source of daylight seemed to have intensified.

She was just turning her head to look when an inviting burst of light washed around the centurion in front of her, and a section of wall disappeared like a wife's dress falling away upon removal of a Tara broach at the shoulder. Only this wall fell away to one side!

She watched as the centurion absent-mindedly let go of the root and stepped over the threshold into the brightly lit room.

As she lost sight of him in the brilliant light, it dawned on her that he looked so relaxed and at peace, as if returning home. The thought made Neasa think that the Roman truly was entering Tir na nOg.

The moment he made contact with the *radix arboria*, tree root, Centurion Tappulus understood everything.

He did not know how he knew, and if he were asked he would not have been able to explain in any great detail, but all of the uncertainty and questioning that had been in his mind only a moment before he made contact with the tree root had suddenly disappeared.

He now understood the answers to his most pressing questions. He understood that the purpose of the tree roots – as he now understood them to be – was to communicate with the entity that controlled the ship.

He now understood that it was, in fact, a ship. A ship that would soon take them away from the ground, and up *ad astra* – to the stars.

He now knew that any time he wanted to enter a chamber *intus astrum navis*, inside the starship, all he had to do was think about the intent while making contact with a tree root.

The brilliant flood of warmth and light, while initially harsh on his eyes, soon felt as comfortable to him as it would to any Roman, about as intense as a sunny spring day in Hispania or in Rome.

As he stepped into what he understood from his contact with the tree root to be living quarters for a *mating pair*, a man and a woman, Centurion Tappulus knew that he was looking at one of 216 such chambers in the *astrum navis* , starship. He did not think it strange at all that despite never having entered such an unusual object, he understood that only 108 of the pods were for people, and the rest for livestock and feed.

He did not wonder how it was that he understood the purpose of the oddly shaped protrusions molded into the walls in the chamber. He simply *knew* that the oval object at the far end of the chamber was the sleeping surface. He went over to it and knelt down, reaching out to feel what he knew would be a soft material, yet as firm as a young woman's buttocks.

As he thought this, he looked up and saw two Hibernian women peeking into the chamber. One was very young, and seemed to be the leader. The other was slightly older, perhaps in her mid-twenties, and was the attractive one that Tappulus had noticed as he had entered the starship. She looked regal and unafraid, yet it was clear that she did not have the coherent understanding that the tree root had given him.

"Hibernian woman, go on, touch the tree root," Centurion Tappulus said to the attractive one, gesturing to the tree root nearest the woman.

She looked at the tree root with skepticism, and then at the younger woman. While she hesitated, the younger woman darted her hand out and grasped the root, fiercely, as if expecting it to hurt.

Just as she did so, Centurion Tappulus saw a fellow officer from Legio II join them, leaning into the pod inadvertently bumping his forearm onto that of the young noblewoman, who was still clutching the tree root. Tappulus was about to say something to Tribune Avitus, when he saw the moment of Equanimity occur.

He saw it in the change of expression taking place on both the young Hibernian woman's face and, simultaneously, on the Tribune's face.

Without a word between them, the Tribune Marcus Avitus and the Hibernian woman exchanged a form of knowing agreement, and entered the chamber to examine it together.

Centurion Tappulus surmised that the enlightenment he had experienced upon touching the *radix arboria* had occurred for the Hibernian woman, and that the experience had been conveyed *through her body* into that of his friend, Tribune Marcus Avitus.

It told him something important about how the *radix arboria* conveyed information.

"Tribune Avitus, do you understand this the way I do?" he asked.

"Yes, Centurion Tappulus, I do. It is remarkable! These Tuathii are amazing beings, and possess great power."

"Tuathii?" asked Tappulus.

"Yes, Tuatha De Danann, in the Hibernian tongue. The magical beings who take people away from Hibernia to an otherworldly realm, Tir na nOg."

"How do you know this? It was not infused into me when I touched a *radix*, of one of these Tuathii."

"Well, Tappulus, you simply have not made contact with the right Hibernian woman," he said, smiling at Princess Neasa warmly.

It seemed very strange to Centurion Tappulus, who still bore the scars from a Hibernian she-wolf he had barely defeated earlier in the battle, to see a fellow Roman, an officer no less, suddenly behaving as though he were deeply in love with an enemy woman.

Thinking of the wild attack the scraggly old woman had launched at him in the battle, Tappulus slipped his right hand under his lorca segmentata body armor to feel the wound from the sharp claws of her unusual weapon.

He found only a raised welt where there should have been a long cut in his skin from what must have been an eagle's claw tied to a stick.

"My wound! It is healing very quickly!" he said, pulling up a layer of his lorca segmentata to show Tribune Marcus Avitus his bare ribs.

"I see no wound, Centurion Tappulus, only a welt. Are you sure you were wounded? This is no more than a whack, not even enough to bother a milite, recruit."

"It is certain. Feel the wetness of the blood on the leather? A she-bitch had shoved an unguis, claw, into my side before I got her in the throat with my gladius."

"You are right. There is blood inside your leather, yet your skin is whole. This is a mystery. But is it necessary to speak so disparagingly about the warrior you so recently honored with a valiant death?"

Tappulus looked at his friend as though he were insane.

"They are the enemy, Marcus. Why is it that you have suddenly come to see them as worthy of such respect? Why do you look at this she-wolf with love in your eyes? he asked, accusingly.

As the Romans talked, Neasa had moved to a wide, oval-shaped protrusion in the far corner of the chamber. Without the slightest compunction, she pulled up her slip as she spun around and sat back, resting her rear thighs on the lip of the platter-sized surface, her privates centered over a hole in the seat.

Watching with curiosity as she defecated and urinated on the brilliant white surface under the seat-hole, the two men stopped arguing.

It was not so much that the woman was immodest, as they looked at her as they would any other soldier unburdening himself. It was that they were interested to see what would happen to the solid and liquid waste when she was done.

From their own moments of Equanimity they had shared with the *radix arboria*, they understood that where the woman was doing her business was the correct place, but their knowledge went no further than that.

Now, observing the excrement and urine falling onto the white surface, the men expected to see splashes of liquid and for the feces to lay on the surface. But the liquid and solid waste simply disappeared into the surface, as if it had passed through the white material without leaving the slightest residue.

"Astonishing. I wonder where it went?" was all that Tappulus could say.

"We can find out more about that later. For now, we need to tell the men what is going on, and what to do," said Marcus Avitus.

"How do you want to do this?"

"Well, I think we should do as the Tuathii want."

"Agreed. In fact, I feel compelled to do as they want. Do you suppose that they have somehow made me feel this way, when they infused me with the knowledge about this sleeping chamber? And why only about this chamber, why have they not given me more knowledge, like where did the scat and piss go to?" said Tappulus.

"You said 'compelled'. Yes, that is the correct word for this. I also feel strongly inclined to pair up with this Hibernian woman. Before this instant, I knew nothing about her, yet now I know that her name is Neasa, princess to the mac Cassan clann. *Formerly* of the mac Cassan clann, that is, as I intend to make her my woman and make this bedchamber our very own. Can you believe it? Where did this come from? From the the *Tuatha*? That's where this intention was originated, I am certain, and it feels like something urgent, something that I *must* do. But I also feel compelled to first organize the men and women likewise. Should I fight this compulsion, or go along with it?"

"We have no choice, Marcus."

"Agreed," Marcus said, reaching out to touch a rectangular metal protrusion that responded immediately by extending out of the wall, making a place to sit and think.

Centurion Tappulus activated a similar chair, and then a table-surface at knee-height smoothly extended between the two seated men.

"Marcus, why don't you carry on with your normal administrative duties as Tribuni Angusticlavii – find out which senior officers are present, and what our orders are?"

"I am with you, Tappulus. Meanwhile, I take it you will play Praefectus Castrorum, and see to the men? – How many are in this ship, what their condition is, and how is their morale?"

"Precisely. What about the she -," he paused mid-sentence, "the Hibernians?"

"I have an idea…" said Marcus as he got up and reached out for Neasa's hand.

She took it without hesitation, sensing what he had in mind.

When Marcus Horatius reached his hand out to her, Neasa reached for him with eager anticipation.

Any thought of her husband, Oengus, one of King Findmal's captains, had long since left her heart and soul. It was as if he no longer existed to her, or more accurately, that he had been relegated to her distant past like a childhood memory.

Hand in hand, Neasa and Marcus reached out together with their other hands and made contact with an appendage of the *radix arboria*.

In Marcus Avitus's mind had been the question he wanted to ask her, of what she understood to be their situation.

In Neasa's mind was a similar question about how the Romans understood their circumstances, and, on another level, she wanted to know if Marcus had feelings for her.

Had she reflected on it, she might have thought it strange to have such strong feelings for a man who she knew nothing about, or wondered if she had been manipulated by the strange tree-like entity, which she thought of as *Tuatha De Danann*, but for now she simply accepted her new feelings, and put her mind to more pressing tasks.

After a shared moment of Equanimity, their questions felt resolved. She knew that he felt love for her, which, while still incomprehensible to her, settled the matter for the time being. She also knew that the Romans were going to instruct their men to go along with the pairing compulsion that they all felt, and find out who was aboard this ship, who had died in the battle, and who must be on the other ship.

Marcus Avitus, similarly, knew with certainty that the woman, Neasa, was now his wife. Nuptials were nto required, but it might be appropriate to have a formal Roman wedding at some time. However he had no doubt that she was now his partner for life.

He knew that their feelings had been enhanced, or at least facilitated by the *gens arbustus tuathium*, the tree-like creatures who controlled the starship and had the ability to convey thoughts and information through touch, but somehow he did not see a problem with that. Their purpose seemed reasonable, to make the travelers comfortable and content for the long voyage.

He felt a strong compulsion to get on with the task of organizing the other officers, finding out what the strategic plan was, and then getting back together with Neasa...

As Tappulus made his way along the corridor to assess the condition of the men, and he observed Roman men and Hibernian women talking quietly and exploring chambers identical to the one he had first discovered, it was evident that many of them had made contact with the Tuathii and activated more chambers.

Tappulus was surprised to see that some of their horses had also been herded into the ship, and were being settled down into the animal pods in the most unusual way. He watched as one frightened horse had been led along the corridor by an immune, while two others had waited until the horse was passing a tree-root. The men shaved hard against the horse's side, causing it to bump against the tree root. In an instant, the frightened equus suddenly seemed quite at home, entering an animal pod as if returning to its well-familiar stall.

Word of how to do so was spreading quickly along the corridor, but there seemed to be a great many more men and women than there were chambers, and he thought that he knew the solution.

Finding a corner at the end of a block of six chambers, Tappulus turned left along an interconnecting hall that was at right angles to the main chamber. This new pathway progressed a few strides until it tilted upwards at a steep angle.

Not entirely certain what would happen as he moved forward, Centurion Tappulus stepped confidently onto the steep incline. Just as his center of mass passed through some invisible line, where more of his body was beyond the line than behind it, suddenly his front foot seemed to be the one on a flat surface, and the trailing leg felt as if it were elevated behind him.

He knew, from his contact with the Tuatha, that he had transitioned from one angle-surface of the ship to an adjacent angle-surface, but it felt "flat" for him the entire time. And even though he had never studied trigonometry, he recognized that the cross-section of the ship was a six-sided conical shape.

Had the interior geometry of the egg-shaped ship been explained to him by as great a teacher as the mentor of Tacitus, Vibius Metellus, he would have had difficulty comprehending it. But with the infused knowledge-message that was delivered directly into his brain by the *radix arboria*, it was as though he had been given all the information he required to have a basic understanding of how to find his way around the starship, but not much more than that. His mind was filled with questions.

He strode the few paces to reach the central corridor of the second surface, which he thought of as the second level, Deck II, and then he looked to his right.

Sure enough, as his infused understanding told him what it would be, the central corridor extended the length of the ship and was intersected in three places by secondary corridors identical to the one he had used to get from Deck I to Deck II.

His mind now accepted the unusual geometry. Had he understood the notion of gravity, he might have wondered how he could feel that he was walking on a flat, level surface and yet arrived there by stepping onto a sixty degree incline. But his urge to explore seemed to be temporarily satisfied, and he now knew where to take the Romans and Hibernians, to Deck II, where they would find additional bedchambers.

He returned to the crowd on Deck I, and encouraged the Roman men to use the *radix arboria* to assist them in pairing up with Hibernian women and to claim a vacant bedchamber. He felt a sense of urgency about getting his men paired up and distributed to the chambers as fast as possible, as if something was going to happen soon which required them to be settled.

Not all of the Romans, or Hibernians for that matter, had heeded the reassuring words and instructions of their leaders. In one case, he witnessed a very brief and dramatic courtship. Two soldiers were struggling to drag two Hibernian women into a pod.

One of the women broke free and moved back, unsure if she should rejoin the fight to save her sister, or if she should run away. A few hours earlier, it would have been perfectly normal behavior for Roman legionaries who had gotten their hands on an enemy woman after the battle was won. But now, in the context of this strange starship and the moderating influence of the Tuathii, the behavior now seemed simply *wrong*.

Centurion Tappulus continued to watch, wanting to intervene while at the same time curious to see where this would end.

It did not take long for things to get very serious. The struggling woman got a hand free, pulled a small two-pronged forked stick, and shoved it into one man's neck.

Blood sprayed from the deep gash, clearly a mortal wound.

The dying soldier fell back into the wall, still holding on to the woman with one hand and his profusely bleeding neck with the other while his friend reached out to help him.

One of his legs bumped into a Tuathii root near the floor, and suddenly all three people shared the sudden calmness of Equanimity.

Watching from nearby, Aulus Tappulus was curious as to whether the three would form a love triangle and what would happen to the dying man. *Will he fall in love only to die a moment later?* Tappulus wondered for a moment, but his intuition had already answered the question.

Whether as a compulsion from the Tuathii, or by something that had passed between them, the wounded soldier and his former hostage emerged from the encounter as a couple.

She switched instantly from fighting for her life to deep concern for the man who moments earlier had intended to rape her. She lovingly pressed her hand against his wound, which had almost completely stopped bleeding.

She had his blood on her hands, and shared a prolonged period of peacefulness with him as they pressed against the root. Soon it was clear that he was going to live.

The bleeding had stopped.

The third man had no interest in her now, and turned his attention to the very young female warrior standing wild-eyed in the corridor.

"Don't be afraid, little sister!" called out the first woman, "We do not have to fight! He won't hurt you now," she said.

The second girl, Niamh, daughter of Queen Noichrathach from the hills north of Tara, would have none of it.

Brandishing a wickedly sharpened three-pointed antler in one hand and a simple pointed stick in the other, she lunged at the foot-soldier who was approaching her with his arms open.

"Do not be afraid," he said, as he reached for her in the middle of the corridor.

She ducked under his left arm and slid past him, driving the antler into his groin.

The man fell to his knees in agony, blood pouring down his legs and then he crumpled to the floor.

Watching yet another skirmish which was also destined to be short-lived, Centurion Tappulus decided not to intervene to save the man, an *immune* – a legionary with special skills and exempt from normal duties – despite recognizing the man as Immune Antoninus Commodus, from his own unit, the Eighth Cohort of Legio II.

Tappulus stood by, watching, letting the incident play itself out to its inevitable conclusion when the woman jumped on the dying man and drove a wooden stake into the man's eye. She was just about to drive the palm of her hand onto the base of the stick, to drive it home into the soldier's brain, when the blond-haired young Hibernian whose temperament Tappulus had just seen converted by the Tuathii, leapt onto her, wrapping her arms around the young warrior's arms and pulling her to the floor.

Tappulus decided it was time to act, and with the help of the first soldier, he dragged the man towards an empty pod,

Tappulus activating the door with a touch as if he had done it a thousand times.

They dragged the mortally wounded Roman into the sleeping chamber and lay him on his back.

They were unsure if they should remove the stake from his eye, or give him a chance to stabilize, but Tappulus believed that the man would heal just as he had himself had done, and prepared to remove the stake.

He did not get a chance to, as the two Hibernian women moved in. The blond-haired girl confidently pushed Tappulus aside with the second girl, Niamh, in tow. Niamh was clearly unhappy about being in such close proximity to more Roman soldiers and was angry about being told not to attack them further. *She has not been initiated into this Tuathii influence,* Centurion Tappulus realized as he stepped back to observe.

The first girl held young Niamh's wrist and put it on the wounded soldier's chest. Then she took the girl's other hand and put it on a Tuatha root that extended down from the corner of the room, conveniently within reach of the table.

Then the moment happened. Niamh's rage disappeared. Her mood visibly softening from anger to that of caring concern. She reached out and gently put her hand around the stake in the eye-socket of the man she had done her very best to kill a scant moment before. Singing a beautiful song that sounded like a lullaby, she yanked the stick out.

Bits of sinew, flesh, and pieces of eyeball were stuck to the stake. The eye socket was filled with dark, venous blood which began to trickle out onto his face. Yet the man did not cry out.

Tappulus noticed that the soldier's assailant had reconnected the man with the tree root, hooking the man into the seemingly miraculous source of Equanimity.

The blood stopped flowing, and the man began to heal rapidly, before Tappulus's eyes.

Minutes later, his damaged eye was closed and purple, but no longer the garish wound it had been earlier. He opened his good eye and stared at the woman who had almost killed him, and smiled at her. "Niamh, I am yours," Immune Antoninus Commodus said.

"I know, and I am yours," Niamh replied, in stilted Latin, embracing her newfound mate as he fell into a deep, healing sleep.

Tappulus had just finished his assessment of the condition of the men when he and the other officers were interrupted by an immune, a specialist soldier, whom Tappulus recognized as a carpenter from the First Cohort of the Legio XX.

"Primus Pilus, this immune is one of yours," Tappulus said. "Take his report, out in the corridor; there are too many people in here already."

No sooner had the centurion from the prestigious First of the Twentieth left the room than he returned, excitedly, to interrupt the senior officers yet again.

"Praefectus! Tribune! we have news!"

"What is it, Spurius Sallustius?" said Marcus Avitus.

"The doors have re-opened! Two at each end of this ship!"

"The doors have opened? Are there more people arriving? What had the immune seen? – Bring him in!"

"Apologies, Praefectus, I sent him back to post sentries at all four portals, to bar exit until we send further instructions."

"Good thinking, Primus Pilus," said Tappulus. Now what more did he report?"

"We should go and look for ourselves. It is impossible to believe."

"With all haste, then, let's go look!" said Tappulus, pausing for a moment to compose a question-thought in his mind before leaving his pod, which was directly across from the one that Marcus Avitus and Neasa had taken. Centurion Tappulus thought that if he focused on a thought or question, a 'question-thought' as he was conceiving of it, then when he made contact with a Tuathii root, the strange life force that seemed to control their fate, whose root tendrils seemed to be throughout the starship, then perhaps he could get something of a thought-answer.

After placing his hand on a root, he continued down the corridor in a relaxed manner. The other officers had rushed ahead, curious as to what they would find. Only Tribune Marcus Avitus looked back to see what was keeping Tappulus.

Seeing the look on the Camp Prefect's face, Marcus Avitus realized what Aulus Tappulus must have done, and stopped to wait for him instead of rushing to the portal to join the others.

"What did the Tuatha tell you?"

"It told me that the ship has moved, despite the lack of any feeling of motion. We are now sitting in a meadow on an island the Hibernians call '*Inis Thiar*', it is a small, fertile island in the open oceanus on the west coast of *Éire*. The other starship – identical to the one we find ourselves inside – sits not far away in another pasture, and soon the men will be eager to go out to forage for the plants, fowl, goats, and feed."

"Provisions? We have moved to another place, to gather provisions?"

"Yes, however we do not need much. Just enough to reach our destination."

"How long will that take?"

"Think-ask the question for yourself, why don't you?"

Marcus Avitus pondered his questions for a moment, and then touched a root nearby. Moments later, he understood that the *astrum navis*, starship, had enough water for the journey and that it had some manner in which urine would be cleansed so as to provide additional drinking water, to add to what he now understood to be a significant storage of water in the bowels of the ship.

He also had an answer to the '*how long*' question. He knew that, with today being one day from the end of February, by the Roman calendar February 26th, they would arrive at their destination in sixteen days, on the Ides of March – 15 March, the same day as the dictator Julius Caesar was assassinated.

"That is an inauspicious date for whomever, or whatever, controls the power of these Tuathii and their starships," offered Centurion Tappulus.

Thinking of the omens, Tribune Avitus remembered his duty to appease the gods, lest they become enraged by what was taking place.

"Centurion! Make sure to gather as many live animals as you can. We'll need chickens to sacrifice and throw into the sea, to please Neptune, the god of the water and the Oceanus;we'll need oxen, pigs and sheep to honor Pales, patron of shepherds, goats and sheep; and many more animals and fruits to satisfy hungry Mars, the god of war. And more, for sacrificial feasts. We don't want the gods to abandon us, do we?"

"Live animals, and lots of them – Right! I'll get started, but can you send out more men to help round up the animals?" Centurion Tappulus asked, thinking more of his hungry stomach than sacrificing perfectly good animals to the gods.

As he saw to the details, Tribune Avitus had a new question, but did not bother to ask it just then. He would find out soon enough what was to be done with any villagers who attempted to intercede. *We'll probably just have to kill them,* he thought to himself.

Several hours later, judging by the arc the sun had made in the partly cloudy sky, Marcus and Tappulus watched the last of the men return to the ship. Their ship, they both thought instinctively. It was all consistent with the task that had been imprinted on the men by the Tuathii.

Standing next to each other, the two senior officers were the highest ranking Romans aboard what they now knew to be the second of the two alien ships. The primary ship, simply by virtue of being the one which carried the commander, Legatus Agricola, and his second in command, Tribune Cerialis, stood off in the distance. Focused on their task and somehow inhibited them from doing anything other than to gather supplies, the Romans and Hibernians had not attempted to make contact with their people on the opposite ship, other than to waive encouragingly at each other.

While the two largest of the Tuathii ships sat on the ground to gather supplies, and the 3 others remained aloft as if on patrol, Centurion. Tappulus had communed with the Tuatha, asking if they could send the *aquilifer*, the standard-bearer for the legion, over to the first ship.

For the first time in his experience with the strange tree-like being that inhabited the ship, there was a sense of confusion in the exchange of thoughts. The Tuatha did not seem to comprehend the sense of urgency Tappulus attached to ensuring that the battle standard of the newly-formed Legio XXVII, with the Pegasus of Legion II flying overhead and the Boar of Legio XX on the ground below, must at all times accompany the legatus when the legion travels at sea.

The Tuatha had acceded to the request, however in doing so had also conveyed what seemed to Tappulus to be a reflection or thought that the request was seen as incomprehensible – devoid of any purpose or logic.

Tappulus made good use of the transfer of the aquilifer to the other ship. He sent along a hastily assembled report on the status of the legion's personnel aboard the second ship, and the names of the senior officers present. He received a reciprocal report from Tribunus Laticlavius Cerialis regarding the status of the other starship.

Through reports from his men, he calculated that, onboard both ships was a total of three hundred and ninety nine Hibernians and Romans combined.

Having communed with the Tuatha about the bed-down of personnel and livestock, the Praefectus Castrorum had learned that there were to be 108 pairs, 108 males and 108 females, and sufficient livestock collected during the stopover to be enough to feed them for fifteen days, plus an equivalent number of livestock, intended to be delivered intact as breeding stock at their destination, presumably at what the Hibernians called Tir na nOg, the otherworldly realm.

There were 216 pods in the ship, 108 of which seemed more suited to livestock than to human beings, not equipped withseating places for defecating or with chairs, tables or sleeping mats. These more basic pods were larger than the 'people pods', and were located on the lower deck. They were equipped with basins that magically stayed full at all times, no matter how much water was withdrawn, perfectly suited to supply water to all manner of livestock. This, in contrast to the on-demand basin mounted on the wall of the people-pods on the main deck, led to the conclusion that one type of pod was designed for civilized people, the other for animals. *We'll have to relocate some people out of the animal pods,* Tappulus realized.

With two people in each people-pod, there would be 216 people on each ship, and 432 if both ships were fully populated.

There had been another one problem. When the combatants had been herded into the ship, there had been over two hundred and twenty people. This number had been decimated to fewer than two hundred in the first few minutes, when some Hibernians and Romans had killed each other, leaving his ship eighteen short of the intended quota, as communicated by the Tuatha. Of this shortfall, they were short by two men and sixteen women.

As the ranking officer aboard the second ship, it had fallen to Tribune Marcus Avitus to give orders to the most suited centurion, Primus Pilus Spurius Crispus, before they sent the men and women from their ship out to forage for livestock and feed from the local village.

"Centurion Crispus, the gens arbustus Tuathium wants us to have 108 pairs aboard this ship before we leave. Tell the men who have not found mates among the Hibernian women to find women in the village. Also grab two young men from the village, and two girls who seem to be associated with them, to round out the numbers..."

"Our men will be eager to carry out that order. But what of the Celtic men?"

"You are referring to the two Hibernian men who have no women?"

"Yes, Tribunus."

"Their queen has given them similar instructions. Tell your men to back them up if need be. The other ship is raiding the hamlet on the far side of the field they are landed in, to make up fifteen women."

"You want our soldiers to back up the Celts? Won't the Hibernians simply tell their cousins what they want?"

"Are you crazy? There may be Celts here too, but they may as well be complete strangers, or enemies for that matter. No, I would expect some fairly determined resistance from the men of this shit-hole. Kill them as you go, to keep things from getting out of hand when they realize we are taking their women."

"Tribunus."

"And make sure that strange priest, the Druid Allanon, takes a woman."

"Priests! They don't seem to know what's really important in life! And they are the last people I want to take advice from."

"Exactly. Anyhow, he serves a purpose in their culture, so make him take a woman even if he does not know what to do with one. See to that yourself."

"With pleasure, Tribune. Do you want me to show him how to fuck his woman, when we get him one?"

"Well, if the *gens arbustus* can't make him understand which hole his cock is supposed to go into, maybe you'll have to sho him…"

Marcus had meant that as a joke, but from the look on Centurion Tappulus's face, Marcus was not sure. He got the distinct impression that Tappulus might have taken him literally.

For a young boy travelling to his village on the western island of *Inis Thiar,* the dramatic arrival of egg-shaped objects from the sky momentarily stunned him. A simple goat-herder, he tried to comprehend the unusual sight in terms of the legends and myths of his people. He sat on a pile of rocks some distance away from the village, and watched with fear and fascination.

It was exactly as the Druids had told him, in the stories he had heard them recount on his visits to the village. *Sometimes, the Tuatha De Danann come to take people away to Tir na nOg.*

That these particular Tuatha De Danann looked like Romans, that they killed all the men inside the village, and took only the best of the women away with them into their ships, had been the most difficult part for him to accept, but that is what he saw. When he later retold the story in a much larger village, they found his account impossible to believe.

IX

APTANS
{ Adjustment }

Legatus Quintus Julius Agricola watched as the aquilifer approached from the second ship. He was pleased to see that the man did not rush the sacred task of delivering the battle standard to him, still very much in command of a proud Roman legion despite the incomprehensible events of the day. As the boar of Legio XX and the Pegasus of Legio II became visible on the small square of fabric just below the golden eagle atop the battle standard, and the letters *LEGIO XXVII HIBERNICUS DOMITIANUS* became readable, with *SPQR* – Senātus Populusque Romanus, 'The People and Senate of Rome' – in gold lettering on the bottom of the standard, Legatus Agricola looked at the faces of the men who had rushed to the entry portals to welcome the legion's battle standard to what they had taken to calling *their* ship, Agricola's command ship.

He had last looked upon the legion's battle standard much earlier in the day, but it now seeming like a lifetime ago. When last he saw it, he had been riding out to the front lines to check on the progress of Primus Pilus Crispus, leading COH I of Legio XX up the incline towards King Findmal's force, and into the battle.

Though inexperienced, he had easily absorbed the information displayed on the numerous *centurial signamii*, spear-shaped standards decorated with disk and moon-shaped medallions and the names of each of the centuria within the First Cohort, to get a clear picture of the disposition of the cohorts and centuries under his command. These were the visible signs of progress, as the actual combat at the front centuries of COH I LEG XX were obscured by dust and distance.

When he had watched his units maneuver and carry out the initial stages of the battle plan, he had felt the exhilaration of command that his father had often talked about, and for which he had studied for years under the tutelage of Vibius Metellus and the other wise men of his father's retinue.

But his own enjoyment of a command position, leading the newly formed Legio XXVII Hibernicus Domitianus into battle as its Legatus Legionus, had been short-lived to say the least. And rather than stories of glory to impress his father, and the honor of being sent reinforcements to swell the ranks of his legion as he continued onward to conquer all of Hibernia, Quintus Julius Agricola was certain that he would never again see Britannia, nor his father, Governor Gnaeus Julius Agricola.

He was in the hands of fate now, with some unknown destiny fast approaching. All he could do was stand up like a man, try to show the confidence and surety of a courageous and honorable leader – the very tenets that the philosophers Vibius Metellus and Fabius Quintilianus were always arguing about.

He wanted to show that he was ready for command, ready to face any danger. So the arrival of the legion's battle standard was an important opportunity to hold the men together. He could shore up their courage and morale in the face of such extraordinary circumstances. He needed to convey that they had a brave and capable general to follow, and that they all served Rome.

As he read the dispatch that Praefectus Castrorum Tappulus and Tribune Marcus Avitus had sent with the aquilifer, Legatus Agricola thought about how the camp prefect, would have the men on his ship squared away much as he had done when establishing the camp, their tents perfectly lined up according to cohort and century, on the Dubh Linn lowlands in the days leading up to Proelium Dublinensis, the Battle of Dubh Linn.

Agricola knew that he had to ensure that the senior officers aboard his ship, *navis primus*, were equal to the task, placing discipline and military concerns ahead of all else. They were, after all, still a legion of Rome, or at least the core elements of a legion. As long as they had blood in their veins, officers to command them, and an enemy to vanquish for the glory of Rome, Legio

XXVII Hibernicus Dominitius would remain operational, despite the disconcerting circumstances they now found themselves in.

Nostras Hibernias postmodo constraprobimus, we'll fuck our new Hibernian women later. This last thought made him think of the one man who, like himself, had so far refused to follow the strange compulsion of the *gens arbustus Tuathium,* Tuatha, as the officers from the second ship had termed them in their report. His close friend and second in command, here with him in the first ship, Tribunus Laticlavius Kaeso Cerialis, had deliberately held off from taking a woman despite the strong urging he felt after his own contact with the Tuatha.

Kaeso Petillius Cerialis had consulted with Agricola on the issue, and explained his ambivalence. Despite fearing that failure to comply with the strange entity's intention could bring harm to his most trusted and closest friend, Agricola had agreed. As for himself, he had taken a woman but not linked with her, as he had some doubts about the matter and wanted to hold off before taking any risks. He was, after all, in command.

After consulting with Fabius Quintilianus Legatus Agricola and Tribune Cerialis sought out the senior Hibernians. He had soon found two regal women: Queen Laelie mac Cassan, and a visibly angry young woman, Princess Maura mac Cassan. While Princess Maura stood in stony silence, her sister-in-law, Queen Laelie, greeted the Romans in passable Latin.

"Legatus Agricola, it is an honor to finally meet the leader of this fine pack of fools who thought they could conquer our proud people. I must compliment your soldiers for taking well to being given to our women as their bed-slaves," she said, as she reached out to grip the Agricola, hand to wrist, as two peers would do within the Roman military community.

"Call me Quintus Julius, in private, Queen Cassan."

"Thank you, Quintus Julius. Your friendship is returned. This beautiful lady, Princess Maura Cassan, is the sister of my husband. In his absence, she is of higher status than I."

"My lady. I offer you my friendship as well," said Agricola.

"You may address me as Princess Maura in public, and Lady Maura in private," she said, offering her arm in the Roman style, but speaking with a sharper tone than Queen Laelie had used. "However I am afraid I cannot extend the same level of friendship to your companion with the old man's balls!" she said as she glared at Tribunus Laticlavius Cerialis, the man who had raped and brutalized her the night before; the enemy who had tried to manipulate her with a poorly executed scheme of deception.

The Hibernian princess had seen through it, of course, and taken it as a sign of weakness on the part of the inexperienced young Legatus Legionus that he would attempt such an obvious ploy.

Tribune Cerialis glowered at her, as much for the intolerable insult she had made as for his own embarrassment for what would be asked of her.

"My lady, Princess Maura, we have a request. It is one that must be handled in a....delicate manner," started Agricola. He knew from his mentors that pairings, like marriages, are political opportunities. Advantage could be gained by conducting the negotiation in a manner that gave the other side the impression of having the upper hand, allowing them to decide the outcome while never revealing the intended result.

But this was the first time that he had ever conducted such a negotiation, and it seemed to play out far faster in reality than when he and Marcus filius Fabius had discussed it with Tribune Cerialis.

"Quintus Julius, my dear friend, my sisters have already told me what you seek. And the answer is no."

"But," replied Agricola

"But nothing. Sure, Tribune 'old-man-balls' must have a woman, lest we offend the Tuatha De Danann, but I will not give him any choice in the matter. And your interceding on his behalf will do him no good at all."

"Go on my lady."

"We have a suitable woman for him. And if you will accept my judgment in the matter, if you will trust me in this, then I will grant your wish. But dry-sack over here will not be happy about it."

"What do you have in mind, my lady?" Agricola asked, unsure of how he had so quickly lost the initiative. The young Celtic woman was behaving as a veteran Roman noblewoman in similar circumstances, as if she held all of the good in the barter.

But he knew enough to keep his mouth shut, and let his opponent reveal her intentions first.

"For the old man, who proved so ineffectual with me last night, we have a woman equal to his condition but far superior to him in status."

"Who is she?"

Princess Maura sneered as she replied: "Were it not for the fact that she had last night sworn an oath to serve Clann mac Cassan, to follow the orders of my brother, Findmal, she would be the second highest-ranking Hibernian on this ship, and your man would have to beg at her feet. But as I am, by blood and by oath, of elevated status at present, I will tell Lady Achal, wife of King Fedelm Noichrathach, that she must pair up with Tribune dry-balls. However, there is something you both must know, and it must never be repeated."

"We are all ears and without lips, my lady," said Agricola.

"She has entered her final years as a woman. She cannot bear children, and has other problems in that region as well. She must not, and will not, copulate with dry-balls. In public, she will appear to be his mate, and will do the female duties to make their bed-chamber a comfortable, if not intimate, retreat for your fine officer."

Agricola sensed opportunity at the sudden change of tone coming from Princess Maura. It seemed that the Hibernian woman had no idea of Cerialis's true desire, and had wrongly assumed that he would have wanted one of the younger women, more pleasant in appearance, to go with his high rank. He also discerned that from the Hibernian perspective, pairing one of their nobility, even a wretched old woman who must be well into her fiftieth year, to the Tribunus Laticlavius – second only to the Legatus Legionus himself, would be a prudent political move for the Hibernians. It would strengthen their internal power structure and cement the bonds between the mac Cassan and the Fedelm Noichrathach tribes.

But if this was her strategy, and she was uninformed about Cerialis's desire to not actually wed, but rather to remain loyal to the spirit of his deceased wife, then there was yet more opportunity to exploit.

"My lady, your candor is noble, and your careful understanding of our issue is commendable. However, you ask for too much. Were we to accept such an arrangement, it would bring great disrespect upon our nobles, and could be seen by our men as having acceded too easily to your demands," he began, hoping she would talk herself into the trap he had laid.

"That fear is understandable. What do you propose?"

"To balance the transaction, we would need a major concession from all of the Hibernians, and it is one that I fear you may be unable to arrange."

"I am in command of the women in this vessel. They are loyal, and will do as I command," she bristled.

"What we would require, for the Romans to ever accept that the Tribunus Laticlavius be paired with such a barren old wench, would be for her, for you, and for all of your people to speak to Romans as masters."

"Are you insane? We could be asking the same of you, that your people address our people as *"brigh"*, for 'noble', each time you mention their name. You should address me as "brigh Maura Cassan!""

"Let me continue, my lady," he said, using the quiet voice and calmness that he had learned during his training in the art of rhetoric and influence.

In a whisper that Princes Maura could barely hear, even with her head inclined close to his own, Agricola gave her what she needed.

"It would only be for public display. In private, your women will rule over their men. In the privacy of the sleeping pods, the traditional Roman rights over the wives shall now be contingent upon the woman's choice," he said, knowing that if word of what he had just proposed ever reached Rome, he would be the laughing stock of the empire.

But from his point of view, with the loving feelings that his men had suddenly gained for the women they were pairing with, he knew that none of the women would be mistreated in the usual way. None would be seen as slaves, concubines or Hibernian whores.

What he needed most was something to reinforce discipline, and the appearance, and therefore the fact, of Roman rule over the Hibernians.

"So you are proposing that my women and I command in private, and you and our men command in public. And that we must address you as 'Dominus'? What of our nobles, when addressing the lowest of your soldiers?"

And now Agricola had her. With just a simple nod to the nobility amongst the Hibernians: the queen; the princess; the queen of the Noichrathach and her daughter Niamh; the Celtic lawgiver or poet or whatever Daffid Og was; and the Druid priest on the other ship, they would all be given special status – and thereby fall under Roman authority.

"Your nobility, I believe six persons? Will be addressed as Domina and Dominus by all but our senior officers. They will be addressed by title by our senior officers, or by their names if they grant that degree of informality. Simply put, your nobles will have status."

"Seven. You missed my cousin, Neasa, who is paired with Tribune Avitus. So all of our nobility will have elite status? Thank you. But that is not enough, Legatus," said Princess Maura.

"What more would you have me offer?"

"Two things, easy for you to give to conclude the barter."

"What are they?"

"First, I have avoided contact with the tree roots as well. You must find me a husband of equal rank to my noble status. I would have chosen you, but out of love for my brother's wife, and in deference to her great leadership of the women of Clann mac Cassan, I will ply my influence from the sidelines, behind the curtains, just as your philosophers do. In fact, I want you to pair me with that Vibius Metellus character. I understand that he, too, has avoided being randomly paired by the tree roots. He is a ridiculous looking, bald old man, but he speaks to our people with respect. He and I will be a good pair, politically speaking. And that leaves the stage clear for Queen Laelie and you to pair.

"But I have a woman in my domicile already," said Agricola, playing out his hand masterfully.

"Laelie wants you." Lady Maura said, bringing a rush of pink embarrassment to Laelie's face. "It makes sense from our point of view, and I am certain from yours as well. And the girl you chose, the blond-haired one with the large breasts and the pretty face? – She tells me that you ordered her into your chamber but that you still have not connected with her through the Tuatha. Is this correct?"

"That is correct. It is my intention to take her when I settle for rest, but there have been more important things to attend to. I am certain that she will provide satisfactory service," he said, hoping not to give away how he really felt.

The lowly girl, pretty as she was, had been a poor choice. Certainly she would satisfy his need for sex, but she did nothing for his status, other than to tell the men that their legatus had chosen the most attractive woman for himself, which would be typical for a noble of such high status.

But such would not have been up to the higher moral standards that Vibius Metellus, his mentor, always tried to instill into him. Vibius Metellus was part of Agricola's father's retinue, one of his personal rhetoricians and advisors. Back at the garrison of Legio XX, at Deva, Vibius Metellus was put to use mentoring Agricola the Younger and his fellow student, Publius Cornelius Tacitus. Agricola the Younger had received a heavy dose of ethics and logic from his mentor, and knew full well what Vibius Metellus would have said: *You know what is right, a priori, so if you are good, you must do the right thing.*

"Please forgive my rudeness, Princess Maura." Agricola started, and then turned to face the other noblewoman directly. "However, as we are talking about this beautiful lady at your side, would it not be more respectful if we asked her opinion?"

The warm smile that Agricola gave Queen Laelie, and the gracious way he passed the control of the situation to her, visibly impressed her. After a nod from her sister-in-law, Laelie understood that it was time to embrace the leadership role that had been offered to her.

She took his hand in hers, placing her other hand on top in a warm and intimate manner. "I would be willing, Dominus, to share a pod with you," Laelie said, with a sincere smile on her face and a mischievous twinkle in her eye.

I wonder what that look portends, Agricola thought to himself, aroused by the sensual way that Queen Laelie stroked his hand.

Resuming the negotiations, Agricola continued to hold hands with Laelie and spoke as though the deal was not yet finalized. He addressed Laelie directly now. "But even if I would give up my wench and take you as my woman, which I do not object to with any vigor, what would the second concession be?"

"That you give status to our – to Laelie's – captains as well," Princess Maura responded.

"Captains? How many are there? And how many Hibernians does a captain command?"

Laelie, comfortable discussing leadership roles as one of the many subjects she constantly drove home with her young warriors, answered the question: "It varies from family to family, but in our culture, a captain is the leader of a group of warriors, and they follow her as long as she has their confidence. If she has no followers, then she is no longer a captain, and a new captain emerges. It is not something I control, but rather, something I observe and respond to as leader. Our people know who their captains are, and will let your men know. It won't be difficult. Hibernian woman have little difficulty making their thoughts known."

"Of that, my lady, I have no doubt!"

"But we can put a limit on it, as in one in every eight, similar to your contubernium, tent-groups."

"But that would far outnumber our own officers. We have no senior officers below centurion, who lead groups of eighty men."

"But you must have five or six centurions here, and yet they command only one hundred men, if not less. And you have those others, the immunes, who seem to be like officers, only they are not in command of any groups of men. What do they do, and why do they do so little to help the munifex, the common foot-soldiers?" said Laelie, now clearly playing the role of leader of the Hibernians.

"What you say about the centurions is true, but the immunes are not senior officers. They have special skills and duties, and are used across the full range of the legion, doing administrative tasks. That's why they are 'immune' from some of the more common tasks, which are better suited to the soldiers."

"Well, then, can we say our younger, less experienced captains shall be equivalent to immunes, and say one handful of our more powerful captains, the ones with the largest followings, shall be equivalent in status to your centurions?"

"Agreed. They shall have status, and you and I shall pair. When would you like to see our new home?" Agricola said, unable to hide his feelings any longer.

Queen Laelie was wise enough to not mistake his enthusiasm as an indication that he was enamored with her, which he certainly was. However there was something she had missed in the negotiation, and this bothered her.

I will have to grind it out of him later, Laelie thought.

X

CONSILIVM
{ Planning }

Quintus Julius Agricola had never experienced anything like it. He had performed a variety of sex acts with exotic women from different places in the Roman Empire, but had never experienced anything quite like what his new partner in life, Queen Laelie, introduced him to.

Of course, he knew that she was not a queen in the way Romans might think of one, because in Hibernia, a man was declared a king if he ruled over a clann of any size at all. But Quintus Agricola liked to think of her as a queen because of the delightful contradictions that came with her. By the unkempt way she liked to keep her hair, the crude scents from her rarely-washed body, and the vulgar way she spoke to him in private, one might think her an uncivilized person, a savage, as the Romans had thought of all Celts. But she was a member of the Hibernian nobility, and had some ability to speak Latin.

From what he gathered, Clann mac Cassan operated a fleet of trading, and occasionally raiding, ships out of the shelter of Malahide Bay, near Dubh Linn. This gave them constant exposure to Romans and to other Irish clanns who traded with the Romans, and with other Celtic clans from the west coast of Britannica.

From the stories that her people told of Laelie's exploits in battle, and confirmed by eye-witness accounts from some of his own personnel, his queen was capable of great courage and a merciless, efficient, ability to kill.

At first it seemed strange to Agricola that she had embraced the pairing that he and Lady Maura had negotiated. He thought that her rapid adjustment to her role as his partner had been due to more than simple political expediency, and more than the intoxicating effects of the Equanimity that came with Tuatha-linking the two had ultimately gone through. But when he had pried with questions about her husband, her cold, stony, reaction indicated her unwillingness to discuss the topic. Eventually Agricola let it go, but suspected that Laelie's lack of mourning or pining over her removal from her husband may have had something to do with the fact that King Findmal had been an old man of fifty years, in contrast to her much more youthful and vigorous twenty-five years. Perhaps their arranged marriage, a political union that brought peace between the mac Cassans and the Caucis, had been a loveless marriage. It certainly had been a childless one, but then again, in his mind's eye Agricola did not see Laelie holding babies. Holding weapons, yes, but a brood of children did not appear to be her focus.

Whatever the cause, it seemed to Agricola that her heart was open for him, as were her legs. She was wise beyond her years, intelligent, educated, and yet had the characteristic coarseness and wildness of the Celts.

But the most exquisite aspect of her surprising personality was the way she handled her lover in bed, or on the floor to be more precise.

It was just as Maura and Laelie had negotiated. The Hibernian women were in charge in the bedroom, but obediently referred to their Roman men as "Dominus" in the corridors or when others were visiting their domicile. Laelie began to suspect that Roman wives probably did not refer to their husbands in this way. To her, it seemed to be the sort of thing you would have a slave say. *That 'Dominus' thing will have to go*, eventually, Laelie had determined.

The first full market-day cycle, eight days, had settled into an almost boring routine. Life aboard the starship was stressful in one sense, caused by not knowing their destination or their ultimate fate. The Tuatha was revealing, in small bits and pieces divulged to various people who linked-in to the strange master of the ship, that they were indeed travelling and that they would not arrive until fully three market day cycles plus four days had past –

twenty-eight days since their departure. However, the basic human needs were being met: food, water, shelter and community were all available to them on the starship. And while Agricola and Laelie returned to each other frequently throughout the day, finding sanctuary in their pod, they were free to seek out others of their nation, as much to hear about what their people were learning of the starship as to instill confidence that, whatever was taking place, their leaders were seeing to their well-being.

And, when the Tuatha dimmed the corridor and pod-interior lighting to simulate night-time, Queen Laelie and Legatus Agricola returned from meeting with their people, and sat together in the privacy of their domicile to talk.

Their evening conversations always began with comparing thoughts of what the Romans and the Hibernians had learned, and what issues each of their leaders had dealt with, out of mutual interestt for each other as leaders of their people. Soon enough, however, the mood would invariably shift from business to pleasure.

Their lovemaking had been repeated frequently over the ensuing days, and far outpaced their interpersonal understanding of each other. The effect of their increasing emotional bond made them feel as though they belonged together, regardless of their differences or how they had come to be together. It was as if they lived two lives, one as near strangers, the other as though they had been together forever.

It took some time for their relationship to become established on a more intimate level.

Eventually he got to know her moves and became playful with her, while never completely shaking the notion that she could bring him great pleasure, but was equally capable of slitting his throat – she was that powerful of a personality.

The relationship power balance tilted slightly towards him, but she did not lose the edge she maintained over him in bed. As he grew more experienced in how to deal with her, he tried to tease her at times, to provoke her – and then enjoyed the reaping the consequences.

'*Numquid, cum crisas, blandior esse potes? Tu licet ediscas totam referasque Corinthon. Non tamen omnino, Laelia, Lais eris.*' Agricola said, provocatively: "Could you possibly be prettier as you grind? You learn easily, and could do everything they do in Corinth; but you'll never be Lais, Laelie!" Agricola said, provocatively.

Laelie had no idea who this beauty 'Lais' was but she suspected that she had just been rated 'second best' to the woman, and Agricola had implied that it was *he* who had been teaching her the art of lovemaking, adding insult to injury.

Knowing the limits her new man could endure, she took him right to the edge of agony as she spun around on top of him, not losing him, but wrenching him painfully as she turned 180 degrees. She accelerated the tempo in the unusual sexual position, and just before he climaxed, she eased back, letting him penetrate yet deeper, and then she doubled over towards his feet, locking her legs around his thighs, lifting his buttocks off the bed and causing him to involuntarily arch his back in the erotic submission-hold.

As the blood rushed to his head and it seemed the bloodflow to his legs was being cut off, she held him there, controlling whether he could release or not, and then she let him have it.

"With a small movement of my hips, Dominus, I can break your *sopionis*, cock, like a dry twig – or I can give you something far more pleasant," she said, to the man she held at her mercy. "Tell me why you agreed to our terms so easily, regarding Kaeso Cerialis?"

Barely able to speak, and in a state of terrifying incipient climax-or-agony, he had no choice but to answer.

"Kaeso is grieving his lost wife. He wanted to be paired with an unfuckable woman so that he would not put himself into a position where he would come to love another woman and betray his wife's memory."

Having received the information she had sought, she relented, letting the blood flow once again. His climax was unlike anything he had ever experienced. The sensation verged on torture, yet was profoundly satisfying.

Afterwards, Laelie lay next to him and studied his face. "Did you know her? What was so special about her?" she asked, a tenderness in her eyes that spoke of sincere caring.

"I knew her well, and loved her. Her name was Julia, after her father, of course. It is our tradition that a woman's *praenomina* is changed when she is married, so she became *Julia Cerialla* when she married Kaeso. They had a son, Appius Julius, but he died shortly after *natus*. Then Julia died during her *puerperium*, soon after giving birth, from grief."

From out of nowhere, Laelie felt herself becoming jealous of this deceased young woman, Julia, who meant so much to the stranger upon whose chest she now rested her face, the man she had once wanted to kill, and now, the man she loved.

"Were Kaeso Cerialis and his wife together long?"

"Yes. We all grew up together, in Ostia. Our fathers worked together and our mothers were part of a very close circle of friends. Julia, Kaeso and I were inseparable as children. We loved to climb up into the *cercis siliquastrum.* "

"Cercis siliquastrum? What is that? I don't understand. Is it a kind of tree?

"Yes, it is a very special tree. As kids, we called it *arbor roseaus*, Rosebud Tree."

By the whimsical way he looked away into the distance and was brought to the time of his memories, Laelie knew that this arbor rosea – or the places associated with it – was central to what made this great and powerful man who he was. It was a sacred thing for him, and she liked the way he glowed with love and joy as he spoke of it. She wanted to know more.

"Tell me more about arbor roseaus," Laelie encouraged.

"Most of the time it is a simple tree, about three times the height of a man. In the spring time, before green shoots begin to sprout out of other trees, a glorious sea of pink emerges in the Seven Hills of Rome. In the center of Ostia, the original site of Rome, where I spent my childhood days. Long pink buds, shaped like…" momentarily embarrassed, and then mischievously he continued, "shaped like the button inside your vulva, emerge. First as firm nubs, then they open into heart-shaped flowers all over the bare tree, making a sea of deep pink. But that's not all. The smell! They smell wonderful, like sweet cake fresh from the baker's oven, like honey mixed with vanilla. They smell, to me, like *happiness.*"

"What a wonderful memory. This was your childhood with your friend, Kaeso Cerialis? Climbing these wonderful rosebud trees, chasing girls?" Laelie asked, still fighting the feeling of jealousy, yet actually very pleased that her newfound lover had such warmth in him.

"There's more," Agricola said, conspiratorially.

Intrigued, Laelie moved her head next to his, and whispered, "Tell me, Dominus. I can keep a secret."

"There is a new name for *arbor roseaus.* A name which Romans are forbidden to use."

"What is it?"

"*Arbor Judae*, the Judas Tree," Agricola whispered.

"Why is it forbidden to call it that?"

"Because there is a war going on in the heart and soul of men. It is a war that is whispered between a man and woman, between friends and family, and not openly discussed."

"How mysterious. Who are the leaders? What people are involved?"

"It is very complicated. I can introduce you to my two philosophers, Vibius Quintus Metellus and Marcus *filius* Fabius Quintilianus, who can explain it better. But the way I understand it is that it is a war between the gods."

"Oh, I know something of your gods. You have so many, but I think there are twelve that are most important?"

"Well, there are twelve: Six gods and six goddesses, to whom we make offerings most often. With all that has happened, we have not been diligent in conducting the *lectisternium,* offering to the principal gods: Jupiter & Juno, Neptune & Minerva, Mars & Venus, Apollo & Diana, Vulcan & Vesta and my favorites, Mercury & Ceres. But we will do that soon, I hope."

"So if you have all of those gods on your side – and I have heard the stories of Venus myself, she is my favorite – then who are the gods that your gods are fighting? Are they the Greek gods? – Zeus, Hades, and the others?" Laelie asked, quickly exhausting her understanding of Greek mythology. "- Or are they like our Celtic gods: Demiurge, the life-force; Ishiti, the snake goddess; and Oranah, the monstrous stag-god?" she asked, realizing that having many gods was something that she and her impressive new man had in common. *I could get to like this, talking about such interesting things with this magnificent man,* she thought, looking at his serious face as he replied.

"No, those Greek gods, and yours as well I suspect, are much the same as ours, not the enemy. No, the enemy is only one. The 'one god.'"

"One god? Who has only one god? Even we have many gods of our own. What nation has only one god?"

"Not a nation, but a following. There are many followings that originate with one crazed prophet or another. But the one we are at war with is the "one god" spoken of by a Jewish man named Jesus. As is commonly done when these so-called messiahs gain too large a following, Jesus was crucified on Pontius Pilatus's orders – nailed to a wooden cross and left hanging until dead."

Confused, Laelie wanted to return to the point. "So what does this have to do with the rosebud tree?"

"Before he was tried by Pontius Pilatus, this man Jesus was betrayed by one of his twelve closest followers, a man named Judas Iscariot."

"Judas betrayed his friend Jesus?"

"Yes, he sold him for thirty pieces of silver. But the story goes that he felt so guilty about it that he hanged himself on an *arbor roseaus.* Thus, the followers of Jesus and his twelve apostles, called 'Christians' – prefer to call *arbor roseaus* as *arbor judae,* the Judas Tree."

"So why do you know so much about the Christians, if they are so bad?"

"It is merely a fad, but it is gaining popularity amongst the slaves."

"The slaves, why?"

"In Rome, wealthy families require good slaves. To cook, to clean, to tend to clothes, manage the children, harvest the crops and so on. Lately, a large number of slaves have been coming into the slave markets of Rome from Judea, the province where Jesus Christ was crucified. These slaves are telling the stories attributed to their messiah. The stories are harmless, and on their own they have their appeal, especially to the down-trodden people – like the slaves. Because it promises them a better life in the next life, and speaks of wondrous miracles that give people hope, and great entertainment."

"So these stories, they are told in the homes of the rich and powerful, by the slaves who watch over your children?" Laelie asked, feeling a sense of anger rising.

"Yes, that is true."

"So a generation of Roman children are being influenced by this slave religion, and you Romans stand for it?" Laelie was now thinking of how Allanon was always seeking out the children of the Cathair, telling them stories and having them keep secrets, which always bothered Laelie.

"It is harmless, and a passing fad. There are so many religions now, all competing for the same sheep," said Agricola.

'Really? Then why is it taboo to refer to the rosebud as the Judas Tree?"

Agricola thought about it for a moment. "Perhaps because our nobles do not like mischief being carried out under our very eyes. Perhaps because they have chosen Christianity as an example to be made, to suppress all other such cults."

"But to simply refer to a tree by another name, what is so terrible about that? How does that related to the war of many gods against one god?"

"It's quite simple, Laelie. Rome is a great and powerful *idea*. Rome is an empire, based on the *fasces*, bundle," said Agricola as he picked up a small twig that had been imbedded in his battle-armor piled by the side of the sleeping area, to demonstrate. "You see, an individual, even a city-state, is weak on its own – like this *virga*, rod," he snapped the twig. Then snapped the two remaining pieces, four short twigs together in a bundle. "But when put together in larger and larger numbers, as a bundle, a *fasces*, then it becomes much stronger." Agricola pretended to be unable to snap the bundle of four twigs.

"I understand. Is that why your men stay so close together when they fight?"

"Yes, but that's not the point. Rome is all about power, conquest, and war. Our economy, the entire empire in fact, requires constant inputs of new resources, new slaves, and new territories. And to continually expand our empire, we must have the most powerful military. That is what has made the Roman Empire so successful for over eight hundred years. The gods give us their blessings in many ways, and have helped Rome vanquish each and every enemy we have faced."

"So what does this have to do with the war between your gods and the one god of Jesus?"

"Can you imagine what would happen if we allowed gentle pillow talk of Jesus and his teachings to become adopted widely in the Roman empire? A pacifist religion? It would be the end of the Roman Empire. So there can be no open talk about "love thy neighbor" and 'thou shalt not kill' and all of that nonsense."

"So this one god cannot be allowed to defeat the many gods of the Roman people? That is the war between the gods? The war between the Romans and these Christians you speak of," she said, rhetorically.

Laelie noticed that the peaceful, loving mood was broken. Something about this Christian religion, and its idea of only one god, and teaching about peace, individual freedom, and love, was deeply threatening to the Romans. *They would have to give up being what they are, Laelie realized. They would no longer be warriors, and they would be weak.* Laelie now understood why such talk must not be allowed to flourish in the Roman world.

Changing the subject back to the issue of Kaeso Cerialis and old Queen Achal Noichrathach, Laelie tried to bring back the sweet smelling mood of the Rosebud Tree.

"So what happened in your love triangle, between Kaeso Cerialis and his future wife, Julia?"

Sighing, Agricola allowed himself to return to the story "Well, as Julia matured into a beautiful young woman, Kaeso and I got into a lot of fights over her. Eventually, Kaeso's family's offer was accepted, and he and Julia were married. But within a year of their *nuptia*, wedding, the day came when Appius Julius had arrived and departed, and Julia Cerialia had died. But before that fateful day, it had been a happy year for them both, until grief overtook them, that is. A grief that has not yet let go of Kaeso."

"You loved her too?"

"Of course. She was my younger sister, Julia."

Laelie was shocked, and then embarrassed for presuming that Julius Agricola's fights with his childhood friend had been as competitors for the love of a young woman, when clearly it had been to defend the honor of his little sister, Julia. She wished she could have taken back the 'love triangle' comment, but it was too late. She felt that she had accused Julius Agricola of incest. Certainly incest was not uncommon, at least within the highest levels of the ruling class, who wanted to preserve the purity of their bloodlines. However, in general, incest, between a brother and a sister, was as taboo for Celtics as it probably was for most Romans.

Laelie remained silent as her mood soured further. She began thinking of the harm her husband's sister-in-law Princess Maura had come to at the hands of the very Kaeso Cerialis that they had been discussing. But that had been war, and everything in her universe had changed in the days since.

"What did you fight with Kaeso Petillius about, then? Did he hurt Julia? Is he a cruel man?"

"Cruel? Why would you ask that?" Agricola asked, and then remembered the hatred that Princess Maura had in her eyes for Kaeso. "Look, what he did to your sister-in-law, that was war. We are required to be brutal to our enemies. That does not mean that we are brutal to our loved ones," he tried to reassure Laelie, so that she would not condemn him, or fear him, for what a soldier must do in war."

"I understand. When we raided the Caucis last winter, to capture sheep and tubers so that our people would not starve, I personally castrated a young Cauci warrior, and let him live to tell the tale. That had been war, and it now seems a very long time ago. If I saw that boy today, I would probably regret what I had done, and wish I had left his manhood intact. Everything has changed now. So no, I do not see Kaeso as a cruel man, even if Maura will probably never forget, and never forgive. So let us return to my question: what did you two fight about?"

"I wanted him to be my *friend*, not my brother-in-law. A friend can be loyal, but in the Roman world, you sometimes have to kill your brother-in-law! Besides, by keeping them apart – hopeless as it was – I guess I wanted to keep us all young and carefree a little longer. Those were happy, peaceful, days."

"And he mourns her still, after so many years..."

"Yes. I don't think she will ever let go of him."

"But even so, as a soldier, he could rape an enemy woman, even kill her without compunction, but in his personal life, his heart is broken?" Laelie asked, certain that she now understood.

"Sadly, yes. There are times when a leader, particularly a tribune, has to set an example for the men. We have to get our hands bloodied so that the men will have confidence in us. That is also why we do not bring our women with the legions; their moderating presence would interfere with our soldierly duties."

"Have you had to do such things here in Hibernia?"

"No. I was too busy planning to defeat your men. There was supposed to be plenty of time to brutalize you and your women in the years to come. But then your innocent, defenseless girls flew across the Dubh Linn bog, and began shoving those antler weapons up our asses..."

By the strange look on Agricola's face, Laelie understood that he was giving her a peace offering.

"And we could do it to your men again. Never forget that. The women of Éire fight for themselves, and we are definitely not property. If we choose a man, or we are required by our families to wed a man for political reasons, we are loyal and dutiful wives until the end – but never property."

"My queen, I will not treat you like property. That is not the Roman way. True, the man of the familia, *pater familias*, is the head of the household and the ultimate authority. But women have great power and influence within the domicile and within our religion. Daughters have the same stature as sons, and women can own slaves and other property. They just cannot hold positions of real power, or any high office."

As they discussed the status of women verbally, their non-verbal communication also progressed. As they resumed the affectionate cuddling and stroking, the loving mood was restored.

"Maybe I should get Maura to stop harassing him about his 'old man balls'."

"I think that would be best, Lais – oops! Laelie!" he joked.

Laelie reacted as any self-respecting queen of *Éire* would...

Ten minutes later, as Laelie prepared some herbal tea for her new mate, the red welt of her open-handed slap across Agricola's face was still visible on Agricola, and the sense of contentment in his heart was still evident.

They spent the rest of the evening talking about the people under their shared leadership, and how the two cultures were coming together.

He was impressed at how intimately she knew the thoughts and feelings of her people, and how deeply she seemed to respect, even revere, each and every one of them. To her, exploring the diversity of characteristics and personalities of her people, sharing countless hours of stories and idle talk with them, seemed to be endless fun. Now, he wanted to move on to more strategic issues.

When Fabius Quintilianus arrived with his Hibernian mate, the presence of the rhetorician, a man trained in philosophy, argument and logic, changed the focus of the discussions.

To both men, it was a welcome respite from the topsy-turvy domestic lifestyle that they were constrained to for perhaps more time than they were accustomed.

These were men of action, and being cooped up in a small room with anybody, let alone these strange Hibernian women, could wear one down. Getting out of the ship, and moving on to whatever was to come, would be a much-needed change.

While they could not do anything to hasten it, they could and did do everything they could to gather intelligence on their captors, learn as much as possible about them, and try to infer their true nature.

To accomplish this, Agricola and Laelie had agreed to divide the task, with the Hibernians concentrating on having frequent contact with the Tuatha, taking specific questions with them, and then comparing notes with each other. This required countless hours of group discussions to develop a coherent picture of how best to pose questioning thoughts in order to obtain the most information.

A few of the immunes and other well-educated Romans who spoke any of the Celtic language were involved in this project, documenting the key findings so that they could contribute this information to the Roman efforts to learn as much about the ship itself, the Tuathii, engineering details about what gave the ships their power, and anything else they could learn of value.

These two projects were in addition to the ongoing coordination of the animal husbandry, butchering, cooking, cleaning, laundering and personnel management. The ship was well stocked with provisions and livestock from Inis Thiar.

These day-to-day tasks had been the focus for everybody at first, constantly going to the Tuatha to emote questions or concerns, such as "where can we make a fire to cook our meat" and "is there any firewood here?"

The Tuatha had responded to the firewood question with a feeling-tone that could only be described as dis-equanimity. Rather than the pleasant, golden feeling-tone that generally accompanied contact with the Tuatha, those who had thought-asked about wood to burn had come away with the impression that the Tuatha saw this notion as deeply repugnant.

Their hosts had given them the silent treatment, after at one point suggesting to the humans that maybe they could burn some of their own arms and legs.

"These Tuathii are sensitive beings, after all. They don't seem to like the idea of burning wood. They are trees. Not just using trees to communicate with us, but the creatures themselves, they truly are trees, and we should not think of them as people, but rather, from the point of view that a tree might have," suggested the philosophical Fabius Quintilianus.

Fabius's new Hibernian wife explained that she had been thinking about heating up some water for tea, and had bumped into a tree root. The Tuatha had passed the idea to her that food could be cooked by simply placing it into an orifice in the wall, which opened to the touch. The people had learned that by thinking of how they wanted the meat to appear, taste, and respond to the knife after being cooked, and thinking all of this while touching an appendage nearest the orifice in the wall, the meat would cook perfectly.

The first time Laelie reached in to take out a rump of lamb, she burned her hands in the fraction of a second she held the hot piece of meat. In her surprise, she sent the food flying across the room, amusing Agricola and everyone who saw it.

Soon enough, they learned that everything they needed was available in their pod: suitable places to butcher a carcass, a means of disposing of the waste material, and a basin to wash meats and vegetables.

They also found smaller compartments with surprisingly strong, light, and thin metal pots. They learned how to activate a flat surface onto which a pot could be placed, to boil water, make soup, or even to cook eggs.

For the Celtic women, who had experienced starvation from time to time when winter was particularly harsh, access to the bounty of livestock, grain and other commodities was a dream come true. They enthusiastically learned a great deal about how to cook tasty meals – not just butcher animals and heat the meat up, but the art of *seasoning*, from their Roman men.

The cooking implements were easily washed with a strange kind of moving sand, which could be sprinkled onto anything dirty, even edible tubers, rubbed around a bit, and then shaken off. Some of the engineers theorized that the sand was actulally little creatures, or perhaps machines, but so small as to be inpossible to see with the naked eye.

The white sand seemed to have something inside of it that gobbled up dirt and grease, taking it into the waste disposal system to be converted into something that the Tuatha described with the thought: "useful byproduct', but would not elaborate upon.

Now, after nearly fifteen days onboard the ship, a great deal had been learned, but so many unknowns remained.

Getting information out of the Tuatha, or figuring out how things on the *astrum navis*, starship, functioned, was like trying to fill a bathhouse with water wrung from wet cloths. A great deal of effort was expended, to negligible effect.

"Fabius Quintilianus, what have we learned from the Tuatha today?" asked Agricola, the two women listening while maintaining their 'seen-but-not heard' role while the two Roman men acted like Romans. It was all a charade, in a sense, but it the role-playing worked well for both cultures.

"We broke through the wall in one of the animal-pods, but by the time we found someone from the Second to take a look at what was beyond, the wall had miraculously repaired itself."

"Did you get a look beyond the wall yourself, Fabius?"

"Yes! I saw a great many long ropes, going into perfectly shaped holes, or into little boxes, where they seemed to join with other cords," he began. "When one of the men tried to cut a piece of the rope, his bronze blade bent, without cutting the snake. It is made of some type of metal, only in a way that allows it to be flexible. So a centurion took a swipe at the snake with his gladius – much stronger steel – and the cord was cleaved. There was a brilliant flash of light where the cord was cut, and the centurion was thrown back as if struck by a lightning bolt! We have since passed word that nobody is to cut into any of these lightning-snakes again, until we know more about them."

"Where is this lightning-snake that was cut?"

"That is the most unbelievable thing. It is no longer there! We were busy carrying the centurion back to his pod, so that his woman could tend to him – he had burns on his hands and feet and could no longer speak. By the time we returned to the scene, the snake had been made whole again! Someone must have come to replace it with a new one, or perhaps it restored itself. So we explored further, and found that there is a corridor, or perhaps many corridors, for those who keep this ship in good repair."

"That is important to know. Well done, my friend. Did you see any of these beings? Or their footprints?"

"No. It was too dark. But I did *hear* things. Sounds that we do not hear on our side of the walls."

"What kind of sounds?" asked Agricola.

"A strange brushing sound, and the sound of things being dragged. But that's not all."

"What else?"

"The *smells*. There were two. One was a horrible smell, putrid like death," said Fabius, who then seemed at a loss for words.

"And the other?"

"That's the strange part. It could just be my mind playing tricks on me, but it smelled like, like *arbor roseaus,* a rosebud tree. Do you remember how sweetly they smell, Legatus?

"Oh I remember. I too have come across that scent, but thought my mind was playing tricks on me."

.

XI

DISCIPLINA
{ Training }

The dangerous task was assigned to Centurion Spurius Sallustius Crispus, Primus Pilus of the First of the Twentieth. Fabius Quintilianus and the other academic, Vibius Metellus, had prepared him as best they could. From what they had seen when the engineers from the Eighth of the Second had cut through the wall in a domicile pod, they believed the key area to explore was above the main corridor, not below.

They had cut a hole in the ceiling of a pod at the end of the line, near what they considered to be the rear portion of the ship. With no sensation of movement, there was even some dispute as to whether the ship was moving, and if so, how high above the ground it was. Agricola and his key advisors, however, were certain that they were moving. They had found a few places on the starship which were extremely cold, even colder than the snow-covered tops of the *Alpes Cottiae*, the Cottian Alps. Agricola and a few of the tribunes had crossed the Alpes on journeys between Rome and Gallia. It had always impressed him that there could be snow at the higher elevations, while it was warm in the valleys down below. Based on this, he believed that for the hull of the starship to be so cold, they must be very high indeed, *perhaps as high as the heavens.*

At fully three full market day cycles of eight days according to the time-keeping immune's estimate, the travel to the distant land the Hibernians called Tir na nOg should not be much longer. So Agricola had assigned information-gathering missions to be more aggressive in their efforts to gain information and insights into true nature of the Tuathii and, ultimately, their intentions, to arm himself with as much knowledge as possible before they arrived at their destination.

To give Spurius Crispus an advantage after he climbed up into the hole cut through the metal ceiling, Kaeso Cerialis had come up with something to distract their captors. At the opposite end of the ship and one deck below, a soldier was to hack at a Tuatha root as thick as a man's leg. The idea was that by cutting off the main appendage leading into an unused animal pod, little harm could be caused. But given what Laelie's people had learned of the Tuathii sensitivity to the idea of burning wood, the Romans expected a swift response. Hopefully the distraction would allow Crispus additional time to complete his task.

To ensure success, the soldiers watching the tree-root being hacked at had not been informed of the true purpose of their task. The soldiers had been told to think about how much they liked the tree root and that they wanted to show their respect by eating it. Hopefully this would yield more clues about the Tuathii while confusing them about what the humans were doing at the same time.

Once Spurius Crispus had climbed into an opening above the pod, and his eyes became adjusted to the much darker space, he paused to let his senses report.

The first thing he noticed was the smell. There was a strange combination of unpleasant odors, which reminded him of rotting seaweed drying in the hot sun. But somehow, there was also the underlying pleasant aroma of vanilla, just as Marcus Fabius had reported, the scent of *arbor roseaus*, the rosebud trees of Ostia and of Judea.

The putrid, death-like smell that Fabius had reported sensing in the lower levels of the ship was not present in these upper reaches. That made sense to Spurius Crispus, as it was the same in any ship he had ever been on. The deeper you went the more corruption, piss and shit could be found.

He made his way forward onto what was like a walkway, towards an area with more light. He noticed that on both sides of the walkway there were long poles, perfectly straight, at knee and hand height, as if placed there simply to hold onto while walking. *These hand-hold-poles could be helpful if the ship were to encounter rough water. But is there water in the cosmos? Is there air?* Spurius Crispus wondered, as he moved along cautiously.

He had not taken more than a dozen steps when he saw movement, and froze.

From ahead of him, a horrible monster approached. It had four legs and two arms, and a series of shields across its back. As it neared him from the opposite direction, it suddenly veered to the right and entered onto another walkway, lower and to the left of where Crispus stood. The hideous beast paid him no heed.

The creature was much larger than centurion Crispus, about a head higher. Its head was larger than a man's, and had a wide flat helmet-shaped bone protruding behind the head, like an armored shield over the back of the neck. It had two eyes, but where a nose and mouth should be there were numerous thick large whiskers that ran along the jaw line. Sharp, prickly looking spines extended from the ends of each successive layer of hide-armor, and two long feelers moved about in front of its mouth, dangling over from the back of its head. The feelers were constantly in motion, as if sampling the air and spaces around the beast. Centurion Crispus noticed that one of the long feelers was strapped backwards and affixed to a harness that was secured to the creature's back. It looked uncomfortable, and for some reason it reminded Crispus of the bridle used to control a horse.

The creature's legs were long and appeared to be powerful. A second set of legs, coming out at the waist of the creature, seemed to be used alternately as legs and arms, with powerful claws that also seemed to be quite useful. At times, the creature gripped the lower of the handrails with this middle pair of legs, and at times it used them on the ground, as a dog might.

As the creature neared an illuminated area ahead, it stopped and sat its large rump down on the walkway for a moment, and reached out a smaller, upper-arm to hold on to the upper hand-rail.

Spurius Crispus realized that both sets of hand-rails, while metal, also had long thin Tuatha roots. So the monster must be 'talking' to the Tuathii.

Soon enough, the hideous monster resumed its transit, at a much quicker pace.

To Centurion Spurius Crispus, the beast reminded him of a *Siphonapterist*, a flea. But due to its monstrous size, he thought of it as a *Siphonapterist monstrum*, monster flea. He had once looked at one through a viewing-lens, and saw the same sort of massive legs, ugly head, and hideous overall appearance.

He became more cautious as he neared the well-illuminated area. He could hear movement ahead, and decided to get off the walkway lest more of the giant fleas come his way.

Careful not to touch the Tuatha roots on the railings, he climbed down onto the same sort of panels as he had cut his way through from the pod at the other end of the ship.

As he moved forward stealthily, something orange appeared ahead, illuminated by the light coming from what he thought must be the center of the ship.

It was another monster, only this one was not that much larger than a man, and certainly smaller than the Siphonapterist.

The smooth, hairless creature was covered by a waxy orange skin and had white dots on its bumpy head. It had two rather large eyes protruding from the sides, where a human would have had ears.

It reminded Spurius Crispus of the creature in the legend he had read in a copy of Pliny the Elder's book, *Naturalis Historia*. Spurius Crispus had only seen a few books in his lifetime, but had been shown the drawings contained in the book, part of the personal library of the academic who travelled with the Twentieth Legion, Cornelius Tacitus.

The two had argued about the notion that a monster could live in the sewers of coastal cities, such as Cisalpine Gallia, where such legends were common.

Spurius counted, and determined that the orange creature had eight legs, just like the octo-polypus of legend, or *octopodes*, as Pliny had termed it.

Crouching down, Spurius moved closer to observe.

After he rounded the corner and passed between a large obstruction that rose from floor to ceiling, he found a perfect place to hide and watch the Octopoda.

The Octopoda creature seemed much more intelligent than the Siphonapterist monstrom.

Spurius Crispus looked around the bright room, which was situated slightly higher than the various walkways that all seemed to lead to this platform, which he thought of as a bridge between the various walkways.

Spurius then looked for Tuatha roots, and saw that progressively larger Tuatha roots also converged on the bridge, disappearing behind a tall obelisk-shaped object he could not see past, where the light also seemed to be the most intense.

He was about to move around to get a glance past the obstruction when he saw a half-dozen creatures – four Siphonapteristii and two Octopodii – rushing from the bridge and heading forward along the main walkway.

He imagined that this might be the Tuathii response to whatever diversion Agricola and his advisors had created.

That left only one Octopoda on the bridge.

As Spurious Crispus watched, the Octopoda seemed to be continuously moving two or three of its arms over some sort of collection of small protrusions on a table situated around three sides of the creature, and occasionally touched a fourth arm to a nearby Tuatha root. The creature also pressed his face toward what appeared to be a pot that was on the desk, and seemed to be concentrating on whatever was inside of the pot.

Suddenly, the Octopoda climbed off of the simple chair it had been perched on, and glided down the corridor in the direction of the other creatures.

It moved with grace, its eight arms reaching out ahead on the floor of the walkway, one at a time, making the creature's progress through the ship seem effortless, smooth and calm in contrast to the jerky, jumpy movements of the Siphonapterist.

Crispus saw his opportunity to learn more, and rushed to where the Octopoda had been.

The bridge was empty, as far as he could see. He looked briefly at the table where the Octopoda had been working, and made his way around the final obstruction to the area of intense yellow light.

As he rounded the corner, he shielded his eyes from the bright light, and was astonished to find an *arbor rosea*, Judas tree, standing in the middle of the bridge.

The many Tuatha roots all led from this solitary tree, it seemed.

Its branches, reaching up to the ceiling and spreading out at the top, were in full blossom. The soft, sweet aroma of the Judas Tree filled the air of the bridge with the pleasant aromas of freshly baked treats, honey, and vanilla.

The warm yellow light coming from the ceiling reminded Spurius Crispus of the pleasant equanimity feeling that he felt whenever he made contact with the Tuatha root.

He was tempted to touch a nearby root, but decided against it. So far, his reconnaissance mission of the ship had gone seemingly undetected, and he wanted to keep it that way.

He looked at the strange pot that the Octopoda had been peering into, and carefully placed his face on top of the rim, just as the Octopoda had.

There, inside the pot, was a blue and white marble.

As he looked at the marble, he tried to focus on it and suddenly, *it got larger!* When he tried to reduce his focus on it, it became smaller again. It was as if the pot he was looking into could discern whether he wanted to close or expand his focus. He concluded that it was similar to the Tuatha roots, that it could sense his thoughts, at least in regard to what he would see in the pot.

He concentrated his thoughts on looking even closer, and the blue, white and brown of the marble became clearer. The blue now appeared as water, in the way it looked when looking down at the ocean from a high cliff – or from a mountain top.

The white seemed like clouds, and seemed to be moving slowly across the water.

The brown clearly was land, with areas of green, sandy brown and grey colors.

The image continued to become larger and larger. It made him feel as if he were falling to the ground from a great height. He continued to look into the viewing pot, which he considered to be greatly magnifying what his eyes could see, almost like a sailor's looking glass, only far more powerful and responsive to any change in his intensity or direction of focus. He experimented with looking up, then down. His view changed accordingly. Soon he was able to move his focus and aim-point around at will, as easy as using his own eyes to explore the ground that he considered to be far below the starship. *Am I with the gods, looking down on the land?* he wondered.

Suddenly he saw something in the pot, moving about on the ground. Tiny at first, the specks grew larger. Suddenly it was clear what they were. *Siphonapteristii monstrom*, monster fleas!

In amongst them were another type of creature, but he could not believe his eyes.

To Spurius Crispus, they appeared to be *people*.

They were humans.

The humans seemed to be *herding* the Siphonopteristii towards a cave in the side of a hill, into which they disappeared.

Simply by his thinking, the focal point changed, moving past the hole in the mountain and moving on to another hole not far away. Siphonapteristii were coming out of this hole, but seemed to be carrying something, and proceeding in a line, with humans apparently shepherding them.

As he pulled his face away from the pot-shaped device he wondered how such a small vessel could somehow hold something that could grow and shrink in size. It added to all of the strange things he had experienced, seen, and been confronted with. It was almost too much for the mind to grasp. *Is this some terrible magic? What fate is in store for us? Are we doomed?* He felt fear and frustration.

He tried to pick up the viewing pot, but it held firm to the table. He looked under the table and found that the potl extended under the table, down into the floor, and disappeared. It made him believe that it was all based on bouncing light along tubes, lenses and other things he was familiar with – *there is no magic here, only machines and things that I have not yet come to understand.*

His confidence and curiosity so encouraged, he put his face into the viewing-pot again, and once again the view was of a blue and white marble. After adjusting his focus to confirm that his eyes had not deceived him, and that he was able to look more closely at the tiny marble, he tried to move his focus away from the marble, to see what was beyond.

He saw stars.

Moving his gaze around between the stars, it suddenly became very bright inside the viewing pot, until somehow the brightness was muted, and no longer painful to his eyes.

He found himself looking into *sol*, the sun!

He continued to explore and noticed that the viewing pot seemed to follow his thinking, and another marble appeared, this one absolutely white.

He thought of pulling back, to see where each of these marbles were in relation to the others, and to the sun. He was soon presented with an image that somehow felt like reality and yet also like a drawing, with circles and lines now 'drawn' on what he could see, like a navigator's chart.

The circles went around the sun, and each circle went through the middle of a marble. Something told him that the marbles were going around the sun, and the sun was stationary.

Other than the sun in the center, there were five marbles that circled it. One brown one, small and close to the sun. The next was the white one, fairly close to the sun, then one that was blue and white, which he now recognized as where he had seen humans walking on the ground, and finally two much larger ones very far away from the sun.

His eyes and brain ached after looking at the images through the viewing pot, and he decided he that he had seen enough.

In his last look at the blue and white marble, he had the impression that it was turning. As if it was a spinning marble, in the stars.

These marbles are planetae. Each one of them is a world onto itself, and that blue and white one, while small because it is far away, is very, very large. Large enough to have lands, with people living on it, perhaps nations? Spurius Crispus realized, his brain alive with the possibilities. *We are in a ship in the stars, looking down on a planeta, probably not Terra, but a planeta with people on it!* he concluded.

He broke away from the viewing-pot and continued to investigate the bridge, taking a long moment to stare at the array of small objects embedded into the Octopoda's worktable. Then he began to step back, preparing to depart the bridge while trying to absorb as many details as he could for his report.

He noticed a few other such workstations on the bridge, almost like a collection of stations for *scriptores*, scribes, or perhaps *clerici*, clerks.

He made his way around the large obstructions in a different path than when he entered, and saw that on the face of the large obstruction was a window. The window was made of the clearest glass he had ever seen.

Peering through the glass into the dimly lit interior of the large metal box, at first he could not make anything out.

And then he saw movement.

Suddenly he realized that he was looking into the angry looking face of an Octopoda.

He ran, terrified, and unable to shake the look of anger in the face of the Octopoda. He would have given anything to be back at the Legio XX castra, Deva, in Britannia, where life made sense.

What he had seen on his reconnaissance mission was unbelievable.

The carnage in the pod where the munifex had hacked the Tuatha root to pieces had been swift and brutal.

Even to an experienced soldier such as Kaeso Cerialis, the blood and body parts strewn about the room spoke of terrible violence.

The two milites who had witnessed the event were still in battle-shock, unable to report what they had seen. All they could say was that terrible monsters had suddenly come through the walls and ripped the soldier apart.

They had disappeared quickly, before the officers and soldiers in the corridor could react.

Placing his hand on the shoulder of one of the young milites, Kaeso Cerialis spoke in a reassuring tone.

"Listen carefully to me. I know you are terrified by what you saw. You are a brave young man, and from what I hear from your centurion, you are well on your way to being considered one of the more trustworthy milites in your cohort, likely to advance much faster than the other trainees. So I will speak to you as if you were a munifex, an experienced soldier of Rome," he began.

"Tribune," was all the boy could say, but he appeared to be a bit less terrified.

"The creatures you saw, they are not monsters. We know what they are," Cerialis lied. "They are our enemies. And by coming out to kill one of our men, they have fallen into our trap. The trap our genius commander had set for them. You see, we tricked them into responding, by cutting one of their roots. What we had hoped for was to provoke them, and to have an eyewitness report of what they looked like, how they moved, what weapons they used, and so on. Do you understand?"

"Yes, Tribune."

"Well then, I want you to calm down and tell me where you were before this happened?"

"I was standing sentry with my sentry-partner, Milite Opiter Paccius, as I had been ordered. We watched as Munifex Seppius had been chopping away at the root for some time, and the others had all gone out of the chamber and into the corridor to watch for a response from the Tuathii," he paused, looking worried.

"Go on, boy, you are doing well."

"Tribune. We all expected to see something, maybe a person or a monster, coming down the corridor from the end of the ship. Nobody expected them to come at Seppius from within the walls. Anyhow, he never saw them coming. Two terrible monsters, with long hairy legs and maybe four arms each, grabbed hold of him and simply tore him to pieces and ate him. Then they returned into the walls."

"And what weapons did they use?"

"They had no weapons. They used their bare hands, or what we would consider as hands. They were like the claws of an insect, only much larger than a man's hand. Even bigger than that of an *ursa*, bear."

"They tore him apart with their hands?"

"Yes, Tribune, in just a few seconds. It happened so fast."

"Did they speak?"

"No, Tribune. They did make some kind of squeal, but nothing you could call words."

"Did they look at you or the other milite?"

"No, Tribune. They simply came to kill, eat, and then left."

"And how large were they?"

"They were about this tall," the milite held a hand about an arm's length over his own head. "Their heads were small, their lower torso was very thick, and they were covered in armor or scales. That's all I saw."

The milite appeared to have not moved since, as if his feet had been welded to the floor.

"Very well done, soldier. You have acquitted yourself as well, or better, than any man would be expected to under the circumstances. Now, do not talk to anybody about what you saw, only that you made your report to me and that you succeeded in your task. Now go, take care of your sentry-partner. Tell him that everything is fine and he did well. It is important that you both not make contact with a Tuatha root, unless you are ordered. If you do so by mistake, then concentrate on happy thoughts, perhaps a memory of Britannia or having sex with your woman. Do not think about what happened here today. Do you understand?"

"Yes, Tribune. It is a military secret, and it will die with me."

Later, when Cerialis, Agricola, the two academics and Spurius Crispus compared notes in Agricola's pod, the discussion became very heated.

They had agreed to put off the analysis of what Spurius Crispus had seen, and to focus on what to do about the chunk of Tuatha that had been chopped off by the munifex.

"I think we should leave it where it lies, and see what the Tuathii do about it," said Metellus, the historian.

Agricola responded firmly. "That would be ceding the battlefield to the enemy. No, I want it brought here, right now."

"But —"

"Now!"

"Legatus." said Metellus, ceasing to argue.

Kaeso Cerialis nodded at Centurion Flavus to complete the task without delay.

"What do you mean to achieve by provoking them further?" asked Vibius Metellus.

"The men are afraid. Rumors of what happened have already passed throughout the ship. I need to show them that I am unafraid. And I have a plan: I will connect with the Tuatha, thinking about how unhappy we are that one of their sacred roots has been defiled, and that I will keep the segment of root close to me, to display to our people, as a constant reminder that we must never again harm a Tuatha root."

"And what purpose will this serve?" asked Fabius Quintilianus.

"I hope that it will satisfy them that we have learned our lesson. But more importantly, I will put it on display in some manner, so that whenever I speak to our people, we can remind ourselves of how tenuous our existence is. We are at their mercy, but we are not cowed by it. Far from it, we are preparing for the day when we can cut them to little pieces and make a bonfire out of their sacred appendages," he said, drawing hopeful smiles from his closest confidants.

"We must play the obedient slave, waiting for the chance to cut the master's throat. And today we learned something of what makes them vulnerable, how we can provoke them when the time comes. But for now, let us focus on what Spurius Crispus has reported. And Spurius, thank you for that excellent report, you have given form to our shadowy enemy."

"Legatus."

"From the description you gave of the Octopoda creature you saw on the bridge, it appears that both these Siphonapteristii brutes and these strange Octopodii are quite different, not only different from us, but different from other animals we know of on Terra. Vibius Metellus, you think that this is important?"

"Yes, Legatus. I think it means that the Tuathii use different beings to do different jobs. Perhaps based on what jobs need to be done, or perhaps based on the capabilities of these beings. And I further believe that we can deduce that we are simply another form of being which the Tuathii intend to use for their purposes."

"Is that an important deduction?"

"Yes, Legatus. Because it means that our captors need us in some way. That means we are safe, at least for the time being. We are captives, perhaps slaves, but it also means that the enemy has some sort of deficiency or vulnerability. This may give us an advantage at some point. We need to know more.

"Well, that is what we are discussing, isn't it? What do we need to learn, and how? Vibius, go on, continue to lead the discussion."

"Legatus," continued the rhetorician, "there are three categories to consider. First, what do we know of the function and status of the ship? Second, what do we know of the crew, these smelly Octopodii and the hideous Siphonapteristii? Third, what did Spurius Crispus actually see in that looking-vase?"

The men argued into the night, and made considerable progress, however they could not agree on whether the Tuathii served the Octopodii, or vice versa. There was unanimous agreement that the monstrous fleas, the Siphonapteristii, were merely brute force. They also believed that what Spurius Crispus saw was a mine, with humans acting as slave-handlers and Siphonapteristii performing physical labor. However this led to an impossible conclusion, which only one man believed could be possible.

"I grant you that we cannot doubt what Spurius Crispus says he saw. He thinks that he saw humans and Siphonapteristii moving about on land, not far from the sea. This could be our destination, and if Metellus is correct, then this looking pot is actually not a pot at all. It is a very special type of spyglass, one that can see very far, very close, and all around. But on the other hand, the blue-and-white marble may simply be a distortion of light, as light travels through a thick piece of glass, making the sides look round when in fact they continue to the sides but beyond view," argued the other philosopher, Fabius Quintilianus, trying to strengthen his hypothesis that they were not travelling in the cosmos, but merely over a different piece of land, on *Terra*, planet Earth.

"But Fabius Quintilianus, if that were true, then Spurius Crispus must have been looking down through the bottom of the ship, through the inside of the column that he described as being under the table. That could make sense, if we are flying in the air, over the land, however that does not account for also being able to look down on the sun. You can only look up at the sun!" said Kaeso Cerialis.

"Let us step back and consider an alternative explanation."

"By all means, Vibius Metellus, why not bruise my brain further with your unending variety of possibilities! You philosophers, you must take great joy in sharing your sophistic fantasies!" said Agricola.

Respectfully, Metellus countered. "Legatus. If you will grant to me that being inside a ship that floats in the sky, as we appear to be doing now, is not impossible, and that the engineering and shipbuilding skills that allow the Tuathii, or the Octopodii – whoever is in charge – to do so is very real, then maybe what hampers our ability to understand is our inability to let go of our assumptions. And the one assumption you all continue to hold is that this land we are travelling to, or may have arrived at, is part of the same world as Rome, Hispania or Hibernia.

But suppose that what Spurius Crispus saw was actually a sphere, not some distorted view of the land below. Then we are not travelling over land, rather, we are travelling through the cosmos from one planeta to another. The planeta below is not Terra."

"But I still have trouble understanding that we are standing on a sphere. I have heard these theories before – they come from the Greek, Aristotle, do they not? What I can never get my head around is this: Why do we not fall off?" asked Agricola.

"This I cannot explain. I have read accounts of how the Greeks understood it. What I recall are the facts which we know today to be true: That is, the seven celestial objects we can see – Sol, Luna, Mercury, Venus, Mars, Jupiter and Saturn – these all revolve around Terra. That means that Terra is a planeta, which is a very large ball floating in the cosmos. Everything else, out there in the firmament, does not revolve around Terra. Or if it does, such as the constellations of the night sky, then they are very far away, and revolve around Terra.

"There is another conception of cosmology, and that is that actually *sol* is the center of the universe. This theory has many advantages, as it explains what astronomers observe of the motion of the planetae, and perhaps even explains why there are summer and winter seasons, but it would also require that Terra is moving around sol, and yet we do not feel any motion. Therefore this so-called 'heliocentric' model could not be true. That is, would not be true unless Terra is such a very large *globus* that we simply cannot feel the motion, just as you don't really feel all the motion a ship is making while you travel on one.

"But suppose that this globus, Terra, is so large that somehow we can stand on it and not fall off; something about it makes things stay connected to the surface. And we know from

Aristotle and others that if the world is a sphere, spinning in the heavens, then the way the stars change at night stands up to reason. That's why the men of the Second were able to navigate their ships, by making reference to the stars. Now add one more idea, that the stars are themselves very large, and very far from each other," said Vibius Metellus.

"Why do we need to imagine that? Because Spurius saw sol in the viewing pot as being much larger than other stars? Maybe it was the way things are made smaller or larger by the viewing pot?"

"That could be it, Legatus, but suppose each star is a different sun, and around each star there are spheres, going around just as in the heliocentric cosmological model. Certainly this matches the circular lines around the sun that Spurius Crispus saw in the viewing pot."

Frustrated with the unending discussion of complex mathematical and geometric shapes that the two philosophers had dragged the senior officers through, Agricola gave up.

"Suppose you are right, and we have left our sphere, Terra, and have now arrived at another sphere, at another star in the heavens, and now float above another unknown sphere. What then?"

"Legatus, I believe that what you just said is the simple truth. And if it is true, then there are many important conclusions. First, these Tuathii have been to Terra before, or else how could there be humans on this other planet? If this is true, then they may have been taken from Hibernia, as the Hibernian legend of the Tuatha De Danann speaks of strange beings that come to take people away to an otherworldly realm, from which they will never return. Suppose that is true, then perhaps we are to be used as slaves, to shepherd those Siphonapteristii into doing exactly what Fabius Quintilianus said – that they are working in a mine inside the mountain."

"So lay it out for me, Metellus. Are we to be used as *custodiae servi*? – prison wardens?"

"Perhaps. It is indeed possible. If the dominant race here is the Tuathii, like the one that Spurius Crispus saw situated on the bridge in the center of the ship, then they must require the use of other creatures to labor as slaves. They can achieve this by some trick of nature that lets them convey thoughts and feelings in a very pleasant way, simply by contact, into the minds of man or beast.

"If this is how they operate, then these Octopodii, while apparently smarter than the brutish Siphonapteristii, must be the next highest ranking creatures. Perhaps they are the immunes, those with special skills and training, like operating the ship itself. It stands to reason that the Siphonapteristii can be difficult to manage, and maybe the Octopodii are not all that suitable for serving as custodiae. Maybe that is why they require humans."

"Legatus, I think Vibius Metellus is on to something. And from what Spurius Crispus says, the Octopoda he saw inside the chamber on the bridge may well have been immersed in water. If that is true, and we can find out easily enough, then it could explain why the Octopodii are not suited to the role of *custodiae* on land. They must need to spend much of their time in water," said Fabius Quintilianus.

Agricola took a deep breath, massaging his temple as he tried to reduce the headache that resulted from such a theoretical discussion. The possibilities, he was learning, were well beyond his range of experience. He reflected how his studies in the military arts and strategic planning did not prepare him for this, and then continued.

"So if all of this is true, then the one tree in the bridge of this ship controls everything on this ship by touching other creatures and giving them thoughts? – such as, go fix this, go do that? And that is how they control the creatures that do their bidding?"

"Precisely."

"So how do they know what needs to be done? Do they ask their minions if something needs to be done?"

"Yes, Legatus, I think they do. Consider the viewing pots. They require the Octopodii to operate these devices, to look down upon the planetae and stars, to determine where the ship is."

"Why do they not look for themselves?"

"Ttrees do not have eyes!"

And then it hit him. Everything his two philosophers had argued about must be true. That the Tuathii need other races to manage their affairs. They do not have eyes or ears, and they gather their information from the thoughts and perhaps visual images being experienced by their minions in contact with them through their root appendages. If this were true, it would mean that there was great opportunity for the Romans. But one question had not been answered.

"And what of my lady, Queen Laelie's suspicion?"

"Which?"

"She suspects that the Tuathii have taken root in these ships, but they could not have been the ones who designed and constructed them. She believes that these ships are stolen from some other race."

"I had not considered this idea," said Metellus.

There was a long pause as the mentally exhausted men considered going into yet another line of considerations and logical discourse. And then the simple soldier, Honestus Flavus, interrupted them.

Honestus had retrieved the thick tree-root that had been chopped off, and dragged it into the pod.

It was long and bulky, and brushed up against some of the men as he dragged it along.

Not wanting to divulge their thoughts to the Tuatha, the men instinctively pulled back.

"Don't worry, it doesn't work. Go ahead and touch it."

Agricola touched it first. "It feels dead, and stiff. Like a dried log."

"It is. And I have an idea.

"What is it, Honestus?"

"Legatus, why not let me and some of the carpenters from the Eighth of the Second cut this up and make a *solium* for you?"

"A chair of state? To sit on?"

"Yes, Legatus. It would be perfect. You could tell the Tuatha that it is our way of honoring their sacred limb. But for us, it will be an amusing reminder that ultimately we will defeat our enemy.

Each time you sit on your throne and flatulate on their sacred root, it will remind us all that we will one day have mastery over them, and throw them into the bonfire!"

"That would be audacious. Yes please. Do so discretely and do not let any of the carpenters think too much about it, or communicate with the Tuatha. We could be playing with fire."

"Legatus."

"And what about the question we were discussing before Centurion Honestus returned?" he asked the others.

"What question, Legatus?" asked Honestus, happy to be involved in the discussion with the senior officers.

"Whether it is possible that the Tuathii have stolen these ships from some other race."

"Anything stolen can be stolen again," said Honestus.

XII

PLANETA METALLORVM
{ Mining Planet }

Based on what he had gleaned from his thought-discussion with the Tuatha about the chopping incident, Agricola was confident that the probe of the ship's command deck by Spurius Crispus had not been detected. Because there had been no recriminations against Centurion Crispus, Agricola believed that the Octopoda had not reported seeing the human. After thinking about it further, he attributed it to the possibility that the Octopodii were in the same fix as the humans, having been abducted by the Tuathii and in all probability about to be forced to do their bidding on the nearby planeta.

An alternative suggested by Vibius Metellus was that the Tuathii simply chose not to reveal that they knew.

Regardless, Agricola had decided that it was time to press their master for an audience, or to force the issue.

Grasping a Tuatha appendage, and linking with Queen Laelie, the two leaders passed on a singular thought: *take us to you, we need to know more.*

The Tuatha responded by imparting unto Agricola and Laelie the route to follow to the bridge, and emitting a welcoming feeling-tone.

They told Cerialis that they had been invited to the bridge, and then headed off in the direction that was indicated by the Tuatha, which led them through the ship into a blank wall. After touching a root-appendage nearby, the wall opened, revealing an upward-leading ramp.

After ascending a ramp, they found themselves standing on the bridge deck, which appeared very much as Spurius Crispus had described, however there were none of the creatures he had seen.

They approached the central chamber, where the light was brightest, and found an *arbor roseaus*, a Judas Tree.

Looking around the command deck, Agricola saw that there were actually six work-stations, two of which were outfitted with what appeared to be viewing glasses. The four other workplaces each had arrays of small shapes embedded in their surface, as if for the ease of touching. Each of the small shapes seemed identical, except for some sort of lettering or label applied to each.

He knew from the intention-message that the Tuatha had passed to him and Laelie that he was supposed to connect to a nearby appendage, but he decided to delay. He mused, *if they truly are blind, and we do not make ourselves known, then how would they know if we have arrived?*

But then he saw a creature lurking in the background, just behind one of the large rectangular-shaped water tanks, presumably a swimming closet for an Octopoda. He saw that the creature did indeed appear to be a man-sized Octopoda, and that there were tree-roots wrapped around its head.

When he looked into the eyes of the creature, he felt that the consciousness looking back at him was not only that of the Octopoda, but also that of the Tuatha, so he did not delay any longer and grasped a nearby root that was wrapped around a handrail.

He immediately felt the connection with the Tuatha, and an urging to move closer to the Judas Tree.

Taking Laelie by the hand, he moved to where he understood he was supposed to be, and then knelt with Laelie in front of the trunk of the Judas Tree.

A large orifice in the base of the tree opened, momentarily bringing the inviting image of a woman's vulva to mind. Agricola quickly chased the image from his thoughts, and inserted his head into the cavity, as he understood he was required to do. Laelie did likewise.

The feelings of connectivity with the Tuatha, and with his lover at the same time, were far more intense than any he had experienced before.

He felt a wave of understanding pass between himself and the tree, and with Laelie. Yet he also felt that he could control what was passed, at least what was playing in his own mind for the Tuatha, and Laelie, to see. He was conscious of a reciprocal trading of information occurring, thoughts of *I'll show you where I come from while you show me where you come from*, and just as he thought that the exchange worked best if voluntary, the thought was confirmed, *Yes, sharing works best when given freely*.

He wondered about the many appendages that had now wrapped themselves around his head. *Yes, to really see your thoughts there must be many close connections.*

In the span of an instant, a thought-conversation took place: "So what are you?" *I am an old being, what you think of as a 'tree'.*

"How old are you?" *On the next passage of the life-giver at maximum extent, I will be two thousand and two hundred of your years.*

"Life giver?" *The nearest Equanimity sphere, what you call a 'sun'.*

The complex web of thoughts and feelings that the Tuatha conveyed, in an attempt to explain the meaning of Equanimity, was overwhelming to Agricola. All he took from it was that somehow the source of power in nature, and seemingly for the starship itself, was also the source of that wonderful feeling of peace and resolution – the equanimity he experienced when in contact through the Tuatha – and that this was a deeply revered part of the Tuatha conception of the universe. He would have to talk to his philosophers about it, as delving into such noumenal and philosophical subjects made his head spin.

Agricola moved on to other thought-questions.

'Where have you taken us?' *To a place where you can be of use.*

'What use will you put us to?' *You will control the stupid ones.*

'The stupid ones?' Agricola thought, to which an image of a horrible monster came to his mind, along with images of the monsters being shepherded into a mine, forced by whip and cane to do a variety of tasks that Agricola recognized as mining. Then came images of the monsters carrying away handfuls of metallic ore.

When he reflected that it seemed strange that the monster was not using buckets, wheels, or baskets to make their work more efficient, the Tuatha thought-replied: *We don't do things that way. The stupid ones produce the needed material at a suitable pace; anything faster or more efficient would be insane.*

The Tuatha's mood suddenly changed when it began to communicate to Agricola about another creature found on the nearby planeta, and the fact that they were to be killed on sight. The humans were expected to consider them a pest to be eradicated. What surprised Agricola was the intensity of the hatred he felt when the Tuatha described *'Those who cut us down with their teeth'*. To Agricola, they seemed like the soft-furred creatures whose pelts he had first seen on display in the Pantheon in Rome, when as a boy he would go with his father to see the treasures displayed for the citizens of Rome, and hear the stories retold by the legionaries who had conquered some new territory.

He had once purchased a pelt of one such *castor fiber*, and given it as a wedding gift along with a vial of liquid extracted from the creature's scent gland. The gift had been expensive, but was so well received by the young bride that he had ever since enjoyed favor from her husband, an up-and-coming young equestrian, a man of wealth. Whether the medicinal elixir made from the scent gland of the *castor* was beneficial, as so many rich women believed, was uncertain.

After having experienced first-hand the high price that the nobility were willing to pay for the pelts and the oils, Agricola the Younger had considered the animals to present an economic opportunity upon his return to Britannia. With his family so well established in Britannia, there seemed to be an opportunity to establish trade with the Caledonians in the north, who had occasionally tried to sell the local variety of castor pelts to Quintus Petillius Cerialis, his best friend Kaeso's father, on many occasions.

Trade in castor pelts could lead to better relations with the northern Celts, he had once believed. But that now seemed to be a long-forgotten memory.

The image of the castor creatures of Planeta Metallorum was drastically different than those of Terra in that these *Castorii* had very strange fur. Their bodies were covered in what seemed to be short feathers, but they had the same enormous teeth, wide, flat tail and, from the images the Tuatha conveyed, built their homes out of trees and branches, just like the Castorii of Terra.

That must be the cause of the hatred, thought Agricola. *The Castorii cut down trees with their teeth, and the Tuathii are trees. They must take it very personally...*

That left unaddressed the question of the relationship between the Tuathii and the local trees. Were there Tuathii living in the local forests? When he tried to ask this question, the Tuatha did not respond and emitted an unpleasant feeling-tone that he took to mean: *You do not need to know this.*

And so it went on for a considerable time, Agricola thinking questions and the Tuatha replying with images, thoughts, and feelings when it suited, or with evasive thoughts when it did not.

From time to time Laelie interjected thoughts of her own, questioning about *how their people were to live, what are the rules to be? What is it like on Tir na nOg?* What Laelie and the other Hibernians had been calling the nearby planeta.

The Tuatha at first seemed confused by the notion of Tir na nOg, but then probed her with thought-questions and then came to understand: *Yes, this can be your 'Tir na nOg'. It is an otherworld for you, and it is true that we are the ones who brought you here, so we can be Tuatha De Danann for you. We would have brought many more on our other expedition to your homeworld, but two of our three starships were lost, somewhere on your planeta, at places we will not return to.*

The image conveyed with this thought matched with Agricola's understanding of the known world, which seemed to tell him that the Tuathii had sent three starships to Terra many millennia ago, with the two lost starships having landed in the vicinity of Judea, or perhaps Egypt, and the second, coincidentally, near the future site of Rome. He could only imagine what may have befallen the Octopodii and Siphonapteristii crewmembers, and the single Tuatha, that had been aboard the lost starships.

The Tuatha did not seem all that interested in prying into either Laelie or Agricola's private thoughts, or about Hibernia or Rome, other than to confirm that Agricola and Laelie understood what their people were to do in the service of the *'Many-one'*, as the Tuatha thought of itself.

Agricola pressed with more questioning, *Why us? Why have you chosen humans to do this work for you? Can we ever leave? Why not?* but the Tuatha emoted anger and impatience, and a very unpleasant feeling-tone which made the humans want to break contact, understanding that the Tuatha had given them all the answers that it would, for now.

Gently, the Tuatha appendages were removed from their heads. However, before Laelie and Agricola removed their heads from the cavity at the base of the tree; they each understood that they must take a deep drink of the liquid pooled in the bottom of the cavity.

It had a nectary sweetness that was deeply satisfying. They both wanted more, but felt a deep compulsion to return to their people and communicate what they had experienced.

As they made their way from the Tuatha's trunk through the bridge, they saw a few of the Octopodii and Siphonapteristii. The creatures were all in close contact with the Tuatha, and were seemingly on display for the humans.

While Laelie looked at the many unusual objects that were on the bridge, Agricola stopped to put his face into the looking-pot that Spurius Crispus had described, hoping to see a planeta, or a star, inside. But unlike Spurius Crispus, he saw nothing, only blackness.

Feeling a mild connection with the device nonetheless, he thought of the sky, and imagined being shown the sky. Suddenly the viewing pot became bright to his eyes, and then adjusted the intensity, making it less painful to look at. It was as if he had opened his eyes and looked upward into a blue sky.

As he thought of looking around, the viewing pot showed him the terrain, as if he were looking through the window of his chambers at his father's castra, Deva, in Britannia Major.

He could see grassland with a herd of sheep. Thinking his view forward, he now saw that the hills beyond were actually covered with an unusual kind of tree, with bright green leaves, which he had never seen anywhere before.

He cast his thoughts to the right, looking for anything else to see, and the viewing pot showed him what lay to the right.

Suddenly a massive egg-shaped vessel came into view. It was just as he had seen in Hibernia, one of the Tuathii *astrum navis*, starships, appeared in his field of view.

It was settled on the ground, on several legs that jutted out of the lower reaches of the egg, but the portals were closed.

As he thought of the portals, the viewing pot made the starship appear much larger, as if focusing in on the side of the ship. Suddenly Agricola could make out the shape of a portal on the side of the starship. His vision got closer and closer, until he felt that he could reach out and slip a finger into the gap between the portal door and the side of the ship.

His mind reeled at the drastic change in perspective, and he thought of moving his focus back away from the ship, and the viewing pot obediently backed off so that the starship now looked smaller and was fully in view.

Agricola felt something pushing against him. At first he thought it was just Laelie, who was with him moments before, but he smelled something awful, and pulled his face from the viewing pot to look up.

He found himself face-to-face with a hideous monster looking down at him. The ugly, scaly little head, with its two feeler-whiskers wiggling and the many spiky hairs leading to its mouth writhing in a terrifying way, glared down at the human as if it was about to bite into his face.

Agricola ascertained that, for the time being, he was no longer welcome on the bridge, and departed with Laelie.

Agricola and Laelie spent the next hour telling their officers and other key people what they had learned, and that they were all to leave the ship soon.

It had come as a surprise to the others that the second starship had already landed on the surface of *Planeta Metallorum*, as they now called it, Mining Planet.

"There must be something about the manner in which these starships travel that tricks us into not feeling the motion," concluded Metellus, who then had a distant look on his face, as if pondering the cosmological implications. *So indeed, one does not have to feel a sense of motion while on an object travelling in the cosmos. Therefore the holeocentric model may well be – certainly appears to be – true. Planetae revolve around suns. Around each star in the constellations there may be planetae like this one below us, to explore.* He realized excitedly. *Imagine the possibilities…*

"More importantly, what do you suppose was the purpose of having you drink the water from the cavity in the Tuatha?" asked the other philosopher.

"Oh, I am sure that I know what that was for, Fabius Quintilianus," said Laelie.

"Please explain."

"The Tuatha told us. A great many ages ago, when they were simply trees, they, what is the word? Oh yes, *evolved*, they evolved the ability to hold some water in a cavity near the ground, and to change the way the water tasted by modifying it with various flavors minerals and fluids, to make a variety of different tastes. This fluid, and the aroma that it carried into the air, would then attract small animals who would come to the tree to drink the nectary fluid.

While the little animals drank the fluid the Tuathii would touch them with their appendages and gain some understanding of the creature's life. As the Tuatha recounted to Julius and I, as they evolved over a great period of time they developed the ability to wrap more and more appendages around a creature, to increase the flow of information. And now, after eons, they are able to actually see with the creature's own eyes – as long as they have a strong enough connection."

"Astonishing," said Fabius Quintilianus, "but if they do not have many appendages wrapped around a creature, such as a simple hand-contact we use to activate our domicile pods, do they not receive the information that they seek? Are they blind?"

"Yes," said Laelie, "They cannot see with our eyes, or hear with our ears, unless they have our heads shoved up their *cunnis arbustum*, tree-vagina. They can only convey a few simple thoughts, intentions, or desires. But as we all learned when we were enticed into our pair-bondings, even these simple intentions and desires – and the pleasant feelings that they are accompanied by – are enough to have even sophisticated creatures like we Hibernians, and you simple Romans, to do their bidding!"

"Laelie!" objected Agricola, giving his woman a stern look.

"Dominus!" she replied, simulating obedience to her man while smiling at the Romans in a friendly but sarcastic manner.

"You mentioned something about talking with the Tuatha about your Hibernian mythology?" asked Vibius Metellus.

"Yes. I asked if this planet was Tir na nOg, the mystical realm which the Tuatha De Danann take the people to."

"Is it?"

"Yes and no. This is an 'other world', and it is where they have taken my people – this time, and one time before – but this is not actually Tir na nOg and these Tuathii are not the real Tuatha De Danann, if there ever were any such beings."

"How can you be so sure?"

"Because in our legends, the Tuatha De Danann are wonderful, magical, godlike, but also very much like people. These trees, if they are all like the one on this ship, are interesting creatures, with interesting capabilities, but they are not gods. They are not *draoidh*, magical."

"But they could be the source of your legends?"

Queen Laelie paused, reflecting on that. "Yes, I suppose our legends could have their origins in a previous abduction by the Tuathii, and then changed over the years, but I don't want to accept that they are the Tuatha of legend, even if our Druid, Allanon, believes that they are."

"So what do we call them?"

She paused, and then answered. "I am unsure, Vibius Metellus. It may serve us well to continue to think of them as Tuatha De Danann, and to consciously hold them in high, godlike, regard – at least whenever we interact with them."

"Certainly this would be a form of flattery which could serve us well. It seems to appeal to them to be thought of in this way. Besides, as long as we do not let many of our people stick their heads into the tree's cunnis we can keep this information to only those of us in this room. After all, we must keep our people from despair," said Metellus

"For my people, especially those who listen to the Druid, Allanon and the *Filidh*, story-tellers, perpetuating the religious myth, this may help keep them happy,"

"Very astute, my Hibernian Queen," said Agricola. "It shall be the same with the Romans. Nobody shall shove his head up into one of those tree's cunnis without my permission. And we shall all refer to them as if they are the Hibernian's Tuatha De Danann.

"Meanwhile, we have much more to learn about them and how things are done here on Planeta Metallorum." Agricola got up, and picked up the simple wooden throne that Centurion Flavus and the boys from the Eighth had fashioned out of the lopped-off Tuathii appendage.

"So without further discussion, I think it is time to form up the legion and march with pride out onto our new homeworld and see how the rest of our people in the other ship have fared!"

After a brief 'we are ready' contact from Agricola to the Tuatha, the four main portals of both ships opened.

XIII

INIMICVS INIMICI MEI
{ Enemy of my Enemy }

The first impression that Agricola had of Planeta Metallorum was the smell of grass in the air as the entry pods to the starships opened. He could see that the ten or twelve horses being led from his starship were hesitant to eat the strange smelling grass, and he hoped that they would take well to it as there seemed to be no alternative.

Having become acclimatized to the artificial light within the starship, the splendid brightness of natural light outside was painful to the eyes at first, but his eyes soon adjusted as he and his people emerged from the two ships.

Agricola sensed excitement amongst the Hibernians, who believed they had arrived on their mystical Tir na nOg. His men, in sharp contrast, felt as if they were marching onto a battlefield.

He could feel the fear and tension in his men, and decided to do something about it.

"Kaeso, have the horn-blowers sound a triumphal march," Agricola ordered his Tribunus Laticlavius. "The men need to know that we are marching home in victory, not marching into slavery. Give them back their pride for now, and we'll give them victory one day."

"Legatus." Cerialis mounted one of the horses and rode a few strides ahead. He could have simply run up to the Primus Pilus standing immediately behind the three *cornicens*, horn-blowers, to give the order, but understood that Legatus Agricola wanted full military pageantry.

"Centurion Crispus, have them blow out a triumph!"

"Tribune!" replied Spurius Crispus, understanding immediately what was intended. He then turned his head and barked an order to the munifex in the first rank of the cohort behind him. "Miles Gregarious! Lead the men in song!"

After the soldier shouted out the first couple of words, the men behind quickly joined in.

Looking over his shoulder at the column as it advanced past him, Kaeso Cerialis observed how marching together in parade formation lifted the men's spirits, and put them in in a better frame of mind.

The pleased look on Legatus Agricola's face told Cerialis that his commander was pleased with the result. The men were standing taller, more confident, ready to face whatever lay ahead.

Not far away, in front of the second starship, Tribune Avitus watched as the Praefectus Castrorum Tappulus got the men from the second starship into a similar formation. When the sound of the marching song began to rise from the column headed their way from the first ship, Marcus was impressed that they had chosen a Gallo-Celtic tune, which made reference to places in Britannia that even the Hibernians knew about. This had a positive morale-enhancing effect on all of their people. It carried beautifully in the still air of Planeta Metallorum, and somehow made the planet feel less alien. And from what he could see from outside the portal, the planet was much like home, with forested hills, grassy lowlands and white clouds in a blue sky. It was welcoming, compared to the strange starship in which they had all been confined.

"Praefectus! Send an immune out to hold the men stationary. I want the Hibernians to be led out in front, to join in with the Hibernians at the rear of Agricola's column. The men from our ship will then form the rear phalanx in column of route," Marcus Avitus ordered, imposing Roman order on what would have otherwise become a disorganized crowd.

"Tribune!" replied Centurion Tappulus.

With no idea where Legatus Agricola was leading the people, Tribune Avitus thought it best to blend his Hibernians and

Romans into what resembled a triumphal parade, and simply trust that Legatus Agricola and the other nobles from the command ship knew more about what was going on than he did.

That he was free of the confinement of the starship, and being re-united with the command elements of his legion, made Marcus Avitus begin to feel that there was indeed a reason to celebrate – despite all the uncertainty about whether they would ever leave this place and return to Terra, planet Earth.

Once the two groups had formed one long procession, with Romans marching in perfect step at the front and rear of the column and the Hibernians making a chaotic gaggle in the middle, Tribune Avitus and Centurion Tappulus rode ahead, to the front of the column, to join the officers from the first ship.

When they arrived, the lead elements in the formation were nearing the top of a grassy hill, and an *eques legionis* cavalry scout was riding back from the summit to report.

On an order from the legatus, the column was halted.

"Salve! Legatus!" Tribune Avitus said. "You have no idea how relieved I am to see that you are well, and that this terrible journey seems to have concluded without harm to you or the other nobles!"

"Salve, Tribune Avitus. I am indeed well, and happy to see you are in such high spirits. We can talk more in a moment, but for now just ride with me. We'll send Centurion Flavus to take over the rear of the column, so that the good Centurion Tappulus can join us," Legatus Agricola said, then turned his attention to the nearby Patrician.

"Honestus, take over the rear of the column. Pass on the basic details of what we learned on our journey here. Tell them that this is to be our new home and that the Twenty-Seventh Legion and the Hibernian people are now one," Agricola said, with a nod to Queen Laelie.

"Legatus!" said Honestus. Before he could depart, however, Laelie spoke up.

"Centurion, wait!" she said, and then addressed the old woman riding beside her. "Queen Noichrathach, sister, go back with Centurion Flavus, and have the *Filidh* Morcant the Widluios attend to me. Tell our people from the other ship that I am now the wife of the Roman General, and that the legatus is now our leader – with me at his side. But he is not to be called "king" – that would be to call him a tyrant. We are a united people now, under Roman law and Roman military command. I want our people from the second ship to know this from the lips of someone as noble as yourself."

"Yes, sister-queen. And I suppose by having me do your bidding in this way, it won't be lost on them that I am the number two queen here?" she said, with just enough sarcasm.

"That's right, elder sister. Now be about your business. I know you are eager to check on your daughter, Niamh."

"Domina!" said Queen Achal Noichrathach, smiling. She cast a quick look at her Roman husband, Kaeso Cerialis, who nodded permission to her, and then she rode off with Centurion Honestus Flavus.

No sooner had Honestus and Queen Achal departed, when the *eques legionis* cavalry scout halted his horse a few paces from legatus, to make his report.

"Give us your report, Eques," ordered Kaeso Cerialis.

"Tribune!" he replied, "There is a village at the bottom of the next valley. It is of the Celtic style. There are a score of those roundhouses atop a knoll. It is fortified with a tall mound around it. I estimate fifty people living in the village, Legatus. Of those that I saw, all were people like us!"

"Very well. Are there any people headed this way? They must have seen the ships arriving."

"No, Legatus. There are none. They know that we are coming, however. Their main gate is open, and there appears to be a party waiting just outside their oppidum."

"That is just as the Tuatha said it would be. They will not approach us, so that we may take time to become familiar with our new surroundings. Tell me, Eques, did you see any dangers, any of those ugly Siphonapterist monsters?"

"No Legatus, I saw no signs of danger. But there appears to be more activity leading into the hills on the far side of the compound. This trail we are on now, from where we left the ships, it leads to the village. From there, several well-used trails leaving the far side of the village to the mountains and forests beyond. Do you want me to scout around to the far side of the village?"

"No, Eques, that could be misunderstood as hostility. I will take a look myself. Dismissed."

"Legatus!" said the scout, before moving off to join the remaining cavalry, formed up near the front ranks of the column.

With a firm squeeze of his legs, Agricola accelerated his horse ahead. The other nobles understood that they should ride along with him, as did the contubernium of eight personal guards who followed the legatus everywhere he went.

Agricola paused at the front of the column, to personally oversee the transfer of the legion's *aquilifer* battle-standard into the hands of one of the mounted personal guards.

The mounted contingent of nobles then rode to the top of the hill to get a look for themselves while the column waited.

It only took a few seconds for Agricola to satisfy himself that there was no danger, and that things were as the Tuatha had promised.

He and the other nobles rode down to the village, expecting to be welcomed. Being soldiers, however, they were watchful for any sign of concealed danger and occasionally put their hands on their own short swords, out of an ever-present readiness to engage in combat.

But there was no need.

The humans who greeted them at the entrance to the modest sized hill-fort were a bedraggled, impoverished-looking bunch. They reminded Agricola of some of the weakest of clanns that he had seen in the Celtic areas of western Britannia. A conquered people, with seemingly no heart.

For a moment, he was ashamed for them. It was as if their human kinship with the Romans had brought shame on the Romans as well. But by the way their eyes lit up when Queen

Laelie spoke to them in their Celtic language, he saw a glimmer of hope in them.

After several minutes of incomprehensible dialogue between her and the local chief, Agricola spoke up.

"What does he say?"

"I did not understand all of it, but it sounds like he is happy to see us!" said Marcus Avitus.

"You speak the Celtic language?" asked Queen Laelie, for the first time acknowledging the tribune from the second ship.

"Yes, Domina, I do."

"Well, you have a strange accent. What land did you learn it in? Germania?"

"No, Domina, I learned it in Lugo in Hispania, when I was a boy."

"Well, it is better than this old man's. He is their chief, and he speaks like a *Scraelig* from the most isolated tribes in Hibernia. He knows nothing of Terra. It seems that he is descended from Hibernians taken a great many generations ago, perhaps as far back as the time of *Si an Bhru* of the *Bru na Boinne* people," she said.

"What significance does that have?"

"These people speak a language that is so old I can barely understand him. But I can see from his tattoos and some of the artwork – there on that gate, for example," Laelie said, indicating the spirals carved into some rocks and logs that made up the haphazard looking entrance to the fortress, "that these are indeed my people. They are ancient Hibernians. They must have been brought here by the Tuathii."

"Ask him how many of his people there are. Are there other villages?"

After watching the dirty, unkempt old man struggle to understand the barrage of questions, and coming to his own conclusion about the general conditions, Agricola estimated that the Hibernians of Planeta Metallorum were few in number, not well organized, and essentially harmless.

Agricola and his group rode into the village without invitation.

The old man simply moved aside without protest, as a slave would do.

"From what I understood, there are two other villages, but this one is the largest," Laelie said, "and there are no more than two hundred count of their people. He said that there were once many more, but the beasts and illnesses have killed more of them than could be birthed and raised, so their numbers have declined over the years rather than risen."

As they rode through the collection of primitive huts made from logs and mud, as if they were built by a down-trodden people, perhaps devoid of steel tools, it became obvious to everyone that the village could offer little to the new arrivals.

The few domesticated animals, artisan workshops and other resources could prove useful, as could any local knowledge, but other than that the local situation was far more austere than Agricola had assumed from what he had learned from the Tuatha on his ship.

"Laelie, would you agree that this village is in much worse condition than the Tuatha thought-told us?"

"Yes, Dominus, it is. But I think that is because it was told to them through the eyes of the old man himself."

"What do you mean?"

"I mean, from his point of view, this village is absolutely normal. In fact, if it really is the largest of the three villages, then his own home may be the most luxurious. He may see himself as a king. Perhaps that is what was conveyed to the Tuatha."

"Can't they see it for themselves?"

"With whose eyes? The Octopodii? The Siphonapteristii? No, the only beings who could assess the quality of this place would be the people, and these people don't know any better."

"They truly are wretched. And their fortifications are pathetic. No wonder they are falling prey to the Siphonapteristii. Is this man really their chief?"

"That is difficult to understand. He is their chieftain, but as an elder. He stays here in the village, and does not work in the mine."

"So who is in charge of their warriors, at the mine?"

"His son, Drustan. The old man offered to have one of his daughters take us there, after we decide which of the roundhouses we want to take as our own."

Looking at the hovels, Agricola was unimpressed. He looked up at the sky, trying to assess the weather, but found it to have a strange look. To him, it seemed as if there was one continuous cloud, with no variations in shading, so it was impossible to assess.

But from the soggy appearance of the village, and the many streams and puddles he had seen on the ride over from the ships, it appeared to be a very rainy place, like Hibernia.

Seeming to read his mind, Laelie continued. "The chief said that it will be dark in a while, so we had better make the best of things for the time being."

Agricola nodded at his second in command.

"Praefectus Castrorum!"

"Tribunus!" replied Aulus Tappulus, who had already tabulated the number of Hibernians and Romans from the command ship – Agricola's ship – from the reports brought to him by an immune from Agricola's ship. He was busy combining the numbers with those he had recorded from the first ship.

"Determine which of these hovels are in the best condition, and allocate space to the people as much as possible. For now, keep the soldiers separate from their women, and we can mix the Hibernians with the locals. Use that big one for the officers," Cerialis said, indicating the central roundhouse, which was clearly in better condition than the others.

"Tribunus. But what of the animals back at the ship?"

"The Tuathii are taking care of that for one more day. But they want us out of the ship, so we have to stay here or out in the open," said Agricola, thinking of how the Tuatha had put it: "After one cycle of the life-giving light, you must come back and take everything from these ships," to which Agricola had thought-asked: "Why? What happens after that?"

The tree had responded, strangely: *The ships must be made as new again, and I must put my legs into sustenance, my arms into life-giving light. There must only be eight-leggeds and stupid ones left on the star traverser, to carry out the repairing tasks,* the tree had replied, with its eccentric way of describing things.

Agricola understood the imagery to mean that the Tuatha would very slowly extract its appendages from the holes throughout the ship, slowly shifting its main trunk out of the bridge area and reposition outside onto the planet's surface. There, with its roots in the soil and the leafy branches exposed to the natural light of the life-giving sun, the Tuatha would begin to recover from the long journey.

In that one exchange, Agricola had learned a great deal about the Tuatha. The trees could move! Slowly, yes, but they could shift their roots, even their trunk, and as the tree had put it, reposition themselves. But the most important thing that Agricola had learned was that the Tuatha did not fully understand the details of how to operate all of the devices aboard the ship. Neither did the Octopodii, and certainly not the Siphonapteristii. *What other races are involved here?*

What Agricola now understood was that Queen Laelie had been correct. The Tuathii were not the ones who had built the ship. They had somehow inherited the ships from another race, and learned how, with the help of the Octopodii race, to operate the shipboard systems. But even the Tuathii did not really understand the overall design and how it all worked.

He turned his attention to the matter at hand.

"Cerialis, while we are out at the mine, have Praefectus Castrorum organize the immunes of the Second to come up with a design for a castra. I want it close to the forest, over on the opposite side of this valley, as far from the starships as possible.

"Have the men focus on throwing together some animal pens so that by tomorrow afternoon we can move the animals from the ships."

"Legatus. But what of the men from the Twentieth?"

"Have them begin to harvest wood."

"But Legatus, the men will protest. Usually it's the men from the Second who do that sort of thing, while the men of the Twentieth see to their military training. I was thinking that we would use the men from the Twentieth to take charge of the management of those brutes at the mine."

"Certainly that is in line with our mandate from the Tuathii, but I think we have to put the emphasis on our own well-being first. We'll employ our men in the mines gradually, and keep their numbers low. That will allow us to focus on building up our castra, our defenses, and our artisan capabilities. If we throw too much into doing the work the Tuatha want from us, we will end up like these ancient Hibernian wretches."

"Legatus."

"Besides, this space smells like a stinking dung heap. How long do you want to be sleeping here? You can also have the Camp Prefect remind any men who complain that as much as we still recognize the proud history of the Twentieth and Second legions, we are all united as the Twenty-Seventh Legion, Legio XXVII. Any who complain or who do not throw themselves enthusiastically into their labor shall be given appropriate punishment."

"As far as death?"

"Much worse, long-term billeting in this *annulus merdus!*"

The officers shared a laugh; the collection of roundhouses within the encircled fortification really was a circle of shit.

After receiving orders from Tribune Cerialis, Centurion Tappulus soon headed out with a collection of specialist immunes in tow, to gather some of the better carpenters and engineers to begin working on the great tasks ahead of them.

Cerialis also detailed four parties of cavalry to scout the terrain, and a fifth to work with Aulus Tappulus, scouting the forest on the opposite side of the valley for a suitable location to build a fortress to house the people. It would be called *Castra Metallorum.*

Agricola and the other officers had seen enough of the inside of the ancient Hibernian roundhouses, and had nearly vomited at their fetid odor, when the old Celtic chief arrived with a skinny young woman who he introduced as Princess Roisin, his eldest daughter.

Travelling with Roisin and the Roman officers on their way to visit the mines, Laelie had gotten what information she could from the girl, using archaic forms of *gaeilge arsa*, the Celtic language of Éire. It seemed that life in the village revolved around simply surviving to work another day, with little thought to improving their condition.

While the Celtic men worked in the mine or hunted game in the forest, the women foraged in the meadows for edible roots, berries and other food.

Clearly their hunting skills were mediocre at best, or the game was scarce – or both – as evidenced by the scrawny condition of the villagers.

Once they arrived in the mine area, Agricola recognized that the procession of Siphonapteristii going into the mine was very much as Spurius Crispus had described.

Up close and personal, the Siphonapteristii looked even more terrifying than the ones he had seen on the ship.

These ones were slightly larger but with even smaller heads, as if the ones smart enough to work on a starship, dumb brutes as they were, were the more refined of their species. The ones relegated to the mines, just as slaves working in Roman mines, were the larger, stronger type.

The resentment apparent in their ugly eyes and menacing vibrations of their feelers showed an open hostility toward their Celtic guardians.

But these Celts were more impressive than the old men and the women seen in the village. These men were muscular, and had the weathered, leathery look of men who knew how to fight.

Their leader, the old chieftain's son Drustan, was equally impressive. He had the confidence and swagger of a man in his prime, one not accustomed to being contradicted.

Agricola liked him immediately, and chose to treat him with a measure of respect. Not quite as an equal, but certainly as a leader of the ancient Celtic people.

Through Laelie's best efforts to translate, Agricola and Drustan discussed the situation. Marcus Avitus quickly picked up on many of the unfamiliar words in *gaeilge arsa*, the ancient Celtic language, and was able to participate more and more in the very simplistic conversation, much to the delight of Laelie, who found the job of simultaneous translation to be very tiring.

Drustan had been told by his father that people would be arriving. Their people had been told this for generations, which seemed confusing to Agricola. He left it to his two philosophers, to investigate how, and by whom, the arrival of the Romans had been foretold. But it seemed clear to Agricola that it had taken many generations for the starships to make the round trip to Terra to collect more humans. What confused him was that it had only taken them twenty eight days to travel from Terra to Planeta Metallorum.

He would have to ask the Tuatha about that. It did not make sense how it could take many hundreds of years from the perspective of those on the planet, and yet only be experienced as a barely one month from the perspective of those travelling in a starship...

Prince Drustan was more than happy to show the Romans around the mining operation. The tour of the mine facility did not take long. One mine is like another, simply a hole in the side of a mountain from which ore is removed.

The actual removal of the ore was much like that of the mines that Agricola had seen in Britannia. Men – or in this case Siphonapteristii brutes – toiled with hand tools to break rocks off of the face of the mine tunnels. Then the rocks are broken into smaller pieces and transported out of the mine.

What was unusual was that the brutes did not use anything other than their four arms to carry the burden out. There were no baskets and no carts.

It seemed that the human presence was required occasionally, to whip, kick and poke the brutes if they stopped moving along in the long line transporting the rocks, or if they ceased hammering, chiseling or otherwise toiling inside the labyrinth of tunnels inside the mine.

Following the line of brutes out from the mine, Agricola saw that the material was deposited onto large flat rocks where other brutes smashed the rocks into progressively smaller rocks, until the material was reduced into a powder form.

This material was then collected with small brushes made of a natural material, likely switches from a small bush of some kind, and then transported on leathery-looking plant leaves to a small building. The structure was of a material similar to that of the starships. It was clean and smooth, and bore no tool marks. Clearly it was not made by the ancient Celts.

The inside of the building was off-limits to the humans, but given that there were a few Octopodii operating in and out of the building, Agricola's advisers reasoned that it had something to do with the starships.

Then an orifice opened and a brute emerged with a finely crafted long narrow cylinder, about the length of a man's arm. Agricola was impressed at the craftsmanship that must have gone into making the strange object. He assumed that this was the end product of the mining operation.

Peering inside the building for the moment that the orifice had been open, the Roman had seen several Octopodii working at strange tables, touching strange objects on their tables while a procession of Siphonapteristii entered with the powdered mineral at one end of the building, and left from another.

Other than whatever took place inside the strange building, the entire operation reminded Agricola of an ant colony, with an unending procession of beings working incessantly, out of instinct or obedience, rather than with any great individual understanding of the overall purpose of the activity.

What purpose there was in the enterprise, seemingly culminating in the production of those long metal rods, as Fabius had termed them, was clearly focused on providing something related to the starships, as that was where the metal rods were ultimately delivered to.

The party was then shown the outskirts of the Siphonapteristii infestation. It could be described no other way. The brutish beings, when off duty, were confined to a large oval area about as large as the Flavian Amphitheatre in Rome. There were two such ovals.

Inside the large circumference of the first oval was a giant forest, where great trees grew. At the base of the trees, on the forest floor, was lush undergrowth. Moving around in this undergrowth were large, slow-moving beasts that resembled oxen, grazing contentedly on the grass. They were only a bit smaller than oxen, but by the strangely fluffy appearance of their fur – perhaps feathers – they looked like they were of some alien origin. Agricola assumed that they were not from Terra.

Inside the second oval, jumping around, from tree to tree and onto the backs of other Siphonapteristii – who then kicked the attacker away with great force in a ludicrous display of jumping energy – were the off-duty Siphonapteristii.

The grotesque creatures behaved like monstrous fleas, befitting the name originally given to them by Centurion Spurius Crispus.

They seemed to be easy enough to keep within the confines of their oval infestation, as all around the perimeter, which was a path perhaps four paces across, there were human sentries armed with tall rods.

The poles seemed highly unusual to the Romans. They looked like lances, about the length of a man, but seemed to be very light and easy to wield.

The guards within the mines had carried similar, if shorter, variants of the weapon.

The tour continued with the group riding along a well-trodden path towards the forested area on the opposite side of the valley. The group soon encountered a pair of local humans coming out of the forest, carrying a long pole from which was suspended the carcass of some sort of animal, about the size of a deer. The four-legged creature had a feathery hide instead of fur, the creature had strange, closely cropped ears, but it certainly looked edible.

After the hunters got over the shock of seeing unfamiliar people, they were ordered to continue onward to their village. The excitement on their faces said everything. Nothing this big had happened on Planeta Metallorum – ever!

"Why have these people not built a proper bridge over this creek?" asked Kaeso Cerialis through Laelie.

"They don't know how to build one that will last for more than one season. When they do try, it is usually washed away by the heavy rains in the winter season," was the eventual answer.

"Oh? What season is it now?" asked Kaeso Cerialis.

"Summer!"

"Yuck. This place is as wet and cold as Hibernia!"

"Yes, wonderful, isn't it?" said Laelie.

"They don't know how to build? It's as simple as that? I would have thought that the problem was that they cannot fell trees. You know how sensitive the Tuathii are about cutting trees," said Cerialis

"No, I asked him about that. The Tuathii don't monitor what goes on with the local variety of trees. They really hate the Castorii, who sometimes swarm out of the forest and chomp off appendages from the Tuathii themselves, but they have no idea what goes on in the local forest, and don't seem to care. There are no restrictions against cutting 'stupid' trees."

"And they don't use stone?"

"Other than the food-preparing slabs and a few other uses, and for burial slabs for the chieftains, they don't do much with stone," said Laelie, "but the stone seems as good here as anywhere else."

"So where do the Tuathii live? Are there many here?"

"There is a forest of him, on a peninsula on the other side of that hill where the ships landed."

"Him? Is that what this Roisin said to you? Should it not be 'them'?"

"No, you understood her correctly," interjected Daffid Og. "It is 'Him'. Apparently all Tuathii are basically parts of the same single being, and when they inter-link they come together as one being. Roisin here says that the people stay away, and only the chieftain and the senior Druid are allowed to commune with the Tuathii, and then only rarely. The humans are required to keep the area between here and the Tuathii peninsula clear of trees, so that the Castorii have no reason to encroach on the Tuathii peninsula."

When the conversation turned to the hunt for Castorii, the Celtic prince broke out laughing.

"Those rats are harmless. The trees only hate them because the rats like to eat trees. The Castorii don't bother us, as long as we leave them alone, they leave us alone," Drustan explained.

"But don't you have to hunt them, to please the Tuathii?"

"We make a show of killing one or two every large-moon cycle, but actually we use bodies of ones left for us by the rats themselves. The trees don't know that we are not actually cutting into their numbers."

"How long has this been going on? Aren't you afraid that the trees will catch on?" Laelie had asked.

"Not at all. They are stupid. They think we are stupid. They think the brutes are stupid – and they are. They think everybody is stupid, who is not a tree. We've been fooling them for generations. Besides, they are the ones who are the most afraid."

"Afraid? Why?"

"That's hard to say. Our elders believe that it is because they are probably easy to kill. They are trees, after all. We could just chop them up and be done with it, and then kill the brutes."

"So why don't you?"

"Because of you. Or the promise of you, anyhow. They have held it over our heads forever, or at least for as long as there have been people on this world. Our legend is that we will one day be returned to our homeworld, and until then, we must wait. It is my generation that has always been foretold, by our legends and by the trees, that we are the ones that will be freed. One day we can kill these crazy trees and return to our homeworld," Drustan said, for the first time showing any real emotion.

The next day, a party of centurions and immunes were sent to the mines to master the task of managing the Siphonapteristii brutes. Meanwhile, with the combined efforts of almost all of the remaining humans, an area for a robust castra had been cleared of 'stupid' trees and compounds to house the sheep, goats and horses brought from Terra had been hastily constructed.

The men were highly motivated, after a night in the stinking, crowded roundhouses of the ancient Celts. They put their shoulders into their work, knowing that the sooner it was done, the sooner they would live like civilized men.

After clearing the land, the more difficult task of actually building the castra then began. Unlike the regimented layout of a traditional Roman garrison, the castra for Legio XXVII, Castra Metallorum as it was being called, would be the first one in Roman history to be designed around the family unit, providing each couple with a private domicile within a barracks constructed from logs, in the Germanic style that the Second Legion was familiar with.

There had been little opposition to the new concept, other than from some die-hard centurions who wanted to keep the soldiers behaving like obedient soldiers, and less like domesticated husbands or over-indulged citizens.

The men seemed to work harder than was expected, which seemed understandable given the prospect of having privacy for themselves and their women.

Within a month, a variety of specialty buildings had been constructed, including those related to agricultural purposes, animal husbandry, butchering of livestock, and the structures that would house the full array of services that a small town required. There had been resistance to this, from Centurion Aulus Tappulus, Praefectus Castrorum, the Camp Prefect, who had wanted all stores to be warehoused in a military manner, with personnel assigned to their safe-keeping and control. But when Agricola explained the idea of combining military life with urban commerce, and that a shopkeeper family would be given the role of warehouse-master, allowing for a local economy to be created, Centurion Tappulus seemed to embrace the notion.

For his part, Aulus Tappulus found that he had reason to support the more civil scheme of organization. His Hibernian wife liked to bake, and he loved to eat tasty food. He was suddenly inspired by the image of serving tasty treats to men, women and children of the new village.

And then his mood darkened, as his fantasy lifestyle conflicted with his duty as a soldier, to contribute to defeating the Tuathii enemy and find a way to return to Earth. *But then again, that may take a very long time. No harm in eating well in the meantime,* he thought.

The first building to be started out of stone was, of course, the bathhouse. With ample water coming down from the forested hills, and with a seemingly infinite supply of firewood that could be collected from deadfalls within the forest, it soon became downright livable, albeit rather crude.

But the lack of suitable implements and materials had been the limiting factor in their progress. The source of iron was limited to the swords and other implements they had brought from the battlefield in Hibernia and had attained in the rapid pillaging of the village soon after.

There being no enemy to conquer, nor any threat of an enemy, meant that a great deal of human energy could be expended on making improvements.

To make their lives simple, the immunes responsible for the overall castra design had simply adapted the design of their home castra at Isca Silurium in Britannica, to fit the local terrain of Metallorum.

The men seemed particularly intent on completing the military bathhouse – for men only – but they were also making rapid progress on the grand, elliptical-shaped building they were constructing for Legatus Agricola, who, at the suggestion of their officers, the men were now calling *Legatus Augusti Pro Praetore Planeta Metallorum* – Provincial Governor of Mining Planet.

At the end of the first month, Agricola was satisfied that progress was being made in transforming the village into a more habitable locale, and given the ease with which the men from the Twentieth had taken over mining operations, Agricola and his advisers then set their sights on exploring the unknown territory farther inland, hoping to make contact with the Castorii.

They had heard a great deal about the industrious animals, but had yet to see one for themselves. Whether they were an intelligent being, a useful beast of burden, or perhaps a tasty source of meat was a question the Romans wanted answered.

Before this, however, they had to take an enormous risk.

Fabius Quintilianus had come up with the idea himself after discussing their options.

The problem was that nobody knew how to communicate with the Castorii, should they find them. It was not as simple as inviting a Castor to link with a human using a Tuatha, given their mutual enmity.

But when Agricola had gone to visit the Tuatha from the command ship, which had relocated many of its roots to reach into the soil outside the ship, and whose canopy now reached out through the oculus at the upper side of the starship, he acquired considerable new information.

As he approached, he noticed that not only had the tree made its way a fair distance from the bridge and had spread its roots over ten paces from the starship, but it had also extended one long appendage across the grassy plain – and made contact with a similar feeler from the Tuatha of the second starship. *They must be communicating*, he thought to himself.

While his personal guards stood watch over their commander, watching in horror as Legatus Agricola prepared to shove his head inside the cunnis of the tree, Agricola noticed something unusual. A very small tree, which he had seen growing nearby, had changed its location. It had only moved a short distance in the market-day since his last visit, when the Tuatha had only begun the slow process of relocating itself from the bridge and had only reached one appendage outside, into the earth, where the small tree had been last seen. Agricola was certain that the little treeling was making its way towards the Tuathii peninsula.

So when he made a strong connection with the Tuatha, he thought-asked about the sapling.

"Tell me about the little tree nearby." *It is a little-me I have grown, to send word to the rest of me where I live, adjacent to the sea.'*

"How long will it take to get there?" *'It will take a few large-moon cycles.'*

"Why did you not land the ship closer to yourself?" *'Because it would be harmful to me. The Nesslessness-Thing field hurts me, if I am too close when a starship operates.'*

"What is Nesslessness? And what Thing?" The Tuatha tried to thought-explain the concept but it was too strange for Agricola to understand. He would have to ask his philosophers to explain it, later.

"What if the little-you comes to harm? Suppose a terrible castor finds the little-you, and eats you?" Agricola asked.

The Tuatha emoted terrible fear for an instant and then recovered. *'That would be unfortunate for little-me, and I would have to grow a new me and start again. No matter, I have lots of time.'*

On the ride back to the hub of activity that was Castra Metallorum, Agricola reflected on what he had learned. *The Tuathii are unable to communicate with itself at a distance. This is important. It fears the Castorii, perhaps because it is so vulnerable? And most importantly, the Tuatha associated with a starship are completely isolated when a ship is travelling.*

As he entered the castra, he sought out his advisors for consultation on what the Tuatha had revealed about the source of the ship's power, this 'Nesslessness-Thing' concept.Later that evening, after an intense session of argument, the Romans and Hibernians had formulated a plan. It was risky, but the payoff could be enormous.Agricola concluded the strategy planning session by putting it succinctly:

Inimicus inimici mei amicus meus est, the enemy of my enemy is my friend.

XIV

CAUSA VIS
{ Source of Power }

It was an audacious plan. It all depended on how wary the Tuathii were to deception, and how well the humans could control their own thinking when communicating with the Tuathii.

Once again, the mission was assigned to the reliable Primus Pilus, Centurion Sallustius Crispus.

Centurion Crispus, a contubernium of eight legionaries, Queen Laelie, Marcus Avitus and Princess Neasa set out under the cover of darkness. It was the first time any of them had been outside of the castra during the evening hours and had the opportunity to carefully observe the strangely illuminated night sky of Planeta Metallorum without the distraction of the 'light pollution' from the stump-burning bonfires in and around the castra.

Through the veil of clouds, he could see two glowing light-sources, one larger than the other. The philosopher with the greatest knowledge of astronomical sciences, Vibius Metellus, had explained that the two moons had differing orbital periods. Such heavenly details were beyond Spurius Crispus's ability to fathom, other than to understand that on some nights there would be little or no moonlight, while on other nights – like tonight – there would be a great deal of light from the two moons.

It made their approach that much less stealthy.

Other than the ancient Celts from the local village, on patrol to net or spear any Castorii that ventured too close to the Tuathii areas, there were no other beings actively monitoring the area. Once they reached the sentries, Avita Neasa approached one of the ancient Celtic women, and conversed with her for a few moments. The woman sent the others away, leaving Centurion Crispus's group in sole control of the area.

It took them little time to find the sapling, now several strides farther down the hill between the landing area and the Tuathii peninsula far below.

They stopped their advance when they were just a few strides from the little tree. They watched the sapling in the bright moonlight as it slowly extended one root-leg after another in a continuous and steady creep, with the occasional lurch as it shifted the weight of its small trunk off the ground and repositioned it a few meters farther ahead.

The sapling had no awareness at all, until Crispus's men moved in to grab all six of its main root-legs and attempted to heave the tree up onto their shoulders.

The little tree would not budge.

Somehow it was holding fast to the ground.

Upon examination, Spurius Crispus saw that the root-legs themselves had extended tiny hair-like tendrils into the earth.

"Men. Think to yourself a happy thought of how you are doing what the Tuatha at the ship told us to do, to carry this lovely young tree to where it is going," Spurius Crispus ordered.

"Primus!" the men replied. After a few seconds of their reflection, the tree let go of the earth, and withdrew the tiny root-hairs.

"That's better, little sapling!" one of the men said aloud.

The Roman officers had not told the men the details of their mission, lest a wayward thought betray their true intentions. It was enough for them to have their centurion give the directions.

Making a big military secret out of snatching a little tree seemed a bit silly, but the men still felt that they were on an adventure because their officers seemed to take the task so very seriously.

Once the sapling had let go of the earth it was not difficult for the rugged miles gregarious of the First Cohort.

They shouldered their burden and followed Spurius Crispus.

By the time they reached the outskirts of Castra Metallorum, the men were given a short rest while they waited for a rendezvous with scouts from the cavalry alae.

In the light of the two moons, Castra Metallorum was silent. However, in the bright double-moonlight, it was clear that the growing collection of barracks, temples, bath-houses, and marketplace structures had really taken shape as a vibrant little town.

After meeting with the mounted scouts outside Castra Metallorum, Crispus's men continued with their burden, carrying the little tree for another two hours into the 'dumb' forest and unexplored terrain inland, until they reached an isolated marsh area that Spurius Crispus believed to be consistent with the plan.

He had never seen a castor himself, but understood that the busy creatures were wonderful engineers, building dams from trees, branches, sticks, and mud so that in the winter, even if the surface of the water freezes, there would be sufficient depth of water to enable them to swim in and out of their dome-shaped homes.

The Castorii of Planeta Metallorum were no different, he soon learned. However their dome-shaped homes made of sticks and mud were much larger than their Terran counterparts.

After choosing a suitable spot on one bank of the creek, just below the dam, the contubernium gently placed the tree onto the ground.

"Think happy thoughts of how the tree will live here in this spot for years to come!" commanded Centurion Spurius Crispus.

The men smiled as they complied, still holding the tree.

Soon the little tree had extended its roots deep into the soil. Spurius Crispus thought that he could hear a crinkling sound as the thin roots reached out and took hold of the rich, moist soil.

The tree looked content; the men removed their hands from the tree, and sat nearby, waiting for the arrival of a castor.

It did not take long before one approached.

At first it was hesitant, poking its face up out of the water to peer at the sudden appearance of a sweet-tasting moving-thinking-tree, and some humans.

This particular castor had seen humans on many occasions, and understood the implied contract between humans and Castorii, whereby, as long as they provided the humans with the occasional carcass of an unfortunate castor, the humans would leave them alone. The castor that would be provided was usually dead from old age or other natural causes, but occasionally were killed by their own kind for good reason. In return, the Castorii limited themselves to only occasional raids of the thinking-tree forest by the sea.

So for humans to come this close to a Castorii colony, and to carry with them a young thinking-tree sapling, was unusual.

He thought about returning to his den to discuss the situation with his colony, and perhaps sending some pups to other Castorii dens nearby, but worried that another colony of Castorii would pick up the scent and devour the thinking-tree sapling before he made up his mind. So he moved closer to investigate, slapping his broad, flat tail on the surface of the water to alert his colony that something was happening.

As he climbed up the edge of the bank to sniff out the humans, he could sense the movement in the water from others of his colony coming to join him.

Soon all sixteen members of his colony were lined up along the bank, watching him intently.

He moved closer to the one human who seemed to be in charge, based on the fact that the others were grouped farther off while the first human was crouched closer, between himself and the thinking-tree.

The outstretched hand of the human did not flinch when the castor put his wet nose to it, and licked it.

The human had a nice salty taste, and seemed harmless enough.

As the human's paw moved back and forth, it seemed to the elder castor that the human wanted him to approach the tasty little tree.

Could this be a dream? the castor thought to himself. *Why would a human bring me such a treat? Maybe it is an offering, or some kind of negotiating tactic.* He decided that it is a gift, and that the humans will want something in exchange. *Perhaps more territory?* He wondered, as he moved closer to the tree.

Just before the elder castor could take a bite of the small tree, the human reached one of its paws out and grasped a tree root. His other paw reached out and took hold of the castor's leg.

Any thought of biting into the thinking-tree was suddenly forgotten as the thoughts of the human, of the tree, and of the elder castor himself were combined into one shared thought-forum.

It was confusing at first, but a feeling of peace and contentment filled the elder castor.

There seemed to be two conflicting conversations. One, who the castor knew must be the tree, contributed a series of thought-questions. *Why did older-me have me taken to this spot? What is this monster castor going to do to me? – I hope it does not eat me! I was supposed to report to the many-me by the sea. What is taking place? Where am I?* the Tuatha thought into the thought-conference.

From the human was a more sensible series of thoughts. *Hello my little Castorii friend. Are you wise and senior amongst your people? We need to think-discuss some important issues. My people are new on this land, and do not know which of you is the one to talk to. We need to use this little tree for our discussion. Little tree, your new purpose is to facilitate discussion between my people and the Castorii – that is the task your older-you has instructed us to carry out, with your assistance. You will not be harmed.*

The castor was somewhat disappointed to hear-think this. It seemed that the tasty tree was not going to be his to eat after all, yet something about the way the human's thoughts were shaped made him optimistic that what the human had thought-said to the tree was not the full extent of the story.

I am an elder of this colony. There are many other colonies within this water-draining-system, and I am well known amongst them. The den of our elder-elder is a long distance from here. Do you want me to summon him now? thought the castor.

What do you think, flat-tail? Are you suited to these discussions? thought-asked the human.

Yes, I am sufficiently known as dominant. I can send word to the other colonies that these discussions are taking place. Their nearest elders will come to join us here in my pond, and elder-elder will make his way here in time.

*Here is the situation. The thinking-trees have brought a large family of us here to your world. We are constructing our dens now at...*Crispus thought of the hillside location of Castra Metallorum, paying particular attention to the streams and ponds, which he imagined to be the way the Castorii mapped out their world in their minds' eye, *and we are taking over responsibility for the protection of the thinking-trees from the great Castorii.*

How many of you new-people are you?

We are twenty-seven of your colony group, was the thought he conveyed, somehow the Tuatha-linkage converting the Roman number 432 into a proportion the castor could understand, in groupings of 16, for 27 times the size of his own colony.

That is a large colony of humans. Are you the elder-elder, or merely breeder-dominant in your pool?

Finding the Castorii perspective of social order to be very strange, Crispus tried to keep it simple. *No, but I speak for my elder-elder and will retell to him whatever we agree upon here.*

So what is the agreement you seek?

There are many. First of all, that you not eat this little tree.

Again the human's thought did not ring true to the castor, as if what he was saying was for the benefit of the tree but that another meaning altogether was meant for the Castorii. It fit with the idea long believed by Castorii that the thinking-trees did not understand not-truths, and interpreted lies as statements of stupidity, in that the thought-spoken statement did not match reality, therefore it must be stupidity or insanity. The Tuathii had not developed or acquired any understanding of *deception.*

The half-truth imbedded in the human's thought-speak seemed like when young Flat-Tails say things that are not true, so as to avoid consequences for their misdeeds. That sort of behavior is eventually replaced by the wisdom of truthful speaking, but it takes several seasons before young Fflat-Tails understand that not-truth is foolish. Yet the human seemed trustworthy. The elder Flat-Tail understood instinctively that he must think-speak acceptance of the notion that no harm shall come to the little tree, and guard his intuition that added 'for now'.

This thought was instantly acknowledged with a feeling-tone of great relief from the tree.

On another level, the castor understood that the tree was being used to serve both Flat-Tail and Human interests.

I understand you completely, human. No harm will soon come to this nice tasty tree. What next?

We want you to not swarm the other thinking-trees.

Again the feeling of not complete truth was sensed by the castor.

We will stop swarm-eating the thinking-trees, thought the castor.

We want to increase the number of Flat-Tails that we will kill, just as the other humans have killed your kind, doubling the number of your corpses that we can display to the thinking-trees, thought Spurius Crispus.

There was great fear from the little tree for a moment as it waited for the castor's response to the human's proposition that an increasing number of Flat-Tails were to be killed by the new group of humans.

We can increase the numbers of our kind that you kill, in the same way the other humans have killed us.

The castor understood the deceptive code intuitively to mean that no Flat-Tails would be actively killed by these new humans, but the Flat-Tails would be required to deliver twice as many corpses to the humans, to display to the trees.

The tree injected a confused thought: *It has thoughts that do not match other thoughts that it also has. Is it insane?*

The elder castor understood that some of his reflective thinking was leaking through his surface thinking, perhaps revealing the truth. He redoubled his efforts to disguise the truth.

Your killing of our kind is having a great impact on our numbers. If this continues for many sun-cycles, I fear that we will perish. He lied-thought.

The tree was ecstatic.

There is more, the human thought into the conference. *Little tree will generate many more little-little trees. Humans will come to transport these saplings progressively farther inland. These will beget more little-trees, and be farther transported, so that a little tree will be growing beside the pond of each and every castor colony in this water-draining-system. And each of these trees will then expand their numbers into growing clusters of thinking-trees beside each of your colony-ponds...*

The little tree was apprehensive, but accepted that this plan must be coming from older-self. The fear was replaced with the image of a vast forest of thinking-trees extending deep into the unexplored lands of the planet. The Tuathii had long wanted to expand its colonization of the planet, but predation from the Castorii had kept them confined to just the one peninsula. *The increased culling of Castorii, as promised by these new humans, is going to allow the we-me to begin to finally colonize this entire planet!* the little tree thought.

Unable to disguise its thoughts, the palpability of its excitement was clear to the human and castor, who both felt the same level of satisfaction at the progress of the deception which the humans and Castorii had achieved.

And then the elder castor countered with a subtle negotiation tactic of its own, hoping that it had understood the undertones correctly.

What will be the consequences, the castor began, deliberately not think-speaking 'what would be', *if some of our kind accidentally bite off the occasional limb from the thinking-trees growing so close to our colony ponds?*

The tree became terrified at the prospect.

Until your numbers are sufficiently eradicated from this territory, it is likely that such incidents will occur, replied Spurius Crispus. *I suppose it will happen about as often as the dual-moons are at maximum brightness?*

That is about how often I think our younglings will be so foolish as to do something as forbidden as biting into a thinking-tree's roots.

Are you confident that they will only bite off one root-leg, so that the thinking-tree can easily recover from the insult?

Yes, that is about what will take place, one tree-leg in every dual-moon, maximum.

The tree was still petrified.

Then as long as you little-trees can grow vigorously, and replace the one leg-root for each dual-moon cycle, and you are able to increase your numbers locally and also provide seedlings to continue the expansion of thinking-trees inland to all of the colony-ponds, then this will be a sustainable compromise, Spurius Crispus thought to the Tuatha and the castor.

I can regrow at that pace, the little tree thought-replied.

One other thing, elder castor. To assist the new humans in making our shelters, can you send some of your kind to cut down a number of stupid-trees? We have such poor teeth and our hand-tools are not nearly as effective as Castorii teeth.

Certainly, if we can remove the smaller limbs from these dumb-trees. How will we know which trees you want cut down?

Well, we can mark them for you by wrapping their bases with a garland of small branches woven together, Crispus thought of an image of some interwoven branches making a ring around the trunk of a large tree.

Yes, that would work. And if you add any branches dropped from a thinking-tree into this ring, we would appreciate the treat.

Agreed. And when we need a log to be cut again, such as in the middle, can we put a grass ring around it, and Castorii will come and cut the tree there also?

Certainly. If your people display a grass ring, and wave their paws, like this – the castor thought of a human waving his hand with a small grass ring in his hand – *we will follow this signal to the segment of trees you want cut into pieces and we will do this for your tiny-tooth people.*

That will be perfect. We will gather as many discarded branches from the Tuathii as we can find, as a reward for this assistance.

We are agreed. Let us pause from these negotiations for now, so that I can communicate with my elder-brothers.

Agreed. Spurius Crispus let go of the castor and continued think-speaking to the Tuatha.

We will have humans near each of your little-little-yous to protect you from these castor monsters. If they break this agreement, we will bring more humans here and kill them even faster than the doubling we have agreed with them, he thought reassuringly to the terrified little tree.

So we will be safe, this close to the sharp-toothed monsters? And we can increase our numbers vigorously? it thought-asked, insecurely.

Soon your numbers will be growing so fast that the dumb trees of this planet will have to give way to forests of yous.

Just as Spurius Crispus let go of the tree-root he felt the wave of relaxation and peace of mind that the tree was experiencing.

After about an hour of sitting with his men, watching the castor pond churn with the excited movement of swimming Castorii, Spurius Crispus had solid evidence that the castor was successful in ratifying the alliance agreed upon with the humans.

The elder castor returned, moving towards Spurius Crispus. It placed a paw on Crispus's hand and then turned its head back towards the pond, as if to say: *watch this.*

Moments later, the surface of the pond was broken by a series of Castorii. Each wave of Castorii turned out to be two large males, each dragging a Castorii corpse.

They dragged the corpses out of the water and deposited them gently on the ground not far from the little Tuatha, and then returned to the water.

Looking across to the opposite side of the pond, Spurius Crispus saw a procession of Castorii coming from the creek that led into the pond. Castorii were arriving from more distant ponds, dragging Castorii corpses to the water on the far side.

Soon there was a veritable battle-field of Castorii corpses lying on the forest floor. And then the elder castor did the most amazing thing.

It put a paw on the hilt of Crispus's short sword, clearly indicating its intent.

Taking the cue, Crispus gestured to his men to follow suit.

He took his sword over to a Castor corpse and stabbed into it. Once his men had done likewise, and had completed the staged scene, he made contact with the Tuatha, partially placing his head into the tiny cunnis of the little tree, and then turning awkwardly so as to be able to look back over his side, to the gruesome scene in the valley beyond...

Do you see with my eyes? We have now killed a great number of the Castorii monsters. There are so many more to kill, but you can rest assured that we are keeping you safe.

The Tuatha replied. *No, I cannot see with your eyes, but I sense and understand what your eyes see. When I am larger, you will be able to connect yourself better with my liquid-bowl and I will be able to see with your eyes. But it makes me very content to know that you are surrounded by dead Castorii. I can now begin to grow little-little-me's, to be carried to other Castorii ponds,* .the tree thought-said with satisfaction. *Please tell older-me that I am settled nicely into the soil here, and will soon be surrounded by a stand of other-me's. This is a great day for my- selves.*

I will pass this on to older-you, Crispus thought-said, before releasing the root.

Back at Castra Metallorum, the humans discussed the success of the mission.

The deception had been an overwhelming success. From this moment on, the Tuathii would be expanding inland, growing clusters of rosebud trees aside each of the colony-ponds of the Castorii. The Tuathii had no idea that these new clusters of tasty, thinking trees were ultimately destined to be lambs to the Castorii slaughter. From the Tuathii point of view, agreeing to a few limbs nibbled off, in exchange for peace, was a rock solid agreement. They were simply not mentally equipped to imagine that, when these small clusters of Tuathii had grown near the Castorii ponds, and at a time of the Roman's choosing, the Castorii promise not to harm the Tuathii would be revoked.

In exchange for the agreement, at least for the time being, the main Tuathii forest and the Tuathii in control of the starships and the mine operation would be unmolested.

Furthermore, the added help in felling and cutting to length the enormous "dumb" trees would contribute to the continued improvements to Castra Metallorum.

The critical element in the Roman plan was to keep the two groups of trees from communicating with each other. Thankfully, the little tree had been too distracted by fear to consider this. So as long as the Tuatha at the command ship believes that the first little tree had come to harm, and sends a replacement messenger-self to the peninsula forest, the deception will be complete. A grand alliance between humans and Castorii had been established, with the blind assistance of the young Tuatha sapling.

The enemy is vulnerable now, and we have a great ally in the Castorii, thought Agricola.

A month later, thanks to the vast improvement in productivity created by the cooperation with the Castorii, Castra Metallorum was taking shape faster than hoped.

Most of the men had settled into their domiciles, Spartan as they were, along with their Hibernian wives.

Many of the women were pregnant, and eagerly making the little improvements that would convert the rough-hewn wooden structures into comfortable homes into which a child would soon be welcomed.

The operations at the mine had become greatly improved, with the Siphonapteristii having quickly learned that the new breed of humans had zero tolerance for any testing of their mettle. The dozen or so monster fleas who had tried them on had been quickly dispatched by their Roman masters. To make the job easier, most of the Romans from the First of the Twentieth had taken to using the long staff-weapons provided to the humans by the Tuathii.

The weapons had a terrifying power. The Romans had learned that when activated by twisting a sleeve just above the handgrip a seemingly magical power was activated. The Romans had feared the magic of the weapon at first, until Vibius Metellus had examined the device and consulted with the command ship's Tuatha.

After discussing his findings with Agricola, Metellus had been given permission to explain what he had learned to the men. The intent was to have them become comfortable with the alien technology, and to begin to master and adapt it to their own purposes.

The men were assembled in the central clearing at Castra Metallorum, where Vibius Metellus explained what had been learned. With the legatus seated on the throne fashioned out of Tuathii lumber, the philosopher stood holding one of the staff-weapons in his hand when he addressed the Romans and Hibernians:

"My friends. You have been told why you are here – to learn about the Tuathii technology. Well, this is a weapon-staff," he held up an example. "And understanding it is essential to understanding all of their technology, so listen closely, as if your life depended upon it – it does!

"This is not a magical device. It is simply a tool. As you have seen by watching the ancient Celts, this weapon-staff must have small cylinders occasionally inserted into it, such as those produced in mine-processing building, where the Siphonapteristii bring the mineral from the mine. Think of these as drinks of water. A man, like these weapons-staffs, must have frequent replenishment of water, correc?" Metellus asked rhetorically. "Well these weaons-staffs are the same. They must have fresh cartridges of thorium fuel inserted from time to time.

"This is where it all starts, and what you must understand and become comfortable with. It is part of a larger circle of activities that you are familiar with at one end – harvesting ore from the mountain tunnels – but which have implications and consequences at the other end of the cycle which you will find unbelievable at first. I assure you, however, that all of this is true.

"I have learned from the Tuathii that there is a cycle of power that can do a great many things. Providing power to these weapon-staffs is only the simplest example.

"It all comes down to the material produced in the mine. It is the most important substance to the Tuathii. It is very precious to the Tuathii, and is the reason for our presence on this planet.

"The Tuathii think of this substance as 'thunder', so we will give it the name of the Germanic god of thunder, you know as Thor. This 'thorium' is precious as it is the source of all power in the alien technology cycle.

The cycle starts with the ore from the thorium mine. This ore is crushed manually and then refined into a fine powder by machines operated by the Octopodii who work inside the production building. They have devices that separate one substance from another, much as cream and butter are separated from milk at a *bovae agri*, dairy farm.

"Most of the material is then discarded, which we now use as mortar for the new stone buildings we are building at Castra Metallorum – such as the military bathhouse.

"Legatus Agricola has also found a way to extract *aurum*, gold, and *argentum*, silver, from the mine by-products. Who knows, perhaps these will one day be minted into coins for our new commercial enterprises. But I digress...

"The thorium is purified in the processing complex and then formed into those lance type objects you have seen being transported to the starships. These are called 'fuel rods'. Inside the starships, and also inside the processing complex, these pellets provide fuel for devices the Tuathii call a 'Molten Salt Converter Reactors'. These reactor uses the thorium fuel rods to release the power of thunder inside a vessel, where it turns a wheel. This turning wheel creates electro-thunder, which can be transported through strands of copper metal called 'wires' to provide heat, cooking power for those cooking surfaces your women used on the starships, and to power the flameless illuminators you recall from the domicile chambers in the starships.

"Another use of this power from the thorium reactor is to generate the 'Nesslessness-Thing field' that enables a starship to fly between the stars.

"It is all very complex, but in a conference think-discussion with the Tuatha and an Octopoda, I have seen how this operates. I can assure you, it is no more magic than is the conversion of wood into heat when you burn Dubh Linn peat or firewood to cook game on a spit. Yet even that would seem as magic to a beast, and we are not beats. We can come to understand the technologia used by the Tuathii.

"Let's look farther than simply cooking. How does as starhips fly? Well, the thorium fuel produced in the mines here on Metallorum: it is used to make a type of fire called a *Nesslessness-Thing cloud*. It is akin to having a quantity of the very substance that makes a sun provide heat and light to the sky. This is the core substance in the cosmos, and the alien technology can create small quantities of this. The substance is called 'Equanimity', for it is the resolution of the primordial pair of opposites in the universe, 'Nesslessness and Thing.'"

The glazed-over expressions of his audience told him that he had lost them. The technology was simply too complex for them to understand.

"I know that this is next to impossible for you to understand, but I want you to hear it. You will hear it again and again until you understand it, so keep listening and try to remember at least the main words." Metellus paused, and looked at the Tribunus Laticlavius for support.

Tribune Cerialis had gone through the same thing himself, receiving several lectures from Vibius Metellus before he and the other senior officers finally grasped the main concepts behind the source of the alien *causea vis*, source of power.

"Centurions! Any officer who fails to learn this material before the next market-day will be executed," Cerialis proclaimed.

"Tribunus!" replied the centurions.

As word passed through the assembled Romans and Hibernians, the audience sat up in rapt, if uncomprehending attention. They would learn the words and master the explanation no matter how many times it would have to be repeated, as if, and as, their lives depended on it.

Metellus continued, this time trying to get through to them another way.

"We are Romans, not ignorant savages. We have a long history of mastering the technologies, customs, artisanship, science, and philosophy of those we trade with and those we conquer.

"Now, here on Planeta Metallorum, we are in the process of mastering the power of the technology that the Tuathii have introduced us to. There is some doubt as to whether they are the original crafter of this technology, or whether they have adopted it from another alien race. We will find the answer to this question in time. Our Tuathii captors are not presently willing to divulge this.

"But what we do now know is that the thorium fuel rods are like logs onto a fire. They are inserted into devices that convert this fire into lightning, but lightening that is stored inside devices called *causa vis*, 'power-supply', and can be transmitted along 'wire' just as water can be transferred through a clay pipe."

To test his audience, the veteran teacher of rhetoric singled out a milite seated on a stump near the back of the audience.

"You there, the milite with the damaged ear!" he shouted at the young man who had lost an ear in during the construction of Castra Metallrum.

"Dominus!" the young trainee replied.

"What is the name of the substance that is refined from the mineral we are mining on this planet?"

"Thor!"

"Thorium, but you were close enough! Well done! And if this inexperienced young milite can grasp that much, then all of you veteran legionaries should be doing at least as well, so I will continue!

"The starships use this *fulmen impigritas*, electrical energy, produced by the thorium fuel rods, to create a sort of cloud around the starship. That is why the ships are shaped like an egg, as that matches the shape of the energy-cloud that is created by the cloud-making device on a starship." Metellus turned his attention to another person.

"You there, the munifex with his hand up that young woman's shirt!" he shouted at a nearby soldier, sitting with his arms wrapped around his woman in a decidedly un-Roman posture."

The soldier sat to attention, jettisoning his woman off of his lap in the process.

While others around him laughed, he listened for the life-or-death question that would be put to him. *Make it an easy one, please, gods!* the soldier thought to himself.

"What is the shape of the starship?"

"An egg, like an energy cloud, Dominus!" *Whew, that was easy!*

"And why is it shaped like an egg?"

"Because that is the shape of the cloud? – Dominus!"

"Correct, munifex. You may continue living!" said Metellus, clearly enjoying such a large and attentive audience.

"So this cloud. It is called an 'Equanimity Cloud' because it contains two parts of the one thing that is the source of all things in the universe: Equanimity. That is the pleasant, golden feeling-tone you feel when you link with a Tuatha. It is the happy feeling you get when you go from the moment before you get something you want, like *fututio*, to the moment after you are done fucking – for some of you that is a very short moment, as I am sure your women would agree!" – uproarious laughter followed from the Hibernian women and a few of the men.

"So then, this Equanimity, it is the combination of two powerful parts of the universe. One part is called 'Thing'. Thing is light. Thing is raw energy. Thing is *materia*. Thing is any 'thing' you can detect. But the universe also has an equal quantity of the other part, called 'Nesslessness'. Nesslessness is that which cannot be detected but is there nonetheless.

"You there! The woman without a man!" he shouted at his own woman, Princess Maura, sister of King Findmal.

"I have a man, Dominus. Why don't you ask him about his little moments of Equanimity?" Maura said, shooting it back at her husband.

"Thank you, Maura, my dear. But here is a question for you. What are the two parts of Equanimity?" he demanded, with a serious expression that completely hid his delight at her performance.

"Nesslessness – that which is not detected – and Thing – that which can be detected in some form," she replied, having heard this conversation already a dozen times in their home.

"Well done. Now then, the effects of creating a cloud of Nesslessness and a larger cloud of Thing around a starship is that a ship will want to move from the Nesslessness towards the Thing. Think of it as a slippery piece of soap squeezed between your two hands. It will not go anywhere, but if you open up one end of your grasp, making a gap, the soap will fly out, correct?" he asked, rhetorically. "And it is the same with a starship, by adjusting the amount of the Thing-cloud on one side of the ship, the Nesslessness pushes more on all other sides, and the ship is propelled in the direction where there was less Thing."

He paused, looking at the confused faces in the audience. From the knots on their faces, he knew that they were trying to understand, but having difficulty. That was enough for the first exposure to the sophisticated scientific explanation. So he moved on.

"Now then. The weapon-staff uses the same principles. It makes a cloud of Nesslessness around the staff. The staff itself is made up of what?"

"Thing!" came the reply from a few people in the front row.

"Good. So we have both parts of the universal source of power, Nesslessness and Thing, wrapped around the power staff in very close proximity. Somehow, and I do not yet understand it all myself, the staff-weapons can sense the material that makes up the man holding the weapon, and somehow connects this with the 'Thing' of the staff itself, and wraps the Equanimity Cloud around the person as well as the staff. So what do we have? – We have a human safely ensconced within an Equanimity-cloud. But if something should try to penetrate that cloud, what will happen?"

This time the question was not rhetorical, so he waited for a reply.

"The intruding object becomes a flash of light!" came the reply.

"I see you must work at the mine! So come up here to demonstrate. And don't worry, you won't play the part of the intruding object. For that, I will use a large rock!" said Vibius Metellus.

The soldier from the First Cohort got up proudly and took hold of the weapon-staff. It was not the first time he had used it, but this time the weapon did not generate the same level of fear in him that it had when he had first been shown how to use it, at the mine. This time the feelings were more like the intimate connection that soldiers throughout time have had for their favorite weapons: *trust*.

"I am ready, Dominus!" he said, confidently.

Vibius Metellus moved back a few paces and made ready to heave a rock the size of a man's head at the soldier.

The rock smashed into his chest, cracking some ribs and knocking him down.

The crowd cheered, some of them nearly pissing themselves with laughter.

"It helps if you activate the power supply. Twist the shank, Munifex!"

"Dom...Dominus!" the injured man replied, getting up slowly, in a great deal of pain.

He then twisted the shank of the weapon-staff. There was no obvious change, other than the slight increase in warmth that the man felt, and the occasional flick of golden light that seemed to spark at various places along the length of the shaft.

"Now for those of you who have not seen this before, you must always consider these weapons to be extremely dangerous. If they are left lying around, they are harmless. However, in the hands of a person, they are quite deadly. As long as the person has the brains of an ox, and remembers to activate it!"

The soldier cringed at the insult, but stood his ground, still proud to be of service to the legion at such an important moment. His ribs would heal, and the pain was not too intense to endure.

Vibius Metellus picked up the rock again, and hurled it at the munifex. The soldier flinched slightly, despite knowing what was supposed to happen this time.

The rock burst into a bright golden light the moment it penetrated the invisible cloud.

Most of the audience had never seen the Equanimity effect, and few had even heard of it, as it had been a military secret up to this point. They let out a collective gasp of surprise.

"Where is the rock?" one of the women asked.

"Where is it? Were you listening child? Can anybody explain it to her?" Metellus demanded.

One up-and-coming young discens, a specialist soldier who had shown great promise with the engineers from the Third of the Twentieth, stood up formally and proudly responded to her question.

"The rock has been converted to Equanimity because it penetrated the Equanimity-cloud boundary between the invisible Nesslessness and the visible Thing we call 'Munifex Petronius'. The one part was transformed into light, the other into more invisible Nesslessness!" he replied.

"Precisely, Discens Blasius. I could not have said it better myself. Now sit down and stop grinning! Who is your mentor-officer?"

"Centurion Gaius Hortensius Hadrianus, Dominus!"

"Centurion Hadrianus, have this discens elevated immediately to fully trained immune and then have him report to Tribune Lucius Antoninus Commodus with the Eighth of the Second. He will make himself useful working with the other technologia specialists."

"Dominus!" said Hadrianus.

That the philosopher had given orders without consulting properly with the military chain of command was not lost on the senior officers present. However when they saw a slight nod from the legatus, they accepted the oversight, having the subtle confirming order given non-verbally by their legatus. Everybody knew that the secret activities under the supervision of Antoninus Commodus, and the specialists of the Eighth of the

Second, was where all of the mysterious questions were being investigated and where so many answers seemed to be coming from to a wide variety of questions.

As the young man resumed his seat, glowing with pride, his fellow – now former – discens looked at him with admiration. *That's how you move up the line around here, learn the alien technology!*

"Have any of you noticed the much smaller flashes that happen every now and then?" asked Metellus.

"Yes, Dominus!" replied many.

"Those are the same as what happened to the rock." He kicked a cloud of dirt at Munifex Petronius, creating a sudden flurry of tiny golden flashes of light. "Whether a bug, a raindrop, or an errant hand," he then stuck a twig into the cloud, the end of the stick converting into golden Equanimity as it was devoured at the Equanimity-cloud boundary, "whatever encounters the cloud is treated the same - obliterated into Equanimity."

Vibius Metellus then moved closer, and swung his fist at the man.

The crowed recoiled, expecting to see the philosopher's hand disappear into a flash of Equanimity. Instead, Munifex Petronius stammered backwards a few paces, in as much surprise as the audience.

"But if you are protected by your own Equanimity cloud, as I am," Metellus said, opening his tunic to reveal the handle of a weapons-staff that had been connected to his belt, "you are also protected from the Equanimity effects of another man's weapon-staff." Metellus had a flair for the dramatic, and had the audience spellbound as he continued the demonstration.

"Now then, Munifex, disable your staff."

The man complied, and had the presence of mind not to hand the shaft to the philosopher. He laid it on the ground in front of him and carefully backed away from Metellus's lethal force-field. He then resumed his seat, hoping he would not be called upon for any more demonstrations.

"As you can see by the careful way this courageous soldier has sought the safety of his seat, this technology is exceedingly dangerous. Those of you working at the mine, or on sentry duty near the starships, or out at the edge of the Tuathii forest, you may be given the weapons-staff. Some of you have already had the honor. In fact, I can now tell you that Munifex Petronius from the Third of the Twentieth was the first to convert an unruly Siphonapterist monstrom into Equanimity."

The crowed murmured in respect, while the munifex nodded in acknowledgement. However, the kill-joy himself, Primus Pilus Spurius Crispus, glared at him to remind him not to overdo his moment of glory.

"So unless you are specifically given such an honor, you are not to touch, play with, test, or in any other way come into contact with a weapons-staff or any other Tuathii technology. I understand that Legatus Augusti Pro Praetore Agricola and his officers are deadly serious on this point – this technology is off-limits. Any violation of this decree will be met with dire consequences."

Kaeso Cerialis nodded appreciatively at the philosopher, for putting it so clearly to the people. Hopefully that would end the whining from the soldiers and others who had been pestering the immunes with requests for alien technology to make their lives easier, such as using the weapon-staff to cut lumber. They would have to rely on their hand tools, and the help from the Castorii, to do their work.

"I have one final note to offer you, which I deliver with the permission of our great leader, Legatus Agricola." Metellus began, with a bemused expression that showed a warmer, fun-loving side that told the men that the formal part of the lecture was over.

"You may have noticed the segregated-off area, where the baths are to be? Well, the baths are now operational! And there is more. By the hard work of the immunes and men of the Tenth Cohort, and with complements of Pilus Prior Crispus, there is an allotment of two *quartarius* of liquid waiting inside for each and every man, which I trust you will share with your women."

"What liquid?" asked the Princeps Prior, Decimus, highest ranked centurion from the Third of the Twentieth, knowing full well the answer.

"A strange and powerful elixir made from the barely edible berries collected from the soggy pastures of this planet. By filtering their juices through fabric and charcoal, and fermenting for fully three market-day cucles, the men of the Third of the Twentieth have come up with something that tastes like falerian wine, but far more potent. So don't drink this as if it were simple fermentum, for you will not only use up your allotment too quickly but you will also be so completely inebriated as to be of no use to your woman!" Metellus concluded his remarks, and moved aside so as not to be trampled by the horde of eager men and women who sprang to their feet in cheer – the men cheering at the prospect of something to drink, the women at the prospect of having a hot bath.

As their people swarmed into the military bathhouse, where a veritable banquet had been prepared by the local chieftain's best cooks, Agricola and Laelie looked on.

As Metellus, Kaeso and the other key nobles gathered around them, both leaders felt a wave of satisfaction at what they were witnessing.

"We are a people now, aren't we?" Laelie asked.

"Yes, my queen. But we cannot let ourselves get too comfortable here."

"Why not?"

"Because no matter how viable life on this planet under Tuathii rule may appear to be, I will not allow our people to become slaves."

"We are slaves, here aren't we?" Laelie asked, reflectively.

"Yes, but not for long."

XV

APCESSVS REPENS
{ Unplanned Departure }

Laelie knew it was too good to be true. After six months, Planeta Metallorum had begun to feel like home. More to the Hibernians than to the Romans, on account of the wet climate, but home nonetheless.

The pair-bonding of her women to the Roman men, facilitated as it had been by the Tuathii, had proven to be successful. None of the couples had lost their closeness, and many of the women were pregnant.

They had made the most of their new surroundings, and each couple had personalized their living quarters very well. The homes were comfortable and well-constructed. Thanks to the help of the Castorii for making felled and cut logs so plentiful, the homes had solid log walls and each had a fireplace and hearth made of real stone, mortared together with the sandy concrete made of waste materials from the Tuathii processing facility.

But it was when Queen Laelie had thought about how their numbers were soon to increase, and contemplated the wonderful improvements that the Roman engineers were envisioning for their community, that it all was taken away.

She would never forget the moment when it happened, as she had seen it taking place on her man's face. She and Agricola had gone to the Tuathii forest for what she called their monthly 'meeting of minds'. It was while Julius Agricola had his head shoved into one of the trees that it happened.

Laelie could see part of his face. She saw the shocked expression, and then waited for the bad news. He soon emerged and sat on the forest floor, clearly at a loss for words.

"What happened!" she asked, afraid that she already knew.

"He-they are pleased. We are victims of our own success."

"What do you mean?"

"They have 'pondered' the situation on this planet, the greatly increased productivity we have provided them. They have decided to send humans to other planetae, to be of use in some of their other locations which are, in the thought-words of the Tuathii, 'progressing without successes.'"

"I don't understand. We are to leave this place? How many?"

But Agricola was still too shocked to try to explain. He abruptly stated: "We have to convene a war council, to decide how to respond. I know what I feel *compelled* to do, but I need my advisers to help me to decide what I *should* actually do," he said, rising slowly.

The walk back to Castra Metallorum seemed to take forever to Laelie, carrying the burden of not knowing while her man carried the far heavier burden of knowing, what was to follow.

The military council met at the usual place, sitting on log benches surrounding a small fire in a large, round, hall with an oculus in the center of the ceiling. Through the smoke wafting through the large round hole, bright stars and, on occasion, one of the two moons of Metallorum could be seen..

The hall was separate from the din of Castra Metallorum, but still close enough to the center of the town to be seen by everybody as the place where major decisions are debated, decrees and news distributed, and ceremonies conducted.

Tonight, however, sentries had been posted to ensure that no curious people could approach within ear-shot, particularly those who were not well trusted, such as the mischievous Druid Allanon and his cadre of acolytes.

Only the senior officers – the five tribunes and the four most trusted senior centurions along with Queen Laelie, a few Hibernian nobles, and the two philosophers, were invited to participate.

After disclosing what he had learned from the Tuathii, Agricola concluded his opening remarks.

"So there you have it, friends. I feel compelled to do as they require, and deliver one hundred and eight couples – half of the total number of us taken here from the battlefield at Dubh Linn – and a corresponding number of livestock and provisions to the command ship, by mid-day tomorrow.

From what they thought-told me, those who are sent will never return to Planeta Metallorum. However the ship will return here for another stockpile of fuel-rods once this 'grand tour' is completed in one hundred and fifty years."

"But I thought you said that this tour would take only thirty days, how can that be one hundred and fifty years?" asked Honestus Lartius.

"From what I understood, there is a difference in how time is experienced while travelling *ad astra* in comparison to that experienced here on the surface of Planeta Metallorum."

"Simply put," interjected Fabius Quintilianus, the mathematically-inclined philosopher, "those who travel in space do not age very quickly while those on a planeta do so at the normal rate. So if anybody did come back with the starship after the trip, they would not really have aged that much, but then they would meet the great-grandchildren of their great-grandchildren."

"How is this possible? Did the tree explain that?"

"Yes, Honestus, it did. It has something to do with their philosophy."

"Their philosophy?"

"Yes, they call it 'Timeconsciousness'. Something about how all things in the universe come from the same origin, Equanimity. It is also related to the fact that the use of the Nesslessness-Thing propulsion system in the starships exposes passengers to a higher proportion of Equanimity than they would normally encounter on the surface of a planeta. This is because..." said Agricola, pausing in frustration. "No. I've lost it. I thought I had it, but now I am lost again. I can't stand thinking in this esoteric manner. It makes my head hurt."

"Legatus, may I?"

"By all means, Vibius Metellus. I recognize that the esoteric appeals to your sophistic nature."

"Thank you, Legatus. Their Timeconsciousness philosophy also relates to the science by which the starships and other alien equipment derive their awesome power, that contrast between Nesslessness and Thing. You have to think of it this way: When we are on the ground here on Planeta Metallorum, we are 'Thing' standing on 'Thing.' There is no 'Nesslessness' anywhere around us. But out in space, so far above the surface of the planeta that rain, clouds – Hades, even the air that we breath – are all below us. That is where the boundary between Nesslessness and Thing begins.

"Beyond that boundary, out in the cosmos, there is plenty of Nesslessness. Now remember that Nesslessness *pushes* in all directions. But Thing does not push at all, it just takes up space in the cosmos. So the Nesslessness pushes down onto the surface of the planeta, like this:" Metellus picked up a round piece of fruit and poked his finger onto it. "But if we stood on the bottom of this planet, Nesslessness would push us up against the bottom of the planeta, like this:" he poked his finger up onto the bottom of the fruit. "So anything close to the surface of the planeta gets pressed against the surface, like an apple falling from a tree, so there really is no top or bottom, only outside and inside the outer circumference of the object. To put it another way, it is all relative to where you are on the surface, and down is always to the center, and up always to the cosmos."

"So things are pushed to the surface, by Nesslessness?"

"Yes, Honestus."

"Why are things not pulled to the surface, by the materia that comprises it up, like the Greeks believe?"

"That conception works in some ways, but the Tuathii see it in the opposite way: things are *pushed* to the surface by the nothingness of the cosmos, the *material negra* – dark matter if you will, the Nesslessness. But if we are in space, inside a starship, we are so vastly distant from any large collection of materia that there is very little 'Thing' to be pushed down onto. Somehow this slows down the manner in which *time* occurs. There is a connection between time and energy, or between time and materia – Thing. But in space, with so little substance, there is little experiencing of time to speak of."

"Does it matter how fast we are travelling?"

"That's a difficult question, Honestus. From what I gather, there is something to your question. But I am confused by the Tuathii explanation, what they call *relativistic effects of space-time-consciousness*. It could be that I lack the knowledge necessary to understand, or, it could be that they do not fully understand it either. They seem to believe that the faster you are going, the greater the distance from material, such as stars and planetae, so the rate at which time passes is different. This change in the nature of time is caused more by the absence or presence of large quantities of 'Thing' more than it is by the speed at which you are traveling.

"One example they gave is that if you were alone in a remote region of the cosmos, not travelling at all relative to your home planeta, you would age very very slowly. But on your home planeta, everybody you knew would continue to age at the normal rate. In what may seem as an hour to you might be a month that will have passed on your planeta – all because you were distant from any large concentration of 'stuff', this Thing we call *metria*. And in this example, relative velocity is irrelevant."

Metellus's explanation was interrupted by a question: "So if we go away on this grand tour, and return in seventy days as you say, and one hundred and fifty years passes on Planeta Metallorum, then many generations will have passed. Babies will have been born, grown, had new babies, and then aged and died. So how many people will be here when we return?"

"Honestus, you ask a lot of good questions. But I think that Fabius Quintilianus has anticipated this one. Am I correct, Fabius?"

"Yes. Thank you Vibius Metellus. Now it is my turn to bend minds to these amazing facts," Fabius Quintilianus began. "So, given that they want us to take eighteen-twelve-groups with us,"

"What?"

"Oh, sorry. The Tuathii look at things in groupings of twelve."

"Why do they do that?"

"Look, Honestus, do you want me to answer your first question, or explain how they evolved their sciences?"

"Apologies, Dominus, please go on," he said with a smirk.

"Dominus my ass! We are all brothers in this forum, Honestus, and you are patrician while I am merely equestrian. In any event, we have digressed. Back to the point. Suppose we assume that due to the healthy population of women here – mostly pregnant already – and the lack of predators and illness, with any luck we can expect the population here to grow faster than it would have on Terra, where there are frequent wars, famine, and disease which reduce the rate of population growth. Given some assumptions that the bean-counting immunes and I have played with, and the traditional age at which the Hibernian women begin and end their child birthing years, we have come up with a growth rate of three per cent. That is higher than what we experienced in Rome, of course, their not having any form of birth control on Metallorum."

"That's all well and good, but what does it mean in simple numbers?" Honestus persisted.

"It means that when the starship comes back in one hundred and fifty years, the two hundred and sixteen of our people left behind, plus the two hundred of the ancient Celts in the villages, will have grown to a small city of thirty five thousand, one hundred and ten, plus one man to count heads, for a total of thirty five thousand one hundred and eleven," concluded Fabius Quintilianus.

Silence fell on the room as the men contemplated this.

"And the valley will have changed considerably. Those left behind may well have pushed inland or along the coast, starting new settlements where useful resources or favorable terrain may be found. There is an entire planet here to explore, after all."

"But that number far exceeds the number the Tuathii would need to manage their mine."

"True, Aulus Tappulus, however as long as we don't let anybody who knows the truth stick their head up a tree's cunnis, they will have no way of knowing the true extent of our propagation."

"Let's move on to other sides of this question, shall we?" suggested Vibius Metellus.

"Certainly, go on."

"Thank you, Fabius. I would like to know more about where this grand tour will take us."

Agricola sighed, not eager to resume the esoteric, philosophical, and scientific discussion. "I was shown a barrage of images of planetae, seemingly through the eyes and thoughts of a variety of beings. One planeta, the first one we would see, I think of as *Planeta Scientiae*, science planet, which appears to be where most, if not all, of the metal-based technology, from starships to weapon-staffs, originated. The Tuathii want to take the supply of thorium there, for onward distribution to a variety of power-hungry devices band starships on that planet.

The next planet is the Tuathii homeworld, *Planeta Arborum*, tree planet, as I think of it. A planet infested with massive forests of *himself*, with little or no technology. There are a variety of other species there, mostly in the oceans but a few who crawl on the surface or fly through the air. Many of these creatures are tied closely to the Tuathii."

"Are the Octopodii from Planeta Arborum?"

"No, Honestus, they are from some other planeta that I did not learn about. Now, the next planet would be *Planeta Terraformata*, the damaged planet, where they need a goodly supply of thorium for some machines that are designed to repair the environment. Some sort of disaster befell the reptilian beings there, something that was deeply upsetting for the Tuathii to think about. All I remember from the Tuathii image of it is an image of massive ugly hillsides of burned-out forests, terrible, unbreathable air, and a brown skyline.

After that, we are to travel to *Planeta Bellorum*, battle planet, where there is some sort of battle going on between the Tuathii and some other alien race, competing for some prized planet they both want. It seems that this war has gone on for millennia, as it takes so long for each to bring in reinforcements. I have the impression that it is strategic, something to do with there being some limit as to how far a ship can travel without stopping, and this planet being in the middle of some gap that separates Tuathii territory from the 'terrible destroyers' on the other side of the gap. And this is the worst of it, they want to deploy one hundred and eight of us`humans there, as seed-stock to build up a local human population to be used in the war in some manner."

The notion of traveling so far, only to die for their enemies, brought a feeling of gloom over the men.

"I feel the same way," said Agricola, but there's more. After that, we would visit what I think of as *Terra Caedum*, massacre planeta, where the Tuathii have massacred an entire alien race."

"Why did they do this? Were they at war?"

"No. This race proved difficult to manage. In their words, the Tuathii thought of them as insane. This last assignment is interesting, to me at least."

"Why is that?" asked Kaeso, sensing a military dimension.

"Because there are a number of starships with special weapons and capabilities that I did not get much information on, only that they are 'potentially useful' to the Tuathii in their war on *Planeta Bellorum*, Battle Planeta."

"Or to us, for that matter?"

"Precisely, Kaeso."

"And there is one other factor to consider," offered Agricola, knowing what the response would be.

"And that is?"

"The hairline, and sexual exploits of Vibius Metellus!" said Agricola, only half-joking.

"What?" said Spurius Sallustius.

"Do any of you remember how bald and fat he was, back in Britannia?" Cerialis asked, looking directly at the shocked Vibius Metellus.

"Sure. And I mean no disrespect, but I also heard rumors that you had ceased visiting the brothels altogether, lost your appetite for sex – women or boys," said Fabius Quintilianus, unable to resist taking a well-placed jab at his rival in the philosophical art.

"No offense taken. It is true. I had gotten old and fat, and almost forgotten about how much fun could be had with my cock. And yet, now I have sex almost every day, and twice on market days!" Vibius Metellus said, proudly.

"*An refert, ubi et in qua arrigas?*" commented Fabius Quintilianus, snidely.

"Well you should care about 'who made me erect, and when', my dear Fabius, if you think about it for a minute. My hair is restored, and my hunger for women is once again like that of a young man. Now even *you* make me hard, on occasion," Metellus.

"Granted, your hair and sopionis are back, and certainly Emperor Domitian could use a little of that himself – at least in regard to his pathetic bald head – but what is the military significance of it?"

"It's not only me. So many of our men, and the Hibernian she-wolves, were healed while travelling in the starship, do you recall?"

"Yes. I forgot about that. You may be on to something. Are you suggesting that something about spaceflight in a starship is good for the health, that it is rejuvenative, or restorative?"

"Yes, Fabius, I am. And I asked the Tuathii about it. They say that close proximity to the effects of an Equanimity-generator has a restorative effect on the minutest particles of which we are comprised. The Tuathii call them 'cells', and these cells have diagrams inside them that tell them what to be, even from the moment of conception. And when a seed grows in a woman's belly, these cells read a map, and become legs, eyes, ears, lungs, heart, and so on."

"And you believe this?"

"I have thought-seen it with my own eyes, through the eyes of some other beings as recalled by the Tuathii. You can think-ask for yourself, but what I understand is that as a seed of a baby grows, it makes more and more of some basic building blocks, like the bricks that we use in Rome to build wonders like the

Flavian Amphitheatre and the Pantheon. These cells read their maps and add to other cells, making the organs and parts of the body. But when we age, the maps inside these cells become damaged. Not all of them, but enough for new cells to be made with new mistakes. These mistakes accumulate, and become arthritis and other illnesses that are associated with old age, and which eventually kill us."

Skeptical, Fabius had to admit to himself that as hard to believe as it sounded, he had never known his colleague to be reckless in his logic or in his understanding of science.

"Well if that were true, that exposure to the Equanimity-generator in a starship helped repair these so-called maps in our so-called cells, then would the cells repair themselves to the extent that we could live forever? Is immortality an actual possibility?" he asked, incredulously.

"Yes. Well, no. I'm not sure. There was something about another type of cells, also important, called thymocytes, which are helped by the Equanimity-effects. These so called 'T' cells do something important in helping the body repair itself, and when we get older, their ability to repair us is reduced. But under the influence of the Equanimity-field, these T-cells are rejuvenated, somehow, and then are much better at helping the body to restore itself," he said, and then added, "I got the clear impression that our lives would be greatly extended, perhaps adding scores of years, maybe a century or more, but we would not become immortal."

"Well if this is true, and by the evidence of your hair and your cock, I for one want to go on this trip. I'm just not too keen on being thrown into battle for the Tuathii. Can we do anything about that?" asked Spurius Sallustius.

"I think Primus Pilus is on to something here," started Kaeso Cerialis. "I mean, we could learn a great deal more from our enemies. They seem easily enough to deceive, after all."

"That is true. It is as if they have no understanding of the notion of deception, let alone the strategic use of the tactic," added Fabius Quintilianus.

"They have none. I am sure of that," said Vibius Metellus. "Our deception of that sapling we planted to reward the Castorii was proof enough. But also, they seem to think that any being that lies to them, the fundamental root of deception, is simply insane or stupid. And they seem to consider stupidity and insanity as fundamentally evil traits."

"You know," said Agricola, "that reminds me of something the Tuatha thought when think-showing me something of Terra Caedum. They wiped out every last one of those lizard-beings, simply for being crazy. Maybe there's more to it than that."

"So what do you all advise we do. We are running out of time, and if we don't parade half of our people into the ship later this morning, they'll just take whoever they can herd with that moving wall of theirs."

"Legatus, I have a plan," said Marcus Avitus, as he got up awkwardly after sitting so long on the floor in the cramped quarters.

After Marcus had completed his proposal, the two philosophers were the first to comment. Without exception, all of the others echoed in agreement with their analysis.

It may have been an unplanned departure, however by the time the contingent of Romans and Hibernians selected for the task had marched aboard the first starship, all of those affected had been told their role in the plan, whether they liked it or not.

There was no dissent.

XVI

FALLACES COGITATIONES
{ Deceptive Thoughts }

It was a strange request, but Praefectus Castrorum Centurion Tappulus was the most qualified to carry it out - at least on the Roman side. He had been ordered to find the three most sycophantic men, those who would do whatever they could to garner the appreciation of anyone in a position of power and authority.

Such behavior was always frowned upon in the Roman military, but there were invariably a few who, out of their need for attention, or a more carefully calculated effort to be given recognition or promotion, had fallen into the habit of deferring obsequiously to those in power.

They were usually called such things as *frustra es homo*, annoying, and yet under the present circumstances, their unpleasant disposition now seemed essential to the interests of Rome.

On the Irish side, Queen Laelie had already chosen three women who had the same inclination.

To ensure that he chose well, and without being influenced by Queen Laelie's choices, Centurion Tappulus had not been given the names of the Hibernian women selected.

He had narrowed the field down to just five men. Three of whom were of *ordo equester,* order of knights and therefore nobility, and had risen about as high as they could without the concerted effort of a powerful benefactor. They were immunes, of course, having found that by taking on their respective responsibilities as bean-counting administrative officers, architects, pay-masters, and surveyors, they could avoid the more dangerous combat and ever-present general-duty physical efforts required by regular soldiers – and still gain prestige through military service, albeit in the rear echelons, but that's where men like these preferred to be.

The other two were common soldiers: one a milite, the other a veteran munifex.

Walking up and down the main corridor of the starship, Tappulus sought out each in turn, to observe their behavior more than to interview them.

He soon eliminated two of the immunes due to the fact that they were actually quite involved with the engineers and other skilled people from the Second, who were focusing on mastering the Tuathii technology. That would make them security risks, given the mission at hand.

The third immune was focused on counting hens' eggs, rations of cured meat, bales of grass-feed for the livestock, and other provisions. He also hailed from the Twentieth, so he had not been exposed to any important secrets. He would be fine.

The milite and the munifex were both involved in the medical arts, trained as they were in stabilizing battlefield wounds, removing injured soldiers from the battlefield and helping surgeons cut off damaged limbs or stitching up gashes that the front line soldiers earned in battle.

When Tappulus handed in the sheaf of paper with the names and units of the three candidates, he was surprised to see the look of amusement on Tribunus Laticlavius Cerialis's face.

"What is so amusing, Tribunus?" he asked, worried that he may have chosen poorly.

"Nothing. It's just perfect. All three of these men chose their women well."

"How so?"

"Look for yourself. Here is the Hibernian list."

After reading the list, he noticed it immediately. The women had retained their Irish first names, but now as cognomen. They had taken their Roman husband's cognomen as their first names, in the Roman tradition. So despite the unfamiliarity with their Hibernian names, the irony jumped out at him right way. The two lists were identical.

"How can this be? Is this some kind of joke?"

"Nope. It must have something to do with how 'birds of a feather stick together," Cerialis said, still amused.

"Must be. It will certainly make my job a lot easier. So now what? Bring them in for their assignment?"

"Queen Laelie will do that. We want as much plausible deniability as possible, just in case one of them shoves their heads too far up the trees' cunnis!"

The men laughed, and then turned their attention to other matters.

Laelie and the three couples settled into the domicile-pod of the immune selected by Centurion Tappulus, but the briefing had not yet begun. An uncomfortable silence descended on the room.

Fulvia, the wife of Immune Laurentius did her best to break the tension. She seemed to be maneuvering to get herself and her Roman husband into a leadership role, by virtue of his being a higher rank than miles gregarius, Ovidius, and the milite, Albus. The wives of these other two ambassadors had already been told how things would be, with Fulvia laying into them in *gaeilge arsa*, their Celtic language.

"My dear Queen, can I offer you some tea? It is humble, but I have prepared it from the last of my spirit-root tea, and I would be honored if you would share a jar of it with me," said Fulvia.

"That would be wonderful, sister," Laelie replied, allowing the young woman to ingratiate herself upon her and ignoring the overly forward way the girl spoke to her. Something of her husband's status as an officer from the Third of the Twentieth had gotten into her head, as if she saw herself as an officer as well.

It made Laelie think of how amused her Roman husband and his second in command had been that all three of the chosen, *bum-lickers* as he had put it, had somehow found themselves pair-bonded to the three most annoying, obsequious, women in all of Éire.

They were all so perfect for the job that it made Laelie begin to like them.

As she sipped the strong tea, the taste and aroma of Hibernia brought back memories of her life with King Findmal. She did not so much miss her lost husband as she missed being Queen of a proud and noble people. She missed the coming and going of the merchants into Malahide Bay, and the stories of the distant from where lands they had travelled.

She missed their wares, and the delightful challenge of bartering a good price for the more exotic and unfamiliar objects. The bartering trade on Planeta Metallorum had been boring in contrast, with only the objects brought from the battlefield of Dubh Linn and raided from that Scraelig village in western Éire to trade, or the wooden and wooden objects handcrafted in the workshops of Castra Metallorum.

But now, confined to the starship once again, with only one hundred and seven other couples to interact with, things would become downright boring.

At least she would have the new assignment to keep her busy, and managing these three couples would be amusing enough. And she had the help of one of her most trusted captains, which would make the isolation that came with secrecy less stifling.

A knock at the portal preceded the arrival of the final participant.

"Oh, Lady Achal, thanks for joining us at last. Have you completed the task I gave you?"

"Yes, Domina. Word has been spread."

The three couples stared at her in polite ignorance. They had been deliberately left out of the lightning-fast rumor mill that the Hibernian woman used to convey orders and gossip throughout their people.

They did not need to know that these three couples had been declared *personae non gratae*, unwelcomed persons, to be kept in the dark about all the secret happenings.

"Let's get started, shall we?" said Laelie, and then continued. "As you all know, my elder sister here, Queen Achal of the

Noichrathach is now the wife of Tribunus Laticlavius Cerialis, second only to my own husband, Legatus Legionus Agricola," she began, unnecessarily invoking rank.

She knew that these three couples, more than any others on the starship, were deeply aware of the rank and social status of all of the important people. People they desperately wanted to please.

"We have selected you three couples from all of our people for an important task." Laelie paused, to let the fact sink in.

She saw the young men's chests rise, as though they wanted to show how brave and ready they were for any task. She looked into the eyes of the young women and saw the excited glimmer of hope for an improvement in their status.

"If you are successful in this task you will have earned great honor and status among our people, and the title and rank that goes with such a great accomplishment. Simply put, your task will be that of ambassador to the Tuathii. From this moment on, none of our people, other than you six, will be permitted to commune directly with the Tuathii."

Seeing confusion on their faces, she explained further.

"Communing with the Tuathii has been a closely guarded military secret. You should not have heard of it, and if you have, give me the names of those whose lips have uttered it to you, for only the highest ranking among us have thus far been privy to this secret.

"So what I am about to tell you, you may never discuss with others, not even of higher rank. Your only discussions may be whispered amongst the six of you, or in the reports you shall provide my sister here, Lady Achal Cerialis.

"You may, on occasion, be directed to re-tell your report, or be given important information to convey to our masters, the Tuathii, by the Tribunus, or perhaps even myself or the legatus, but not by any others. Do you understand this, so far?"

"Yes, Domina!" murmured each of them, as she looked at them in turn.

Knowing what was to come, Lady Achal kept silent and tried to show neither emotion nor reaction.

"Some of the information we will pass to you, which you can share with the Tuathii at your own discretion, may seem at odds with what you may expect our people to think."

"Domina?" one of the women spoke up, "I am not sure I understand the nuance. Are we to lie to the Tuathii?"

"Not at all, but it may feel that you are betraying our people."

"Betray Rome? – Never!" said one of the men, heroically.

"What do you mean?" said his wife.

Laelie continued: "What I am saying is that we are a conquered people. In order to survive, we must accept that. We must never do anything contrary to the intent of the Tuathii. We must never conspire to harm them or interfere with them in any way. We must, in short be their humble and obedient slaves."

"Dominus! That is treason! Why would you and the Legatus have our people grovel so?"

"It is not groveling, when you face reality with dignity. Even a slave has pride, if that is what is necessary to preserve his people!" she said, with mock indignation.

The three women looked at Lady Achal for confirmation.

Lady Achal nodded her head somberly, showing that it was the sad truth that they faced. Caving in to their masters, so as to save their people.

After a long pause to let that sink in, Laelie then gave them the real bait, the one morsel of information that she wanted them to communicate loud and clear to the Tuathii. The message that Agricola wanted to have delivered by these naïve innocents, with no hesitation or doubt in their hearts.

"We do this so that the babies in our bellies will be safe. We do this so that we can live another day."

"Domina," replied the six, quietly, and nearly in unison.

Good, she thought, *they're coming together as a team...*

"And never forget, you serve Rome and you serve Hibernia, when you help us as ambassadors to the Tuathii. You will come to be respected by all of our people. As long as you do not shatter their illusion of pride, their fantasy that one day we will be free. We will never be free, and as their leaders, Legatus Agricola and I, and Tribunus Cerialis and Lady Achal here, and you six – we ten leaders are the only ones who can know that we have accepted our fate, and committed ourselves to serving the Tuathii as if they were our new emperor, our new king."

"So we must not tell our people about this?"

"No, Immune Laurentius. You must simply not engage in any such conversations. You will hear people talking, simply smile and nod your head appropriately, as you might when a child boasts of all that they will one day do, and do not say anything that would undermine their hope. After all, that hope, however poorly grounded, is all they have at this time. They do not have the abilities that you have, nor the inside knowledge we have shared with you. They could not handle it," she said, certain that the six ambassadors were now correctly prepared.

"Now, in addition to your role as ambassadors, conveying messages between us and the Tuathii, you have one additional mission."

They sat up, continuing to listen attentively.

"You must come to know as much as you can about any Octopodii or Siphonapterestii that you encounter on the bridge."

"The bridge?"

"Yes, that is what we call the place where the Tuatha who commands this starship resides. It is a place, one level above this level, where there is a light-filled chamber where the Tuatha lives. You will go there momentarily, to be initiated into the communing ritual, and you will share happy thoughts with the Tuatha, our master. You will think-explain to it that from now onward only you six may communicate with them, as it helps to keep our people content and able to focus on serving them in whatever way they require.

"But you will also learn as much as you can about how the starship functions, how the Octopodii and Siphonapteristii and any other beings fit into the Tuathii empire," she paused, looking for any indication of doubt from the new ambassadors.

"But Domina, why do we want to collect this information?"

"So that we can earn our way to positions of greater responsibility, of course!" she said, excitedly. "The more we know about how things are done, the more we can show that we may be useful to them, and thereby we will be that much more secure. It is as things are done in Rome, from what my husband tells me. In times of strife, or when the economy weakens as it had during the year of the Four Emperors, sometimes a household has to sell off a few slaves. Only those slaves who can demonstrate their utility through their contribution have any degree of job security."

"And we report this information to Lady Achal Cerialis?"

"Yes, whenever you think-receive it. At times Lady Achal will require you to re-tell it to others. You may need to make drawings, as well. That is why you must always be observant, always be acquiring information. And most importantly, try to be subtle about it. We do not want our competitors to be aware of our intentions."

"The Octopodii. We want their jobs," added the immune, making his move to be the leader of the six.

"Precisely, Ambassador Laurentius. Precisely."

Judging by the expression on his face, Laelie knew that he liked the way that sounded.

XVII

PLANETA SCIENTIAE
{ Science Planet }

Just one market day plus two after being promoted to high office, one of the ambassadors came rushing along the corridor, shouting "Where is Queen Laelie? Where is Lady Achal?" People had to jump out of his way as he ran madly along the corridor toward the Agricola pod.

The Legatus himself opened the door to his knock.

"Ambassador Laurentius, you have something to report? Why have you not given your report to Lady Achal?"

"Apologies, Legatus, but this is news that you must hear!" he said, excited to have reason to interrupt the legatus.

"Come in, then, and give your report. Would you like some water, Ambassador?" Agricola said, with feigned respect.

"No, Legatus. No time! We have arrived!"

"So soon? Where have we arrived?"

"We are in orbit around a planeta!"

"Orbit? – Oh yes, going around in circles, among the stars yet close to a planeta. Is it Planeta Scientiae?"

A confused, disappointed look came over the young man's face, as if the legatus had stolen something from him.

"You knew? I thought only we ambassadors were allowed to commune with our masters."

"Boy, you have lost your place! Never speak to me in that insolent tone again. I am your ruler, do not forget!"

"Legatus!" The former immune had let being an ambassador go to his head, and had to be reminded that despite having such an important role, he still served Rome and his life was always contingent upon the good graces of the Legatus.

"Go on, boy."

"Legatus. The Tuatha thought-showed me an incredible variety of starships. Some are as large as this, but arranged differently inside, as though for larger creatures than our kind. Other ships are much smaller, as though for making short trips in calm seas. Scout-ships, I think the sailors from the Second would call them. And still others seem to be for rolling around on the surface, carrying burdens. These did not seem capable of flight. And Legatus, most of the ships are dead!"

"Dead?"

"Well, unable to move. From what I saw in the Tuatha-mind, these ships were like that ages ago, when the Tuathii inherited...or received, or something, this planet of wonders. And there were other things, which I sensed that the Tuathii still do not comprehend."

"Well done, my boy. Now what does the Tuatha want us to do here, at Planeta Scientiae?"

"Nothing, really. We are to assist the Octopodii in unloading about half of our cargo of Thor's fuel rods. They will be used to activate one of the sleeping ships."

"Only one ship, with all of those fuel rods in the cargo pods?"

"Yes, Legatus. The ship they are reviving is very special to them. They have only two other such ships in operation, at a planet where there is a very ancient war being fought against their great enemy, the Dupli-Tri, at *Planeta Bellorum.*"

"So this is a warship, then? What manner of weapons?"

"That I did not seek, but will do so when I merge with the Tuatha next, once we are done talking here now."

"Yes, find out as much as you can about the warship, how many beings, and what type are required to operate it. What principles and actions do they take to operate the weapons, and so on. And also, try to learn if there are smaller things on that planeta, unusual tools, hand-weapons, more of those weapon-staffs or unusual machines of any sort."

"Why, Legatus?"

"We want to ask our masters for anything that can help us serve them in ways they may not have considered. And this may be our only opportunity, here at Planeta Scientiae, before we move on to their homeworld, Planeta Arborum.

Again that look of disappointment from the young man, but he recalibrated himself quickly, as if reminding himself that he served two masters.

"So we are to ask for these objects to be brought to this ship?"

"Precisely. Even those things the Tuathii do not yet understand should be brought here. Their purpose could be discovered on our way to Planeta Bellorum, where the war rages."

"That is all I have to report, Legatus. Is there anything else for us to pass on to our masterrr...to the Tuatha?"

"Yes, pass on my excitement for their task, and how proud we are that the thorium fuel rods we helped prepare on Planeta Metallorum are proving useful to the Tuathii. And for you, Ambassador, find out what you can about how the actual transfer of fuel rods is to be carried out. Do the Octopodii do it? Does the ship land on Planeta Scientiae, or are they transferred onto a smaller ship? What is involved in activating a dormant ship, and so on. Do this subtly, so as not to annoy our master with nuisance thought-questions. Do this by observing the Octopodii, and then make notes or diagrams, as always, and pass them on to Lady Achal. Do you understand?"

"Legatus," he nodded his head as he prepared to leave.

"And Ambassador, remember who you serve. You serve the Senate and People of Rome. You serve Emperor Domitian or his descendants, anyhow. And you serve me. Our masters are masters over our people, but the line of authority goes from the Tuatha to me directly, and from me to our people. Never forget that. As an ambassador, you are like one of those tree's appendages, a conduit for information. No more, no less. I can cut you off and have you replaced if I have any doubt of your loyalty to me. Or I can reward you with special honors and entitlements, if you continue to serve as well as you have."

Ambassador Laurentius seemed a bit unsure why all of this talk was necessary, but he thought it had something to do with mixed loyalty.

"Legatus, I am Roman above all else. I am honored to serve as ambassador, and perhaps I have had too much of the Equanimity fluid from the bowl inside the Tuatha. Please excuse my overly enthusiastic representation of our captor's will."

For the first time, Agricola had hope for the boy.

"Perhaps you are right, Ambassador Laurentius, too much of the Equanimity drink may affect judgment. I will have Lady Achal draw up a schedule, so that none of you six commune too often with the Tuatha. And, you must all begin to limit your consumption of their nectar."

"Legatus."

Just to ensure the boy understood the seriousness of the addiction, he continued.

"Your addiction to the fluid reminds me of what happened to a sentry back at Castra Deva. Because of over-indulging in vinum, when he returned from a night visit beyond the castra walls the sentry did not recognize my father, Legatus Augusti Pro Praetore, and spoke rudely to him."

"What happened to the sentry?"

"My father knew who the milite was. The sentry was the son of a close friend of his, a tribune attached to the Second of the Twentieth, I believe. Anyhow, despite his affection for the boy, it was necessary to have discipline, you understand…"

The boy looked up fearfully at Agricola, sensing what came next.

"He split the boy's stomach open, to let the wine out of his belly," Agricola said, pausing dramatically before continuing. "You are a milite too, just like that sentry, aren't you?"

Choking down a swallow, the boy-turned-ambassador-turned-boy was barely able to croak out: "Legatus."

Agricola slapped him firmly on his back with one hand as he activated the domicile-portal with another, and the boy was propelled out of the pod.

Ambassador Laurentius stumbled along the corridor in the direction of the access-portal leading up to the bridge, once again in a suitable frame of mind for a milite in the service of Rome.

A market day later, as the starship made its way towards the Tuathii homeworld, the leaders discussed what had been learned from the devices brought aboard from Planeta Scientiae. Their conclusion was that there were a great many devices which would take careful study to understand, and that these devices could be too dangerous to experiment with while travelling in the cosmos. Some appeared to be simply *causa visi*, sources of electro-power for other devices, which appeared to be sustained by power that was conveyed from these thorium-fueled devices by means of a slender tube, like the metal rope-snake that a soldier had chopped and caused an electro-thunder explosion. However, all of that was in the hands of Marcus Avitus, Antoninus Commodus, and the other engineers of the Second to explore in the fullness of time.

Simply discovering everything they could of what there was to see, piecing together a full inventory as it were, was the primary objective.

It had been quite risky, but Agricola had agreed to let Spurius Crispus make one of his visits to the out-of-bounds areas of the starship.

While Laelie and Lady Achal kept the six Ambassadors confined to a pod, ostensibly – and actually - going over everything they had learned of how the Octopodii carried out their functions, Primus Pilus Crispus had snuck into the storage chamber near the exit portal at the far end of the ship, just one level below the human's quarters, where thorium fuel rods and other bulk goods were stored.

It was not far from the more bulky mid-ship areas where a few Octopodii and a number of Siphonopteristii operated the devices required to recycle the liquid and solid waste generated by the humans, livestock, and other beings aboard the ship. As there was no activity in the storage pods, Spurius Crispus was able to move around unobserved.

The problem, however, was how to open the access pod without touching a tree-root, as that would inform the Tuatha that something was afoot.

But he had a plan for that. He reached into the satchel he was carrying and took out a chicken. *This is no ordinary chicken*, he thought to himself with a grin, *this is Ambassador Chicken!*

The *pullus,* chicken, had been prepared for the mission with a leather strap wrapped tightly around its beak, so as to keep it silent, and a wooden strip tied to its legs. The feathers on the chicken's back had been plucked, making a bald spot on its back.

He held the little ambassador up by the stick, and rubbed the bald spot against a Tuatha root next to the orifice, and it opened obligingly for the chicken. *Good, the Tuathii can be fooled.*

Moments later Spurius Crispus emerged with a sack full of small artifacts, the plucky little ambassador, and two of the smaller-sized thorium fuel pellets that the Romans had learned the Tuathii had stockpiled, yet for which the Tuathii had not determined the use of.

Hours later, as the senior officers and a select few of the experts from the Eighth of the Second examined the artifacts, everybody was stumped.

Nobody could figure out what any of the strange objects were for. They spent hours and hours considering the possibilities, manipulating the objects in a variety of ways and listening to endless speculation from the two philosophers.

Just when they were all getting frustrated and at their wits' ends, Spurius Crispus had an idea.

He slipped out of the pod to speak to one of his most trusted men, and then returned.

He let the others continue the discussion a few moments longer, before he broke the news.

"Brothers!" he said, "I have some terrible news, and I have some good news."

Seeing the grin on his face, Kaeso Cerialis knew that it would be good fun, as did the other officers and nobles.

"Let us have it, Primus Pilus!" he commanded.

Crispus went back to the portal and opened it.

His wife came in, along with Queen Laelie and one of the few Hibernian men, one two couples from the ancient Celtic tribe found on Planeta Metallorum who had come along on the journey.

Everybody knew the man, as he had gained a good reputation with the Romans for his culinary skill.

He carried a platter, with a leather cover.

Just as the Hibernian man was reaching his free hand to remove the cover, the man spoke with an over-the-top air of seriousness, showing that he was making great strides in learning Latin:

"*Codriali saluti a tutti i liberi e laeie*," he began, "I present to you the unfortunate, dead, Ambassador *Pullus Primus*! – Senior Ranked Chicken!"

The carcass was still hot from the cooking-box in the chef's pod, filling the room with succulent smells and a variety of unusual fragrances that had made his reputation as a chef so legendary.

"Now that is a great way to keep a secret!" shouted Agricola.

Everybody closed in on the meal, which Primus Pilus himself cut to pieces with his *pugio* dagger.

"The time may come when we have to do the same with the six other chickens!" joked Marcus Avitus.

"Come, now, Tribune Avitus! The ambassadors are doing their job very well. And when the time comes to use them to best effect they will not let us down," said Lady Achal, in defense of her charges.

"Truly? They have not started to sprout leaves, after all of that tree-sap they have been drinking?"

"Well, now that you mention it, they are starting to smell a bit like cake," said Agricola, only half joking.

The reference was lost on those who had never seen a Judas Tree in season. Seeing their blank stares, he explained.

"The Tuathii resemble *arbor roseaus*, the Judas Tree, found in the more sunny climates of the Empire, but mostly in Judea, around the Seven Hills of Rome, and Ostia. When in bloom, the Judas Tree has a sweet smell, of sugar and vanilla. I found the same fragrance and sweet taste in the elixir when I had my head shoved up inside the Tuatha's cunnis," he said, remembering fondly the one time that he and Laelie had shared communion with the Tuatha.

Laelie must have been thinking the same thing. "I remember. It tasted so lovely, like the most succulent treat any baker ever made. Do you suppose, after we defeat our captors, that we can find a way to domesticate them? – to harvest their elixir and use it in our baking?"

"Oooh, that would be nice! A sweet, tasty dessert to have after such a fine meal as Pullus Primus here..." said Spurius Crispus, as he gave serious thought to how he could approach the task.

XVIII

PLANETA ARBORVM
{ Tree Planet }

It never ceased to amuse the senior Romans whenever they saw any of the six ambassadors on the hunt.

Ever since the Tuatha had told them of the incursion into the storage room, by a monstrous chicken, they had been scouring the ship, looking for the creature who had stolen some items from the Tuatha.

"Any luck finding *profugus pullus*, fugitive chicken, Ambassador Laurentius?" asked Spurius Crispus, after tracking down the former milite.

"No, Primus Pilus. We have found no sign of it. Nobody has seen a chicken anywhere near as tall as the Tuatha believes it must be.

The tree must have been confused when I held the chicken so high, when I activated the storage room door with it, thought Crispus. *It must believe that there is a giant sized chicken on board this ship!*

"Have you gleaned anything about what the missing items were for?"

"Yes, Primus. Some of the devices have something to do with preparing the minerals at Planeta Metallorum. Others were intended for Planeta Terraformata, another of the Tuathii-controlled planets in this celestial region, which the philosopher Fabius Quintilianus has termed 'Locus Capricornus' by virtue of an observation which he and Vibius Metellus had arrived at," said Laurentius.

"Oh, what observation?"

"The two philosophers had spent several nights laying out on the ground at Planeta Metallorum, examining the night sky.

"They both agreed that most of the constellations were skewed, as if their locations had been altered. Yet some constellations, such as Centaurus, Hydra, and Pyxis appeared normal. And other constellations were completely absent, such as Capricornus, Aquarius, and Delphinius. The conclusion that they drew was that neither Terra nor Sol were the center of the cosmos, but were only single points amongst a multitude of stars and the planetae that orbit them. They confirmed this theory by having an ambassador think-ask the Tuatha about celestial navigation, and learned that the Octopodii were actually quite adept at it. In fact, they learned, with just a little training, how to use the viewing pots on an extremely out-focused mode, using the starships' optical systems to track their position in the cosmos by virtue of the location of various bright star complexes – the same constellations as mankind has gazed up at in the night sky for millennia – and to plot the path which the starship shall take by mentally designating the intended arrival locus or constellation.

"In a three-way thought-discussion with the Tuatha and an Octopoda, Marcus Avitus confirmed that Planeta Metallorum, and eight other Tuathii-controlled planetae, were all situated in what the ancient Greeks had termed Capricornus. Therefore, being right in the middle of the stars that constituted the constellation, other than those which were actually far beyond the locus, it is impossible to see them as forming any pattern. You would need to be far away from the stars to see their patter, not right in the middle of them. So for those constellations which were essentially on the opposite side of the galaxy, however, located along line extending from *Locus Capricornus* through *Locus Terra*, and projecting a great distance to the far side of Locus Terra, this line would then pass near *Locus Pyxus*, *Locus Hydra*, and *Locus Centaurus*, whereas *Locus Sagittarius* and *Delphinus*, being ninety degrees from this line, were distorted so much as to bear almost no relation to how these constellations appear from the vantage point of Terra.

"Wow, that's a mouthful, ambassador. But I think I follow you. It is like if you observe a fleet of ships. If you are right in the middle of them, with ships all around you, you cannot see their pattern, or the larger picture of their deployment. But if you are on a hilltop near the Oceanus, looking out over the water, you can see the orientation of the fleet. So the idea here is to look for the constellations which have not changed, and those will be at one extreme of our sky map. Those at the opposite – where we are in the middle of the constellation – will be unrecognizable, and therefore, our location.

"That is right, Primus. It is rather fascinating. And you know, celestial navigation was one topic which the Tuatha positively rejoiced in think-discussing. It seemed that, having gained access to the cosmos by virtue of the starships, the Tuathii were finally able to explore the cosmos which, up until then, had been frustratingly out of reach.

"From the Tuathii point of view, the multitude of galaxies, stars, and planetae represented great potential for finding new places to expand itself, and a great variety of creatures that could be used to expand the Tuathii awareness.

"In order to achieve this expansion, they required a considerable number of fuel rods for the starships that sat idle. And with each new planeta, new challenges arose. In the case of Planeta Terraformata, they needed thorium for machines that had something to do with cleaning very bad soil and air. The mental picture I got from the Tuatha was akin to when fields have been salted, making it impossible for crops to grow. The entire planeta seems to have been rendered useless from some form of warfare that poisons the air, water, and soil. The Tuathii take great offense at this, and intend to colonize it in a few milennia, after it has been cleansed of toxins.

"There are also some small items which they have no idea of their purpose or manner of use," concluded the ambassador.

"Interesting. Are you referring to these?" Crispus showed the ambassador a small object that had a receptacle for a tiny pellet of thorium fuel, and a similar object that was somewhat larger.

"Yes, Primus. Have you divined the use of these items?"

"No, Ambassador Laurentius, we have not," he lied. It had been Agricola himself who had figured out that the spring-loaded flap on the back of the smallest object seemed just right to be used to affix the object to one's belt. He had a volunteer clip one to his belt and activate it. At first it seemed that nothing had happened, but when a fly buzzed across the room towards the immune, it suddenly disappeared in a bright flash, less than a pes from the man.

After some experimenting, they learned that the belt-clip device was an Equanimity-generator that would protect a man in much the same way as the larger field generated by an Equanimity weapon-staff. With the belt-clip, a man can move about without destroying objects he encounters, through some unknown aspect of the device's design. But when a living being – or an object connected to a living being breaches the field, it is converted to Equanimity.

They all recognized the military applications of the device, and the danger it presented if used in mixed company. They theorized that the larger version of the same device was used to create a large protective field, perhaps the size of a genera'ls command tent, but they did not want to experiment with it in the confines of the starship. It gave them a clue as to the warlike nature of the race that had conceived of and manufactured the devices. This made them that much more motivated to discover other powerful inventions. Keeping all of this under wraps, particularly from the Tuathii-loving ambassadors, had been only prudent, however, they also began to trust Laurentius, Albus and the other ambassadors, and began to share some military secrets with them on a trial basis.

"Would you like some help finding the fugitive?"

"Yes, by all means. I'm sure that our master won't mind. What do you have in mind, Primus Pilus?" asked Ambassador Laurentius.

"Come with me, I'll take you to them. I've got two men from the Second who will accompany you on your next sweep of the lower decks. Two others from the Second have already been assigned to help your brother and sister ambassadors, searching in the bridge area and the upper ductwork."

"So I am in command of these two men?" the eager young man asked.

"Not exactly, but your knowledge of the ship, how to access every nook and cranny, will certainly help. And when opening doors, certainly, that will be your honor. We do not need to confuse the Tuatha by having them respond to so many new people – that is your role, Ambassador.

"I have told them their task, and they will carry it out along with you. They are to look into every compartment, every crevice, and in every space throughout the ship." *Hopefully they will find additional useful objects and secrets without the Tuatha becoming aware of the end-to-end search of the starship*, he thought.

"Primus," said Ambassador Laurentius, before heading out with an important mission that would serve both of his masters.

Spurius Crispus had not been entirely lying to the ambassador. The men from the Second were ostensibly looking for the fugitive "Pullus" Primus, who had long since been digested.

The fact that the Tuatha believed that there could be an enormous chicken revealed much to the Romans, in their continued efforts to get to know everything possible about their enemy.

Crispus entered the Agricola pod, to meet with the others.

"How goes the search for the monster chicken?"

"We have our best men on it, Legatus, but I fear that we may never find the dastardly fugitive," said Crispus, grinning with the others who understood the inside joke. "But this is a great opportunity to snoop through the ship. By the end of the day, we should have enough details, paced-off measurements, and observations for Immune Commodus to complete his schematics of the ship."

"Very good. And Lady Achal, what can you tell us of the role the Octopodii play in operating the ship?"

"Dominus," she said, rising to make her report in a somewhat formal manner, enjoying sharing what she had learned almost as much as she enjoyed the intellectual challenge of divining the purpose of every motion, every touch of the tentacle, and every visit to the Tuatha made by the Octopodii.

"I have so much to report that I don't know where to start," she began, and then seemed to become sure. "Let's start with first principles."

"The Socratic method, yes, by all means," said Agricola.

"The Tuathii are deaf and blind. Everything they know, they learn from other species. This is true?"

"Uhuh."

"And none of the species we have seen thus far seem to know how to work with the type of metal this ship is made of. It is as if the Tuathii have somehow inherited the starships, the mineral processing devices, the weapon-staff, and so on."

"Yes."

"So I wondered, what happened to those who made the ship? I focused on trying to infer what type of beings they must have been."

"How did you do that?" asked Metellus.

"I realized that there were three ways to approach it, and gave the pieces of the puzzle to the lady ambassadors. First, I had Laurentia Fulvia focus on getting to know how the Octopodii do their work. She accomplished this by becoming friendly with them."

"Not too friendly, I hope!" said Aulus Tappulus.

"Get serious. That's disgusting!" said Laelie.

"She found that they really don't like to get too dry, but sometimes they have to keep working on a task until it is done, and cannot climb up into their tanks to enjoy a leisurely swim. So she began experimenting with ways to get them wet. Eventually she learned that if she simply carried a goat-stomach sack filled with wet cloths, and occasionally wiped their heads, body, and even down their long tentacles, they would vibrate, kind of like a cat does when it purrs."

"So they like to be wiped down?"

"Yes, Dominus. They seem to love it. But doing that for them also let Laurentia Fulvia spend a lot of time observing how they did their work. Something seemed strange to her, and she alerted me to it, and I observed it when we pretended to be searching for "Pullus" Primus. Anyhow, it seemed clear to me that the Octopodii don't really know what they are doing."

"What do you mean? They have all the critical jobs, don't they?"

"Sure, but they seem able to only do a few things like make the ship fly, open doors, and maintain the function of the water and solid-waste recycling systems. But even then, they have to keep returning to the Tuatha to seek guidance. And there's more. They really don't like sitting on those knobby chairs.

"That got me thinking. The chairs aren't designed for them. And then I realized it. Most Hibernians, other than queen Laelie and the other nobles, cannot read or write. Well, the Octopodii can't read either! And yet, all the levers, those little push-stones, and those flat symbol-displays, they all are labeled with written symbols."

"So how do they understand the writing, if they can't read it?"

"They seem to guess."

"Are you saying that we have been taken into the stars, and travelled from planeta to planeta, in a ship run by fools?"

"Basically, yes."

"How can that be? How can they *guess*?"

"Dominus, that really bothered me. So I tried a few experiments, and that brings me to two other questions I wanted to answer. The first, as we discussed, was to understand how the Octopodii did their jobs. We'll come back to that in a moment.

"The second thing was this, have the Octopodii always performed this job, or have some other beings done it for the Tuathii? Did the Octopodii know anything about the original masters of the starship?"

"How did you approach that question?" asked Fabius Quintilianus.

"Well, by asking them."

"How?"

"I had Ambassador Albus go into the Tuatha with one of them, to ask about another matter. But really, the plan was to learn what life on the starship was like before our masters were present onboard the ship."

"That was risky, my dear..." said her husband, Cerialis, who had not been aware of her strategy, busy as he was with military matters..

"I know, but it worked out well enough. Laurentius went in there seeking to know whether humans could serve by learning how to clean the overfilled vats of recycled solid waste."

"*Tramas putidas*! yuck, those tanks are disgusting. I've always wondered why they are so full, and why nothing is done about them."

"Me too. Anyhow, Albus was also supposed to suggest that humans could replace the Octopodii on the one job they seem most ill-suited to carry out, that of inserting fresh thorium fuel-rods into the receptacles in the rear portion of the lower deck. The Siphonapteristii can't do it, they don't have the dexterity and coordination, and when the Octopodii do it, they are constantly dropping them on the floor – their tentacle-ends can't grip them well, and when they attempt to wrap their arms around them, they have great difficulty getting the rods into the small orifices.

"The Tuatha seemed surprised that Ambassador Albus had dragged an Octopoda into the cunnis, but still considered the two propositions. At the same time, the whole life of the Octopoda became clear to Albus. The more inquisitive his thoughts, the happier the Octopoda became, sharing the information like an eager child. And according to Albus, the Tuatha did not seem to care that the human and the Octopoda were busy having a thought-discussion on the side. Albus could sense that the Octopoda was thinking through a sequence of events, each task that the twelve Octopodii would normally complete, and then comparing what the outcome would be if they did not have to spend so much time managing the fuel rods. When the Tuatha then thought-considered the offer of humans clearing out the overfilled shit-vats, it was clearly dumbfounded. It was as if the Tuatha understood the notion of an empty vat, but had no idea how to make that happen.

"So when Albus thought-asked the Octopoda how the vats are emptied, the Octopoda had a clear moment of recollection that answered the question. The image of another life form, with three legs and three arms, using some sort of flexible tube that sucked the scum out of the vats, came to the Octopoda's mind. This proves that there were Octopodii present inside the starship before the Tuathii took it over from some other beings – perhaps the ones with three legs and three arms, the Dupli-Tri as I like to think of them. And you know, those strangely shaped seats on the bridge, with their three-sectioned cushions, may be just the right fit for a triple-cheeked ass," said Lady Achal.

"I am not sure that I understand," said Agricola.

"Well, from what Ambassador Albus said, the Octopoda made a thought-image of a three-legged being seated comfortably on the knobby chair, with one leg sort of draping over the gap between each of those three lumps on the top of each stool. A perfect fit, so the being seated in the thought-image was the one the stool was originally designed for. The being had a slender torso, and three arms. Each arm had two fingers and an opposable thumb, and the same for the legs, making for twelve digits and six thumbs," said Lady Achal.

"That is significant, isn't it, Metellus? The number twelve?"

"Yes. So many things around here are in threes, fours, nines and twelves. Like the number of pods, eighteen times twelve, for example," Metellus said.

"And the way the thorium fuel rod receptacles are laid out, four rows of three. And the number of finger press-points on the cooking apparatus, and other such finger press-pads throughout the ship!" added Laelie.

"In that one thought-image, Albus also noticed that the being at the work-station had something strapped around its torso-head, like a garland wreath, with strings leading from it. And that's not all."

Just when Metellus was about to press her with questions, Kaeso raised his hand to cut the detail-obsessed philosopher off. "Go on with the main points. Metellus can pester you about the loose ends afterwards. Continue."

"Dominus. In the time of the Dupli-Tri, there was no Octopoda tank on the bridge, only in passenger-pods and in the bowels of the ship. And where the Tuatha sits, in that splendid light, there was only a long table, with a few other Dupli-Tri beings seated around it, as if a meeting chamber for their officers."

"Dupli-Tri? That's what you said before, and that means three legs, and three arms?"

"Yes, Legatus. That's how the Octopodii think of their former masters, the starship-builders."

"By the way, did they have heads?"

"I've got Albus working with the Hibernian sketch-artist Daffid Og Briogan and the architects from the Second, making drawings of what she saw in the Octopoda's mind's eye. We can look at them later, but no, she says that the way their arms hung off of their torsos looked like willow-tree branches, dangling down from their trunks."

"Oh boy, not another tree!" said Cerialis.

"No, Kaeso, not a tree, but still kind of stumpy. Albus said that where you might expect to see a head was just a flattish dome. But it had eyes, three big ones, one below each arm.

"So where was its mouth?"

"She did not see, but when she wondered about it, the Octopoda indicated that the Dupli-Tri was seated on its mouth."

"Something like a starfish?"

"Yes, something like that, I think."

"What else?"

"That's all about the second line of investigation. Now, for the third line if inquiry, to which I tasked Ambassador Laurentius and his wife, Laurentia Fulvia, to look into. I wanted to learn if there was anything that the Tuathii controlled directly, or if they are simply passengers on this ship."

"Well that's easy, they control the doors into the domicile pods," said Aulus Tappulus.

"Not so, Praefectus," said Lady Achal, "There is an Octopoda work-station where the creature's only task is to sit with a tentacle touching a Tuatha root appendage, and press down on a sequence of little press-pads whenever ordered to do so by the Tuatha."

"How do you know that there is a relationship between this task, and that Octopoda's job?" asked Tappulus.

"Well, first of all, that is the busiest job during the waking hours. And second, I have observed it myself, when Ambassador Laurentius and two soldiers passed nearby and sought access to a pod used to store the grubs and dried fish the Octopodii eat. An instant after Laurentius touched a root appendage, the Octopoda seemed to get a signal or something from the root at its workstation, it quickly pushed on press-pads, and the orifice opened for Laurentius.

"Between the ambassadors and I, we have made similar observations of each of the work stations, and discerned what they do. We know which knobs are for activating the ship, which are for navigating our path through the stars, which are for seeing to the recycling systems and which are for the management of the thorium causa vis, energy-maker. Others are clearly for the pod doors, and a few only seem to be active when we are in orbit around a planeta. There are others which we have not seen being used, but we compared the symbols, press-pads, and levers on these and we think that one must be to control that energy-curtain that forced us into the starships back at Dubh Linn. Another, which seems to have a diagram of a long series of eggs linked like sausages, must be for connecting a number of starships together while in flight, and finally, there are two unused ones that might possibly be used to control some type of weapons."

"Weapons?" asked Cerialis, sitting up attentively.

"Yes. I found one of those head-garlands and put it on my head, and looked into one of those viewing-jars that some of the stations have, and while it only looked out into empty space, I had the sensation of knowing that there were a number of choices I could make. I did not understand them, but there was a clear image in my mind, something asking me if I want to release something powerful. It was like when an archer draws a bow, the feeling of power, and the ability to aim at anything you want, and to let loose the arrow at any moment, that's how it felt. So, given the sensations that I experienced, I think of it as a means to control powerful weapons."

"We need to know more about this," said Cerialis. "Legatus, didn't you say that we will come to a planeta where there is a war going on at some point in this odyssey?"

"Yes, Planeta Bellorum. But that's three planetae from now. We should be at their homeworld next, as you know, Planeta Arborum, and then that one they want to put some cleaning-devices on, Planeta Terraformata. What are you thinking?" asked Agricola.

"That we should have our ambassadors continue to observe these workstations. Have them stroke or wash those Octopodii to keep them content, and have us assigned every dirty job to enable us access to all parts of the ship so we can master all of these things."

"Yes, that's what we need to do. Make it so, Lady Metellus, Kaeso. And Kaeso, maybe you should skip some of our endless philosophical debates about the purpose of all those objects we have stolen, and work with your find Lady Achal, on this. Take personal charge of mastering the weapons and other important capabilities of these starships. I am sure that Tribune Avitus will need to be involved as well."

"Legatus," Cerialis said, not certain if he had just been criticized for not talking with his elderly wife, or if had just been about making her research a higher military priority. Thinking about Achal, and the way she was always quiet around their pod, made Kaeso feel something for her. Not exactly love, or pity, but perhaps a desire to know her better as a friend. He made a point to sit with her to drink tea, as she did, perhaps introduce her to chess or other games he liked to play with his male friends.

A few days later, the starship arrived and took up orbit above the Tuatha homeworld.

The ambassadors had been successful in part, getting humans tasked with loading and unloading fuel rods from the thorium reactor. This gave their leaders a chance to rotate all of the officers through the bridge in groups of six or seven. It was clear that as long as only one person touched a Tuatha root to activate the access portal leading up to the bridge, the Tuatha would have no idea how many people were coming and going. Certainly the Octopodii were no threat, happy to have been relieved of the more frustrating tasks, and enjoying the wipe-downs and other attention lavished on them by the ambassadors.

So when the ship settled into orbit, Agricola rushed to the bridge to see for himself.

The Octopoda had no objection to the large human who pressed his face into the viewing pot at the navigation station.

Agricola placed the wreath on his head, loosely, until the Octopoda reached up to pull on a string, tightening the apparatus to fit as snugly on his head as a well-worn hat.

It only took Agricola a few moments to master his controls of the focal point, as the wreath seemed to make the man-device interface that much more efficient. He wondered how the device worked, and sensed that somehow it was watching his own eyes for cues as to what he wanted to see. That, or it somehow read his mind, but he felt that to be highly unlikely.

Looking at the blue, white and brown marble was mesmerizing. It sat there, so beautifully in the blackness of space, and looked so fragile.

He focused in to look closer at the planeta, and saw that it was mostly land, with a smaller proportion of blue, which he sensed was water. He also saw the occasional cloud pass by, momentarily obscuring his view.

It was just like laying on his back as a child, with Julia and Kaeso, looking up at the clouds passing over them, only now he was looking down from the sky, he understood.

Thinking of his youth made him yearn to be looking down on Rome. *One day*, he thought to himself, *I will be home.*

For a moment, he thought he was looking down on the Ostia of his childhood, as he recognized a cluster of Rosebud Trees. But then as the viewpoint grew nearer, he saw that it was actually a cluster of Tuathii.

He looked around, and saw no roads, no structures, and no sign of any kind of people. Then suddenly, he saw some animals. Strange, slender animals, moving amongst the trees.

He spent a goodly amount of time looking around the planeta, as it seemed to roll gently like a ball under the starship. In all of that time, he did not see anything other than trees, fields of green, rocky shorelines, oceans, and a variety of animals he had never seen before.

It seems like a beautiful planeta. Boring, yes, but it certainly seemed to be a nice place to settle, if it were not for the dominant species.

As he wondered what sort of life it must be for the trees, to just stand about in the sun, growing roots into the ground, spawning other trees from their roots, as the Tuathii had done on Planeta Metallorum, he thought of it as a suitable way for a tree to live. *But so much more could be done with the planet. Great cities could be built. Ships could ply the oceans, perhaps bringing treasures and oddities from one place to another. Commerce could take place, and, if there were enough people contesting the best territories, then wars of conquest could be fought,* Agricola imagined, with satisfaction.

The thought confused him for a moment. *What if wars did not need to be fought? Certainly life on Metallorum had shown some potential for happiness, with no hostile species or race to compete with. But is that enough for a man? To just live in peace, like a tree?*

Agricola thought not.

He withdrew from the viewing pot, removed the garland from his head, and moved about the bridge to see if he could divine the purpose of the other workstations as the activity on the bridge intensified.

He knew from his session with the Tuatha, before they departed Metallorum, that the purpose of the visit was to rendezvous with a scout-ship, which would transport a number of Tuathii saplings from the Tuathii homeworld into the starship, and take them onward to unite with Tuathii on other planetae along their itinerary in order to pass large quantities of information that had been accumulated for a great many years.

He was not sure if he understood the purpose correctly, but it seemed that as much as they were all one being, in a sense copies of one original, it seemed that there was a degree of differentiation between them. Not so much that they had personalities, or individuation as his philosophers put it, but they had different information, different memories, at least until they linked with themselves to cross-share all of the information they had collected or experienced.

To Agricola, it seemed like an absurdly slow way of doing things. And that brought to mind something that one of the ambassadors had said. Something about a signal. Just before coming into orbit, Ambassador Albus come to the Agricola' pod and told him that "Our masters inform us that we are soon to arrive, and that all is well on the homeworld."

At the time, he had thought of nothing more than his desire to be on the bridge when that happened, to observe everything. But now, as he waited for more to happen, he realized that there was something important in what the young man had conveyed.

They have a way of communicating with their homeworld at a great distance. Where is it? How does it work? he wondered, looking around the bridge.

On the pretense of learning better how to take over unpleasant duties from the Octopodii, the ambassadors and a few of the technicians from the Eighth of the Second had probed the Octopodii, and at times the Tuatha itself, on specific questions. The reports were passed through Lady Cerialia Achal and Kaeso Cerialis, but the analysis of the information was managed by Vibius Metellus, who formed an increasingly clear picture of what had transpired on Planeta Arborum, the Tuathii homeworld.

What Metellus was able to piece together now formed a clear picture. It all began when the first of the starships had appeared on Planeta Arborum. It had not taken long for the Tuathii to take notice of the strange new creatures. The most important of these, to the Romans understanding of the chain of events, was the sudden arrival of both the Octopodii, the eight-armed beings, and the Dupli-Tri, the three-armed-three-legged beings.

The way that the Octopodii thought-told the story was that they had been stranded on Planeta Arborum when the shipbuilders – the Dupli-Tri race – had landed en-masse with their fleet of egg-shaped starships.

The Dupli-Tri had immediately begun to clear land to build an initial outpost while their engineers explored the planet for resources. The Tuathii had tried to communicate with the Dupli-Tri, to ask them to stop, and the Dupli-Tri had ignored them. The Tuathii had then summoned all manner of creatures, and murdered most of the Dupli-Tri. It was the Tuathii's first experience with war, and they had no conception of strategy, of gathering intelligence, or of negotiation. They had simply come to the conclusion that, despite several attempts to influence the Dupli-Tri – who seemed largely immune from the motivation-imprinting capabilities of the Tuathii – they refused to stop cutting Tuathii. To make matters worse, the Dupli-Tri found the largest, oldest, and therefore most wise Tuathii to make the best lumber, and were well on their way to laying waste to the ancient heart of the Tuathii race, cutting down the oldest stand of Tuathii. The Tuathii had responded with a determined mindset of total war, the intention to completely obliterate the Dupli-Tri.

The first action of the war had been a relatively small skirmish. They had sent a large number of the fiercest indigenous animals to kill a team of Dupli-Tri who were setting out to cut down one of the oldest incarnations of the Tuathii tree-self. However, not all of the Dupli-Tri were killed when the critters had departed, the Tuathii imprinted order only lasting so long before the creatures lost interest in the task, and returned to their normal lives.

When one of the injured Dupli-Tri accidentally rested up against a Tuatha root, it had been enticed to commune with the elder tree. No longer seeking to simply influence the enemy race, the elder Tuatha had made overwhelming contact with its cunnis-tentacles, wrapping the creature's head with a great many roots, and unleashed all of the mind-contact power it could muster against the mind of the Dupli-Tri.

Linked with other ancient Tuathii, it-they collectively overcame the mental resistance of the Dupli-Tri, and sought out the reason these creatures hated the Tuathii so. There was no reason, it seems. They just wanted to build cities, clear land to grow food, and find other materials they needed.

The thinking-trees had kept enough of the Dupli-Tri alive, for a time at least, to experiment on them. The Tuathii did not have any technology of their own, but they did have a great deal of access to the flora and fauna of their environment, and soon learned what was most toxic to the Dupli-Tri biology.

The Tuathii discovered that the venom released by a simple creature, which the Tuathii had long cooperated with, would become their weapon of choice against the Dupli-Tri. In fact, the venomous creature, a tiny flying insect, was one of the messenger-species the Tuathii used to gather information about their own planet.

Going from the mental images they encountered in their thought-discussions with the Tuatha, the ambassadors had experienced some initial difficulty acquiring a clear understanding of what these strange flying bugs were, but eventually understood them to be about the size of a gnat – almost invisible to the naked eye.

While the gnats would come and go into the nectar-bowl in the tree's trunk, attracted to the sweet liquid, they occasionally landed on a root. Their simple brains would allow the tree to recall from the creature's recent memory a glimpse of what it had seen. Other messenger species, which crawled about on the forest floor and onto the limbs and leaves of the tree itself, provided additional information to satisfy the Tuathii's constant hunger for information on the land, the planet, and ultimately the universe around it.

Accessing information from the smaller creatures was much easier than accessing the visual memory of larger creatures, whose more complex brains were cluttered with thoughts and feelings so as to make it very difficult for the Tuathii to acquire the desired information.

To extract more than the creature was willing to give, the thinking-trees had long known, could be unpleasant for the creatures, and result in the species avoiding contact with the Tuathii in the future, and thus, isolating the tree from part of the biosphere. And the Tuathii had a deep reverence for all life, for all things in the biosphere, which the Tuathii thought of as the source of everything interesting in their world.

But the little gnats, simple as they were, presented no such difficulties.

And once the thinking-trees had learned that the gnat's venom was highly toxic to the Dupli-Tri, that a simple bite could kill a Dupli-Tri in only a few days, the Tuathii realized it had a weapon of mass destruction.

The Tuathii had been fortunate that the Dupli-Tri had not seen them as a threat when they had first arrived, quickly assessing the planeta as a safe place to land all nine of their colonist starships and the three larger warships as well.

They had let their guard down.

Had they known that the trees were thinking-beings, and had the ability to kill, then they would probably have been more cautious. Perhaps they would have used their intelligence and advanced technologia to dominate the thinking-trees. Had they done so, and retained the initiative, they may have succeeded in colonizing the tree planeta. But they had been excited about having access to the bounty of what seemed an undefended planet, and had paid for this mistake with their lives.

Up until that point, the Tuathii had not thought it possible to depart from their planet. They had observed the cosmos, in cooperation with a variety of seeing creatures, sharing their vision for a time in exchange for nectar. Those creatures which saw better at night had been most helpful in observing the stars over countless millennia.

Over time, the Tuathii had deduced the nature of stars, planetae, comets, and asteroids, but had little knowledge in other things. Until the arrival of the Dupli-Tri, they had considered the cosmos completely out of reach.

But when they had their encounter with the Dupli-Tri, and had been unable to bend them to their own will, they were left with a new problem.

The Tuathii knew, from their mind-invading interrogation of the Dupli-Tri, that a much larger force from the Dupli-Tri homeworld would soon come to investigate what happened to them. That homeworld was what the humans had come to understand as *Planeta Scientia,* by virtue of the bounty of Dupli-Tri technology that they now understood originated there.

The Tuathii had learned that it would take as long as twelve revolutions of their planet, just twelve day-night cycles, for a starship to travel back to Planeta Scientia, and yet in that short time there would actually be twenty of the much larger cycles of Planeta Arborum orbiting its nearby sun. The concept of time dilation and the use of the Equanimity-Field, the power created at the boundary between Nesslessness and Thing, the power source at the heart of the Dupli-Tri technology, made sense to the Tuathii. It merged with their cosmological understanding and deep ecological philosophy about the relationship between matter, energy, and consciousness. But how the starship *actually functioned,* and the operation of the devices onboard, was another story.

They could not think of a way to operate the starship on their own. No matter how knowledgeable they were, there were some things that a thinking-tree simply could not.

Even if they could use another creature's eyes for a time, it would not permit them to do the multiple tasks required to operate and navigate a starship. And the size of even a young adult Tuatha was such that no more than one or two could fit in the confined space of the bridge, let alone replace the dozens of Dupli-Tri that were normally required to operate a starship.

And then the Tuathii considered the passengers on the ship, the relatively dumb but seemingly harmless eight-legged Octopodii.

The Octopodii had been spared during the war, as many had fled to what they thought of as the relative safety of the sea.

The Octopodii had thought they had found a marvelous new ocean to inhabit, but soon found themselves being preyed upon by a wide variety of creatures that dominated the seas on the strange planet. So the Octopodii had sought refuge in the tidal pools at the water's edge, close to the very starships that they had fled when the Dupli-Tri extermination began.

Eventually some Octopodii had ventured back onto the land in search of food, the ocean being far too dangerous. While food from the sea was their normal sustenance, they became desperate enough to eat grubs, worms and other land-based food they found on the forest floor. In seeking food, they came into contact with the Tuathii and, after willingly think-explaining their origin and purpose, worked out a compromise: If the Octopodii would help the Tuathii to operate the starships, to be their hands and eyes, then the Tuathii would try to help the Octopodii find their way home.

The trouble was, the Tuathii had not extracted enough information from the Dupli-Tri to know where the Octopodii homeworld was. And while the Tuathii had every intention of honoring their promise to replace the Octopodii with another suitable race, and to release the Octopodii on a suitable watery-world, this goal was yet to be achieved when the Romans had come into the equation.

That had been the agreement between the bewildered Octopodii and the Tuathii – the new and completely unsuited masters of the Dupli-Tri fleet of nine colonist-ships and three warships.

Still possessed of the determination to exterminate all Dupli-Tri in their simple-minded cause of total war, the first matter at hand for the Tuathii had been the complete destruction of the Dupli-Tri on the Dupli-Tri homeworld. The Dupli-Tri were an insane race, and from what the Tuathii had seen in theirmemories, the Dupli-Tri homeworld had become nearly uninhabitable.

The Dupli-Tri had to be stopped, or they would come to Planeta Arborum in greater numbers and chop the last of the elder Tuathii. The Tuathii also believed that the Dupli-Tri advanced understanding of how to manipulate materials, energy, and their powerful devices would also enable them to identify and overcome the danger posed by the gnats, the one vulnerability that the Tuathii could exploit. But that would take time, and, from what the Tuathii had extracted from the Dupli-Tri, time was something that the three-by-three species did not have.

They had consumed the vital resources of their planet; expanded their population at a grotesque, logarithmic rate and as a consequence of their unrestrained, irresponsible consumption, squandering of resources, and disregard for the well-being of their natural environment, the three-by-threes had transformed the atmosphere of their planet into one that was increasingly toxic.

The Dupli-Tri were on the verge of catastrophe. Their bid to colonize the planeta of the Tuathii, along with a few other habitable planetae within range of their homeworld, had been a last, desperate, attempt to maintain the existence of their species. As pressure built between the out-of-control population growth and the accelerating collapse of their resources, the powerful elite of their kind had tried to mask the truth. They had tried to control their population by euphemism and propaganda, promoting the fantasy hope that each and every Dupli-Tri would have a chance to win a seat on a colonization ship.

This helped keep the masses at bay while the most powerful and influential Dupli-Tri readied plans to abandon the homeworld to the ignorant, luckless many. In reality, there would only be billeting for a small number of colonists to travel in these colonization ships. This reality was kept secret while the last of the planetary resources were thrown into the effort to build more starships, to horde the meager reserves of thorium fuel to power the starships, and to outfit some of the largest starships as *warships* – lest there be any type of resistance on the planetae they intended to colonize.

All that was known of the selected sites was that they were within the range limits of their Nesslessness-Thing Equanimity-Drives, and that the atmosphere had the right diurnal variations in temperature, along with a nitrogen-oxygen atmosphere, that was suitable for colonization by the Dupli-Tri race.

Their plan was simple: To arrive with colonists in sufficient number and with advanced technology, and overwhelm any indigenous resistance that may be found in the new worlds.

Planeta Arborum, the homeworld of the Tuathii, was to be the second of their conquests. The first, and most important, was to establish a mining outpost on another planeta which, while endowed with a wealth of thorium reserves, was far too humid and cool for colonization by the Dupli-Tri. As a result, Planeta Metallorum was established as a mining outpost and not a colony. It was outfitted with a mineral processing facility to produce thorium fuel rods for the fleet of starships and other power-hungry technologies possessed by the Dupli-Tri.

In order to manage the production of thorium on Planeta Metallorum, the Dupli-Tri had installed a race of brutish beings they had conquered on another planet, and had employed members of the Octopodii race for more technical tasks, such as the refinement of concentrated thorium from the mineral ore, and the preparation of the fuel rods in the processing plant. The Octopoda being more suited to the damp environment of the place.

With additional supplies of thorium in place and more starships nearing completion, they had then set their sights on Planeta Arborum, what would be the second of their planetary conquests. They committed the bulk of their fleet and resources to establish the initial cadre of colonists, on what was a make-or-break effort – they did not have the resources to make a second attempt at colonizing another suitably habitable world.

Had they succeeded, and resettled the most fortunate of their kind on the planet of the Tuathii, the Dupli-Tri would eventually have abandoned their own kind, back on Planeta Scientiae, to their fate.

Things had not turned out well for the Dupli-Tri, who had seen the trees simply as another resource to be thoughtlessly consumed. Not recognizing any threat from the indigenous species of the planet, the Tuathii, they had lowered their guard and thrown themselves into the colonization effort.

They had been overwhelmed by an unexpected onslaught of creatures of all sorts, each intent on killing a Dupli-Tri. Few of their kind had survived the push-back by the indigenous creatures of Planeta Arborum, which had been orchestrated by the collective effort of the Tuathii many-one forest itself.

Now, with the bulk of their fleet stranded on the planet of the Tuathii, it would have taken another generation and the final resources of their nearly exhausted planeta to mount another major effort. This second effort would include more weapons and technology intended to defeat any opposition, but they had no information as to what had happened to their colonists, other than the fact that they had been overcome by hordes of beasts. From what the Dupli-Tri had been able to piece together, Planeta Arborum did not possess an advanced civilization or any sentient beings, and yet their initial wave of colonists had been utterly destroyed.

With precious little remaining resources, and with no other suitable planetae within accessible range, the Dupli-Tri had no alternative. They pieced together a follow-on contingent, to try again.

They had been near the end of final preparations when the Tuathii had, with the help of the Octopodii, succeeded in developing an understanding of the basic operating principles of the Dupli-Tri starships.

The Octopodii were to be used as the Tuathii's hands and eyes, to carry out the critical shipboard operational and maintenance functions. However, for the Tuathii to exercise shipboard command and control, it was also necessary to install at least one Tuatha inside each starship. The starships, however, were not designed with a tree in mind.

Fortunately, the needs of a Tuatha are quite simple. They need only water, white light, and nutrients for their primary roots. The brightly lit conference room in the center of the bridge, once stripped of the Dupli-Tri tables and chairs, provided a suitable location for the Tuatha.

A single mature Tuatha was placed onto a pad of soil on the bridge of each starship, and was to come to learn as much of the functions of the ship as possible.

One of the first achievements was when a Tuatha had been able to extract, from one of the few surviving Dupli-Tri hostages, how to activate pods from a workstation on the bridge. This came with the knowledge that Dupli-Tri, as well as Siphonapteristii Monstrum and Octopodii, each required sleeping chambers, pods, or in the case of the Octopodii, salt-water tanks so that the beings could feed, rest, and recover, just as the Tuathii required dirt, water, and light for sustenance.

The Tuathii comprehended the notion of the pods, but at first did not see much use for all of the rooms, laid out as they were in rows of threes, sixes and twelves. After contemplating this with the larger Tuathii network, the collective came to the conclusion that the pods would be useful for transporting other, more suitable and useful alien races, so they determined to know all that they could about the operation of the pods.

The same logic was applied to learning other systems. But having never used machines of any kind, or conveyances such as a ship, or even a dwelling for that matter, there were a great many of the shipboard systems that they had not even become aware of by the time they had used up the last of their Dupli-Tri hostages, fatally extracting what they needed to know of navigation, propulsion, control of miniscule repair robots measuring no more than a few nanometers each, and the basic routines of starship maintenance.

The Tuathii were not suited to space travel, and they knew this. They had evolved in a complex manner which enabled them to interact with their environment, making use of their ability to connect with the minds of simple creatures to overcome their many limitations. Despite these limits, they possessed profound intelligence.

But their intelligence was the result their incredibly long lives, millennia of observation, thought, and the accumulated knowledge of other species with which they interacted. It was not uncommon for a thinking-tree to live several thousand years. Furthermore, they considered themselves to be a single being, in a sense, due to their habit of interconnecting with other, genetically identical, iterations of itself, expanding its thinking power and exchanging information.

They were constrained mostly by the limited intelligence of the creatures of their homeworld, but found working with the Octopodii, brought to their world by the Dupli-Tri, to be a way to overcome many of the challenges that they faced in mastering the alien technology. But the Octopodii themselves were a primitive race, lacking the mental abilities and discernment of the Tuathii. The solutions that the Tuathii formulated were awkward, and, in many cases, incomplete. As a result, there were a great many aspects of maintaining and operating a starship that they had been unable to understand simply due to their ignorance.

But their objective was to learn enough to operate the starship on a mission to return to the Dupli-Tri homeworld, to bring the fight to their enemy. They created novel, if somewhat incongruous solutions to the challenges they faced. They learned how to adjust the chemistry of the nectar in a few of their kind so as to secrete a concentrated acid that could be poured by Octopodii to burn holes through the metal that compromised the interior structures of the starships, and how to inhibit the minuscule automatonic repair devices that would have otherwise closed these holes. This allowed them to extend route-appendages throughout the ship, to act as a means of communicating with the Octopodii who operated the ship and with future passengers.

So despite their unsuitability for performing the routine operational functions, through the application of their extensive networked intelligence and with the help of the Octopodii and the less intelligent but far stronger Siphonapteristii, they succeeded in their objective of operating a starship.

They proceeded to navigate their stolen flotilla of egg-shaped starships, which they had linked together like a string of pearls, as they had gleaned from their interrogation of the Dupli-Tri, and had ultimately arrived at the Dupli-Tri homeworld.

They landed all nine colonist-pattern starships in the spaceports in the nine capital cities of the Dupli-Tri homeworld. The three warships remained in orbit, with a Tuatha on each ship linked to an Octopoda, and through the sea-creatures' eyes the three versions of Tuathii bore witness from above.

Each capital city had once been the origin of one of the colonist-ships, and was the focal point of their civilization's remaining resources.

Despite having lost word of the colonists nearly a century earlier, small pockets of the dying race had the power and resources to preserve a degree of civilization, passing the legend of the lost colonies. They held out hope that at least some of the colonists had succeeded, and would return to provide salvation for the withering species before they were totally extinguished.

When the excited leaders of the Dupli-Tri homeworld came to greet what they believed to be returning colonist-ships, to celebrate the success of the initial wave of colonists, the Dupli-Tri had been shocked to see that rather than their own kind issuing out of the four main portals of each ship, a swarm of tiny bugs surged out, a black cloud that soon dissipated into the air.

The toxic gnats of Planeta Arborum had been given three simple intentions by the Tuathii who had lured them in with gnat-attracting nectar, in their billions upon billions. So as they spread out from the starships at the nine spaceports of the Dupli-Tri home planet, the gnats' minds were set on the three simple thoughts: *breed as fast as possible; spread out as widely as possible; and bite as many Dupli-Tri as possible.*

They were a plague on the vulnerable species, infecting their capital cities first, and then spreading out from there. The Dupli-Tri leaders and most capable died off first, by virtue of being the closest to the returning starships when the gnats were unleashed on them. This was the final nail in the coffin for the Dupli-Tri species, most of whom had no idea of where the sudden new terror had originated. All they knew was that death spread across their land, taking the strong as rapidly as the weak, as if some terrible judgment had been passed on their kind. The global population of Dupli-Tri had been completely exterminated within five short years.

During the decades after the invasion by the Tuathii, occasionally Dupli-Tri scout-ships and smaller fleets of colonist-ships returned from other colonization and exploration missions that had been launched to stars more distant than the Tuathii homeworld, and therefore the return voyages took a great many years longer. Arriving to their homeworld expecting to be hailed as returning heroes, the Dupli-Tri crews were completely unaware of what had befallen it.

Each in turn landed into peril.

Octopoda employed by the Tuathii brought the dying Dupli-Tri crews to the small forests of thinking-trees that had been planted not far from each spaceport, so that the Tuathii could gather additional intelligence.

One such returning ship had brought the Siphonapteristii. The Tuathii were disappointed to learn the limited range of tasks which the strong, dumb brutes were capable of performing. The Siphonapteristii were not the replacements which the Tuathii and Octopodii had hoped for. That particular ship also carried Dupli-Tri engineers and geologists, who had returned from Planeta Metallorum with another payload of thorium fuel rods.

Upon interrogation of the dying Dupli-Tri engineers, who had been infected by gnat venom upon landing, the Tuathii had learned of the Dupli-Tri plan to return to Terra for another cadre of humans, as the first small cadre transported from Terra by Dupli-Tri milennia earlier had proven not quite up to the task of managing the Siphonapteristii, the beasts used to mine thorium on Planeta Metallorum. That initial cadre was limited in number due to the small scout-ship that had been used to abduct only ten mating pairs from a rain-soaked island on Terra. And because of the limited genetic pool of the ancient humans, and the high mortality rate they had due to challenges managing the dangerous Siphonapteristii, breeding alone would never solve the problem.

A subsequent mission to gather larger numbers of the useful bipeds was required, to increase the human population and rate of thorium production on Planeta Metallorum, as the Dupli-Tri had found no better candidates.

Understanding the importance of thorium ore production, the Tuathii had attempted to execute the follow-up mission originally planned by the Dupli-Tri. They sent three colonists ships to Terra, to collect more humans. However, only one colonist ship had returned, with two hundred and sixteen breeding pairs of ancient humans from the water soaked island. The two ships that had not returned had come into some unknown circumstance.

Needing more humans to increase the productivity at the thorium mine, the Tuathii had then sent two more colonist-ships along with the three warships to execute the new mission to gather two hundred and sixteen more breeding pairs, hopefully enough to boost the productivity of the mining planet and to provide seed-sock of additional humans to be used on other planetae.

If successful, which would only be known in a great many years due to the length of time involved in interplanetary travel over such great distances as from Locus Capricornus to Locus Terra, it was hoped that once a sufficient number of humans were available to the Tuathii, the thinking-trees would be in a position to make good on their promise to return the Octopodii to their homeworld. Despite the fact that the Tuathii had never encountered a human, they were optimistic that the human race might be just what they needed.

That had been almost six thousand years ago.

Since that time, after they sent ships to Terra and Metallorum, the Tuathii had learned how to integrate their appendages into most spaces and systems within a starship, but they had not been very successful at mastering the wider breadth of the Dupli-Tri technology.

The great many years lost in sending little-trees back to the Tuathii homeworld, and for messengers to return with instructions, made the challenge of deciding what to do with these newfound resources that much more difficult.

They had been able to manage a moderate rate of production of thorium fuel rods. They needed more thorium to power up the increasing number of starships which they had dispatched on a variety of missions, hoping to expand their knowledge of stars in their region of the galaxy, and perhaps to find more species that they could work with to overcome their physical limitations.

Their thinking at this point was twofold. First, to become more secure from outside attack so that nothing like the Dupli-Tri invasion of their homeworld would ever recur; and second, to find more suitable beings to work with, so that that their Octopodii allies could be freed.

Eventually they encountered another hostile species, and a very costly war soon followed. This war consumed much of the thorium that came out of the mines on Planeta Metallorum, and in diverting so many resources, thwarted their long-term efforts to master the Dupli-Tri technology.

The war itself was at a standstill, having reached a steady state, whereby both sides required considerable time to recoup their losses and prepare for the next round of hostilities, with centuries between each battle on the contested planeta, Planeta Bellorum.

Now, with the success of the Tuathii mission to gather humans from Terra to provide the required numbers to stabilize operations on Planeta Metallorum, the next stage in the Tuathii plan was to carry on testing which other roles and which other worlds the bipedal race were suited to.

What they needed most was to install some of these seemingly intelligent and resourceful bipedals into all of their colonies, have them breed to increase their numbers, and then use them wherever they proved useful.

They needed to know more about what the humans were capable of, and they needed to determine this by taking a number of humans to their planet to have them commune with the larger, networked Tuathii on the Tuathii homeworld, who were powerful enough to draw the most information out of the bipedal.

A patient being, the Tuatha elder-self had waited nearly two millennia for the fresh humans to arrive. In that time, Tuathii scout-ships had come and gone with reports of a range of planetae which, generally, were not ideal for the Tuathii, and no better candidate than the bipedals had as yet been discovered. Even worse, the Tuathii scout-ships had encountered some very hostile races at some of the constellation loci they had visited, resulting in a number of potential threats. It made the Tuathii insecure, and increasingly eager to have bipedals to train, and perhaps to assist in mastering the unknown technologia and weapons inherited from the Dupli-Tri.

That had been the hope when the Tuathii of Planeta Arborum had learned of the arrival of the colony ship most recently from Planeta Metallorum. The problem was that the ship carrying the new cadre of humans *did not land as it was supposed to,* and therefore did not deliver the cargo of bipedals to interrogate. The colony ship had simply taken up orbit for a short time and then unceremoniously departed from its orbit.

Lacking the ability to communicate directly with their Tuatha-self aboard the starship, the homeworld Tuathii were limited to communicating through reports transmitted between an Octopoda on the orbiting starship and another Octopoda on a starship, parked on the surface of the thinking-tree homeworld, using Dupli-Tri technology aboard the spaceships.

The message had been simple, as always, due to the intellectual limitations of the Octopodii. *There will be no delivery of bipedal subjects, and no delivery of thorium fuel rods. The bipedal race is now in control of this starship.*

The effect of the message on the thinking-tree homeworld had been dramatic.

The networked intelligence of the entire thinking-tree race was enraged. They had thought it possible that the bipedal race would prove a mixed blessing, and some arguments had been considered that using the bipedals was too risky, however they had been confident in their ability to imprint suitable intentions in humans minds. Something must have gone wrong on the thorium planeta, and the bipedals had out-thought the thinking-trees assigned to the Planeta Metallorum task.

I have to act, the Tuathii decided collectively, and set about to do so.

Knowing that the departing starship would be out of range shortly, there had been only enough time to send a single, short message through the Octopodii.

Pass the word to any and all of your kind, and to all thinking-trees you meet in your travels, that the bipedal race is to be exterminated. If you fail to pass this word, your race on Planeta Octopodii will be exterminated. Do not share this with the bipedals on your starship.

Sitting on his Tuatha-stool on the bridge, next to an Octopoda at the communications table, Agricola had a hand wrapped around one of the Octopoda's tentacles.

Sandwiched between the Octopoda's rubbery skin and his own was a short length of Tuatha root.

The root was from a very small little-Tuatha that had been taken from one of the Castorii plantations. The tree was too small and inexperienced to understand much of what was going on between the human and the Octopoda, but did have enough of its collective memory from its ancestor on the starship to know that the information being shared from Octopoda to human, through its own root, needed to be shared with a more mature Tuatha.

I need to share this with others of myself, thought the little tree into the conference.

You will be permitted to link in with your kind on this ship, when it is time. It is not time now, thought-said Agricola, trying to emote sincerity to the little tree-hostage.

The idea of bringing aboard a few saplings from a Castorii plantation had been a stroke of genius. Agricola had agreed with the suggestion, and authorized Tribune Marcus Avitus to keep two of the trees in a pot in his sleeping pod.

The little buggers had quickly linked with each other, and had been reaching their young branches outward to find other Tuathii appendages in the pod when Neasa had snatched them away just in time.

Had they made contact with one of the Tuatha roots in their pod, the ruse would have been discovered and no doubt a violent battle between humans and Siphonapteristii would have ensued, with an uncertain outcome.

As it was, by keeping the little trees in clay pots and only allowing them access to light when they could be observed, they were kept from growing well. They were sickly, and barely able to survive under the circumstances. One day, one of the ambassadors had found sheets of translucent material in a storage room. Without knowing the true purpose, the ambassador had been ordered to steal two squares of the material, which were eventually given to Tribune Avitus. With the translucent material tied firmly to the tops of the clay pots, the two little trees were able to get enough bright light from inside the pod that they could thrive, like an indoor plant, and yet there was no risk that they would link-in with the Tuatha operating the starship.

Over time and with a little experimentation, the Roman leadership had learned how to use the little trees to communicate with Octopodii on the ship. They had started small, three-way conversations with two Romans and the little tree, to develop a relationship with the little fellow, and to spin a web of lies to put the little thinking-tree's mind at ease. They found the naïve and inexperienced little tree to be easily tricked.

Later, the philosophers Metellus and Quintilianus had explained that the thinking-tree race seemed to have evolved without ever having had any awareness of the notion of deception. A lie was simply not something that would occur to a tree. Rather, when a race communicates something that does not match reality or action, the tree sees that race as stupid or crazy. As a result, the trees were fundamentally trusting when it came to facts and reports. The Romans came to think of the Tuathii race as the most intelligent dimwits imaginable, but were also aware of how violently they reacted when they decided someone was a threat, as the poor munifex had learned when he had chopped off that appendage and been so quickly put to death.

They saw this as an opportunity that entailed great risk. The reasoning was, if the Tuathii come to understand the nature of deception, that they have been systematically misled by the humans, then they would likely apply the same complete hostility toward the humans, and set about to exterminate them. So by using this strategy, the Romans understood, they were playing with fire.

Once they were comfortable regarding how to manage the little tree as an intermediary, they set their sights on the Octopodii.

In order to minimize the risk that the Octopodii would report the message to the Tuatha operating the starship, they had singled out a beaten-up looking Octopoda who worked in a rather unpleasant area in the bowels of the ship. It seemed to rarely have need to link-in with the Tuatha, and for some reason there were no appendages in the dank corner of the ship where he worked, supervising some Siphonaperistii cleaning out filth from recycling vats. The circumstances were ideal for the communications experiment conceived by Vibius Metellus, the objective of which was to have direct communications with the Octopodii, without the starship's Tuatha being aware.

Their first surreptitious discussion with the Octopoda told them a great deal. They learned that the Octopodii disliked serving on the starship, and detested working with the beastly Siphonapteristii.

They also learned that the thinking-tree promise to return the Octopodii to their homeworld was growing a bit thin, as it seemed that the thinking-trees would never grant them their freedom.

They were creatures of the sea, and yearned to be free to swim, eat, mate and simply live in the salty waters of their homeworld.

When Agricola and Avitus both thought-told the Octopoda that they intended to release them, once the humans understood how to operate the starships, the Octopoda intuitively knew that they were speaking the truth. After all, the thinking-trees had long promised that the bipedal race, once suitably domesticated and trained to serve the thinking-trees, were to be their long-promised replacements.

That the bipedal race would be in charge, rather than the thinking-trees, was of little importance to the Octopodii.

In addition to being cut off from the mature Tuatha, the old Octopodii selected for their communications experiment with the sapling was actually senior among his race, and that was an added benefit.

After that, the Romans had discrete three-way conversations with Octopodii at each of the work-stations, with immunes from the Second participating so that an accurate record could be made of what was learned. The little sapling Tuatha was strong enough to facilitate the discussions, but as it had no opportunity to tie-in with more mature versions of itself, it had no way of knowing that it was being manipulated, and, as was true for the Tuathii, it had no comprehension of deceit.

With each progressive increase in their knowledge of the ship's functions, the Romans began to assign specific men and women to master the newly acquired skill sets, and at times had humans doing the job side-by-side with the Octopodii.

The transition of humans taking on a greater portion of the Octopodii workload was not without challenges. In one instance on the bridge, a Hibernian female was wiping down the Octopoda with moist cloths whilst the Octopoda was communicating instructions on the operation of a control panel. Water dripping from her wet cloth accumulated on the control desk, and infiltrated inside. Suddenly sparks and flame leapt up from beneath one of the controls, startling the Octopoda and its human ambassador.

They jumped back, looking at the smoking panel and wondering what had happened. Soon enough, as a few people came running up to the bridge laughing uproariously, the young woman learned something valuable.

"What happened here?" asked an immune from the Second, who was the first to reach the bridge.

"A lightning bolt jumped out of the controls," said Fulvia.

"Was that just a short time ago?" he asked, as he examined the damaged control.

"Yes. Why? And what is all that commotion back there?" Fulvia asked, referring to the laughter and noise coming up the ramp from the deck below.

"It appears that whatever happened here caused the sleeping pod doors to suddenly open."

"Which ones?"

"All of them!"

"Oh!" Fulvia replied, and then she concentrated. "That makes sense, because these controls are for opening pod doors. The one that is smoking is the 'activate' control, and is normally used when specific pods are selected, however it can, if rotated all the way to the left, open all of the sleeping pod doors."

"And what made it burn? Was it getting hot before the fire jumped out of it?"

"No, Immune Suetonius, everything was normal. I was just wiping down our Octopoda friend here with some *aqua salsus*, salt water, from its tank."

"You let salt water get inside these controls?"

"Yes. Was that bad?"

"My dear, water and electro-potentia, electricity, do not mix. You must not let water get near any controls or other devices. It could cause a terrible accident. Fortunately, today's accident was more humorous than dangerous."

"Humorous? How?"

"When the pod doors opened, those of us in the corridors suddenly saw into everybody's sleeping pods. It was great fun.

Some people were having sex, and suddenly became our entertainment – there was an orgy going on in Centurion Tappulus's pod!"

"Tappulus's? I thought he and Genovefa were not getting along well."

"They're not. They basically hate each other, despite the Tuatha-influenced pair-bonding. But they sure do have a healthy sex life – seems they are always having noisy sex as evidenced by their now publicly displayed orgy with the Tribune Flavus and his wife. I thought I saw Daffid Og in there somewhere as well, but not his wife."

"Nor surprising. I have never seen them being affectionate to each other, as if they are role playing their pair bonding but not genuinely caring for each other. So what else was seen?"

"In another chamber, a milite was sitting on the solid waste collection system, unburdening himself with great strain. The most amusing pod of all was that of Centurion Crispus. When the pod opened, a group of us were right by his pod. We all got a good look of him wearing a silk dress! We asked him about it, and while he was a bit embarrassed to be caught wearing woman's clothing, he also seemed somehow relieved. He let us feel the fabric, by the way. Have you ever felt silk?"

"No, but I have heard of it. What did it feel like?"

"It was smooth as a baby's bottom! Perfect for undergarments, I think. Anyhow, Crispus said that the silk was from Assyria, or perhaps Indus. He acquired it in Rome."

"Well, I will have to ask Madam Crispus to show me his silk dress," she said, smiling at the image of the powerful man in such a soft, feminine outfit.

After hearing the stories from the immune from the Second, Ambassador Laurentiua Fulvia used a sapling to link the Octopoda to Immune Suetonius, and together they replaced the burned-out control. After passing the word to get people to watch the pod-doors, they tried the repaired control, and found it working properly – opening only the designated pods – much to the disappointment of those who wanted to see more entertainment.

The ship's mature Tuatha never did learn of the communications between the humans and Octopodii, as the saplings used for the conferences never found a way to link-in with the more mature Tuatha on the bridge.

So when the Octopoda at the communications console waved a tentacled arm at one of the humans on the bridge to indicate that something important was taking place, Legatus Agricola was quickly summoned.

He placed a communications-wreath on his head and linked with a little-tree and the Octopoda just in time to receive the final transmission from the Tuathii homeworld, Planeta Arborum.

He had just heard the message intended for the Octopoda race and for the command ship's Tuatha, that the human race was to be exterminated.

The little tree was terrified, and asked again to be linked-in with the ship's Tuatha.

Not yet, little friend. But believe me, we want only peace between our bipedal race and your thinking-tree kind. You serve that peace as long as you trust in me, and assist in our communications, Agricola soothed the little tree.

Think-speaking through the little tree to the Octopoda at the communications console, Agricola knew he had little time to compose a reply to the Tuathii homeworld.

This starship, and many others, are now under the command of the bipedal race called 'Rome'. An ambassador will be sent to you in due time. Peace between our races is possible, if you choose it. Take no hostile actions against the bipedal race, and we will have peace with the great thinking-tree race. He had the Octopoda send the message using the communications console, through the Octopoda on Planeta Arborum, and ultimately received by the network of ancient Tuathii.

This cannot be, the thought reverberated through the ancient forest like lightning, *what possible use could such a primitive species have for the starships, and what will be the fate of the me that is on board?*

XIX

PLANETA BELLORVM
{ Battle Planet }

When the starship arrived at Planeta Bellorum, Legatus Agricola was at first confused.

The humans had been successful in misleading the ship's Tuatha into believing that the delivery of a dozen pairs of humans on Planeta Arborum had been completed, when in fact there had been no little-tree messenger on board the scout-ship when it had arrived.

The Tuatha on the bridge was not satisfied with the report because it diverted from the original plan conveyed from itself on the homeworld. When plans change, as they invariably must, the Tuathii always took great care to ensure that a sapling or young Tuatha was dispatched to update itself on the changed plans and other new information, through direct contact. In this case, the lack of direct contact, with no sapling arriving, and the with no satisfactory explanation being conveyed by the communications Octopoda, the ship's Tuatha thought the humans and Octopodii were being stupid, or perhaps simply insane. However, the Tuatha had no way to independently verify the report and seemed to accept it as an unresolved question. No doubt the tree was still pondering it when they arrived at the next stop on their grand tour, Planeta Bellorum, where the Tuathii were at war with a hostile species.

Ambassadore Albus, the milite assigned with querying the Tuatha for information about the alien race, was unsuccessful in acquiring much of any good intelligence on the topic. All he could report was that the Tuathii had begun to colonize the planet and had then been wiped out by a species which the Tuathii had yet to get their appendages on.

They had never been able to get into physical contact with their enemy, let alone get one to put its head inside a Tuatha for a thought-interrogation.

All that Albus knew of the enemy of the Tuathii was their weapon of choice – comets – from the collection of frozen rocks and particles, much like dirty-snowballs, that were found surrounding the outskirts of the Bellorum solar system.

Apparently, the enemy had a starship that was capable of positioning itself in close proximity to any comet on suitable trajectory that would allow, through some unknown means, the starship to to force the comet to undergo slight directional adjustments to put it on a collision course with a specific location on the planeta. The comet would obliterate the settlement being established by the Tuathii, with little damage to the planet's ecosystem.

Every time the Tuathii returned with another ship full of little-trees to re-seed their colony they would find their beach-head colony had been erased from the planet, leaving no evidence other than a comet or asteroid crater where their colony had been.

The strange thing was that the aliens did not seem to be interested in establishing a colony of their own. It was as if denying use of the planeta by the Tuathii was their sole concern.

But after a few rounds of inquiry, Ambassador Albus had determined that the crux of the issue was the inability of the Tuathii to locate the alien colony, which must be somewhere on the planeta. They had burned a great deal of thorium fuel searching the planet over the centuries, and found no trace. The Tuathii had also assumed that the planeta must contain considerable deposits of thorium, or some other strategic resource, to be contested so hotly by the unknown aliens.

Each time they returned, the Tuathii had used two of the Dupli-Tri warships to hunt down and destroy the alien's puller-ships operating in the comet-fields and asteroid belts of the Bellorum system, seemingly on standby to hurl comets at any interlopers who may attempt to colonize the system's only habitable planet.

The Tuathii would then land and deploy a number of little-trees in a renewed attempt to colonize the planeta. It was a centuries-long game of seed, destroy, seed, and then suffer destruction yet again; a perpetual cycle of pointless violence.

When thought-asked by Ambassador Albus why they did not deploy their trees more broadly on Planeta Bellorum, rather than in one cluster, the Tuatha simply replied: *I like to be together with myselves, so ie can exchange thoughts and information and share perspective with myselves. If I spread out as you say, I would not be with myselves.*

It seemed clear to the Romans that the Tuathii were not very good at strategic thinking.

With Agricola, Marcus Avitus, and many of the other key Romans on the bridge, some looking through the viewing-pots to see images of an enemy redirectional-vessel being tracked by a Tuatha-controlled Dupli-Tri warship, the Romans were witnessing warfare that was far outside their realm of experience. Although they were of a different place and time, the concept of space warfare piqued their interest and excited their imaginations.

"Why do they not simply try to dock with the alien vessel, and board it, as the Second Legion did in the Battle of Actium, against Mark Antony's fleet?" asked Marcus Avitus.

"Apparently, they simply do not know how to do that. The Tuathii know how to slice a ship into pieces with energy weapons, but they do not know how to maneuver in close quarters with their prey," replied Ambassador Albus.

"What about that moving energy-wall they used on us in Hibernia?"

"They have never considered using that in space. They only know of its application for herding 'useful beings' for collection on the surface of a planet."

"Let's suggest to the Tuathii warship that they use their moving energy wall to seize – without destroying – the alien redirectional-ship."

After a few minutes of communications between the Octopodii on the two ships it became clear that the Tuatha and Octopodii crew of the warship did not know how to use the controls of their energy field in space. However, they were open to the idea of letting the recently-arrived colonist-ship make an attempt.

The warship ceased movement towards the little alien vessel, which was hovering near a dirty snowball comet about the size of the warship. It seemed to be taking no action whatsoever.

"Do they not fight back?" Marcus had the Ambassador ask the ship's Tuatha. Albus put his head into the tree's cunnis, and turned to look up to Marcus and Agricola as he provided the Tuatha response.

"No, they do not fight back. Finding them in all of this clutter of objects can take a great many years, and expend valuable fuel-rods, but ultimately the Tuathii warships find them and close with them. They then destroy them by flying through them. Something about how the enemy puller-ships operate when tugging the large objects makes their protective Equanimity Field inoperative, and as a result they disappear into Equanimity when the Tuathii warship's field encounters the unprotected material that comprises the enemy puller-ship."

"But why do the Tuathii destroy them immediately rather than investigate further?" Agricola demanded.

Ambassador Albus thought-asked the Tuatha, and then replied on its behalf: "The Tuatha response was: 'Investigate? There is nothing to investigate. They are in the process of doing the little-me's on the planet harm. If they are not destroyed, they will send more comets to strike the planeta.'"

Agricola and Cerialis gave orders, which the Octopodii crew of the colonist-ship struggled to understand. With help from Marcus Avitus and a few immunes from the Second who suggested ways to activate and to steer-focus the energy field using the viewing pot, one of the Octopoda eventually succeeded in activating an energy field and closing it around the tiny alien vessel without destroying it.

The nearby comet, however, burst into a golden cloud, with the remnants of the comet careening off wildly, after colliding with part of the energy curtain deployed around the puller-ship.

"What now?" asked Cerialis.

"Let's see what happens if we drag the alien ship with us, and have our ship land on the planeta," suggested Marcus.

"Will we be safe on the surface of the planeta?"

"For a time, I expect. But I don't plan on being there for long."

Several hours later, Agricola's ship had landed on the surface of the planeta, with the tiny alien ship coming to rest on the ground just aft of the starship.

After being reassured by the Tuatha and its Octopodii crew that the atmosphere on Planeta Bellorum was similar enough to that of Terra, the Roman officers exited the starship and set foot on another alien world.

"Too bad we are not here to colonize, or to explore. This place looks promising," said Marcus.

"We can always come back some time. Maybe you could be the governor," replied Cerialis.

After finding bearings and taking a quick look around the grassy area, they decided that there was no danger. From what the Tuatha had passed on to them, Planeta Bellorum was somewhat richer in oxygen and, with a greater mass, everything felt heavier. Kaeso Cerialis, Marcus Avitus and a group of men from the Second – along with a little-tree to help with communications – set out to examine the alien vessel.

What they found was astonishing.

There were no aliens inside.

There was a portal, smaller but similar to the exit portal from their own starship. But it was when they got inside, and their eyes adjusted to the darkened interior of the little vessel, that they were shocked to see something veryfamiliar.

"This ship is Dupli-Tri technology!" observed one of the engineers from the Second.

"How do you know that?" asked Marcus Avitus.

"Look at these markings, here, and here," he said, pointing to lettering on the side of a box on one wall.

"It looks familiar," said Marcus.

"It's the same language, the same type of lettering, as on the bridge of our ship."

While exploring the little vessel, they found more evidence of the vessel's origin. They found a power supply, smaller but identical in design to that of the Tuathii starship, with the same slots for inserting thorium fuel rods.

After looking over the spooled-wire and harpoon-like projectiles stored in strange tubes projecting from the rear of the vessel, and the tubes leading throughout the ship, they came to the conclusion that the ship was operated without any beings at the controls.

Later, back in the colonist-ship with Agricola and his senior advisors, Marcus Avitus reported his findings, and the conundrum.

"How can this be? Nobody operating the ship? How does it know what to do?"

"I have heard of this sort of thing. The Assyrians, even the Greeks, have legends of small objects that do things without being told what to do. Some people think it is magic, but the Greeks call it 'automaton', a self-operating machine," said Vibius Metellus.

"That's right. It could be a cleverly devised machine, that has some mechanical instructions that tell it how to harpoon one of those dirty snowball comets, how to drag it into the path of a planeta, and how to steer the comet for final impact on the target. Like a kind of very accurate ballista. The accuracy, to detect and to aim the projectile-comet, must make use of some sort of computational machine. Perhaps some of those systems on this starship, which the Octopoda do not understand. They seem to be doing something all the time, maybe those are also computational machines. In any event, the automatonic nature of these puller-ships seems to work exceedingly well.

"But unlike our Roman ballistae," continued Metellus, "this one can destroy an entire city, or more, I suppose. It all depends on how large the comet is."

"This would have been very useful when dealing with those pesky tribes in Caledonia," added Cerialis, "I wonder if we could use it ourselves someday..."

Two days later Agricola's colonist-starship departed orbit at Planeta Bellorum. Counting the vessels sent to Planeta Metallorum from Planeta Arborum, Agricola's colonist-ship was now just one of twelve major spacecraft now controlled by the humans.

Marcus Avitus had assigned immunes from the Second along with saplings that had been 'programmed' to convey orders from the Tuatha of Agricola's ship to inform the Octopodii and Siphonapteristii crewmembers of the other vessels that new orders had come from the Tuathii homeworld. Blindly obedient to what they believed to be genuine direction, the Tuatha, Octopodii and Siphonaperistii of the two warships were now effectively under the orders of Legatus Agricola and the Romans.

In addition to the colonist-ships and the two warships, the Romans had captured nine of the alien puller-vessels. As each of these was captured, they had been connected to small portals surrounding the aft end of the two warships. It was as if the puller-ships were designed to fit onto the warships, which, of course, they had been.

If adding the scout-ships and puller-ships attached or within each major vessel, the Romans now had a fleet of eight colonist-ships, four warships, twenty scout-ships and nine puller ships.

Looking through the viewing pot of Agricola's colonist-ship, now called the 'command ship', Centurion Tappulus said that they looked like Romulus and Remus suckling the Capitoline *Lupa*, she-wolf.

The three ships had been hovering in close proximity to each other when the Tuatha ordered the Octopoda to do something that the humans had known possible, but not seen put into practice. Using the viewing pods and presumably assisted by the computational machines arrayed on the walls of the bridge, the

Octopoda had flown the command ship to a position in front of one of the warships.

And then it mated with the other starship.

Watching the operation from a secondary viewing-pot, Agricola could not believe his eyes, as both warships in turn linked with the command ship: one in front, and one to the rear.

"This will really simplify things," he said, after explaining what he had observed. "Now we can be assured that all of these ships in our little flotilla will stay together! Too bad we did not know how to do this when we sent those ships we stole from the Tuathii homeworld to Metallorum. We could have used less personnel, and increased the chances that they would all arrive safely. Something to keep in mind for the future, anyways," he said.

Agricola had no idea what the warships and puller-ships would be used for, but was certain that having them could prove useful somewhere. They seemed to be awesome weapons.

The philosophers had debated their purpose, and had settled on the premise that the war between the Dupli-Tri and the Tuathii was ongoing. They rationalized that the Dupli-Tri had sent these automated comet-pullers to the Bellorum system to thwart the settlement objectives of the thinking-trees, or perhaps just as sentries to thwart any potential rival for the virgin planeta. It could well be that there are no more Dupli-Tri out there, and these automatic defenses were put in place millennia ago, before the Tuathii destroyed the Dupli-Tri race. Alternatively, there could be more Dupli-Tri resources, even now, on their way to Bellorum.

Sensing a political opportunity, Agricola had planned a new tactic for use by the thinking-trees to eliminate the Dupli-Tri threat.

Through the ambassadors, Agricola convinced the Tuatha on each of the three ships to generate a few dozen little-trees. These were then deposited in diverse locations across the planeta, separated by great distances so as to protect them by a tactic of dispersion.

The Tuathii were unhappy that their little-selves would be out of contact from each other, and limited in terms of any hope of ever making contact with others of their kind. However, given their long lives, they were optimistic that the promise of a successful conquest of the planeta, and the reduction, if not outright removal of the Dupli-Tri threat was an made dispersion an acceptable price to pay.

As the Roman flotilla of linked starships continued on the grand tour planetary itinerary, one of the two warships was disconnected from the others. It was sent directly back to Planeta Metallorum with Tribune Gratianus from the Third of the Twentieth and a contubernium of engineers from the Second augmenting the crew.

Agricola had instructed Tribune Gratianus to master the warship's technologies and to use the warship to guard what everybody considered a tenuous Roman foothold in the cosmos, Planeta Metallorum, from the threat of Tuathii, Dupli-Tri, or any other adversary.

Gratianus's warship would arrive there in five days. This would be ten years from a planetary point of view, but from what Vibius Metellus understood, well over a century will have already passed since they all had first left Metallorum. So what the situation would be when Gratianus arrived was very uncertain, and good reason for him to be ready for anything by virtue of having mastered the warship's capabilities.

Agricola's colonist-ship and the second warship would arrive back at Metallorum some thirty years from now in planetary time, twenty years after Gratianus's arrival. The difference was due to Agricola's two ships completing a twelve-day side-trip to the final waypoint, *Planeta Caedum*, massacre planet, where the Tuathii had exterminated the dominant indigenous species.

Some of his advisors had suggested that they had gained enough intelligence on the aliens and their various planetae, and that they should return without delay to Metallorum, but Agricola had refused, saying that there was probably a great deal to be learned from whatever had taken place at Caedum.

Worried about wasting time going to yet another planeta when they had learned so much already, some of the engineers from the Second became fixated on trying to understand how it was that the Tuathii on their homeworld were able to communicate with the scout-ship. They knew it was possible when in orbit above a planeta – they had learned that much from the Octopodii while in orbit at Planeta Arborum. *But what if communications with starships was possible over a much greater distance?*

Having conceived the problem, the engineers and ambassadors set about finding the answer.

Soon enough, they sought out Agricola.

"Legatus! We have figured it out! Something the Dupli-Tri called 'tachyon transmission'. It is like an invisible light signal that goes from one starship to another, and it travels faster than light itself!" Ambassador Laurentius reported excitedly.

"Does this mean that we can send a message to Gratianus?"

"We have already begun to try. So far, no luck. He is not expecting us to try, and with the small crew he had, I doubt if he will assign an Octopoda to monitor this 'tachyon transmitter', but we have successfully sent a message to the rear warship in our flotilla. The tachyon transmitter works! And it is *easy*."

"Excellent work. Let me know the moment you succeed, in reaching Gratianus," Agricola said. He then became a bit moody, as he began to have doubts about his rush to send Tribune Gratianus to Planeta Metallorum while continuing to Planeta Caedum with the rest of his fleet. To Agricola, the twelve days of space-time was worth the risk, and the mind-boggling twenty years of planetary time lost in the process was, to his mind, so impossible to believe that he had put it off to "I'll believe it when I see it." In his mind, he still expected to find the same individuals – the old chieftain, his impressive young son Drustan and daughter Roisin, along with the Romans and Hibernians that had been left behind to complete the construction of Castra Metallorum, just as he had last seen them when they departed. He could not conceive of them already having been buried and forgotten by new generations of Metallorians.

XX

PLANETA CAEDVM
{ Massacre Planet }

By the time they arrived at the massacre planet, the humans were fully in charge of the two starships. They kept the three Tuathii content by having ambassadors continue to commune with them, providing new information to digest.

The Tuatha on the command ship, for its part, was of the opinion that the new arrangement served the Tuathii well. The humans seemed to be learning more about the Dupli-Tri technology than the Tuathii had learned in millennia, and the ship's Tuatha was taking notes, in a sense, with the hope of sharing the information with its species. It was also in contact with the Tuatha of the remaining warship, and was able to commune with itself.

The bipedal race seemed to be quite suited to exploration and to war, the Tuatha reflected. Furthermore, if it proved accurate that these bipedals were willing to share planetae with the Tuathii, and not simply kill them as the Dupli-Tri had attempted, then the expansion of thinking-trees to suitable planetae could now proceed at a more rapid, and possibly uninterrupted pace.

In this spirit of mutually-beneficial cooperation, the Tuatha shared more information with the humans than it had previously done. It no longer refused to share thoughts on subjects that would have been taboo in the past, when the Tuatha thought of the bipedals as slaves and not equals.

So when a human ambassador had communed, asking for a full account of what had taken place on massacre planet, the Tuatha had obliged.

The war on Planeta Caedum had been necessary, according to the Tuathii, because the Quadrupedii, the dominant species on the otherwise desirable planet, were insane.

How were they insane? Ambassador Albus had thought-asked.

They were destroying the complexity of their biosphere by overpopulation, predation, and making their atmosphere toxic to life.

So what is wrong about that?

It is wrong to reduce biological complexity.

Why? thought-asked Albus.

Because it reduced the Timeconsciousness of the biosphere.

Ambassador Albus later explained to Agricola and the officers that the Tuathii had developed a philosophy they called "Timeconsciousness," which correlates with their understanding of the energy that makes up all things, and all the non-things of the universe, the very same Equanimity that can be found between Nesslessness and Thing.

"What?" -asked Cerials, who had not been privy to the Philosopher Metellus's previous attempt to explain the Tuathii philosophical perspective.

Not schooled in rhetoric, logic or philosophy, the metaphysical and nouminal, aspect of the Tuathii philosophy was lost on Kaeso Cerialis, but when it was carefully explained to him by Ambassador Albus and Vibius Metellus, he was finally able to grasp the Tuathii concept of the meaning of life.

To the Tuathii, the meaning of life is *to become more complex,* to be more able to perceive and consider the universe in which it exists; to experience and to reflect upon it. To degrade the ecosystem which makes complex beings possible, to destroy the conditions needed for long-lived, complex biological life, runs contrary to the meaning of life and is therefore wrong, evil, insane, and to be opposed. The Tuathii did not see themselves as custodians or owners of the planetae, but rather, as protectors of the life on the planetae. As such, rather than ruling the planetae, they saw themselves as being facilitators of productive interaction between the beings on the planetae, but also as the most suited to take action when action had to be taken, based on the ethical underpinnings of their Timeconsciousness philosophy.

And this is where the Quadrupedii had gone wrong. They had, over the last centuries, created machines and devices which provided them short-term benefits at the cost of long-term consequences. These machines, used to transport them about their planet or to make them comfortable in their homes, and to provide them with distractions which the humans could not understand, were akin to having a fire-pit in a small cave. A very small fire could make little smoke, and have no great effect on the air in the cave. But if there are too many such fires in the confined air of a cave, or if too many wet leaves are thrown on the fire, then the air in the cave becomes choking.

At least, that's the best analogy Ambassador Albus could conjure from the mental images the Tuatha had conveyed. The Quadrupedii had made too much smoke, and changed the atmosphere of their planet. However, it had taken centuries to become noticeable. And in this time, with the help of their machines and other polluting technologies, the Quadrupedii had succeeded in defying the laws of nature.

The fundamental law they had defied was that of equilibrium.

To the Romans, most of whom were from farming backgrounds, the notion of balance in nature was very familiar.

They understood the idea that clean water, clean air, fertile soil, and diversity in nature were fundamentally good. The Romans placed value on a robust, lively hinterland outside of a city, from which the residents could hunt for food, gather fuel, and forage for flora and fauna. This natural resource was fundamental to the well-being of a village or a city.

But if that hinterland is depleted faster than it can regenerate, then something is out of balance. In the end, nature does not like things to be out of balance, and restores the balance by killing off the offending species.

What the Tuathii were most upset about was that the Quadrupedii were so far out of balance, and had so much technological power, that they were beyond the ability of natural forces to counter.

According to their assessment of the trends on Planeta Caedum, the Tuathii had determined that the lesser life forms – the animals, plants, insects, and even types of microbes and bacteria – were all under severe pressure. They were becoming extinct at an accelerating rate.

But what was most disturbing to the Tuathii was learning through a communion with a Quadrupedii captive about the increasingly grotesque diet of the Quadrupedii.

The captive had thought about how the Quadrupedii had once loved to eat small, wet, frog-like creatures along with the grasses and herbs that provided the roughage in their diet.

It was the inclusion of protein in the diet of these former herbivores, millennia before, that had led to their enlarged brains and other evolutionary changes which had made them the dominant species on their planet.

An immune from the second had made a sketch of what the Quadrupedii looked like, from images conveyed by the Tuatha. To the Romans, the Quadrupedii looked much like bovae, cattle, only with very short necks and most of their weight concentrated over their hind-legs. This allowed them to stand upright when desired, so that they could use their smaller, more agile front legs as arms. As their diet improved over the eons, their brains grew larger and more capable, until they became the dominant species. After that, there was no stopping them.

When their population had grown so far beyond that which could be sustained by the normal state of affairs, when the food-pyramid had become so inverted that there was no longer a sufficient base in terms of biodiversity and basic genetic stock, the food-preparation industries of the Quadrupedii began to process dead Quadrupeda corpses into ersatz 'chunks' of simulated frog-meat. They peddled this grotesque creation to the underclasses of the Quadrupedii society without disclosing the truth about the ingredients. For the wealthy, most entitled upper-class of Quadrupedii, there were still genuine, albeit factory-reared, frogs to eat.

From the Tuathii perspective, when a race had become so dominant and numerous as to endanger their atmosphere and all other life forms on a planet to the extent that they became cannibalistic, it was clear that they, the Quadrupedii, were not competent stewards of their planet.

After futile attempts to negotiate with the Quadrupedii, who refused to accept rational arguments or even the notion that what they were doing was worse than suicidal, the Tuathii had given up on the insane Quadrupedii species. But they had not given up on their planeta.

They had given it a great deal of thought in the sixty years it took to send word back to the Tuathii homeworld and to receive the reply – and the resources required arrived in orbit above Planeta Caedum.

The Quadrupedii species is to be exterminated, as a final solution, had been the direction from Planeta Arborum.

Not having a suitable biological weapon to use, as they had in their destruction of the Dupli-Tri of Planeta Scientiae, the Tuathii had chosen to use the only two weapons they had mastered from the Dupli-Tri technology.

First, the Tuathii had deployed a dozen starships – comprised of a mix of colonist-ships and warships – the bulk of their captured Dupli-Tri fleet, to sweep across the planet with their energy-walls set to 'push along' anything not firmly rooted to the ground. Trees and shrubbery remained unscathed, but the Quadrupedii had been shoveled along in great, grotesque heaps of tumbling flesh.

They had died in terror, by being crushed and suffocated. Massive piles of their corpses were left to rot on the shorelines after each over-land sweep of the walls by the Tuathii starships.

The Quadrupedii had proven difficult to eradicate. Not so much because they had tried to fight back as their weapons had proven ineffective against the Nesslessness-Thing boundaries of the Equanimity Drives of the starships. Rather, because the Quadrupedii had a great many tunnels and caves in which to hide.

The overland sweeps had done the bulk of the massacre, but had also depleted the supply of thorium fuel rods, so the Tuathii proceeded to their secondary weapon. They released hordes of the brutish Siphonapteristii, imprinted as they were with the compulsion to tear any surviving Quadrupeda limb from limb, and to gorge on the hot blood of the Quadrupedii corpses.

That was two a centuries ago. The extermination of the Quadrupedii species had been successful, and their mounds of rotted corpses had been broken down by insects, weather, and time.

Ultimately, the humans came to understand that the Tuathii mission that had taken humans and fuel rods from Metallorum to Planeta Caedum had been to provide replacement fuel rods to the starships which had been stranded on the planet surface due to a shortage of thorium fuel rods.

The top Romans and Hibernians had discussed the history of Planeta Caedum, attempting to come to terms with the scale of what had happened. The Romans seemed to have a better grasp of what can happen when a city-state overgrows its environs. Usually something critical like water supplies or food production fails first, followed by a famine, crop blight, or another unfortunate crisis which tends to cull the population.

"Come to think of it", Cerialis mentioned, "the massive improvements of water and other infrastructure that the Flavian Dynasty has brought may only serve to support yet another surge in the population of Rome. We could one day see a population as large as five hundred thousand inhabitants in our glorious city!"

To the Hibernians, such numbers were incomprehensible.

"So how many Quadrupedii were alive on Planeta Caedum when the Tuathii began to massacre them?" asked Laelie.

"According to accounts, as many as sixty billion."

"I don't understand that number.

"Yes. Those numbers are difficult to comprehend. So think of it like this. If your village, Cathair mac Cassan was a handful of sand, this big," said Quintilianus, holding up his fist, "then the number thirty billion would be equivalent to this entire starship full of sand."

"And the planeta would be as full and insanely crowded as this starship that is full of sand!" Laelie said, triumphantly.

"Exactly. Impossible numbers."

"But something like that, with so many humans eating up all the animals, fruits, roots, bugs, and even blades of grass on Terra – could that ever happen?" Laelie persisted.

"Not in a thousand years. More to the point, not in two thousand years!"

"Why not? If it is true that a race can master technologies so powerful that they take control of a planet, more powerful than the gods and goddesses of nature..."

"That would be what we call an existential threat – a threat to the safety and security of the Senate and the People of Rome," said Fabius Quintilianus

"So?"

"So we have a law for that."

"A law against something that can destroy Rome? With whom, the gods?"

"Yes, in fact. We elevate one military leader, chosen from the ranks of our nobility – always a great military man – and give him absolute power over all of our military and society. He would, of course, also be well-schooled in philosophy and science, so that he can make rational, moral, decisions in addition to strategic military ones. Once he has consolidated his grip on power – as there are always those in the Senate who may not agree that a dictator is needed – the dictator then does whatever is required, however brutal, to face and defeat this existential threat."

Laelie thought of the squabbling that occurred each time the great kings of Éire met in Tara to decide who would be appointed as Grand High King. She recognized the logic behind assigning one unified commander, a dictator, to deal with an urgent crisis.

"So what happens when the enemy is defeated?"

"The dictator should return power to the Roman Senate and the people of Rome. He should restore the Republic," said Quintilianus.

"You said 'should'," observed Laelie. "Do they not always do so?"

"Not always. Sometimes they just create a new existential threat and become perpetual dictators. But that's not how it is supposed to be."

"So if Rome was faced with a crisis like too many people making the air and water toxic, like what befell the Quadrupedii, a military leader would be chosen to deal with it?"

"Yes, that is what would happen, without a doubt. Rome would never let it get so out of hand as to allow us become cannibals, let alone permit the population to grow anywhere near the billions that happened here," said Agricola, joining the familiar discussion.

"And this leader, he would be from the military and political nobility? A man such as you, Dominus?" asked Laelie, coyly.

"Sure, or like any number of other competent men. Cerialis would make a fine dictator – as long as he has philosophers like Metellus and Quintilianus to remind the emperor how to be focused on what is best for the people, and not himself. A powerful man can be good and yet also be a ruthless dictator. He draws his right to rule, and therefore the purpose of his rule, from and for the people."

"So, a benevolent dictator?" she asked.

"No, not at all benevolent. The good of the people does not always translate into what would seem good will towards them. The plebes do not always know what is good for them, just as medicine can taste awful, and yet be the required cure. And that is what makes the role of the dictator so complex. How do you decide what is better, when it may require great sacrifice and suffering of the people? To be benevolent would entail minimalizing the suffering, and ensuring that nothing unpopular is done. But that may not be what the people actually need. So it is only when power and responsibility is concentrated in the hands of a suitable leader that these difficult decisions can be made correctly.

"The trouble is when the power remains divided into the hands of a diversity of otherwise good men in a crisis, and you place a hundred such men in a room to argue about what to do – like our senate. They are soon taken with their own personal interests, greedily selling their influence to the money-lenders and fish-mongers. That is when they lose sight of the good of the people, and that is why they cannot unify to face an existential threat – hence the need for a dictator.

"And that's what happened in Rome a few decades ago – sorry, a few decades before the battle of Dublinensis, when we all met, so to speak. The city of Rome was in an economic collapse due to the fires of Nero's time and the squabbling of the Year of the Four Emperors. With the senate focused on politics and their own self-serving causes, the Roman treasury was soon pilfered.

"Without an economy, the armies that hold the empire together cannot be sustained, and that was the existential threat that was faced when the first of the Flavians, Emperor Vespasian, was elevated to dictator. After he died, his son Titus was emperor, but he died soon after. Then we had Domitian, who emasculated the senate by stripping them of their power. With power concentrated in Domitian's hands, he was able to dictate several economic reforms, and undertook infrastructure projects and other measures that turned the economy around, and got Rome functioning again.

"I imagine that soon enough he will, or perhaps already has, restored the Republic and stepped down as dictator," said Agricola, still clearly having difficulty accepting that emperor Domitian was long since dead, with almost a millennia having passed.

"What if a dictator does not step down when the threat is gone?" asked Laelie.

"Then someone who loves him must kill him. A dictator who has outlasted the crisis is no more than a tyrant. We would say *tyranni delendi sunt*, 'death to all tyrants' under our breaths at first, until some patriot of the republic that is Rome has garnered enough support in the senate, and chooses the best time to murder him," said Agricola, with the two philosophers nodding in agreement.

"You said someone who loves him would murder him. What does that mean?"

"We love our emperors, even our dictators, but we are obliged by Roman law and tradition to kill our tyrants. The man we kill is the man we loved, and any good dictator worth his salt would agree that being assassinated by a friend would be far more noble than to hang on for years and years to rule as a hated tyrant," said Agricola, with a look that told Laelie that he was serious.

"So this has happened before?"

"Oh yes. Several times. The best example was set several hundred years ago, when the Republic of Rome was still in its early stages. At that time there were many competing tribes, each vying for some of the same territories. One of these was the ancient people, the Aequi, who lived in the hills above and to the east of Rome. Wanting to push the first Romans back into the sea from which they had come – if legend has it right, we Romans came ashore as descendants from the survivors of the destruction of Troy. Unhappy about the expanding young Roman colony, the Aequi and their allies the Volsci repeatedly attacked Rome. To make matters worse, at that time there were conflicts between the patricians – the ruling class – and the plebians – the lower class of ordinary citizens, and even a slave revolt. So Rome was particularly vulnerable. After a short-lived truce between the Aequi and Rome, the Aequi attacked in cooperation with another enemy, the Sabines, who attacked Rome from the northern hills. Rome raised two armies, one to fight the Aequi force at their camp, the other to invade the Aequi territory. But the Romans had deployed in haste and were poorly led, and one of these armies wound up surrounded by enemies and was on the verge of annihilation.

"A recently disgraced former consul, Lucius Quinctius Cincinnatus, was brought back to the Forum in Rome and declared dictator for a six month term. His duty was to stave off the existential threat to Rome, and all power and authority was concentrated in him. That is the purpose of a dictator.

"Cincinnatus immediately decreed that all able-bodied Roman men of fighting age were to assemble with five days' worth of food and twelve *vali*, long spear-poles. This was unusual, because

Roman soldiers normally only carried one such pole. He then led his new army to the besieged Romans at Aldigus Mons, and had them use the vali spears to encircle the Aequi. The second Roman force then arrived and confronted the Aequi from their rear.

"The Aequi were defeated, however their surviving soldiers were spared, and permitted to return to their territory, except for their leaders, who were imprisoned in Rome.

"With the crisis having been averted by his prompt and creative military leadership, Cincinnatus no longer had a legitimate need for the absolute power that had been bestowed in him. After enjoying a Roman triumph, he publicly celebrated his great victory, wearing the traditional laurel crown, all-purple *toga picta*, painted toga, with golden embroidery. Then, he immediately retired as dictator after only sixteen days, and returned to his modest farm.

"Cincinnatus is a testament to virtue, military leadership and service to the people of Rome. That is how a great military leader must be, if ever called upon to be a dictator. He must not allow personal ambition or other self-serving rationalizations to swell his head to become *dictator in perpetuum*, perpetual dictator – like a king.

"A perpetual dictator would be the same as a king. And that, my dear queen, would be to have crossed over to something that does not serve the idea that is Rome. At that point, the tyrant has lost all moral authority and is therefore an outlaw and must be killed."

Imagining her Roman husband as a dictator, ultimately to be murdered by a friend, made Laelie afraid. "But that sounds so brutal, for a king to be assassinated by those who love him."

"King? We despise the idea of beign ruled by a king. We are a republic! Any emperor who thinks he has a divine right to rule is sadly mistaken. Power comes only from the citizenry, the people that the elites are responsible for, as stewards of the republic. If you lose sight of that, you are no longer fit to hold power, whether as a senator, a dictator, or in any position of trust," said Agricola.

"So if you are an emperor one day, and refuse to give it up when there is no threat, should I kill you?"

"If you love me, my dear, you will. But I will never be emperor. I serve the current emperor, or the senate, depending on the situation when we get there."

"Are we really going home, to Terra?"

"Yes, Laelie, we are going home. Home to Terra. Home to Rome." Agricola spoke in such a definitive tone that everybody understood that the legatus had decided that they had learned enough from their grand tour of the Tuathii planetae. It was time to take stock of what they had learned, and move on.

The Tuathii had taken a deep, primordial offense at the damage the Quadrupedii species had done to their biosphere, and had passed verdict on their right to existence. The sentence had been death. What had motivated the Tuathii to take such drastic action on Planeta Caedum, which the Roman philosophers had termed 'deep ecology', and the fact that the planet had begun to rejuvenate after being liberated from the abuses it had suffered at the hands of the insane species, spoke volumes about how deeply-seated their hatred for toxins – or their love for biodiversity – truly was. It was also stark testament to the brutal efficiency with which the Tuathii could act be if they decided to extinguish an entire species.

The threat that the Tuathii ultimately posed to the human race, should humanity ever wind up on the wrong side of the Tuathii calculus, was taken seriously. Yet, it also appeared that the Tuathii were open to rational negotiation. So after exhausting his curiosity about the conditions on the savaged planeta, Agricola decided to make a gesture.

He approached Marcus Avitus on the bridge, where he was working with some immunes from the Second, theorizing alternative ways to operate the starships, with humans performing specified functions, following verbal commands from a centralized director, the 'starship captain'.

"Tribune Avitus?"

"Legatus!"

"Do we have enough fuel rods to restore all of the dormant ships here on Planeta Caedum?"

"Sadly, no, Legatus. But we can equip a few, depending on the size."

"I guess that's why the Tuathii, and even the Dupli-Tri, placed such a high value on the thorium mine at Metallorum. With all of the time lost between voyages, who knows when their next ship – of either race – will arrive. We must choose with care."

"Yes, Legatus. I recommend we go with a warship and another colonist ship, rather than two colonist ships. Taking the remaining warship would be smart, as it would be like taking the claws off the tiger."

Thinking of a clawless tiger, Agricola was momentarily transported back to Rome. To the Flavian Amphitheatre, and the spectacle of ten poorly-armed slaves forced to face three very angry *leones europae*, European Lions.

On the verge of extinction even when Agricola was a boy, the nobility and power of leones europae had impressed young Agricola so much that from his first sight of a leo, the animal had been his personal talisman. He likened his love for lions to the love that Gaius Julius Caesar had for elephants. In fact, Agricola always carried a few well-worn denarius, silver coins, minted to commemorate Caesar's Gallic campaign. As his thoughts wandered over the vastness of time and space to the Terra he once knew, he rubbed one of the coins, his fingers feeling the shape of the elephant and the name 'CAESAR' on the coin's *exurgue*, the lower curve of the back of the coin. He could feel the roughness of the *cululus*, ritual cup, on the coin's face. *If I ever mint a coin, it shall have a lion on one side*, Agricola dreamed.

And then he had a terrible thought: *what if there are no more leones? What if they too have gone from the world? Would it be because of our hunting them? Our sport with them? Are we so foolish, as the Quadrupedii, as to give up such magnificent beasts as the leo, the giraffe and the elephantus? – surely not! If we are, then we do not deserve to live!*

Unable to shake the horrible thought from his mind, that perhaps mankind had also gone so far down the path of predation as to render the planet nearly uninhabitable, Agricola was inspired to find out.

Agricola thought about it for few moments longer, standing as rigidly as a statue and drawing a few strange glances. Then suddenly he snapped out of his reverie and ordered his two philosophers and his second in command to accompany him to his pod, where he could consult with them in private.

After laying out his thoughts, the other three men thought about it for some time before commenting.

"I agree, it is time. But your plan for Marcus Avitus, that has a great deal of risk," said Cerialis.

Before Agricola could reply, Fabius Quintilianus interrupted.

"But think of the intelligence value! Marcus would be there for years before we arrived. Who better than him to infiltrate their ranks, to determine their power structures and politics?"

"True, Fabius, but what if he is captured and taken to Rome? Would the emperor believe him?"

"Kaeso, after all the years that have passed, we cannot even be sure there is an emperor," said Vibius Metellus, in agreement with Fabius Quintilianus for a change.

"You must be joking. The Republic of Rome, whether in the hands of the senate, a dictator, or an emperor - Rome is superior to any other form of governance. We have the economic might, the technology, the mastery of warfare to overcome any adversary."

"Kaeso, your pride in Rome is commendable, but how do you think Rome would measure up against the technology we have come across in our odyssey through the stars?"

"Not well at all, Legatus. But thankfully, we now have this power. But I take your point. Another power on Terra could conceivably have developed technology that gave them an edge over Rome, but I doubt it. I expect that when we return we will find that the entire planeta is under Roman rule."

"And if it is not?" asked Agricola.

"Then we will…" started Kaeso Cerialis. "I see your point, Julius. In that case we will need intelligence on all the players. We need Marcus to go, as you say, directly. But alone? What of his woman?"

"This brings up an uncomfortable point. We have become a little too soft with our Hibernian wives. Now, as we contemplate our return to Terra, we must think as Romans and not as husbands. Marcus shall go alone, or perhaps with one other man, but they shall not have the distractions of their women."

A somber mood came over the men, knowing how deeply Marcus Avitus loved his Hibernian wife, whom he called his Celtic princess, Laelie's young cousin, Princess Neasa. Rumor had it, moreover, that Neasa was with child, as she had ceased her mēnstruālis, her menstrual cycle. And given that nobody, not the Romans nor the Celts, had found a local source of *silphium*, the medicinal plant used as a contraception, a great many of the women had become pregnant. Horatia Avita Neasa had merely been the first to show signs of it.

"If we do send a second, who shall it be?" asked Agricola.

"Well, it should be someone from the Second. We know that Marcus is suited to unravelling power politics, and has excellent judgment. Why don't we ask him to choose a second?"

"Perhaps that would be wise, Vibius, but what would be his focus?"

"Military technology, strategy, and the disposition of forces, perhaps?" suggested Cerialis, always focused on tactics.

Two hours later, Marcus had been given his task. He chose Immune Lucius Antoninus Commodus from the Eighth of the Second as his companion, and fully agreed that the women could not accompany them on their mission. For Marcus, the painful thought of parting from Neasa, and his sympathy for Antoninus having to part from Niamh, the woman who once jabbed an stick into his eye, was a heavy price to be extracted from the men. But Marcus knew that they were the two most suited for the task.

Marcus also understood that it also meant that he would not see the child that Neasa was carrying in her belly, and would most likely never see her again. The mission was fraught with danger and unknowns, perfect for an inquisitive and courageous young man.

After reviewing the navigational and mission details with an Octopoda, assisted by a sapling, they discussed their mission with a few of the men from the Second. Marcus and Antoninus verified that they clearly understood how to navigate and pilot their scout-ship for their journey back to Terra. They presented their conclusions to Agricola and Cerialis, and together went over the mission plan one last time. When they had finished, they both thought of their little potted sapling, who had acted as such a vital intermediary in their communications with the Octopodii, as the most valuable little tree that had ever been. Perhaps they could have operated their starship without the thinking-tree to back them up, particularly on the celestial navigation, but having the little rosebud tree with them gave them a small boost of confidence. Perhaps even trust.

"So we leave now, and go directly to Terra. The rest of you travel via Planeta Metallorum. When you arrive at Metallorum fifteen days hence, it will be some thirty years later from their point of view, and some one hundred and fifty years since we all left there, what, a month and a half ago?" Marcus began.

"That sounds correct to me. Tribune Gratianus should have arrived there ten years earlier, from their point of view on Metallorum. Unfortunately, we have been unable to establish contact with him on the tachyon device," replied Cerialis.

"Do you suppose he found trouble? Perhaps from the Tuathii or some surviving Dupli-Tri?"

"I doubt it, Legatus. More likely he is busy, and we had not planned a specific time at which to monitor the device. He only has a small crew on that big, empty warship."

"Do you suppose we can establish some sort of plan, as to when to try to communicate with you, Marcus?"

"I don't see how. A day on Metallorum, or here, is quite different from a day on Terra. How would we know?"

"Well, we have the luxury of having lots of people. We can listen, or try to contact you, continuously, from our ship."

Perking up, Marcus understood how it could work. "So then, all Antoninus and I have to do is check in on the scout-ship from time to time, and attempt to operate the tachyon device?"

"Yes. You could do it as often as you like."

Perturbed for a moment, Marcus thought better of it. "No, that would risk wasting thorium fuel. No. Far better that Antoninus and I plan to do it only once in a long time, perhaps once every year?"

"That seems reasonable. You would conserve fuel and also be free to be away from the scout-ship – leave it buried, perhaps," suggested Cerialis.

"Agreed. So you will attempt to communicate – or to hear our more frequent attempts, for one day every year?"

"Yes, Legatus. Now the only question, Antoninus, is what day?"

"How about on Parilia?" suggested Cerialis.

"That, my dear friend, is perfect!" replied Marcus, knowing full well that April 21st, the day of the festival to honor Pila – the god of sheep and shepherds and the best day for a reunion – was the most auspicious day they could have chosen.

As the men now seemed excited to begin their adventure, the philosopher Vibius Metellus shook his head in amazement: "It kind of makes your head spin, to look at things in this way, with compressed time for us as we travel in space, and expanded time for those we left behind."

"Yes. And if everything goes according to plan, and you depart for Terra a few weeks after you arrive on Metallorum, you will reach Terra nearly fifty years after Antoninus and I arrive, correct?"

"Yes. I have gone over it several times with the Octopoda and the Tuatha, and they are certain that is accurate," said Metellus.

"But something does not add up here. It will take Antoninus and I thirty days to reach Terra from here, and twenty eight days for you to reach Terra from Metallorum? Yet it takes you thirteen days to get there from here, whereas I bypass it altogether in just two days?" Marcus asked, confused by the math. "Is the effect of time-squeezing constant when we travel, or does it vary depending on the route taken?"

After consulting with the lumpy-headed Octopoda who knew the ship's navigation system best, and with the insights of the ship's Tuatha, Vibius Metellus came to a new understanding of space-time.

"It varies with your distance from large things, like stars and planetae. So on your direct path to Terra, you will spend more time at a greater distance from things, more time in the Nesslessness. Whereas on our much shorter journey to Metallorum, we will be spending more of our time near material things than you will. We will not reach the same velocity as you will, and we will cover less total distance in the same number of starship days than you will," offered Quintilianus.

"I am not sure I completely understand this, but I will trust that you and the Octopoda do. Just to be sure, Fabius, I will hold you to your forty-eight year estimate. For every month you are late, you owe me one gold aureus!" joked Marcus Avitus.

An hour later, after tearful goodbyes to their women and closest friends, Marcus and Antoninus exited their scout-ship from the storage-bay at the end of the command starship and began their voyage to Terra.

As Antoninus watched Planeta Caedum recede in the viewing pot of the scout-ship, Marcus sat on the uncomfortable three-lumped stool. The lumpy chair may have been quite comfortable for a Dupli-Tri, but even with the quilted pillow provided by Princess Neasa, it was about as comfortable as a post. Looking down on the fragile-looking sapling tied carefully to a table-leg, Marcus was deep in thought, calculating how many years would have passed since he last set foot on Terra.

We Romans and Neasa's Hibernians were abducted in the year of the consulship of Domitianus and Sabinus, the second year of the reign of Emperor Domitian. But maybe it would be easier if I think of it as year 834 ab urbe condita, AUC, since the foundation of the Republic of Rome...

Antoninus and I will arrive one thousand eight hundred and ninety one years after we left. Agricola and the rest of Legio XXVII will arrive one thousand nine hundred and thirty two years after we all left. Excrementum!, I will be forty eight years older, while Neasa will have aged but a few months! And if they are delayed, or take any additional side-trips, I may be a very aged man indeed. Marcus thought.

If they are late, Antoninus and I should do some side-trips of our own, to keep our bodies from aging too much, Centurion Marcus Horatius Avitus decided. *Better to expend some of the precious thorium fuel than die of old age.*

XXI

ITER AD PATRIAM
{ Journey Home }

Legatus Legionus Agricola had seen the men going through their battle preparations, attending to their personal armor and weapons just as they had before that fateful day at Dubh Linn. With the action still many days ahead, he knew that it was premature, but he thought it best to let the men focus on their military craft, to revive their fighting skills. It would be good for morale.

Morale was very low for two of their people, however, and it caused Agricola considerable grief. There was not much he could do, so he left it to Laelie to console the Hibernian wives of Marcus Avitus and Antoninus Commodus, whose men had been sent ahead of the main force.

In the thirteen day journey to Planeta Metallorum, Agricola and his commanders reviewed their battle plans. Lacking any means to know of the current state of affairs on Metallorum, they had to make some assumptions critical to planning.

Their first assumption was that the Roman garrison at Castra Metallorum was intact, and would be loyal to the legatus when he returned. This assumption provoked some debate between the two philosophers, who cautioned that Tribunus Cyprianus Cassius, who had been left in command, could have grown too accustomed to his role as the local commander. That, and given their estimate that the population of Castra Metallorum would have grown to perhaps ten thousand, Tribunus Cassius may have elevated himself to *Legatus Augusti Pro Praetore Planeta Metalloricus*, governor of the planeta Metallorum.

"Well, if that's true," said Cerialis, the ruthlessly efficient commander, "we will treat him as your father treated the traitor,

Legatus Roscius Celius when he mutinied against Legatus Augusti Pro Praetore Britannicus, Marcus Vettius Bolanus."

"Absolutely. We will do as my father did, send in the army and restore discipline. Interesting example you chose, Kaeso Cerialis. After all, that is the event which saw your father elevated to replace Bolanus as Governor, is it not?"

"True, but that still left *your* father as the overall commander, continuing on to heroic victories across Britannia."

"Enough of this reminiscing, Kaeso. Let's get back to the here and now."

"Legatus. Well, as for the prospects of betrayal by Cyprianus Cassius, as unlikely as I see it, we certainly have the high ground. If Cassius is no longer loyal when we arrive, we could simply use the viewing pots to track down him down, and then trap him with an energy wall. We would no doubt make an example of him, and anyone who helped him. I suppose we would also want to reward any who opposed his theoretical treachery."

"Sounds like a good plan. What else do we need to think about?" asked Agricola.

"What if the ancient Hibernians are the problem? Suppose the tribal leader of the day is in charge?" asked Vibius Metellus.

"Do you really think that is possible?"

"Just for the sake of argument, Kaeso," said Metellus.

"Well then, we might use more lethal weapons. What is essential is to salvage as much of the Roman population, especially those trained as soldiers or with skills we need. As for the Hibernians, I am less concerned."

"Would you have said that if your Hibernian wife were present?" asked Metellus, only partly in jest.

"Certainly. But yes, I might have chosen my words more carefully. But don't you agree, we must preserve our Roman nature, the fighting power of the Twenty-Seventh Legion? After all, we won't be able to take everyone with us to Terra."

"And what of any other possibilities?" asked Quintilianus.

"Such as, what if Tuathii, Dupli-Tri or some other alien race has taken over?" asked Cerialis.

"We must consider all of the possibilities."

"Well, I suppose we could take a chapter out of the war book of the Tuathii. We approach the Metallorum star-system cautiously, from the outer reaches first, and peer through the viewing pot to assess the situation on Metallorum. After that, we reassess our strategy, and move in closer. It's unfortunate we do not have the ability to communicate at great distances."

"On that point, are you certain that we do not have this capability?" asked Agricola.

"That is a good question. There are many aspects of the Dupli-Tri technology that we still do not understand. I'll put the question to the Tuatha, and also have some of my men from the Seventh of the Second explore that. After all, if we can communicate from a ship in orbit to a ship on the surface of a planet, it stands to reason that there is some means to communicate from one ship in space to another ship in space."

"Good, Aulus. Inform us of what you learn."

Five days later, Centurion Tappulus rushed into the open portal of the Agricola pod, interrupting a meeting between Agricola, several of the Hibernian captains and Queen Laelie.

"Legatus! We have succeeded! We reached another starship with the tachyon transmitter!" Tappulus reported excitedly.

"So who have you been able to contact with this 'tachyon transmission?' – Gratianus?"

"We received an automaton reply from the scout ship of Marcus Avitus and Antoninus Commodus, and we actually got a reply from the Octopoda onboard the warship we sent from Planeta Caedum!"

"Contact with Marcus and also with Gratianus? Impressive. Well done, Aulus! But explain further. What did you learn? What do you mean by an 'automaton reply' from Marcus Avitus?"

"Legatus, his scout-ship sent some sort of automatic reply in response to our attempt to contact them. But either Marcus and Antoninus do not understand how to operate the communications system well enough, or for some other reason they could not reply. But the Octopodii on our ship say that the signal does confirm that Marcus and Antoninus's ship is still existent, still operational!"

"Yes, that is good news. And what of the warship at Planeta Metallorum?"

"The Octopoda there said that they will pass our greetings on to Tribune Gratianus, and then send his reply shortly! Come to the bridge, Legatus, and you may be in time to speak to him directly. Well, almost directly. There is a long pause of several minutes between communications. From what we can tell, this is due to the great distances involved, and something about contrasting-relativity effects, but we can't figure out what that means, that was the term the Octopodii say was used by the Dupli-Tri."

As Agricola and a few others proceeded to the bridge with Centurion Tappulus, Agricola asked: "Who figured it out? And how are you able to learn what the Dupli-Tri said about this tachyon transmission device?"

"Some of the boys from the Second have made great strides in learning the Dupli-Tri language. Something about there being only forty-eight symbols in their language. Twelve of them are numbers. One of them is a strange number that the boys from the second call 'zero', *nullus*, or 'the number that means that you have none'. Then they have thirty-six symbols for sounds that make up their spoken and written language. By communing with the Tuatha and the Octopodii to explore the sounds, they think that they have figured out the sounds that go with the symbols, and the basic syntax of the Dupli-Tri language. Certainly it has opened a lot of doors to understanding their technology. You should go down to their working pods, where their scribes are busily writing it all out for others to study," said Tappulus.

They had reached the bridge just in time. Agricola saw that one of the technicians from the Second had the communications garland on his head, and was also linked-in through a little-tree to the Octopoda at the communications workstation. Rather than interrupt, he simply nodded at the immune to continue, and watched with great anticipation.

As he waited, he thought about how helpful this wonderful tachyon transmission communications system would be for the Roman Empire. Not only would it be fast, but it eliminated the risk that the tabellarius, courier, could be intercepted or interfered with in some way.

He was certain that the Emperor would be happy to hear of this, in addition to all of the other military technologies that Agricola now had at his disposal.

"Legatus, we have word from Tribune Gratianus. His warship is in orbit at Metallorum, on sentry duty as per your original orders. Gratianus reports that the scout ship with Centurion Tappulus, transporting Lady Avitus and Genovefa, arrived unexpectedly ten years ago!"

"Ten years? But we were only delayed on Caedum by a few days. How can that result in a ten year difference? And what of Neasa? How is she? Did her unborn child live?" Agricola asked, confused.

"She is well, Legatus. And she bore a son. As for how this happened, the ten years, Gratianus does not know. He had not expected to see us until now, so when the scout-ship suddenly arrived, and landed near Castra Metallorum, he was concerned that some terrible fate had come to our starships.

"When he learned that you had sent Neasa Avitus ahead, under the care of Genovefa and Aulus Tappulus, and that otherwise all was well, he was greatly relieved.

"As for the miscalculation, I am not sure. It may have to do with the fact that we had begun to accelerate from Caedum when you decided to go back and collect more alien devices. By sending the scout ship ahead, as we did, we then had to decelerate for half a day, and then travel back to Caedum. So while it seemed like two days, that was starship time, not planetary time. By the time we were finally accelerating away from Caedum, The Tappulus's and Neasa Avitus were well ahead, I guess," theorized Vibius Metellus.

"That makes sense, Vibius. We should have thought about that. So now, what, Marcus Avitus's child, a son by the sound of it, is ten years old? We must ensure that this is passed to him the next time we have contact with his scout-ship," said Agricola. "What else did Gratianus say?"

"He reports that the commander at Castra Metallorum is being called 'Legatus Augusti Pro Praetore Metallorianus'. He is the descendant of Tribunus Cyprianus Cassius, who we left in command some thirteen days ago from our point of view, one hundred and fifty years ago on the planet itself."

"He has elevated himself to governor?" asked Agricola.

"No, Legatus. This Legatus Cassius reports that the population on Planeta Metallorum grew faster than expected, as there have been no wars, major illness, or famine. There are now twenty thousand of our people, all living in no fewer than seven new Roman settlements spread amongst the valleys around the seven hills that surround Castra Metallorum."

"Seven hills? Just like Rome. How fitting. And?"

"And with over six thousand active military personnel and an entire planet to administer, the Metallorian Senate had elevated the previous Legatus to Governor. And there is more..."

"What more?"

"They refer to you as emperor."

"All hail Emperor Julius Agricola!" shouted the other Romans on the bridge, eagerly embracing the notion that their beloved legatus was now the Emperor of Rome. Or at least, of the Roman forces other than those on Planeta Terra.

Emperor Agricola left the bridge in stunned silence. On his heels, Cerialis and the other advisors were very pleased with the news. Not only had the warships and the other colonist-ships captured during the grand tour arrived at Metallorum, but the Roman camp at Castra Metallorum had succeeded, even prospered.

An entire legion now awaited their emperor, and were clearly loyal to him.

As they left the bridge, Cerialis remained just long enough to pause at the communications table to send orders back to Tribune Gratianus in the warship orbiting above Metallorum.

"Send the following message: 'We arrive in three days, planetary time. We will land at the hilltop east of Castra Metallorum. Greet the emperor with a full Roman Triumphal Procession through the streets of Castra Metallorum. Also prepare a suitable facility to serve as *Pantheon*, for we have a great many treasures and war booty to display to the people. And one more thing: ensure that the people of Metallorum refer to Emperor Agricola as *dominus et deus*," he concluded, nodding at the communications officer – a human who had mastered the Octopoda's job – that of sending messages from one ship to another.

Cerialis, having given the orders, received a wink from Metellus and a wide grin from the other philosopher.

The emperor would simply have to accept what everybody else knew to be the right thing to do. *Agricola's destiny is in the hands of his people, after all, not his own.*

After a short time in orbit to practice arrival procedures and to carefully navigate the command starship to the landing field on the hilltop east of Castra Metallorum, Cerialis watched through a viewing pot on the bridge as the reception formation took up their positions to greet him upon his arrival.

Tribune Gratianus had done well, having formed up Legio XXVII, from smartly dressed lines of legionaries at the front, to what was clearly the centuries of the First Cohort, and through the formation to the auxiliary, cavalry, and other special-use formations in the rear.

Kaeso was particularly pleased to see an entire cohort-sized formation, if you could call it that, of Celtic warriors dressed in their traditional, coarse slips with bright green sash, and traditional weapons fashioned from bone, stone, and wood.

Good, the Hibernians have retained some of their proud culture, he thought to himself. *My Lady Achal and Queen Laelie will be pleased!*

Kaeso had been given a full account of the reception details through tachyon transmission in the final hours before arrival, and had approved the plans. But that had put him into an awkward position. Lying to his friend was out of the question, however holding out some portions of the arrangements was a necessary and loyal act, he believed, as he was acting out of one of the most honorable Roman traditions of putting on a great spectacle for the emperor, and that required a degree of surprise.

He had, of course, fully briefed Agricola on the problem of the Allanites. After convening his closest military advisors, Agricola had issued his decree and Cerialis had converted that into specific orders, which were passed in great secrecy to the tribunes and, via tachyon transmission, to Tribune Gratianus on the ground.

The military details tended to, Kaeso then had his accomplice Queen Laelie run interference, confining Agricola to their bed-pod so that Kaeso Cerialis could conduct other planning sessions in secret, without the knowledge of Agricola.

When he heard the clunking sound of a heavy wooden timber striking against the exterior hull of the ship, followed by the agreed upon triple-knock of metal on metal, he knew that all was in place.

As the large exit portal slid aside, the cornicen trumpeted the Imperial Triumphal Salute.

As the portal opened, rather than the grassy field that he expected to see, Agricola was surprised to see that a large wooden stage had been erected as if it were the balcony of the command ship.

He understood its purpose immediately, and proceeded in the manner expected of an emperor.

After he stepped onto the stage, the entire XXVII Legion erupted in cheers, as did the crowds of citizens behind and on both sides of the large military formation.

Agricola was speechless, and felt humbled by the outpouring of love and respect from his people. The adulation was simply intoxicating.

He knew none of them, yet he saw familiar faces. Then he realized that as descendants of the men he had left behind on Metallorum just thirteen days before in starship time – and one hundred fifty years earlier in planetary time – that their features were familiar because they came from those he had left behind. *My friends are gone, and yet, their progeny love me as they did. These are my people, and they accept me to be their emperor,* he thought.

He was still not convinced that it was suitable for him to accept the title. He doubted the philosopher's argument that it was equally likely that Rome had fallen during the thousand plus years since the Battle of Dublinensis. And if there was yet an emperor, Agricola reasoned that he would simply abdicate the title and kneel before the one and true emperor, offering his life to him.

He'll probably take my head, mused Agricola, as he watched the robed men approaching.

These must be my fellow senators, he thought. *I wonder if that round-faced one was related to Tribune Cyprianus Cassius. He would have been the highest ranking nobleman on Metallorum when we left.*

A hush came over the crowd when the elderly statesmen approached Agricola.

Even the rustling of the men and women slipping out of the starship to take up positions on the flanks of the stage had fallen silent. Everyone stood and watched in excited anticipation.

In the silence, Agricola heard some activity behind him, and realized that some of his men were hauling a large wooden throne out of the ship. Despite his initial reservations about sitting on a throne, he knew that he was required by tradition to sit regally, godlike, and look out at his people.

An old man dressed in a close approximation of a true Roman censor, the highest ranking Roman magistrate after the emperor himself, smiled as though he knew Agricola intimately. The old man then began speaking in a loud, strong voice that carried across the now silent Legion XXVII and beyond to the Seven Hills of Castra Metallorum.

"*Primus Inter Pares*, first among equals, General Quintus Julius Agricola, conqueror of the Tuathii, guardian of the Castorii, Octopodii, and Siphonaperistii, discoverer of Planeta Scientiae and Planeta Arborum; Ruler of Planeta Bellorum, Planeta Caedum, and Planeta Metallorum, and humble servant of Rome on Terra of our distant past, we, *Senātus Populusque Universitatis Romanae, SPQVR,* the Senate and People of Rome in the Cosmos, welcome you as our Emperor, *Dominus et Deus, Pontifex Maximus, and Princeps Senatus Augustus Agricola!*"

By the way the censor raised his voice at the culmination of his opening remarks and litany of titles he lavished on Agricola, and by the broad sweep of his hand towards the crowd, the legion and the people of Metallorum understood their cue. They erupted in a heartfelt wave of cheering and applause.

The tears on Agricola's face were genuine, as was the dry brick in his throat. He was momentarily frozen, unable to even move his face. But he felt the gentle touch of his wife, Queen Laelie, on his shoulder.

"Senator, you forgot one of my husband's titles," said Queen Laelie. "King of the Hibernian people!" she shouted, knowing that her people had been prepared for the return of their Queen and her husband, their Roman king.

The cheering from the Hibernians was only slightly more of an eruption than that of the Romans.

The look of appreciation that Julius Agricola gave Laelie lifted the Hibernian queen's heart. He accepted the necessity for what was taking place, and began to transform himself into the mood and disposition of an emperor.

What shall I do now? He thought to himself, but was soon helped out by the most unlikely of sources.

The annoying Hibernian Druid priest, Allanon, approached him, and then turned to face the crowd just as a Roman nobleman brought out a golden wreath. Agricola suddenly realized *That is was not Allanon! Allanon is long dead.* Agricola had been told as much after Kaeso Cerialis summarized what had been learned in the communication with Governor Gratianus. This Druid priest, nonetheless, bore an uncanny resemblance. *This must be a direct descendant of Allanon,* Agricola realized. *But not a member of the Allanite sect...This one serves as a Druid, then,* Agricola reasoned.

The Druid invoked the Hibernian gods, which to Agricola's way of thinking were just as good as Roman or Greek gods. It no longer was a great concern, given the fact that the Romans had largely come to accept the universal pantheism of the Tuathii's philosophy of Equanimity as the source for all things – and the 'nothings' – in the universe. To Agricola and most of the other originals, the ancient gods were extinct, and the traditions were now performed for cultural and social purposes, no longer a serious source of guidance.

Assisted by a Vestal Virgin, a *Septemviri Eulone,* the Roman priest blessed Agricola's laurel wreath made of solid gold from the mines of Metallorum, the philosopher Metellus whispered to Agricola from somewhere behind him. "After you are crowned, and the crowd has cheered long enough, I will look at you when it is time for you to rise and address your people, Agricola Augustus."

After the golden laurel wreath was placed on his head, and the symbolic bundle of narrow wooden arrows wrapped around an axe, the fasces – the symbol of the strength and invincibility of a unified Roman people – was placed in his hands, the moment of coronation was officially complete.

The cornicens blew out a shrill series of notes, cutting through the noise of the crowd, heralding the commencement of the reign of Emperor Agricola Augustus.

With the golden wreath now starting to feel comfortable on his head, Agricola's heart raced as the waves of cheering washed over him. *This could really go to my head,* he thought, and then decided to do something about it.

Without waiting for the nod from Metellus, he put his hands on the arms of the throne, and pressed down as he began to rise. At just that moment, Metellus spoke to the crowd, but was drowned out by the renewed cheering as Emperor Agricola strode forward to the front of the dais.

"Soldiers of the Twenty-Seventh Legion, citizens of Planeta Metallorum, people of Rome, I give you your returned, heroic Emperor, Dominus et Deus, Imperatus Quintus Julius Agricola!"

Metellus and the others nobles moved back, leaving Agricola alone at the front of the stage. His companions, the so-called 'original' Romans arriving with Agricola after their recent grand tour aboard the starship, stood around him on both flanks, making a backdrop for Agricola as he gazed with satisfaction upon the fully-formed Legio XXVII, assembled in resplendent formation before him. After momentarily looking over the silent, disciplined formation, tears streamed from Agricola's eyes. *They are splendid. I have never seen anything more beautiful,* he thought. Only then did he look past the military formation, to the men and women of what could be thought of as a new province in the Roman inter-planetary republic, standing on the grassy rise in the distance beyond.

It was a heady day in the history of Rome, and Agricola's first words did not disappoint.

"People of Rome, I am your servant!" he shouted, holding the fasces symbolically.

He had to wait several seconds for the crowd to settle enough for him to continue.

"It is with a heavy heart that I accept the honor that you have decided to bestow upon me. And I understand that this is a temporary assignment, for I understand that my task is to lead our people to a safe return to Planeta Terra, and to Rome. Once there, if we find that Rome is well and the true emperor lives, my term will come to an end. But if Rome on Earth is no more, then we will together restore Rome on Earth, and build a civilization that this galaxy of planetae and stars has never known before!"

The cheering became so intense that waves of citizens pushed forward into the ranks of the XXVII formations, who were jostled out of position. For their part, the soldiers wept at the prospect of seeing Earth and Rome in their lifetimes, after hearing legends of Earth passed on in their schooling and in the *fabula horae somni* bedtime stories of their youth. Each and every one of them felt deeply honored to be alive at such an important moment in history, to have the chance to participate in such a great adventure.

Seeing that the crowd was about to lose control and crush closer in a human stampede, and having had just about enough of their unrestrained adulation, Emperor Agricola settled them down.

"But before we can begin our adventure, we have a great deal of work to do. We must prepare our starships with provisions and fuel. We must get to know each other, so that we are as intimate as the family that we truly are, and we must make the difficult decisions as to who will remain here on Metallorum, and who will accompany the legion to Terra."

This brought a measure of serious reflection down on the crowd. It did not dampen their mood, rather, it focused their thoughts and calmed them.

"And the *iter ad patriam* is not the only mission we will undertake at this historic time." This statement brought near silence, as the gossip on Metallorum had been concentrated upon a return to Terra. Nobody knew of another mission.

"That is right, my people. We are the beating heart of Rome. But Rome – as great as the people and the idea of Rome – is merely a tiny and insignificant power in the unimaginable vastness of the universe. So it is also our task to expand our reach, to other planetae. We know of no less than six habitable planetae, and it appears that the number of habitable planetae is beyond the counting.

"We will send people to explore the nearby stars, to settle those planetae that seem most favorable, and in all of this, the vital fuel supplies of thorium ore from this planeta will be crucial. So to that end, we also have to greatly increase our production of this vital material. And to do this, we bring you great treasures we have obtained on our odyssey through the stars."

As the emperor turned to this topic, Kaeso Cerialis jumped on the opportunity and signaled for the men from the Second to begin to march out of the ship with a variety of alien artifacts and technology carried on poles by pairs of men.

The crowd stood on their toes to get a better glimpse at the strange objects, as the men proceeded to walk towards the amphitheater at Castra Metallorum. The Romans of Metallorum had modified the classical design of a Roman amphitheater to now include a covering to keep the heavy rains of the soggy planeta from interfering with their entertainment. This made for a suitable location to display the war booty just as the Pantheon housed the spoils of war brought back to the Rome of antiquity.

When Emperor Agricola saw the large wooden-wheeled cart pulled by four oxen, transporting one of the automaton-sentries, he understood that Cerialis had coordinated closely with Governor Gratianus, to have such a cart prepared for the task and quietly loaded on the back side of the ship when the triumph had just begun.

Good, we have close cooperation already between the 'originals' and the Metallorians, Agricola thought.

On cue, the soldiers and others from the command ship joined the arrival procession.

When it became clear that it was time for him to depart the stage and take his place at the head of Legio XXVII, Agricola was pleased to be presented with a magnificent horse.

The expertly crafted leather seat felt just right as he settled astride the large *equus,* horse. With Kaeso Cerialis now at his side on a slightly smaller horse – no doubt yet another detail coordinated by his efficient staff – Emperor Agricola led the triumphal parade from the hilltop towards the impressive stone gates at the greatly expanded Castra Metallorum.

After marching a few hundred *pes,* paces, past the last of the crowd, as the Twenty-Seventh Legion was cresting a rise where the well-trodden roadway forked, the legion suddenly altered course to the right.

It was no longer headed for Castra Metallorum.

For the crowd, mostly to the rear of the legion, but a great many walking along to keep pace beside the legionaries, the new destination was suddenly obvious. *They are marching on the Allanite community*, the locals realized.

In advance of the arrival of Agricola and the other 'originals' – Romans and Celts who had lived on Terra – the local population had gone to great lengths to prepare as genuine a Roman welcome for their returning, victorious emperor as they could. But with a century and a half having passed since the originals' departure from Metallorum, there had been a significant social development.

There had been the rapid rise of Allanism, the new religion that had come to exist in the decades immediately after Agricola's departure, some one hundred and fifty years prior.

At that time, Allanon, had abandoned his role as a Druid priest, and formed a new group. At first it had been no more than a ten-count of devout followers. Having rejected the Roman religion and Celtic Druidism, they listened to Allanon's accounts of Jesus Christ, and to his interpretation of what those stories really meant for them. He told them of his inspiration from the one-god, the god of Jesus Christ, and that he was speaking to them for this God.

With the Roman religious practices in disarray in the first years after settling on Metallorum — due to a lack of Roman women to carry on the sacred rites normally entrusted to them – the Roman and Celtic people of Metallorum began to re-interpret their social and religious traditions.

Some Roman traditions, such as Parilia, the festival to celebrate *dies natalis Romae,* the birthday of Rome, were maintained. A pastoral tradition consistent with the central role that farming and animal husbandry plays in Roman culture, was a good fit for the pastoral way of life that the people of Metallorum had settled into. Laboring to build their homes, expand the flock of sheep and other animals, the annual festival honoring the Roman deity Pales included animal sacrifice, meant to cleanse both sheep and shepherd. It also served to anchor the Metallorum calendar, based on a four hundred and seven day year, starting on the first day of the Metallorum spring, and *dies natalis Romae*, 21 April.

An intensely traditional people, even without the guidance of priestesses and experienced religious leaders, the Romans did their best to restore and re-create their original traditions and beliefs.

But with a new and far more accurate understanding of the nature of the cosmos, based on what they had learned in their journey *ad astra*, through the stars, the Romans found many of the spiritual beliefs of the peoples of Metallorum to be unsatisfactory.

They no longer believed, or feared, the Roman gods. And yet, they needed something around which to anchor their spirituality.

In an attempt to sustain some of the Roman traditions, Governor Cyprianus Cassius, the first leader of the seemingly abandoned inhabitants of Metallorum, had decreed that the old traditions were to be followed, but not to be understood as literal, rather, as metaphorical. He placed an emphasis on community values, rest from toil, and a great deal of good clean fun.

These early attempts to reinterpret and yet preserve their traditions were largely successful, and the Celts and Romans worked together to add some Celtic traditions to the core Roman traditions, many of which had common elements, such as the importance of certain celestial objects, constellations and other cues from the night sky. The eclipse of one Metallorian moon blotting out the other, marking the end of the harvest and the onset of the deepest days of winter, and the start of spring, were other areas of common ground for the two peoples that had blended into one nation, yet preserved their two quite different traditions.

But there were some, those who had listened to the generally unpopular Celtic Druid Allanon, who invented a new path, completely outside of the officially-sanctioned Celto-Romano traditions.

After refusing to obey the decrees of Governor Cassius, despite suffering a near fatal beating, Allanon walked away.

To Cassius, the broken Druid, walking naked and bruised out of Castra Metallorum, was a wretched sight. Cassius had intended to execute the man for his mischievous spreading of stories of Christ and other legends that contradicted the officially sanctioned – and carefully presented new Roman traditions, but had relented out of a desire not to alienate the Hibernians of Metallorum. He let Allanon live.

That had been a mistake.

Allanon's surviving the beatings, and the dignity and grace with which he had walked his own path, had elevated the man to the status of martyr.

Ten people, some Roman men and some Hibernian women, had immediately come to Allanon's aid. They had brought tools, supplies, and their skills to build a refuge for the banished spiritual guide. Soon their numbers grew, as the spiritually unfulfilled and other curious people made the trek to *Cathair Allanon*.

After only a few months, his followers had increased to the size of a small village, and many had taken up permanent residence in huts surrounding the grand roundhouse that was soon erected for their spiritual leader, their spokesperson for the one god.

These people, the Allanites as they were called, were ridiculed and hated for abandoning the Roman castra. They no longer contributed to the labors in the farmland or within the thorium mine, and began to live in a manner that was destined to lead to confrontation.

They lived like free men, doing whatever they wanted, as if answerable to their God, and not to the Romans.

Nudity was the most obvious thing that set the Allanites apart from the Romans. As their messiah had made his departure from the mundane to the sublime by first surviving a brutal beating and then walking naked into the forest, so too his followers would beat each other harshly, or at least simulate such a harsh beating by repeatedly striking themselves with branches and ropes, and then go on long walks into the forest, absolutely naked, to meditate and commune with nature.

As each new member of their community went through this cleansing ritual, they would then be 'saved' by others who had gone before them, and have their wounds and other afflictions treated and the recovery of their health attended to.

They became an extremely close-knit community.

The only attempt to deal with the Allanites during Governor Cassius's time had ended badly for the Romans, when an Allanite devotee had raced, nude and armed with an Equanimity staff, into the ranks of the century of legionaries who had marched on the Allanite commune. The acolyte had taken out twenty men before a similarly armed centurion had halted the zealot's furious destruction of the conventionally armed formation.

It had taught the Romans a few lessons. First, any attempt to deal with the Allanites would result in an unacceptable loss of life. The Allanites had stolen enough of an arsenal of Tuathii weaponry, and possessed such ferocity in their willingness to defend their leader, that any attempt to destroy them could also destroy the Romans in the process.

Second, giving the Allanites the freedom to practice their religion, and to engage in trade and other interactions with this devout and hard-working community, seemed to be a more profitable and prospective approach. The Allanites had built a kiln, and had begun making bricks and pottery. In the Castra Metallorum, the Allanite pottery was in high demand, forming the basis of a trading relationship with the cultists.

Over the ensuing decades, even after their founder Allanon had passed away, the Allanite community continued to grow. Not only in their number, which kept pace with that of the Roman community in terms of birth rate, but also a much higher death rate due to infections and other illnesses brought on by their self-mutilation and other unnecessarily dangerous practices.

Over time, the two communities co-existed, despite the philosophical differences. Some Allanites returned to the Roman community, including some descendants of Allanon who rejected the social controls and self-worship within the Allanite sect, and were drawn to the Druid traditions still embraced by Celtic side of Castra Metallorum.

At the highest levels, the Romans took great offense to the fact that the Allanite leaders were found to be taking multiple wives, and that the leaders – those who descended from Allanon himself – had taken to calling themselves *divine*.

For the Romans, the Allanites contributed nothing to the mining effort. They had at first refused to work in the mines, and then were suddenly eager to do so – until they were caught red-handed stealing Equanimity Staffs. Ultimately an inventory had been taken, and it was discovered that five of the weapons were missing.

After that, and with their refusal to assist in the forestry and agricultural work, the Allanites had been banned from the interior of Castra Metallorum. However, trade was only permitted to carry on outside the Castra perimeter.

Two generations later, when the Governor of the day had confronted the Allanite leader – who went by the name *Spiritus Allanonus*, spirit of Allanon – the cult leader had claimed that he was a representative of God, and the direct descendant of *Allanonus Primigenius*, the original Allanon, and was entitled to be sustained, even served, by the those who were not enlightened.

Now, a century later, the Allanite community numbered well over a thousand inhabitants and had many supporters, secret as they were, within the numerous new Roman communities, largely centered on the Seven Hills of Planeta Metallorum and the capital city, Castra Metallorum.

With the rapid birth rate, these small Roman communities grew quickly, becoming thriving communities in their own right.

All of this had been communicated to Agricola and Cerialis by Tribune Gratianus, by tachyon transmission. The originals had been appalled to learn that the Roman descendants of those left behind with Governor Cassius so long ago had allowed this state of affairs to persist for so many generations.

It would be dealt with immediately upon their arrival.

The orders given by Agricola had been simple, and had been acted upon by Tribune Gratianus.

First had come the decree, from Emperor Agricola, passed out by the Censors of Metallorum. The decree informed the people that those who loved Rome were required and welcome to greet the emperor and other originals upon their arrival. Those who chose to follow the path of the Allanites and wished to live free of Roman law and Roman traditions were invited to remain at the Allanite community for that day. All citizens of the Roman community who had friends or other close ties with the Allanites were encouraged to visit the Allanites for the day, and spend that day contemplating which community they wanted to devote their lives to.

Gratianus had been instructed to do this with kindness and friendship, to ensure that people understood that whichever choice a person made, the day would be a glorious celebration, one way or the other.

Knowing the true intent of his future Emperor, Gratianus had employed his spies within the Allanite community to suggest that the Allanites should show the Romans that their traditions were the more attractive, engendering an effort within the Allanite community to out-do the Romans and their militaristic Triumphal Parade, by putting on a far more joyous festival of Allanon, to showcase their way of life.

As they began to notice the Roman legion now marching towards the wooden gates of their community, however, the Allanite high priest began to worry.

"Sound the alarm!" he shouted, when he saw that the lead century of Romans were activating their Equanimity staffs.

The response that had been raised within the Allanite security forces, however, had not been the one called for by the Allanite leader.

"They've gotten to our weapons! The fuel-pellets have been removed!" said an Allanite lieutenant. "We are defenseless!"

The blood rushed out of the high priest's head as he realized what was about to happen. For a moment, he considered fleeing, taking as many of his people with him, but he knew it was too late. He could see numbers of Romans coming into view on the far side of the valley, cutting off any escape.

He turned, and walked towards the gates, to surrender to the Romans.

No quarter was given.

Agricola had ordered Gratianus to ensure that every man, woman, and child in the Allanite community were murdered, their bodies to be Equanimitized, their temples burned to the ground, and their entire way of life to be blotted out.

However, Agricola had also ordered Gratianus to have the men of Legion XXVII use gladius, pugio, and other traditional Roman weapons as much as possible. He wanted the soldiers to face real battle, even if against an out-matched enemy, to harden the inexperienced soldiers. Other than a few skirmishes and policing duty, the legionaries of Metallorum were paper tigers. They needed to have blood on their hands.

And the blood flowed.

Those few of Gratianus's legionaries who refused to execute the women and children had been summarily executed by their centurions, with several tribunes and centurions of the original Romans interspersed among them to ensure that this was done promptly. None of the new breed of centurions, however, required prodding. They had been well-trained by Gratianus over the past year, engaging in skirmishes with each other to simulate battle – and generate some very colorful bruises in the process. Watching extremely fit and violent warriors fight, in unique combinations and with a diverse range of weapons was, as in antiquity, the most popular form of entertainment.

Later, in the privacy of their barracks, the original Romans had fanned out to visit each contubernia to seek out those who had qualms – or more serious moral concerns – with what they had done. In the case of the lead century of the First Cohort, the entire fifty-nine man group had assembled in an amphitheater, to discuss the matter with their Primus Pilus. Centurion Tappulus had joined them, to assist in the debriefing – and the attitude correction – of the men.

"But why did we have to kill them all? The women? The children?" These had been a common questions, asked by the inexperienced young men, some wracked with guilt.

"What is your name, milite?" asked Tappulus, singling out the most outspoken.

"Milite Egnatius, Praefectus Castrorum."

"I see you know your rankings. Very well, Egnatius. Were you not taught the lesson of General Sulla?"

"No, Praefectus. But I have heard that among you originals, there is a centurion named Spurius Sallustrius Crispus. Is he of the Sulla bloodline?"

"Very astute. I am sure that Primus Pilus Crispus – by all rights entitled to command this very cohort – would claim that he is the great-great-grandson of Sulla," Tappulus said, looking at the Metallorian-born Primus Pilus. While a centurion, the local-born commander of the cohort was not, in any true sense, an authentic Roman in the eyes of Centurion Tappulus. "No matter, I am sure that Emperor Agricola has more pressing duties for Spurius Sallustrius Crispus, so you can relax, Primus Pilus, Centurion Crispus is not about to take this unit from you."

"Praefectus."

"In any case, the lesson. General Lucius Cornelius Sulla Felix was a general of the Roman army and twice consul of the Senate. Just as here on Metallorum, there was something of a conflict between the two social classes. Here on Metallorum, you had only two classes: Romans and Allanites. The Romans are the legitimate authority, and the Allanites were a group of people who believed that they were entitled to an uninhibited way of life, freedom from Roman laws, obligations, and duty.

"This is similar to the conditions in Rome in the time of Sulla, there was a similar group. They were the *populares*, who challenged the patriarchal structure and traditions of Rome. Defending our traditions were the *optimates*, the good men of noble birth and status – the elites who form the ruling class. As the populares demanded more and more freedom, and the optimates struggled to preserve the traditions that made Rome great, ultimately a war, a class war, broke out. It was a civil war –

a war between fellow citizens – that was terribly damaging to the Roman cause and certainly welcomed by our enemies.

"During the civil war, the populares factions supported General Gaius Maurius while General Sulla had the support of the optimates. Both men were great generals and believed in their cause. In fact, they both believed that they were trying to save Rome, however, the civil war was killing Rome. At one point Maurius held Rome and murdered a great many of the nobles who supported Sulla. Then, when Sulla had captured Rome, he killed 1,500 supporters of Marius. And so the recriminations would have continued ad infitum, with the children and other supporters of the murdered taking vengeance on the murderers, populares against optimates.

"Sulla put an end to the civil war. How did he do this, Milite Egnatius?"

"By killing 1500 of his enemies supporters?" the milite replied, with uncertainty.

"No. that was not enough. He went on to kill anyone who had harbored the outlaws, anyone that bore close allegiance to them, and many of their families. By this act of brutality, extinguishing the flame of vengeance, Sulla ensured that the civil war would come to an end and Rome would be ruled as it had always been, by the optimates, the rightful ruling class."

"So the populares lost, for all time?"

"That is right."

"But the plebes, the citizens, do they not have rights?"

"You argue as Meno with the Greek Socrates. I will simplify matters in the Roman style. Plebes, the average citizens, have only those rights that are given to them, and protected, by Rome. Rome is ruled by the elites, and the plebes are lower. Below the plebes, unlike here on Metallorum where everybody is a citizen, are the slaves. That underclass of people who must toil, obey, and live at the whim of their masters. Without such an underclass – in a world where everybody thinks that they have the same rights as the ruling class – there would be no social order, only class warfare and ultimately civil war. So the lesson of Sulla, and the necessary acts carried out by your bloodied hands today, was to protect Rome. There must not be a competition for power. Only one power, Rome, as ruled by the ruling class, may exist. Any opposition to that power, even by friends and neighbors as these Allanites were, must not only be overcome, but eradicated to the last man, woman, and child."

In the silence that ensued, Centurion Tappulus sensed that the Allanite message of freedom to do as one pleases, to form one's own spiritual beliefs, and the right to refuse duty or obedience to Rome, still had a degree of traction with the new generation of Metallorians.

The lesson is not complete. Not for this milite, and not for this soft new breed of Romans.

"Milite Egnatius. I will put it another way." Tappulus approached the young man who, by the body language of his posture seemed to be standing his ground. "Do you believe that Emperor Agricola was wrong to have the Allanites killed?"

After a long pause, Egnatius summoned the courage of his convictions.

"Yes, Praefectus, I do."

Egnatius's head hit the ground before the young man even noticed that Centurion Tappulus had swung his arm. The milite's headless body tilted over and fell like a statue.

"Do any others among you have the same point of view?"

There was absolute silence.

"I can see that you are Romans in name only. You have been infected by an insidious disease. A disease of the mind. You had better come to terms with it, and banish any thought of the Allanite way of life from your mind. You are not free top live as you please. You live to serve Rome. All of us, from the Emperor on down to us common soldiers, to the plebes who do not serve in the military, and to the most lowly slave. Any of us must die, willingly, if it is required of us for the security, continuity and glory of Rome."

Some of the men were nodding their heads, puffing up their chests as if preparing to give their lives – or take lives – for Rome.

"Good. Primus Pilus, give the men their rest and then have them out at the break of dawn for an inspection. I will personally cull this flock of sheep if there is even a hint that tonight's lesson was not well heard."

"Praefectus."

That bloody day, the day of the triumphal return of the emperor and the originals, would also become known as the day of the Allanite Apocalypse.

For the eighth-generation Metallorians, Romans who had never seen Rome, and soldiers who had never seen war, the murder of so many fellow human beings had given many of them pause. But they understood the point that had been made by Emperor Agricola: Roman tradition, Roman values, Roman law, and the absolute domination of Roman power would not allow a competing system to coexist.

From that moment on, any talk of spirituality other than the official Roman and Celtic religious and cultural traditions, was outlawed on pain of torture and death. It was once again relegated to whispers in the privacy of the bedrooms and secret places that those who took it upon themselves to carry the Allanite interpretation of Christianity, the martyrdom of milite Egnatius, or the teachings of any other spiritual leader, risked their lives to convey.

The shock of the complete annihilation of the Allanite people had been a sobering experience for the people of Metallorum. For some, it hardened their resolve to live in the Roman ways and to prove to the original Romans that they were good Romans, worthy of inclusion in the great adventure to come. For others, the departure of the emperor and his brutal companions could not come soon enough.

Two months later, after long days of meeting the citizens of Metallorum, getting to know the officers and even some of the common soldiers of the legion, the preparations for departure were complete.

On the final evening before their departure, Agricola sat with the Roman and Hibernian nobility, senior members of the senate and, as always, his two philosophers, for a final review.

"Aulus Tappulus, go over the figures one more time so that I have them clearly in my head. I'm afraid my head is close to saturated, what with all that we have seen and done these last few days."

"Imperator!" said the Praefectus Castrorum. "Let us keep it simple. We control forty-one operational starships of various types. There are two additional scout-ships and one colonist-ship that are derelict, and beyond repair. However our fleet now includes eight colony ships, four warships, twenty scout-ships and nine puller ships. These are all now fully fueled, and trained crews have been assigned.

"We have sufficient supplies on board, all of the thorium fuel rods – more than enough for the foreseeable future thanks to the accelerated production of Governor Gratianus – and we have a bed-down plan for fully nine thousand men, women, and children – almost one half of our combined population of originals and Metallorian-born descendants.

"We estimate that the Dupli-Tri produced one hundred and forty four ships of various classes, and can only account for thirty seven likely still controlled by Tuathii, just over twenty destroyed by the Tuathii at Bellorum. That leaves approximately sixty unaccounted for that are likely scattered across the cosmos in Dupli-Tri colonies or lost in unknown circumstances. To sum up, Imperator, the forty-one we control represents about one third, or whether there are even now some of their warships or other starships travelling thought the stars. However, we believe that the Tuathii still control a few warships and colonist-ships.

"Now, as to the disposition of our ships. As you recall from our planning session, the plan has been finalized. First, the three warships. One shall remain here with a single puller-ship to protect Metallorum and to serve as a communications link to the remainder of our fleet. We also shall leave two colonist-ships, and seven scout-ships here for exploration of this planet, with a view to establishing additional thorium mines, populating new regions and to build a thriving territory here on Metallorum. This will also allow Governor Gratianus to explore nearby stars, perhaps establish some outpost colonies, and to send emissaries to the Tuathii at Planeta Arborum.

"The remaining eleven thousand citizens of Metallorum will be vigilant for any returning Dupli-Tri or Tuathii, and will either establish trade relationships or will defeat them and seize their starships. No help for Metallorum from our flotilla is possible, given the timeframes involved in our coming voyage.

"Next. One scout-ship has been sent ahead with Tribune Avitus and Immune Commodus. That leaves twelve scout-ships, three warships, six colonist-ships, and the seven planetoid-pullers for our Terra-bound armada."

"Armada. I like the sound of that."

"Imperator. We will move your Aquila, Imperial Standard, to one of the warships, and increase the number of occupants for each colonist-ship from 108 pods for humans and 108 pods for animals to 150 pods for humans and just 66 for livestock. We will also double-up occupancy to two pairs each, four persons per pod – we thought it best for the men to take their wives and children with them, as much as possible – although we have about one half as childless couples. All ships have had additional corrals and cages installed in under-utilized compartments and pile bundles of grass feed in main corridors and under the beds in the sleeping pods, to conserve space. We are have extra some space for potable water storage thanks to changing to dried fish that we are stocking for the Octopodii crew. They seem to prefer dried fish, and this is easier to store than the live fish, grubs and other Octopoda-feed that the Tuathii previously set aside.

"So with the six colonist-ships transporting twelve hundred each, and another three hundred squeezed into each of the three warships the total number of personnel transported to Terra will be eight thousand, one hundred."

"How many of that number will be trained, effective strength, soldiers?" Kaeso asked, despite already knowing the answer.

"Four thousand one hundred and forty. While a large number are immunes, engineers and other crewmembers for the various types of starships, there will be fully eight cohorts available for deployment, Tribunus. Er, Legatus Cerialis," said Tappulus, embarrassed to have yet again failed to acknowledge Kaeso's promotion to Legatus of Legio XXVII. There had been promotions all around, with all of the originals moving up in ranks. This was particularly appreciated by the now Tribune Tappulus, who had now risen to a rank that none of his family had ever reached before. There had not been much movement in the rankings of the Metallorian-born Romans, however, as there can be only so many high-ranking officers, and the original romans clearly had seniority – millennia of it, in fact.

"Eight cohorts? Two cohorts short of a full legion? That may not be enough," said Vibius Metellus.

"It will have to be. We had to leave Gratianus with enough starships to maintain and expand upon our advantage in Locus Capricornus. This is a rich planet, and has a sufficient population to expand our presence. It will also be our first line of defense against our enemies. We, on the other hand, will be travelling to an uncertain reception at Terra. We are taking enough resources to have flexibility and mobility at our disposal," said Agricola.

"Well, I hope you are right, Imperatus."

Smiling with an amused thought of Metellus dressed in a military uniform, Agricola put the argument to rest: "Eight cohorts plus the starship crews. That will be sufficient. If our Dupli-Tri technology is not up to the task, then an extra cohort will not make much difference. So as much as the risk you point out is real, and we have given it a great deal of thought, it is a risk that I am willing to bet my life on – along with yours, Metellus!"

"Imperator."

"So, Aulus, you made an error in your math."

"How so, Imperator?"

"You forgot about Tribune Avitus and Immune Antoninus. They will be old men, but still quite capable of service when we arrive."

"Imperator," said Tappulus, not even dreaming of arguing about the worth of the two old men, or questioning if they were, in fact, still living. That he had aged ten extra years by arriving ahead of the other originals, with his troublesome wife Genovefa and Neasa Avitus, made Tappulus sympathetic to the age, and fate, of Marcus Avitus.

"And of these women and children, how many will be Hibernian?"

"Imperator. Few of the Hibernians men actually wanted to come, as most of the wives are now fully Romanized. The Hibernians seemed to be more interested in expanding on Metallorum or colonizing Planeta Bellorum. Those of the Hibernian men included in our number are cross-trained to fulfill duties as Roman soldiers, so we consider them all to be Romans now."

Just before the pod doors closed, a group of Romans and Celtic warriors rushed out of the starship, grabbed some sacks that had been set aside near the starship, and hurried back inside with one, in some cases two, of the heavy sacks on their shoulders.

It would not be until days later, when Primus Pilus Crispus investigated the noise coming up from an animal pod at the extreme end of the lower deck that he finally understood what had been in the sacks. It had been sand.

Left out of Tribune Tappulus's meticulous list of stores for the upcoming voyage, thirty bags of sand had been prepared by some of the Metallorian-born warriors.

Now, with the sand having been spread on the floor of a large animal pod, a tradition was preserved. The animal pod had been converted into a ludus, a gladiator school.

The Metallorian-born warriors had heard the legends about the rapid healing possible while travelling in starship, and decided that the bare-knuckle fighting and tests of warrior skill they had long practiced on Metallorian, as a way of honing their skills and testing their mettle – there being no actual wars – could now be brought to a much higher level.

Without the knowledge of any of their officers, they had taken to meeting in the animal pod and engaging in near-death combat, using steel weapons and sharpened Celtic weapons rather than the wooden gladius and dulled antler weapons they trained with on Metallorum.

Their individual combat in the ludus of the starship involved the spilling of a lot of blood, and the experience of excruciating pain, followed by rapid recovery thanks to the healing effects of the starship's Equanimity Drive.

Without invitation or being notice, Centurion Crispus watched as two men fighting in traditional Roman style and weaponry went up against two women and one man fighting in Celtic garments and weaponry. It was a test of their two cultures, even if the participants were equally adept at either; the two cultures so well merged and yet their traditions also well-preserved.

In short order, the combat was well under way. The two women closed in on one of the Roman-styled warriors, and looked to be gaining an advantage. It was trap, and the second Roman, who had been drawing his male opponent to the opposite side of the sand floor of the ludus suddenly ran back, catching one of the women unawares. He drove his gladius deep inter her backside, in what would be a mortal wound – anywhere other than on a starship.

He then took his place next to his comrade, and together now faced only one woman and one man.

Crispus watched as members of the audience dragged the severely injured woman out of the arena and into an adjacent pod, where they tended to her as her body healed itself, rapidly stabilizing.

Deeply impressed at what he had witnessed, Pilus Primus Crispus now understood that the new breed of Romans were as tough as any of his time, perhaps even more so, and they were quick to adapt to the military and other possibilities of the alien technology.

We are going to be fine, Crispus thought, *with courageous and innovative warriors like these, nothing can stop us.*

As the Roman armada departed the Metallorum star system, the last person to sit and watch through a viewing pot on the bridge was Tribune Aulus Tappulus. He still found it hard to comprehend, but understood that he would never again see the friends he was leaving behind on Metallorum.

"You look sad, Tribune," said one of the immunes, giving a tour of the bridge to a group of Metallorian noble men and women who had never been aboard a starship.

"Not sad, just thinking of those we left behind."

"You left your wife behind, did you not?" asked an unfamiliar lady.

"Yes. My wife, Genovefa. She and I had our challenges. Hopefully she will find a man that suits her better than I did."

"So is that where your thoughts are? The woman you have left behind?"

"Not at all. In that regard I feel a new sense of freedom. Who knows what I will find of the women of Terra when we arrive. No, it is more that I enjoyed playing a role in building the original Castra Metallorum. It would be quite something to explore the planeta, building a great civilization there."

"But you should look forward to what lies ahead, tribune," said the woman, who appeared to be of noble peerage.

"Lady Cassius, is it? Descended from Tribunus Cyprianus Cassius?"

"Yes, Tribune."

"Alas, poor Cyprianus, I knew him well."

"Why poor? My great-great-great grandfather lived a long and prosperous life."

"Yes, but he was without his brothers. He never returned to Rome. You cannot imagine how important that is to us."

"Meaning no disrespect, my friend, but you have no idea how important it is to be governor of an entire planeta! But I understand your excitement at the prospect of returning home."

"Excitement. Yes, there is that. But I also have a dose of reality sprinkled into my enthusiasm, my lady."

"Reality? Like what? Everything will be wonderful. We will be able to see the wonders of Rome, and take in the games at the Coliseum!" she enthused.

"My dear lady, I hope that you are right. I really do. But for all we know Rome could be in grass-covered ruins, like so many civilizations that came before Romulus and Remus founded our great nation."

Looking at the soldier as if he were insane, she replied: "That could never happen. When our people left Terra, Rome was the greatest power the world had ever seen. They were led by the greatest minds, and had the benefit of the wisest advisors. That's why the Roman Empire stretched so broadly, from Hibernia in the west to the Sumerian and Babylonian lands to the east, and from Germania to the north to the Nubian deserts to the south."

"You certainly do know your Roman history. But do you also know of the weaknesses that had been infecting our people, even then, when I served in Britannia?"

"Weaknesses?" she asked.

"Yes. There were certain religious and philosophical forces at work – amongst the nobility mostly."

"Do you mean the Christian and those other monotheist religions?"

"Yes. Those and other cults, and the hubris of our own human race. We have come to think of ourselves as the pinnacle of all species. As though we own the planet."

"But we do. And we are the custodians of the planet."

"Says whom?"

"Says the gods. Or the one god, if you believe in a single god."

"But what if the philosophy of the Tuathii is closer to the truth?"

"We weren't taught much about that in school. But we are hearing a lot about it from those of you who went on the grand odyssey of planetae. What's it all about, something to do with Equanimity?"

"That's right. Equanimity is the peace you find in the boundary between any two poles in the pairs of opposites that make up the universe, starting with the fundamental pair, 'Nesslessness and Thing', and moving up the line into more and more complex combinations of pairs of opposites."

"Tribune, what you are saying is disturbing. You sound like a priest, or some kind of a cultist. Shouldn't you leave that to the Druids or the Priests?"

"My lady, that is the answer to your question about the philosophy of the thinking-trees."

"OK, I did ask for that, I guess. But does it really mean anything? I mean, if they are right, and everything in the universe is connected by Equanimity at some level, then what? There are no gods looking down on us? Not even one?"

"That's it, exactly. The godhead is the Equanimity that is connected to all things. But to be self-aware, beings need to exist in the realm of 'things,' according to their complexity. So the only beings looking down on anybody are those beings, like us now, thankfully, who have attained the ability to travel through the stars – beings who are complex enough to find the truth about Equanimity."

"That all sounds well and good, really, but what does it mean to how I live my life? Should I not sacrifice animals to the gods? Should I not pray for those I love?"

"You should do whatever it is that most pleases you and makes your life feel fulfilled. However, if you really want to find answers to the mysteries of life, I would suggest you look more closely at the thoughts that underlie those traditions you follow."

She looked at him as if he had said something wise, and wanted to hear more. He continued.

"It's like the Greek, Socrates, said: 'the unexamined life is not worth living.'"

"So that is what you – or the thinking-trees - think? That the meaning of life is simply to examine it?"

"Yes, that, and that protecting life so that life may continue to become more complex, more diverse, is the basis for ethical judgment."

"You mean, like, when those four-legged beings on the massacre planet destroyed most of the life on their planet, that was therefore 'wrong' because it was against this principle of complexity and diversity of life?"

"That's it, fundamentally, yes. That's what the thinking-trees believe."

"But do you believe it?"

"I will put it this way. I think such a belief system could do no harm to Rome. I serve Rome, and will throw my life into the cause of Rome against any enemy or threat."

The noble lady, born and raised on Metallorum as a Roman – schooled in the culture, history, and religion of Rome – was smart enough to know when to move on from such a heavy topic. However, she could not resist asking one more question of the philosophically-inclined centurion.

"So if the people of Terra have become a threat to all life on Terra, just as what happened on Planeta Scientiae and Planeta Caedum, what then?"

"My Lady, that is the 'dose of reality' that tempers my optimism. Who knows what we will find when we arrive."

After the discussion with the centurion, and holding his philosophical thoughts in her head for about as long as her optimistic nature would allow, something deep in her personality decided to reject the concerns of the centurion as simply absurd.

"Well, tribune. It has been a pleasant debate, but I must tell you how ridiculous it all is. Romans, and humans in general, are smarter than all the other species we have encountered in the universe. We are rational enough to recognize trends, to make smart choices about how we live. And if one nation lives in a way that would harm life on earth on such a massive scale as we have seen on those other planetae, then Rome or whoever is the most powerful, smartest nation, would do something about it. And if they don't, then Rome will make them do so," she said, confidently, and then walked away from Tribune Tappulus.

But as she rehearsed what she would tell her friends about the strange philosophical perspective the Tribune had gained from the Tuathii, she felt the grumblings of a doubt in her mind. She tried to wash it from her thoughts: *Humans are smarter than other species. We recognize the dangers that come our way, and then we come together and do something about them. So what could possibly go wrong?*

Gene Skellig

PART TWO

XXII

VALETVDO RES AMERICANVS
{ State of the Union }

I just need four more votes, thought President Russell Ross. *If Vice President Rodriquez can bring in the Latin representatives, I will finally be able to send my tax reform bill to Congress. I better not screw up the pronunciation of those two Mexican-American war heroes' names during the speech.*

It was just one more detail he had gone over for the umpteenth time in the last week, getting ready for his second State of the Union address.

Comfortable as a public speaker, President Ross actually looked forward to having all 100 senators and 435 congressmen and women gathered together in the House Chamber of the Capitol building.

Having the nine supreme court judges, the assembled Joint Chiefs and other top military figures, and all of the carefully-vetted VIPS and popular personages in attendance made this particular audience – and this particular speech – the most important of his political career.

The previous year's address had been important as well. As a newly-elected president with the first ever Spanish-American Vice President seated behind him, he envisioned a time of great transition in America, and hope. His responses to financial and environmental crises were well-received overall, and he had been riding a wave of popular support. However, that support crested as the realities of partisanship and political filibustering undermined the president's ability to pursue his agenda. *The honeymoon is over*, he thought, as he placed the speech down upon the Resolute Desk in the Oval Office.

Looking into the grain of the desk for a moment, thinking about his gradual slide in popularity, he reflected on the history of the desk. It had been crafted from the timbers of *HMS Resolute*, a British warship salvaged by the Americans and returned to Queen Victoria as a token of friendship. After being "paid off", retired, the ship was put to good use: Queen Victoria commissioned the "Resolute Desk" be made, and presented the ornate desk, with the Presidential Seal carved into the center-front panel, as a gift to President Rutherford Hayes in 1880. Other than a few exceptions, the Resolute Desk had been used by each and every President ever since.

Thinking of the desk, and the way that his son, David, liked to play in the front kneehole panel just as John F. Kennedy Jr had done with another populist president, President Ross felt a renewal of his resolve. *This job is a lot harder than I expected, but I am up to the task*, he thought, as he returned to reviewing his speaking notes.

Other key features of his speech included measures to rein in military spending, new accountability laws to ensure that bank and insurance executives would be held personally responsible for the decisions made under their watch; including the re-establishment of certain provisions of the 1933 Glass-Steagall Act which separated commercial from investment banking. Perhaps most importantly, however, were the measures to reassure the American public that there would never be another collapse of the food-supply system, as had happened during the failure of the agricultural supply chain during the previous autumn.

It was one thing when America had to stop providing food aid to the starving masses in the famines of Africa and Europe, that was easy enough to live with. *It's their fault for living where the food ain't* had been the prevailing attitude in the United States, what with so many people struggling stateside.

But then America itself had experienced unprecedented extremes of drought followed by flash-floods and temperature variations that had ruined so many of the few crops that farmers had been able to plant.

Asking for shipments of aid from Canada and Brazil had been a source of national shame for a proud country that had always seen itself as the world's greatest agricultural nation: a powerhouse in farm production and agricultural research and development.

At least we did not have to borrow more from China, he thought. *With our gold reserves mostly transferred to Beijing now, we don't have much left for barter. Maybe we should have taken Russia's offer to buy Alaska. Too late now, considering China now holds it, and the oil that sits beneath it, as collateral for the dollar-yuan peg.* If they ever foreclose, and try to claim Alaska in the process, we'll probably have to go to war. We simply cannot allow the vast quantity of mineral and petroleum reserves to fall into the hands of our enemy – and benefactor – China.

Of course, while it was necessary to touch on the worst points of the past year, the speech was also to inspire America to support the president in bringing about his proposed legislative changes as vitally necessary to ensure a future prosperity. Indeed, it was a year and an administration of re-invention and rebuilding.

Another theme of the speech was how American scientific and technological advances in genetic engineering, hydroponics, 'organo-recycled food products', and 'alternate-sourced protein substitutes' would ensure that each and every citizen in the United States would have sufficient caloric intake. Hidden within the legislation, however, were exemption from FDA-administered food safety inspections and labelling laws for the large food and GMO corporations and total legal protection for their executives. It went without saying that these powerful corporate interests were now using virtually any form of organic material – including some raw materials that the president, upon querying on their composition, had been warned 'do not ask' – and a variety of 'harmless substitutes,' in their food products. These substitutes included wood-cellulose, silica sand, reprocessed solid waste, and types of animal carcasses, including cats and dogs, which the public at large would find repulsive.

That euphemism, 'protein substitutes,' actually meant: *the rich among us will continue to have whatever we want to eat; the poor can eat turd-biscuits and road kill,* but President Ross did not like to dwell on such negative ways of looking at things. *It's their fault for not working harder to become wealthy – they all had equal opportunity,* he reflected, recalling the utterances of the more fiscally-conservative wing of his party. He realized that such sentiments, at least for a president, were better left unspoken.

"Mr. President, one hour,"

"Thank you, Mr. Marsh. Come back when it's 20 minutes."

"Yes, Mr. President," said Irving Marsh, the Ross administration's Chief of Staff.

"What else?" asked Russell Ross, seeing his Chief of Staff hesitate near the door.

"Mr. President. Some of the military staff are still in the Briefing Room, discussing those UFO sightings in New York State last week."

"Are you serious? I thought NORAD already debunked those," said the President. I thought it was a surge in UFO interest after a well-orchestrated series of hoax videos."`

First there had been well-edited video of computer-generated imagery that purported to show a small, egg-shaped UFO fly through the front end of a car in Spain, a few months back. Then there was video from a police car in the Boston area, showing the same UFO flying out through the roof of a liquor store. The robbery of the liquor store had been verified by local authorities, but the video of the UFO, tearing off into the sky after presumably looting the liquor store of a staggering quantity of beer, wine and hard liquor, had obviously been a fake. At least, that was what the NORAD generals had said, in the teleconference held just hours earlier.

"Well, they are not so sure now, Mr. President. Apparently they have data that indicates that there was a strange glitch in their data coming out of EADS, NORAD's Eastern Air Defense Sector, at that precise time. They now consider the reports of some sort of flying object, perhaps a stealth helicopter or a drone, to have some basis in reality. But they assure us that it is not some sort of extra-terrestrial visitor, Mr. President."

"Good, last thing I need is a visit from ET during my State of the Union speech.

"What does that leave us with, for potential media focus after the SOU?"

"We are a bit light on climate change. I really think you should throw in more comments on it, not just on the food security and agribusiness subsidies. It really is in the public consciousness every day. You know, Mr. President, my daughter is so stressed about climate change; she doesn't want to have kids. I told her not to worry, because her kids will get to grow up and have kids before the environment really gets bad."

"Well, given the polar vortex last winter, with that epic dump of snow that shut down Washington and forced us to postpone the State of the Union speech until now, we have to admit that something is going on," President Ross said.

"I think that the public has seen enough new records, extreme heat and drought in some areas, torrential rain and flooding in others, to know that climate change really means disrupted patterns, and an uncertain future."

"Come on, Irving, you know as well as I do that we simply cannot come out and admit that it's beyond control, that we have disregarded it for far too long, and we have acted too late," said President Ross.

"Too late? You could just as easily go the other way, and roll out those speaking points we used during the election. Lots of people, including the Vice President, believe that the entire climate change things is a hoax," said Irving Marsh.

"Do you really think people will be swayed by the line that 'these are natural variations in the climate, not at all the result of human activity'? Or point to the unusually cold winter we had last year as proof that global warming is not real? That would just open us up to ridicule after all the flooding in Florida. No, I am going with my intuition on this and completely avoiding the topic, as if there is nothing concrete to talk about," said President Ross, as he put on his jacket and adjusted his necktie, in preparation for the short walk to the motorcade that would take him from the White House to the US Capitol Building.

As they walked to the waiting car, the President and First Lady enjoyed the warm evening air, and observed the fading sunlight.

"We should hold the State of the Union in April every year," said the First Lady, Katie Ross.

"Why? Because of the beautiful weather?" President Ross said, looking at the cherry blossoms, green grass and well-tended gardens all around him.

"Yes, and because April 21st is when spring really takes off. It is an auspicious time to begin something – far better than January, that's for sure."

"I agree, but we have always held the State of the Union in January, or early February, to coincide with the re-opening of Congress after the Christmas break. Article Two of section Three of the US Constitution requires that the President give this annual update to Congress, and it is the most cost-effective way for a sitting president to get so much free air time," Russell said, with a broad smile.

"Now you're gloating. Do you really think you'll gain enough seats in the mid-term election?" asked Katie.

"Depends on how well I do tonight!" Russell said with a wink, and then he sat forward and knocked on the glass partition, to get the driver's attention.

"What are you doing, Russ?" asked his Irving Marsh, already dreading what he knew was coming.

"This is a perfect opportunity to give them some early footage, in time for the ten o'clock news," Ross said, as the limousine pulled to a stop near the Lincoln Memorial, where a few dozen Romaphiles had gathered on the broad stone stairs leading to the statue of Abraham Lincoln.

Enough time had passed for the media to re-position. Irving gave the President the thumbs up, and offered his hand to help the First Lady work her way to the door, following right behind President Ross.

Looking at the neoclassical architecture all around him, Ross knew that the architects of Washington had intentionally included the symbols of antiquity, even the *fasces*, the symbol of strength of the Roman Empire and the root of the contemporary term "fascism", in the buildings that stood as testament to the very foundations of American power.

Never one to miss an opportunity to expand his voting base, and with the media in close proximity, the President remarked, "We do owe a great deal to the ancients, the Greeks, the Romans, the Muslims, and many others for preserving the great works of philosophy. Heck, our Republic is largely based on traditions and principles borrowed directly from ancient Rome," said President Ross to the Katie Ross, who nodded in complete agreement.

With the agents scanning the battle re-enactors, watching to see if any were about to draw their swords and rush at the President and First Llady, the Romaphiles continued taking their pictures and having their conversations as if the contemporary politician and his security detail were not even there. Standing on the stone steps, all dressed as if out of first century Rome, they looked as if they belonged.

Many of the battle re-enactors were dressed in Roman military uniform that looked quite authentic. A few, however, were in togas, perhaps role-playing as Roman senators. Some were in more sinister looking uniforms, with highly polished black leather embossed with golden artwork. Strangely, rather than the *Aquila*, eagle, that President Ross would have expected, these men, presumably Praetorian Guards, bore golden *leones*, lions on their chests. *That's something I have never seen in the history books, wonder what it means?* thought the President.

As President and First Lady Ross approached, an olive-complexioned re-enactor broke away from the group and approached them, smiling warmly.

"Mr. President. Madam, First Lady. Welcome to Rome!"

"Very nicely done. What's your name?" The First Lady asked, as she extended a hand and turned her head slightly, smiling for a photojournalist to take a shot.

"Eduardo Cuervo, Mrs. Ross."

"Very pleased to meet you. You are one of the organizer's, aren't you? I seem to recall seeing your name on some of the paperwork requesting permission for this entertaining event today."

"Yes, I am one of the organizers. My group, the Praetorian Guards, are re-enacting a scene where the emperor attends a battle. My unit – these fine Romans you see behind me – are the personal guards of the Emperor of Rome. Their lives are sworn to his service and protection." Eduardo said with pride.

"And what is your emperor's name?"

"Emperor Agricola, Mr. President. Quintus Julius Agricola Augustus, to be precise," Eduardo said..

"Agricola? I thought he was killed by Emperor Domitian."

"That was his father, Gnaeus Julius."

"Oh. I was not aware he had a son, or that his son became emperor," said President Ross, with a confused look on his face.

"It's a little known fact of history, Mr. President, something of an untold story."

"Sounds more like an alternative history, my friend," said President Ross, sensing that enough pictures had been taken chatting with the Romaphiles. His keen sense of timing also told him that it was time to head for the Capitol.

"It was nice to meet you, Mr. Cuervo. Enjoy this special day, graciously arranged by the First Lady, when you and your fellow legionaries have the freedom of the city – an apparently full control of the National Mall," joked the President, looking at the small groups of Romans he could see scattered between the Capitol Building and the Washington Monument.

"Oh we are, Mr. President, we are!" replied Centurion Eduardo Cuervo, *Praefectus Praetorio,* commander of Emperor Agricola's Terra-born Praetorian Guard.

After waving goodbye to the Praetorian Guards one last time for the cameras, Russell and Katie Ross joined Irving Marsha in the limousine. The stately motorcade proceded to the security checkpoint on the south side of the US Capitol. they entered the seat of power of the United States of America perfectly on time for the American President`s expected entrance into the House Chamber, at 8:30 pm.

XXIII

DECESSVS PHILOSOPHIAE
{ Philosopher's Retirement }

Professor Avitus was not held in the highest regard by his fellow educators in Boston University's Department of Classical Studies. Several of his colleagues had suspicions as to truthfulness of his curriculum vitae, and were not receptive to his interpretation of history, particularly that of the Roman Empire. His historical views were known to waiver from popular convention, and he was willing to debate anyone on the subject. To his students, however, he was the professor they would never forget. Although diminutive in size and showing every one of his seventy-eight, his charisma and passion for the subject matter made him an almost larger than life character.

Dr. Avitus was a convenient dumping ground for the department's 'toxic waste' – students who seemed to be too enamored with antiquity, particularly Roman and Latin studies, to be successful as objective academia.

And that had suited Tribune Marcus Avitus, Dr. Avitus, just fine.

As Professor Avitus intensified preparations for his long-awaited rendezvous, he had to reduce his teaching commitment and increasingly relied on his grad students to teach his lectures, most notably the Cuervo twins, Eduardo and Nestor.

The Cuervos had been studying under Dr. Avitus for six years, and each twin had recently completed his PhD thesis.

A year earlier, Marcus had enlisted the assistance of a young female PhD History student, Brit Murphy, who was preparing her thesis on Celtic history. A strikingly-attractive young woman with close-cropped blonde hair and a lithe, strong physique, she reminded him of his bride. The daughter of an abusive alcoholic father and neglectful mother, she learned at a young age that peace can be found in a library, and devoted herself to her academic pursuits. An independent woman who had little time for personal relationships, she developed a bond of trust with the fatherly professor, who had assisted her in her studies of the history of Rome and Ireland. When she was given the opportunity to participate in the mission, she accepted the invitation without hesitation.

Marcus had originally intended to take Brit and Eduardo, the brightest of the twins, along with him for the rendezvous with Agricola and the others, but then Nestor became seriously ill with a hospital-acquired infection. Marcus decided to take the ailing young man with him instead, leaving Eduardo behind to lead the Praetorian Guard.

That had complicated matters a great deal, as simply getting Nestor to Spain had been quite difficult. Given Nestor's illness, there had been a risk that the airlines would not let him board the aircraft, or that the immigration officials in Spain would deny him entry. However they had found a way to overcome that obstacle, by placing one of Nestor's healthy legs in a cast. For Nestor, travelling in a wheelchair was much easier, embracing all the courtesy that the airline lavished on the mobility-challenged, first class passenger.

After their arrival at Madrid Barajas International Airport, Spanish immigration officers went out of their way to guide the young man along after validating his passport and tourist visa.

Had they even noticed the waxy, pale skin, or had a medical technician take his weak pulse, they would have attributed it to the leg injury and the strain of the seven hour flight from Boston.

The trio collected their baggage and then summoned a taxi to drive them the short distance to the Hotel Auditorium Madrid. While Nestor slept, Marcus and Brit took a taxi to the Madrid city center where the enjoyed a traditional Spanish gazpacho with freshly baked bread and a sweet local sherry. As Marcus savored the never-forgotten flavors, he reminisced about his past experiences and looked forward to being reunited with his family and colleagues.

Early the next morning, with Nestor feeling significantly better, they rented a van and drove the 500 km to Lugo, where they checked into a suite at the Gran Hotel Lugo and eagerly awaited their meeting with Antoninus Commodus.

As planned, Antoninus arrived a few hours later, having driven from Milan, Italy.

For Nestor, the reunion of the two old men was strange to see. They greeted each other like brothers embracing with the ferocity and strength of warriors, exhibiting the energy of men a third their age.

After being introduced to Immune Commodus, Nestor and Brit decided to leave the two men alone, to catch up on the last thirty years.

Although their contact had been limited in their early days on Terra, initially by mail or telegram, the convenience of modern telecommunications for the last twenty five years allowed them to maintain daily contact by email and, by using simple encryption techniques, they were able to conduct their communications by secure means as they planned for the day of the Return.

Of course, a great deal of the materials had been accumulated over the years. In the basement of Marcus's home was a virtual museum of consumer technology, spanning almost four decades. Marcus had eventually ceased to accumulate computers, diskettes, manuals and other rapidly obsolescent devices, and focused more on research and documentation. In the final years before the planned rendezvous, and with the unwitting help of some of his graduate students, Marcus transcribed, scanned, digitized, and converted the materials into electronic formats, and loaded them into modern-day Non Adiabatic SpintroTronic Yaw, 'NASTY', data storage devices – essentially the same as thumb-drives of the early 21st century, but with twenty times the storage capacity, up to twenty terabytes on a single NASTY thumb-drive. He could essentially store everything he had collected in the last 48 years on a single NASTY drive.

His main focus had been to prepare training materials, lesson plans, reference materials, maps and an extensive collection of video materials. He developed a thorough understanding of the current global geopolitical state, how it arrived at that state, and the issues that impacted the world. Marcus felt he was conversant on virtually any subject on which he was queried, however he prepared detailed briefings on those issues that he felt were most pertinent to Roman plans including military capabilities, geopolitics, telecommunications, global governance, transportation, and the environment. He was also prepared to provide a detailed briefing on the history of the Roman Empire since their departure from Hibernia so many earth years ago.

For his part, Antoninus had a few surprises. First, he had a cat. A Russian Blue to be precise. When Marcus saw Antonius with the cat, he immediately understood.

"Is that the cat that the old man gave us, so many years ago, in Cervantes? It cannot be," asked Marcus.

"Not exactly, old man. It is the twenty-fifth generation of catulus, kitten, from that first cat. I have been living on a country acreage, a winery, and have had many generations of these cats to keep me company. It gives me a better sense of time, to watch each successive generation of these cats, from litter to adulthood, as we wait to be united with our people. In my mind, I imagine the generations of people that will have come to live, love, breed, age, and die, on Metallorum, while we wait. In fact, the twenty-five generations of catulus I have shepherded – like Pales, the god of shepherd and sheep – is about the same number that have come and gone on Metallorum since the day Agricola and the rest of our people left. And soon, we will be re-united with them." Antoninus said, with pride, as he held the large blue-grey cat on his forearm.

"Antoninus, I had no idea you were so tender," Marcus said, sincerely appreciating the metaphor that the catulus embodied. "What is this catullus's name?"

"*Grigi*o, grey, and probably the tenth such cat I have named Grigio," Antoninus replied, handing the cooperative grey cat to Nestor as he turned his attention to unloading the crates he had yet to load into the scout-ship. "These are the best possible cats to breed, you know. They do not suffer from the genetic problems of other pure-bred cats, and they are intelligent," Antoninus said.

The animal-lover side of the engineer, Antoninus Commodus, was in sharp contrast to his engineer personality. He had been responsible for the technical aspects of the mission. Being an engineer living and working in Italy, Antoninus had the opportunity to visit the Cervantes hills over the past two weeks, to pre-position some of the necessary materials. On this final trip, he had brought two dozen cases, some filled with electrical supplies – circuit breakers, conduit, transformer-rectifier units – which he had determined would allow him to hook into a the electrical system of a Dupli-Tri ship to provide power in the right voltage, current and amperage for modern day computers and other electronic devices he had brought with him.

Some of the equipment was intended to augment that on the bridge of the Dupli-Tri scout-ship. Antoninus had realized, as far back as the 1990s, that modern day Earth's remote sensing, digital photography and computer technology had the potential to upgrade the capabilities and ease of operation of the Dupli-Tri starships, as the alien species had not developed anything like computer screens, television, or computers.

Other things provided by Antoninus included small wristwatch-based projectors that could convert any wall surface – such as the walls of a starship's main corridor – into a movie theater or lecture hall, allowing the tribunes and centurions to introduce the material to contubernium-sized and even larger groups.

One of the items that both Marcus and Antoninus agreed must be brought along were the cases of Tequila and Galician wine.

On a previous rendezvous with Antoninus at the scout-ship, years ago, they had taken the risk of activating the power system to verify that it was intact. They were actually surprised to receive an answer from Agricola's command ship through the tachyon communication system. They then powered down the scout-ship and carefully buried it once again in the nearly impenetrable bush lands, not far from the Lugo - Cervantes road, in northwest Spain.

Based on the confirmation of the planned date and location for the rendezvous, Marcus and Antoninus decided that it was too risky to take a side trip. The only real purpose would be to reverse some of the effects of aging. But the risks of detection or some other problem were just too high.

Reflecting back to his youth, and all the changes that had taken place – not only when he had first left Hispania for Britannia, but also since his return to Terra in 1975 and the almost five decades that had passed since – Marcus understood that the best plan was to lie low, as a university professor, and bide his time.

Now, after almost fifty years of anticipation, Marcus was on the verge of completing his task. But the final state would be in another man's hands, and Marcus would be something of a bystander. *It is all up to Antoninus to get us back to our people,* Marcus thought.

When the appointed time had come, and with Marcus, Nestor and Brit watching, Antoninus powered up the ship's thorium reactor and brought the mechanical controls to life.

Having studied the ship throughout his career as an electrical engineer, using digital pictures he had taken on the rare visits he had made for a health-boost and a systems check, Antoninus knew the scout-ship better than any other human knew a Dupli-

Tri craft. He handled it like a familiar car, with love and confidence – and a great deal of excitement.

As the scout-ship began to rise, the Equanimity field obliterating the sandy soil and trees it had been buried under, Antoninus flicked what even Nestor recognized as a modern-day human bank of switches, powering up a trio of computer screens that he had installed on the deck of the cramped vessel.

On one screen, the digital feed from the original Dupli-Tri optical viewing pot was projected. Antoninus demonstrated how to use the track-ball he had installed on the narrow Dupli-Tri work-table that served as the bridge for the craft. It provided them a visual of the winding mountain road that came close to the thicket, where the scout-ship had been secreted all these years. Marcus had eventually purchased the land where it was hidden to keep the secret even safer.

"Hey, there's our van!" said Nestor.

"Do you suppose we can fly over Lugo?" asked Marcus. "I'll get my digital camera."

"Don't bother, Marcus. Watch this!" Antoninus showed how he could click a few buttons on the thumb-side of the track ball, and select 'record.

"You've made this little craft into something far greater than a means of transportation," said Marcus.

"Yes, it truly is a scout-ship – perfect for reconnaissance. But look, it's not as stealthy as I hoped."

"Do they see us?" asked Nestor.

With a few deft clicks and movements of the track-ball, Antoninus closed in rapidly on a couple who had gotten out of their car on the winding road, and were looking up at the scout-ship, the husband taking video with his phone.

"What should we do?"

"Well, we could kill them."

"How?"

"We could just fly down and Equanimitize them. But let's have some fun with this, and give them some proof," said Antoninus.

With a grin from Marcus, Antoninus maneuvered the scout-ship towards the couple, careful not to get too close.

The couple hunkered down, and then fled from their car and tried to hide behind a rock retaining wall.

With the couple now safely away from their car, Antoninus slowly flew the craft towards the car. He did not alter course to avoid it, and deliberately passed through the front end of the car, converting the engine and body – the entire front-end of the car – into bright yellow light.

Leaving a stunned, but still filming, man and woman behind them, Antoninus steered the craft upward, accelerating into space.

Within five minutes of the encounter, high-quality color footage of the car being half-eaten by the small flying egg was viewed by millions on the internet.

The Romans were trending.

XXIV

CONGRESSVS IN COELO
{ Rendezvous in Space }

Agricola was tired. He had tried to keep abreast of the details, but found some of them simply incomprehensible. After their odyssey through the Tuathii-controlled planetae of Locus Capricorns, he was confident that Spurius Sallustius Crispus and his specialists knew what they were talking about, but he was still having problems understanding the concepts.

So rather than botch the explanation by attempting to articulate it himself, he decided to have his Primus Pilus lay it all out for his officers.

"Officers of the Twenty-Seventh Legion," he began, with enough formality that the men knew that this was not going to be one of the informal sessions that their Legatus required them to participate in whenever new information had been gleaned about the Tuathii.

This was to be a military briefing, so Centurion Tappulus had arranged for only the highest ranking to attend. Tribunes, various grades of centurions, immunes and other influential legionaries, were augmented by the brightest of Queen Laelie's captains.

The woman's presentation to them had already begun, in the main corridor of the second largest ship, in the string of connected starships. The latest to arrive were the officers from the Eighth of the Second, who had come all the way from the last starship in the string of pearls, where the bulk of the munifex and milites were garrisoned for the long voyage. Also housed in that last starship were two contubernia of the brutish Siphonapteristii and the livestock required to sustain them.

The practice of connecting the starships in a long line, had been discovered by Ambassador Laurentius, who had happened upon it in a thought-discussion with one of the oldest Octopodii onboard. Once they knew that it could be done, it did not take long for Centurion Tappulus and the engineers from the Second to understand the function of the strange portal at the bow and stern of the ship. With the help of 'Lumpy,' the friendliest of the Octopodii, they figured out the purpose of the coil of telescoping man-sized tubing and the rolls of umbilicus, heavy line stored neatly adjacent to the fore and aft ends of each starship.

The actual activation of the connecting tubes was quite simple. An Octopoda in the bridge of each ship merely had to toggle a series of knobs and the tubing began to telescope outward. A bio-mechanical linkage, by means of the focus-sensing head-band worn at the viewing-pot allowed the observer to direct the operation. The two ships would link by the man-sized umbilicus, and the stronger cable would be used inside the tube for hand-over-hand transit from one ship to another, and to keep the ships tethered to each other. For those transiting from one ship to another, they would experience weightlessness and a daunting reminder of how dangerous open space would be for the unprotected. The engineers of the Second had never encountered, nor conceived, the notion of a "space-suit" or a "spacewalk," but had come to learn of the hazardous characteristics of the vacuum of space.

With the last officers having settled, Legatus Agricola prepared to start things off.

His second-in-command, Kaeso Cerialis, spoke first.

"Officers of the Twenty-Seventh Legion, Captains of Hibernia, I speak to you as Tribunus Laticlavius. Whether you hail from the Twentieth, the Second, or the noble clanns of Hibernia, we are all one family now," he began.

To add emphasis to their new shared identity, Cerialis had chosen this moment to unveil the new battle-standard. With a nod to Immune Laurentius, the most reliable and only Ambassador invited to the more secret briefings, the large, red tapestry was unveiled.

Measuring three pes by three pes, one square meter, the tapestry was a perfect match for the original Battle-Standards of the Twentieth and the Second. However, unlike the charging boar of the Twentieth and the Capricornus of the Second, the mascot of the Twenty-seventh Legion was a tree, arbor roseaus, the rosebud tree.

It was the perfect logo for the newest, most powerful legion in the history of the Roman Empire.

"Well done, Immune Laurentius," said Agricola. "This is exactly what I had hoped for."

"Legatus. The embroidery was done by some of the Hibernian women, with a little assistance from my wife."

"Convey our gratitude to Fulvia and the others, and have them produce one for each starship before we arrive."

"Legatus."

"And that brings us to the salient point to be discussed today," said Crispus. "And while we still do not know the situation in Rome, or even the name of the current emperor, we must remind ourselves of whom we fundamentally are."

"We are Romans!" shouted one of the older centurions, drawing a unified chorus of agreement from the others."

"That is true. We serve the senate and the people of Rome," continued Cerialis. "And we are very soon to return home!"

Thunderous applause came from Hibernians and Romans alike.

By now, everyone had come to accept that those they knew on Terra were long since dead, buried, and lost to the ages. Their thirty-years-in-thirteen-days excursion from Planeta Bellorum to Planeta Caedum and ultimate return to Planeta Metallorum had proven that in the weeks away in space, fully one hundred and fifty years of planetary time had passed on Metallorum.

Seeing the graves of those they had left behind before their grand tour of the Tuathii planetae affected them deeply. They had lost even more of themselves, and therefore the remaining two hundred and thirty of the original group taken by the Tuathii at Dubh Linn became that much closer.

Seeing the new cities and people that had sprung from the fertile soil of Metallorum had convinced them that, while they were not immortal they now had to understand the passage of time locally – on a starship – in relation to the much faster passage of planetary time.

Those who had not travelled with Agricola, who were born and raised on Metallorum, initially had problems comprehending this reality. However their interactions with those onboard Tribune Gratianus's warship had provided a constant reminder that the Romans of Terra were real, and not just legends. They now understood the concept, extraordinary as it was, that they would be returning to a Terra that was almost two millennia older than the one that the Romans had originally known.

But until the rendezvous with Marcus and Antoninus was completed, and they had new information available to them, all they had was what they knew of the Terra they had left some five years – and two millennia – ago.

"People of Rome and our adopted peoples of Éire," Cerialis continued, "I give you the representative of the Emperor himself, our leader, Legatus Legionus Quintus Julius Agricola!"

Thundering cheers from the Romans and, strangely, foot-stomping from the Hibernians, shook the main corridor of the command ship to the terror and confusion of the Octopodii and Siphonapteristii tending to their duties in the peripheral parts of the ship.

The Tuatha knew that the humans would be having some sort of unlinked acoustical connection. Strange as it was for the Tuatha, it was not unusual for the strange bipedal beings to communicate with each other using their acoustical organs. If any of it was of any importance, the Tuatha knew, the humans would link-think it with them afterward.

It was enough to the Tuatha that they had been informed of the planned meeting in advance, and word had been communicated to the Octopodii and Siphonopteristii that the main corridors of the nine linked major starships – six colonist-ships and three warships – were off-limits, so the bizarre humans could prepare for the return to their home planet.

The Tuatha had work to do, preparing for the collection, processing, and storage of the rare minerals that they were going to Terra to collect. At least that was what the ambassadors had told them would be accomplished on Terra. They had also told the Tuatha that there may be a requirement to use some of the ship's energy-curtains in support of accomplishing the tasks on Terra, as there was the possibility of some form of opposition.

Based on their experience with the humans during the visit to Planeta Bellorum, however, the Tuathii in the starships had full confidence that the humans would be competent in their task, and that it was in the best interests of the Tuathii race to do whatever the humans asked, no matter how insane it may seem to their way of thinking.

They are useful to me-us, and I can reflect on all of this when I return to the homeworld and link with my ancient selves.

Agricola rose from the stump-chair made from the segment of Tuatha chopped up by the carpenter munifex, the throne now well-worn by use, and began speaking.

"We have received confirmation that our scout-ship is on its way to the gathering as planned at the opposite side of the orbital path of Terra. For those of you born and raised on Metallorum, the two men you are about to meet will be strangers. For those of us who knew them, they will likely be almost unrecognizable to us as well. When last we saw them, Tribune Marcus Horatius Avitus and Immune Antoninus Commodus were young and powerful men.

"Tribune and commander from Cohort Eight of Legio II, my friend Marcus Avitus, will not be the twenty-six year old man I sent on the mission from Planeta Caedum to Terra – he will be a much older man of seventy-five! Immune Commodus will be almost seventy."

A murmur of surprise followed from those who knew them. Despite knowing that the Equanimity effects of starship travel extended life, they still thought of sixty or seventy years as impossibly old, as the Rome of old seldom saw men older than fifty, and very rarely as old as sixty .

"Marcus and Antoninus will arrive in one hour, their scout-ship will connect to a side portal of our ship, here at the front of the line of starships. They will be met by an honor guard led by Centurion Tappulus," said Agricola, nodding to Tappulus. "And Aulus, you must not show any hesitation when you present Marcus with the Centurial Signum of the Eighth Cohort!" Agricola said.

"Legatus! And don't worry, I am eager to return the command of the Eighth to the rightful commander, Tribune Avitus. Optio Ovidius and Signifer Petronius will be with me to ensure that I do. They served with him in the days of Legio Two in Britannia, so there will be no doubt who the Eighth Cohort belongs to!"

Cheers from the officers of the Eighth Cohort gave evidence of their love and respect for their original commander, Tribune Marcus Avitus.

"Marcus and Antoninus will no doubt have a great deal of information for us. It is my hope that they will provide the answers to the questions I have. Foremost of which is, who is the current emperor? But also, how has the empire grown? Who are our enemies? How has Rome changed? And many more," Agricola said before pausing, to continue with a more serious tone.

"But we must also be prepared for bad news. Rome could have changed a great deal since we left. Rome could be in trouble, in need of our assistance. Rome could have fallen into the corruption and malaise that emanates from the unchecked greed and blindness of a republican senate, as in the final days of the reign of Emperor Nero and the chaotic aftermath." He paused, looking seriously at his audience, making eye contact with several of his officers and a few of Queen Laelie's captains.

"And it is possible that Rome has been obliterated, perhaps even a great many years ago. Rome could be no more."

"Say it cannot be!" shouted a centurion that Agricola did not recognize, probably one from Planeta Metallorum, who would have never seen Rome in his lifetime, only heard legends of it.

Holding his hand up for silence, Agricola replied. "Yes, it could be so. But if it were, then there would be a terrible reckoning for whichever Germanic or other pale-skinned or savage race was responsible. Marcus Avitus and Antoninus Commodus will know who is responsible. And that brings me to the purpose of this gathering. It will take no longer than a few days for Tribune Avitus and Immune Commodus to bring me and my advisers up to date. We will then convene a *comitia curiata*, committee of representatives from all the ethnic subdivisions that comprise our people. Together, with what we learn of present-day Terra, we will carry out a battle planning conference and determine what form our arrival in Rome – or elsewhere on Terra for that matter – will take. Certainly within two market days' time, we will set foot on Terra. Whether this will be a Triumphal Parade or deployment into battle with an enemy of Rome, our long odyssey will soon come to an end!" said Agricola, eliciting cheers from all.

"And now, as we prepare to greet our long-lost friends, I ask you all to make yourselves invisible. Follow the directions of your officers as if your life depended on it. We must show Tribune Avitus and Immune Commodus that no matter what terrible news of Rome they may carry, the discipline and the traditions of Rome live on, with the Twenty-seventh Legion – their legion – and with us – their brothers.

"And if you see them wandering the decks of the ships, perhaps with some of their friends from the Second, perhaps with their wives, and for Marcus at least, the son he has not seen, do not approach them. Do not pester them with questions, and do not disgrace your century with unprofessional conduct," he warned. "To that end, I am now giving the order that should any unit disgrace itself, through poor conduct or any interference with Tribune Avitus or Immune Commodus, I will personally *decimate* the entire unit, including the officers."

The centurions looked at each other, knowing that their legatus was serious. They all knew about what had happened when the Ordovician warlord Caratacuss had wiped out an *ala*, squadron, of cavalry and much of the First Century of legionaries from the Second Cohort of Legio XX. The entire cohort had retreated to the safety of a clearing, out of the projectile range of the Ordovician archers that had ambushed the marching formation. Legatus Agricola the Younger had been tribune in command of the march of the Second and Fifth Cohorts who had been sent by Governor Agricola the Elder to encamp near *Dinorwig*, fort of the Ordovicians, in present day Wales. The area had originally been conquered by Governor Vespasian years earlier, but had been a repeated source of annoyance to the Romans. Governor Agricola had not expected the Ordovician resistance to be so effective, and entrusted the task to his inexperienced son − part of Agricola the Younger's on-the-job training as a Tribune of the Twentieth Legion.

At that time, the young tribune had been incensed that a unit under his command had done such a disgraceful act as to retreat. His response, there in the Ordovician mountains, while the Fifth Cohort cleared Ordovicians from the forest and ridgeline around them, was to assemble the Second Cohort and walk along the line of 480 men while Pilus Prior Cerialis from the Fifth Cohort counted their number. Tribune Agricola the Younger personally hacked, slashed, or skewered every tenth man in the Second Cohort. When he was done, not a man had budged, and forty-eight men lay dead or dying along the line. The unit had been *decimated*.

That the first man he had killed was Pilus Prior Secondus Aurelinaus, a personal friend of his, was irrelevant. Also irrelevant was the fact that the unit was comprised of newly-arrived recruits from Hispania, mostly inexperienced milites and discens rather than the more experienced miles gregarius and immunes of the battle-hardened Fifth.

Inspired to restore their pride, the Second Cohort went on to great success in carrying out Agricola the Elder's next task, also under the command of then-Tribune Agricola the Younger, to completely exterminate the Ordovician people.

That had been a mere four years ago, at least in the timeframe of the officers who had been with Agricola in the Ordovician campaign. Thus, the officers knew that Legatus Agricola was serious about enforcing discipline and maintaining the honor of Rome.

They did not know how deeply the incident at Dinorwig, in present day Wales, had affected the young Agricola. Nor did they know that he had held himself personally responsible for deploying the inexperienced, weaker Second Cohort to the front of the column, where the brunt of the Celtic Ordovician ambush had struck. He should have listened to Cerialis, Tribune of the Fifth Cohort at the time, and placed the centuria of the more experienced Fifth Cohort at the front.

But discipline and Roman law required that regardless of a commander's error or the mists of war, surrender or capitulation is not an option for a Roman soldier. Nor was any other form of disgrace.

That Legatus Agricola had made a point of saying what the veteran officers knew so well made some of the more experienced officers worry about what terrible news Tribune Avitus and Immune Antoninus may be carrying from Rome, and what they may be called upon to have their men do. *The time has come to be soldiers again*, the centurions understood.

After the excitement of travelling in the scout-ship for the first time in forty-eight years, Marcus Avitus felt wonderful.

He knew that part of it was due to the beneficial 'Equanimity effects' that came with space travel in a Dupli-Tri starship. His renewed energy was also due to his opportunity to deliver on the promise he had made to his friend and commander, Legatus Agricola, and the promise of being reunited with his wife Neasa and to see his son for the first time. The old man felt ten years younger, and was brimming with anticipation as the scout-ship proceeded to its destination.

Watching on the video screen that Antoninus had rigged to the scout-ship's viewing pot, the four were now passengers as the scout-ship's automatonic system piloted the small craft to a large double-airlock on the forward side of the lead starship.

Marcus, Antoninus, Nestor and Ruth watched the disc-shaped portal slide up into a recess in the deck-head, and they bent over to peer through the telescoping inter-connecting tube to an identical portal in the much larger starship. The sudden movement of the portal startled Nestor. Back on Earth, Nestor's twin brother, Eduardo, was still seeing to the arrangements that Marcus had directed. The Cuervo brothers were Marcus's closest friends on Earth, and he trusted them with his life. If the young men had shown the slightest hint of disloyalty, of course, Marcus would have killed them.

Having Nestor and Ruth along for the ride made Marcus feel somehow more confident, as they represented living connections to the present day Earth that Marcus had grown to care so deeply about, and in a sense, the boy and his brother were key parts of the plan that Marcus was intending to propose to Legatus Agricola.

After powering down the computer equipment on the bridge and gathering their effects, the four visitors prepared to make their way to the command ship. Carefully proceeding along the tube ahead of Antoninus, Ruth and Nestor, the first thing that Marcus saw was Cohort Eight's battle-standard, held aloft by Signifer Petronius, two cornicens, Optio Ovidius and Marcus's old friend, Aulus Tappulus.

Those first images, the familiar, happy faces, told him that all was well with the legion. The new battle-standard of Legio XXVII, on display with the small group assembled just inside the larger starship indicated to Marcus that the composite legion was whole, if not larger, and with an appropriate mascot. Emblazoned on the battle-standard was the familiar *arbor roseaus*, the Judas Tree.

Everybody looks so young! Marcus thought, as he raised his shoulders, pushed his frail chest forward, and strode through with as much dignity as the seventy-five year-old man could muster.

In the confined space of the corridor leading to the stern portal, the men of Cohort Eight had only enough room to assemble in single file, leaving a few strides of open space for Tribune Avitus, Immune Commodus and their two companions to stand before them and formally be welcomed to the starship.

At the head of the column was an excited young signifer, Petronius, proudly holding a spear-shaft with the Eighth's centurial signum.

The cornicen, from Immune Commodus's unit, came next, blasting away with a short but proud blast from his horn.

After that, Primus Pilus Crispus stood, dressed in full battle uniform, seemingly as prepared for parade as for war.

Next were the Pilus Prior Octavius, Optio Ovidius, and a small group of close friends. Altogether, the reception party numbered eight, keeping the group on the intimate scale of a contubernium, tent group, so as not to overwhelm the aged men when they emerged from the tube.

Agricola and Cerialis wanted to be there, but had decided to let the men from the Eighth have some privacy when greeting one another.

Back in the pod which Agricola used as the *comitia curiata*, conference hall, the Legatus waited along with the Tribunus Laticlavius, Kaeso Cerialis, advisors Metellus and Quintilianus, the most knowledgeable engineers and technicians from the Eighth Cohort and a few of the leaders from Laelie's Celtic women.

The twenty key leaders were packed rather tightly in the back of the pod, leaving room for Agricola and Cerialis to sit with Marcus at a portable table crafted from Metallorum hardwood. The leaders eagerly awaited the imminent arrival of the returning Romans, and the answers to so many pressing questions.

Also waiting for Marcus was his wife, Neasa, and their ten year old son, Avitus Connal. Neasa understood that their small family reunion would have to come after the urgent military meeting. A Roman officer on such an important military mission must tend to duty first, whether that would take hours or days, before being given leave to see his family.

Queen Laelie had already reassured Neasa that once Marcus was free to see his loved ones, they would be given a full day of privacy to become reacquainted. For her part, Neasa was not worried that Marcus would be an old man, or whether they would still love each other. Her only concern was for her son, Connal, and whether he would bond well with the father he had never met.

Fighting the urge to step out and look down the corridor for Marcus Avitus, Legatus Agricola sat in a stoic posture, with Cerialis beside him, facing the open portal.

They could hear the footfalls of a group of men, their hearts lifting as the steps quickened and grew louder. The anticipation was palpable, almost intolerable.

From the beaming smile on the old man's face as he came into view, and the happy expressions on the faces of the men from the Eighth all around him, Agricola knew that the reunion had gone well.

"Hail Tribune Avitus, returned from Terra!" shouted the sentry at the portal, unnecessarily.

"Welcome, Tribune Avitus. Come. Approach and report!" commanded Tribunus Laticlavius Cerialis.

Cerialis had only just completed his words when he was shoved unceremoniously aside; Agricola could take it no longer and bolted out of his seat, pushing past Cerialis to embrace his friend.

Marcus felt the same way, and the two men came together in an intense brotherly embrace.

"Marcus! You old man! I am so happy to see you!"

"As I am, you, Legatus Julius Agricola," Marcus said.

"Legatus," was all that Antoninus could say, choked with so much emotion, that he could not continue.

Agricola tried to put the oldest immune in the history of Rome at ease: "My dear Antoninus, come, sit with Kaeso and me. We'll let Marcus update us on his experiences, and you can join in when you are ready," Agricola said, to the clearly terrified older man as he took him by the arm.

"Thank you, Legatus," Antoninus said, visibly relieved.

"Screw the ceremony," said Agricola, as he led Marcus Avitus and Antoninus Commodus to the table.

Marcus smiled as the other officers assembled in the back of the room, understanding their observer status for his report to the Legatus. He took his place at the table with Antoninus, Agricola, and Cerialis.

Marcus had almost forgotten Nestor, who was removing his backpack, which contained a number of 'gifts' in a white box.

"Legatus," Marcus said, "this fine young man and the young lady behind him both hail from the twenty-first century. His name is Nestor Cuervo, and her name is Ruth Daley."

"Twenty-first century? Of what legion? What sort of a unit?" asked Cerialis, finding it strange to hear of anything more than ten centuries in a legion.

"Apologies. So much has changed. It is how they refer to time now, on Earth – on Terra."

"Oh," said Agricola. "With so much for you to report, I think it best to have you begin, and we will hold our tongues as much as possible. Proceed. And Vibius Metellus. And welcome, young Nestor Cuervo and Lady Daley – sit, please," Agricola commanded, looking over his shoulder to the historian. "Are you ready to scribe every word that Marcus and Antoninus say, so we can review it together after their report?"

"Already started, Legatus!" said the philosopher, seated cross-legged on the floor, in front of the throng of officers at the back of the room.

"Young Nestor was a student of mine at the university where I taught Roman history. I trust him, and he and his brother have done a great deal for our cause," Marcus began, but seeing Agricola looking around as if he expected to see another young man, Marcus explained: "His brother Eduardo, his twin, actually, is still on Terra, seeing to preparations. But we will come to that later. Anyhow, with the help of the Cuervos, and what Antoninus and I had assembled, we have brought you treasures – fit for display in the Pantheon. In fact, good Primus Pilus Crispus is overseeing their transfer from our scout-ship to here, as we speak."

Agricola looked at the strange white box that the young man held nervously in his hands.

"Put it on the table, young man," he said, while motioning in case the young man did not understand Latin, "And breathe!"

Nestor Cuervo put the box on the table, and then moved back to stand behind his old professor's shoulder, only slightly less terrified.

When Professor Avitus, now once again every bit the first century Roman tribune looked back at him, smiling like a proud father, Nestor breathed deeply, locking eyes with his mentor.

"'Imperator' is the correct response, when spoken to by the emperor of Rome and the known universe," said Marcus, encouraging the boy to act like the Roman he needed to quickly become in his new position in this society that he had previously only dreamed might be real.

"Imperator," Nestor stammered, excited to have a chance to speak in his clumsy Latin.

"Well done, boy!" said Agricola, "Now what's in the box, Tribune?"

"Before we get into that, I would like to introduced the young lady, if I may, Imperator."

"Where are my manners? Yes, by all means, Marcus, please do so," said Agricola, pouring on the charm as he turned his attention to the young woman.

Despite being on a starship and confronted by the impossible sight of Romans and Celts from the first century, the young woman stood with poise and confidence. Taller than most of the men in the room, she was dressed strangely from a Roman perspective. She wore an outfit that covered her from neck to ankles, with a brown fabric that seemed to be very rugged. The two-piece suit of clothes had lots of pockets, some of which bulged as if filled with small items. Around her neck was a strap, suspending something fist-sized, that looked to be made by the finest of craftsmen. Over her shoulder was a satchel, much like that worn by the young man in front of her, similarly full of mysterious contents.

Her overall appearance was that of a confident person dressed, and equipped, as if for an expedition.

The men exchanged looks with each other that instantly established their consensus that the woman was very attractive.

Her burgundy hair and voluptuous figure were made that much sexier by the nobility and grace she carried herself with. Looking Agricola in the eye, Ruth stepped forward and offered her hand, introducing herself in perfect, if strangely accented, Latin.

"Imperator. I am honored to make your acquaintance."

"The honor is mine, young lady," Agricola replied, and then addressed Marcus. "Is she your concubine?"

"No, Imperator. She is one of my most promising academics, from the university where I have been teaching Latin and Roman studies for the last four decades. Ruth is an expert scholar, and is completing a thesis – learned argument – on the role of Hibernian women in the political and class structures of Éire of the first century – our time. She is particularly interested to know details of the application of something called the Brehan Law code, and other aspects of women as lawyers in that time."

"Hibernian women act as jurists?" Quintilianus asked, incredulously.

"Yes, or, at least, that is one of the 'facts' of history that Ruth wants to confirm with eye-witness accounts from Queen Laelie and others.

"But we will get full measure out of her as well. She is here to assist me with preparing the Hibernian women for what life is like for a woman of Earth today, as they would otherwise be overwhelmed with a great many changes, affecting women. As for interview, moreover, Ruth is particularly interested in talking with anybody, perhaps Daffid Og Briogan or Queen Laelie, who may have had first-person interaction with High King Tuathal Techtmar."

"What is significant about him? He was just one of the many lesser kings in our time, was he not?" asked Metellus.

"Well, history accounts that immediately after our time, he was somehow able to unify all of Ireland under the rule of a single king."

"Do you suppose that our little war had anything to do with it?"

"What war?" asked Marcus, setting them up.

"The Battle of Dubh Linn, of course."

"That battle, and our entire existence, never happened."

"What?" asked Agricola.

"Emperor Domitian had it stricken from the historical record, to protect Rome from a truth so mystical that he feared it would erode morale."

"These and other details of history are yet another contribution that young Ruth Daley will contribute, Dominus."

I see. Very thoughtful of you, Marcus."

"Thank you, Imperator. I would like to send her on to Queen Laelie, to organize her access to the Hibernians."

"Access? That sounds ominous. Does young Daley here have another purpose, other than to serve?"

"Yes, Imperator. *Quid pro qou*. In exchange for her loyal assistance, I have promised her the opportunity to interview Queen Laelie, Princess Maura, my wife Neasa and others to confirm and to expand upon her theories of how emancipated, how independent and influential, the women of Éire were in their time."

"I see. Very well, I agree with her terms. She clearly is a strong personality, that is obvious. Much like Queen Laelie, in fact," Agricola observed.

"Yes, Imperator. With your permission, I would like to send her on to begin her task."

"Very well," Agricola turned to face his officers, seated behind him. "Men, would any of you be willing to escort young Daley to Queen Laelie's chambers?"

A dozen arms shot up, accompanied a chorus of "I will!"

Loudest among them was the only bachelor in the group.

"Tribune Tappulus. Please take charge of this academic, and convey her safely to my wife."

"Imperator," Tappulus said, nearly jumping out of his seat to take Ruth by the arm, and led her away. The emphasis that Emperor Agricola had placed on safely was not lost on the horny, lonely, man.

No sooner had Ruth and Tappulus departed when Vibius Metellus quipped, "Will she be safe with him?"

"Vibius, the real question is whether Aulus will be safe with her. She is a remarkable woman who can handle Aulus, or any man, for that matter," replied Marcus.

"Very well. Now let's open the present!" said Agricola, returning the focus to what really interested him, Marcus's report, and offering, from Terra.

"This is one of our gifts. The first of many, if you will grant me the latitude, is a very strong elixir that I would like to have Primus Pilus distribute amongst the officers. Would you like to try it?"

"Are you sure it is safe, not poisonous?" asked Cerialis, curiously looking at the golden bottle, with its yellow label and red wax seal. "Well, it is poison, but only mildly so. It is far stronger than Vinum Caecuban, or that of the Appian Way vineyards. And this taste is a completely different experience, and effect, than wine. Men should limit their consumption to a few cyathus, about what they call "shots" on Terra these days. It will put a man into a spirited mood. If you drink this at the normal rate of consumption of vinum, a man will beunconscious within a few hours.

"It truly is poisonous, then?" asked Cerialis.

"Yes, if consumed in excess."

"But it is suitable to celebrate our reunion with? To have a few cyathus?"

Marcus smiled mischievously as he opened the forty-ounce bottle. He removed a bag of small plastic cups from the box and handed them to Nestor, who proudly set them out on the table. Looking around, Nestor counted heads and set out twenty-three cups, hoping that Professor Avitus would tell them of his personal connection to the bottle.

As Marcus began to pour a *cyathus*, a one-ounce shot, into each cup, Agricola motioned for the other senior officers to gather around. They crowded close, eagerly anticipating the drink. It had been quite some time since any of them had drunk anything stronger than the herbal teas from indigenous plants on Planeta Metallorum.

"This drink was invented over a hundred and thirty years ago, by a man named Jose Cuervo," he said, waiting to see if anybody had been paying attention.

"Any relation to the young man you brought from Terra?" asked, the Philosopher, Vibius Metellus.

"Yes, as a matter of fact. Jose was the boy's great-grandfather's great-grandfather, some six generations past, Metellus."

"And this is a product of Hispania?"

"Not exactly. It is from a nation called 'Mexico', which was, for a time, a colony of Hispania. They still speak 'Spanish' there today."

Marcus had finished pouring the drinks. Everybody waited with bated breath as he held out a small cup for Agricola to be the first to taste.

"This is about six times the strength of the vinum you are familiar with, so one drink this size is equivalent to three *vas*, cups, of vinum. It is made from the agave plant, and is described as 'hard liquor' at 41% alcohol."

"Percent?"

"Yes. Pure alcohol is too strong for even the strongest man, and it is the alcohol which gives the pleasant effects of wine and other alcoholic drinks their potency. This drink is particularly powerful, and when a man drinks too much of it, he will go temporarily insane."

"Perfect for soldiers!" said one of the officers.

"Perhaps, for when discipline is relaxed, but it has many effects which are not helpful."

"Such as?"

"It changes perceptions, so that a man may perceive insult where there is none, think a woman wants him when she does not, or thinks a particularly bad idea is a stroke of genius," said Marcus.

"I see. So this is why you call it poison?"

"Yes, when used to excess. As with all such substances – and there are a great many such substances now being used by the people of Terra – this can lead to no end of trouble.

"So why did you bring it here?" asked Cerialis.

"Abusus non tollit usum, misuse does not remove use. I have a fondness for this, in moderation. I thought it appropriate to share in its pleasure, to celebrate our reunion. It is the taste of the world as it is now, and hard liquor is the drink of gentlemen, or those that think they are, and can afford it."

"A taste of insanity, then?"

"How astute, Metellus." Without further comment, he handed the cup to Agricola, and raised his own.

"It is to be drunk in one 'shot'," as he then demonstrated, releasing a satisfied "Haaaah!" sound.

Agricola imitated, downing the tequila in one shot, making a similar "haaaah" comment – quickly followed by some red-faced choking and coughing.

"Babae!, wow, that really has a kick! I can feel it burning in my blood and taking hold of my belly. Fantastic! Give me another. You must try this!" Agricola said, giving his cup back to Marcus and ushering his officers in for their shots.

With a nod from Marcus, Nestor removed a second forty ounce bottle from the box, opened it, and prepared to pour a second round.

After all had their ration, Agricola pulled the focus back to the matter at hand.

"Calix meus inebrians, my cup is making me drunk. Well, now that you have poisoned us all, and put us into this delightful state

of near drunkenness, it's time to give us the bad news. For surely you have lightened our hearts and numbed our minds with purpose?" joked Agricola.

"Imperator can we have a moment, in private. Antoninus and I have a few things that we wish to discuss before the presentation."

By the look of seriousness in Marcus's eyes, and the somber, agreeable nod from Antoninus, Agricola knew that the news was not good. He suspected it had something to do with the fact that Marcus had been addressing his as 'Imperator', when the last time they had met, he had been merely 'Legatus.' *This does not bode well for Rome,* Agricola realized.

Agricola ordered everyone to the corridor.

When the room had cleared, they all sat. Antoninus poured a double round of tequila, and Agricola nodded to Marcus to begin.

"The earth has changed a great deal since we left."

"Continue. And speak slowly. I have no doubt that many things have happened over these many years, and my mind is clouded by this drink."

"I will be brief. You will not be happy to hear this, but I must inform you that Rome is no more. The world has changed, and not for the better. Although there have been stunning technological advances, that you will learn about, mankind has not been a responsible steward of the planet. The environment has been abused. The water is polluted, as is the air. Much of the rich soils have been contaminated with poisons. The climate is confused and does not resemble that to which you would be accustomed. The earth's ability to sustain this population has been stretched beyond its limit."

"Who is in charge? How was this permitted to happen?" Asked Agricola.

"Greed. Greed rules the day. And corruption. There is staggering inequality on the planet. Vast numbers of people live like beasts, while wealthy nations enjoy the lifestyle of nobles. Those who wield the power are more concerned with enriching themselves than exercising any sense of responsibility for the planet on which they rule. They are like the puppet-masters in a child's play. They are as idiots, leading blind sheep."

"Enough", replied Agricola. "We have seen this before on other planetae. What is your recommendation?"

"Rome. We must restore the Republic. Terra is on a rapid downward spiral, there is no other option."

"Very well." Agricola paused for a moment, looking at Commodus, and then returning his look to Antoninus. "Marcus, complete your presentation as intended." He then opened the door to the pod.

All in attendance sat, in rapt curiosity, as Marcus proceeded to the far end of the room to begin his presentation.

"As I recall, you all understand that the Roman Empire, as grand as it was when you last set foot on Terra, was actually very small in comparison to all the lands and all the people of Terra at that time," Marcus began, noticing a number of heads nodding in agreement. Nestor reached into one of the boxes that Crispus had brought back from the scout-ship and removed a desktop-sized political globe and placed it upon the table, while Marcus continued.

"And the time we recall first-hand as when the Tuathii abducted us from Hibernia, we shall refer to as the first century."

"First century? Why? It was 835 AUC, if the year must be numbered, that would make it the ninth century, would it not?" demanded rhetorician Marcus Quintilianus, perhaps the best mathematician in the group.

"No, my dear friend. We have to look at this in the context of the time-keeping system commonly used on Terra today."

"So what is it based on?"

"The months are Julian, as given to us by Dictator Julius Caesar. That will be familiar to you. However, the contemporary people's habit of counting the years is based on years since the birth of Christ. They call this 'AD', *Anno Domini*, as in *Anno Domini Nostri Iesu Christi*, the year of our lord Jesus Christ."

"Christ? The Jew who started that cult that is – was – all the rage amongst the women of Rome?" asked Centurion Vilius Tappulus.

"The same. That particular cult has taken over much of the planeta, with members of the 'Christian' religion numbering as many as two million millions."

"Two million millions? Do you mean two thousands of thousands, for two million?" asked Quintilianus.

"No. A thousand times that number."

"But that is an impossibly large number," Quintilianus protested. "After all, the entire population of the world must be, or must have been in 'our' time, no more than ten or perhaps twenty thousand of thousands – ten or twenty of those impossibly large 'millions.'"

"That estimate is not a surprise, Vibius Metellus, but it falls short of the population on Terra, even in that first century – the ninth century in our system – by a factor of tenfold."

"So you are saying that even then, on the entire planet, with all the lands as yet unconquered by Rome, that all the peoples numbered as many as two hundred millions?"

"Exactly. Your skills with the mathematics of the problem are greater than I recalled, my friend."

"Well mine is not! Explain it to me in a way that the rest of us can understand!" ordered Agricola, seemingly becoming angry at the complexity of the mathematics.

Having anticipated the problem of conveying the largesse of Terra's population, Marcus Horatius removed a glass jar from the box and held it up.

"This is a jar of sand, from Hispania," he began. "In this jar is approximately fifteen million grains of sand. Now if you look closely at this glass vessel, you will see a layer of red paper in the bottom portion of the jar. Do you see it?" he asked.

Heads nodded all around.

"The sand below that line, the bottom stratum, layer, represents the five hundred thousand inhabitants of Rome, including the villas and hovels as far as Ostia to the west, and encompassing all of the *Septem montes Romae*, the Seven Hills of Rome."

Marcus looked around, and saw that his peers understood the numbers in this context.

"So for the population of the Earth – Terra – in that first century, in what we might call 'our time', it would take thirteen such jars of sand, and Rome would still account for only that bottom stratus of just one of those thirteen jars, just one half of one million out of a total of two hundred million inhabitants of earth in the first century."

"This is astonishing. So have we conquered all of these other peoples? They are so numerous! Or have they conquered us?"

"Your comprehension of the problem is impressive, Fabius Quintilianus," Marcus said of the rhetorician. "Sadly, they have long since over-run Rome. We will discuss Roman history in the weeks to come. First I want you all to understand how terrible the situation has become on Earth, and what I advise we should do about it."

"Who destroyed Rome? What people, and do they live still?"

"Imperator, Rome destroyed Rome. The sacking and burning took centuries – hundreds of years – and a variety of peoples took their turn pillaging Rome. They disassembled our great buildings, desecrated our holy sites, and defiled our people. We have a long list of enemies, but they are long gone. Far greater events have since taken place since those times. To explain all of the issues that I consider to be of import will require several days. Because, with every subject that I wish to discuss, I must provide an explanation of how we have evolved to the current state or condition. There is much to be covered, some of which is extremely alarming and some of which will leave you fascinated."

The room fell silent, distraught at the news of the destruction of Rome, and the men and women waited nervously for what was to follow.

"Planeta 'Earth,'is now populated with as many as *eight billion* humans on the plant. Do you understand that number? It means eight thousand million."

"Preposterous. And we know that number, billion, from our discussions at Planeta Caedum. But to imagine the population of earth to have grown so numerous in such a short time.! Why, that would be some fourteen times as many as all the people that lived in our time. How can there be so many? How can they live?" protested Cerialis.

"You are close, Kaeso Cerialis, but not quite right. The numbers are enormous; however the planet is also very large. Also, modern devices, technologia, which they call 'technology', allows men to accomplish great deeds. This allows more people to be fed, housed, or transported than we were capable of doing in our time."

"Are these numbers of people organized into a great diversity of peoples? – Or is there one dominant empire?"

"Imperator. There are about two hundred 'nations', and a great many military camps within each. But there are only a handful of empires. They are not empires as we knew them in our time. They are a very strange variety of states which, through trade and political alliance, compete with each other as money-lenders and merchants, through a system called 'globalized economics', economics that span the entire planeta.

"The greatest of these nations, of which there are very few, do not directly go to war with one another. If they did, due to the size and destructive capabilities or their armaments, there is a strong likelihood of what has been termed a 'mutually-assured destruction' that would have catastrophic results for the countries involved, and the entire planete. Rather, they go to war with each other by sponsoring smaller nations, providing limited arms, expertise, and financial support, and have these nations go to war with each other."

"So like when one *ludus*, gladiator school, puts their gladiators against those of another ludus? These more powerful nations compete indirectly?"

"It is something like that, only on a far more destructive scale."

"Destructive? How so? Too many rotting corpses on the battlefield?"

"No, it is in the destruction of the land, the damage to the cities, and to the environment. These wars leave the earth badly scorched, and less able to support agriculture, and therefore the life of the populations. They convert once productive cities to squalid camps of refugees numbering into the millions."

"How can that be? Surely even if the land has been fired, it will begin to re-grow the next season."

"This brings us to the fundamental problem, and it is one that will take you a great deal of time and effort to understand adequately. This technologia I spoke of, in a way is similar to the technologia we have seen of the Dupli-Tri and their alien races. It is far more capable than any of our now ancient Roman technologia."

"So this truly is as we saw on Terra Caedum?"

"Yes. However there are no Tuathii on hand to exterminate humankind. There are no natural predators, and they lack the wisdom to stop the insanity. So they continue to grow, exponentially. In fact, their entire economic system craves exponential growth, as if it were a blessing."

"But with all of their technologia, do they not see the folly of breeding so many thousands of millions – billions – of people? Why do they not simply cull their populations to a more suitable number?"

"Imperator, they cannot. The scientists and philosophers understand their folly, and even the plebes have concern, however they continue to live as if the problem will be solved by their grandchildren.

"But what of their leaders? Why do they not take action?"

"Because their political life is too short. Taking action would be so unpopular that a politician would not be re-elected at the next election."

The room fell silent again while Agricola pondered what he had heard. His head ached due to the barrage of new concepts and facts to digest, but he understood the main points.

"So what you are telling us is that a great deal has changed. Rome is no more, and the many great powers of the earth are constantly at war with each other, but yet not *totally* at war. That money-lending and commerce are the new mechanism of war, and that this absurd number you propose, eight thousand millions – eight billion – people all strive to live as if they were all elites, entitled to all the comforts and amenities that their technologia can deliver. Does that summarize what you are reporting?"

"Imperator. Indeed." Marcus was steadfast in his assessment and knew that he had not failed in his mission to bring back an accurate assessment of the situation now faced by the legion.

He awaited Agricola's next command, fairly sure he knew what it would be.

"I need another shot of that poison, as I am sure we all do, Marcus Horatius, before you present the recommendations you spoke of."

"Imperator," said Marcus, as he sent Nestor and a sentry out to the corridor to bring in two more bottles of tequila.

After everybody had another shot or two, it was time.

"You mentioned recommendations?"

"Imperator. First, your intention to return to Terra within the next two market days, as Centurion Crispus has told me, is not possible. We will not be ready for months, perhaps five or six.

"Second, not even with the technologia we have from the Tuathii, and the ships you command – how many is that now? Three of the big warships and six colonist-ships and a score of scout-ships and puller-ships? And how many soldiers – less than a full legion? – We do not have the power to take over more than perhaps one of the great nations.

"Third, it may be better to abandon Terra altogether, and use our thorium resources to find other habitable planetae, where we can rebuild Rome," he paused, to see if he was moving too fast. Agricola was keeping up.

"Go on."

"The environment on Terra may already be a lost cause. What can be done to avert the sort of disaster that befell the Quadrupedii on Planeta Caedum may be impossible to achieve on Terra, no matter how drastic a change of direction can be affected. And finally, if we do attempt to influence the events on

Terra, whether by conquest or diplomacy, we will have to first master the use of their technologia, their culture, and a great many other subjects."

"So you are saying that whatever we do, we need to take great care – and time – in deliberating and preparing…"

Marcus simply nodded, silently, as it was clear that Agricola had a sufficient grasp on the situation.

"So tell me, Marcus, with all of their technologia, and incredible numbers of people available to be put to great accomplishments, what exactly do they do," asked Cerialis.

"They consume."

Agricola turned to Cerialis, with a doubtful look on his face, as Marcus elaborated.

"Everybody on earth consumes. In some of the greatest nations, each family has their own domicile that an emperor from our time would find opulent."

"Are you telling me that these eight billion people all live like royalty?"

"Not all of them. Many live in great poverty, but even those plebes in the poorest of nations consume global resources and generate toxic pollution as they strive to become rich enough to live like royalty or to escape the marginal areas they live in. And in many places, the class structure allows them to rise from what we would consider slave status to plebe and on up to nobility – if they can acquire enough money or power."

"And what do the wealthy do, or the not so wealthy do, other than consume? Do they serve in the military, perhaps?"

"No, Kaeso Cerialis, they generally do not serve in the military. In fact, military service is not a requirement of citizenship in the richer countries."

"Not a requirement, not even for the elite?"

"No. The number of soldiers, while large in nominal terms, is a much smaller proportion than in our time. For example, in our time, as many as one in eight or one in ten citizens would be called upon to serve in the military in time of war, but in today's earth, the proportion is more like one in a hundred, or less."

"But then how do people earn their rights as citizens?"

"They are not required to earn their rights. In fact, in most countries, it is considered a simple birthright, along with the concept of 'human rights.'"

"Human rights?"

"Yes, Imperator, human rights. People of Earth today have this notion that there is something special about human beings, above all other animals, that gives them an entitlement to do as they wish, to consume as much as they like, to poison their environment without consequence, and basically act as if they're not responsible for the mess they leave behind."

"What is the source of these rights, then?" asked the philosopher.

"In most cases, the source is attributed to God, Fabius Quintilianus."

"God? Not 'gods'?" asked Cerialis.

"Now this is a question even I can answer, if I may, Marcus Avitus," said Vibius Metellus, the historian.

"By all means, Vibius, explain it to us," said Marcus.

"The Christian cult is a *monotheist* religion. They follow the message of a Jew, Christ of Nazareth, who was active in Jerusalem during the reign of Emperor Tiberius. The Christ-ian religion, 'Christianity', is based on the parables, teachings and activities of this so-called messiah. Well, his followers believe that Christ was the son of God – and that there is only their God – the only God, a God of all men. This God gave mankind dominion over all other creatures, over all of nature, and that they are themselves made in the image of their God, so they are, in a way, Gods – or at least children of God. Does that summarize it well, Marcus?"

"Basically. But you omitted their philosophy of equality and pacifism. While they will go to war, notably in opposition to followers of other monotheistic religions from other cultures, and with other Christian cultures when there is an economic incentive, the fundamental teachings of the Christian cult, which are so pervasive in the nations of the Earth of today – at least in many of the more powerful nations – is the notion that peace and tolerance are the way they should live, and to let others live as they choose as long as it does not interfere with their freedom to do as they wish."

"Goodness, a philosophy like that would be horrible!"

"Absolutely right, Petillius, and that's part of what brought Rome to catastrophe."

"How so?" asked, Quintilianus.

"It is a long story, Fabius. It spans several centuries. We can discuss it at another time. But the shortest explanation is that the emperors believed that they could control a popular new religion by appointing the bishops – the leaders of this new 'church' – and avoid provoking the population by continuing to suppress a very popular new fad – that of the one God, to replace all of our Roman gods. The God of Jesus Christ. However, over time, the influence of this new church grew. It became powerful, and ultimately became independent from that of the emperor. It gained a life of its own, answerable only to God, a higher power. And as this church claimed to be directly linked to this God, it then took control of the spiritual life of its followers, the ultimate authority, in a sense.

"Pagan Roman beliefs faded. The military softened during extensive periods of peace, like bones of an old man that appear strong but have become weak and eroded within. Eventually, with so many legions distributed throughout the Roman Empire, and extravagance and under productive citizenry in Rome, the empire began to collapse under its own weight. Loss of territories and revenues in Africa and Spain led to reduction in wealth, and an inability to support the military. Without the strong military, wealth ceased to flow to Rome, and the Empire could not afford the many legions required maintain control of all the territories accumulated over the centuries.

"Many Roman notables became secretly Christian. The insidious infiltration of the strange 'brotherly love' ethics of the Christian faith, and the incipient failure of the economic system due to the difficulties of managing such a large empire, made Rome vulnerable from within and from without. Certainly the loss of the Roman way of life, replaced by one that was essentially unsuited to conquest and war – at least in the hearts and minds of the nobility if not in the common citizens and soldiers – hollowed out the heart and soul of Rome. Our many enemies from all four directions saw this as weakness, and were emboldened by it. The end result, with the utter destruction of Rome, followed soon enough."

"So the world is run by selfish people, who believe in the God of the Christians as their ultimate master?"

"In a sense, yes, Imperator. Their God can be interpreted in different ways, and even the most vile action can be justified when done 'in the name of God'. However, there are a great many who are non-believers, who follow what is called a 'secular' tradition, but they are suppressed by a much more vocal and politically active collection of religious zealots, and other foolish people are willingly blind to the catastrophe that is unfolding before their very eyes. There are also a great many who subscribe to alternative relations, different gods and different traditions."

"This catastrophe that you speak of, it is the failure of the ecological system, the climate, the environment, as it was on Planeta Caedum, yes?"

"Yes, Imperator. It will soon be the sort of crisis that a swarm of locusts has when it runs out of things to eat, a massive die-off of the pests."

"What makes you think that a die-off is near?"

"As we learned from the Tuathii, about what happened on Planeta Caedum, as the dominant species consumes and pollutes more than the ecosystem can bear, there is acceleration in the extinction of the range of species at the base of the food-chain pyramid. And this is happening on Earth. The number of species going extinct every decade is accelerating. The most fertile soils of the past, through chemical contamination and over-planting, have in many places become exhausted. And perhaps most catastropuic, the stability of the seasons – the weather itself – is becoming more and more unpredictable."

"The winter rains do not come every year?"

"Worse than that, Vibius, they come with savage intensity, in the wrong season, and alternate with extreme cold or with extreme heat and drought. Farmers cannot plant and nurture their crops to maturity, despite great plant-producing technologia. The situation is far beyond any rational predictability. And even the bees, essential as any farmer knows to the orchards and food crops, are becoming extinct."

"The bees, they are killed by the cold and heat?"

"That's just it. No, the bees are being killed by poisons in the air and water, pesticides that are sprayed on and in the soils and the genetic modification of plants of all types. They are dying from diseases that they cannot fight, plagues that they are too weak to fight off. Many believe that electromagnetic radiation, emitted by the communications gadgets that almost everyone uses, are confusing the bees, hindering that inert navigational system, which causes them to become separated from their hives. Myself, I believe that all of these issues are contributing to what is called Colony Collapse Disorder. And without bees, many food crops cannot be produced."

"And how did these poisons get into the air and water?"

"They are used by farmers to help grow crops, or they ooze into the water from mountains of refuse called 'dumps', or they come from the smoke of the engines of their horse-less carriages – automobiles – that most people have access to."

"What a mess. So what is your assessment, then? – Is there any point in trying to intervene? I mean really, what can be done to save Terra? – Maybe we should abandon it now, and not bother with it? There must be some suitable planetae nearby," said Cerialis.

"None of them would be *home*," said Agricola.

After taking a few hours pause to deliberate in private with Marcus, Agricola had his key advisors recalled, to continue the discussion.

"I think we should look at alternatives, determine if there is a way to restore sanity, perhaps take over just one powerful nation. If we can do that, we may be able to build a large enough army to conquer the other powerful nations, and then take the steps necessary – what the Tuathii said should have been done on Planeta Caedum – and perhaps reduce the number of idle people from this mind-boggling eight thousand million to a more sustainable number."

"Well, while we consider this, Imperator, should we not also look for an alternative home, in case we are not able to succeed on Terra?" asked Cerialis, always the realist, always planning an exit strategy should a campaign not go as intended.

"Certainly. We will do that regardless. After all, even after we succeed in taking charge on Earth, we will want to expand our empire to nearby planetae. It is the only way to be secure in the event that Tuathii, or surviving Dupli-Tri, or any other hostile race choose to compete with us in this region of the universe," Agricola concluded, and then pressed Marcus again. "So Marcus, lay it out, what is your assessment of our best strategic approach?"

"Imperator. I am impressed at your grasp of the situation we face. I had expected it to take more time to fully inform you. As for my own assessment, I am only a tribune. I am not a philosopher or tactician; however I have formulated what I believe to be a viable approach for your consideration. I have had a lot of time on my hands, after all," he joked, which brought out smiles from many in the room. The military men, however, exhibited less humor and were intent on dissecting the problem further. Marcus pressed on.

"First, we spend the next few months out here, beyond the detection of the powerful nations of the Earth. I am certain that by following the Earth's orbital path and remaining on the opposite side of the Sun from the Earth, we are safe from the few scientific instruments that could detect us.

"I have prepared a series of tablet-books and teaching moving-pictures to help teach our men English, the most influential language on Terra. We also have to teach the Hibernian women Spanish – and also to those of our men not from Hispania, mostly men of the Twentieth. Here are some examples," Marcus took out a few Latin-English and Latin-

Spanish manuals he had written over the years and then recently printed through a print-on-demand kiosk at Boston University.

"This tablet device is easy enough for a child to use, as long as that child can read and write in Spanish or English. Given time, we could program this to work in Latin as well. However, so much of the information that can be seen with this device is in more common languages, such as English, Spanish, German, and other languages, but not Latin.

"My recommendation is that you have every single one of our people study Spanish and English, using the books and tableta devices that Antoninus and I have brought. We can then begin to teach them how to study other materials on these tablets – and there are so many wonderful things to see and hear – and only then, when our people understand this 'modern' technologia, spoken in either English or Spanish, only then can we contemplate the next step."

"Tribune Avitus, when I sent you and Immune Commodus ahead to gather intelligence, I was confident that you would return successfully to give your report. But I can honestly say no person in the history of Rome has ever provided such an impossible barrage of unbelievable and yet absolutely essential information as you have today," began Agricola.

"My advisors and I will now continue to look through the presentations of moving images that you have provided, perhaps have a few more shots of tequila as we discuss what you have shown us, and deliberate on your recommendation. I ask that Nestor and Antoninus remain, to ensure that these technologia devices function effectively. In the meantime, you have a wife and son to be reunited with. Go now, Honestus will escort you. I don't want to see you again until tomorrow."

"Imperator. By the way, there are some colorful books in the box, which have pictures – captured images – from present-day earth. I have printed a few words to go along with some of the pictures, for your information," said Marcus Avitus, taking out a few coffee-table type books from the box and placing them on the table.

The primary box of samples and gifts now empty, his forty-eight year mission to observe and report now essentially complete, Marcus was now ready to see to his own needs. He followed Honestus out into the corridor, still able to conjure up an image of his young wife and infant son in his mind's eye after all the years.

Standing at what he had learned was the Horatius Avitus domicile; Marcus activated the Tuathii root to open the portal.

The look on the face of the tall boy who stood just inside told him everything.

It was his son, Horatius Avitus Connal, whom he did not know. But Marcus recognized his progeny. It was like looking at himself in a mirror, only seeing himself as he was as a boy.

The complex blend of excitement, fear, love, and enthusiasm on his son's face told Marcus that everything was well. The tears running down the boy's face told him how much his son needed his father, even if he was an old man.

The look on his wife Neasa's face, as he glanced beyond Connal, told him that she still wanted him – that her husband was home. His advanced years had not registered in her mind.

He went into his domicile and embraced them both.

Hours later, only his son exited.

Trying to look and talk like a man, young Connal gave orders to the sentry from the Eighth that Tribunus Avitus and his wife were not to be disturbed.

Avitus Connal walked along the corridor trying to understand the parting words that his father had said, but he had never seen his mother being intimate with a man, so he had no frame of reference from which to understand what Marcus had said, nor why Neasa had looked so happy to see Connal leaving the pod: *"If you see the pod a rockin', don't come a knockin'!"*

XXV

DOGMATI FACISMI
{ Tenets of Fascism }

Word spread rapidly along the pearl necklace line of spaceships. Following the Roman chain of command, it had been a junior *tabellarius*, messenger, born and raised on Planeta Metallorum, who had been given the task of passing the word.

Hungry for information, *Praefectus Navisae*, ship prefects, were standing by at the entry portal to each ship. After being the first to enter each ship, the tabellarius would be greeted by the praefectus navisae. He would then begin reading the edict from Emperor Agricola while progressing through the ship, to the next ship in turn. The second man to exit the portal was Centurion Tappulus, praefectus castrorum for the entire legion, along with Lady Cerialia Achal, who has assumed the same role for the Irish – seeing to the arrangements and needs of all of her people and passing information down to the Irish captains, as directed by Queen Laelie.

Fourth to exit the portal was a milite, carrying the signum, battle standard, of the legion, which had been re-named Legio *XXVII Cosmi Victrix Agricolus*, declaring that Emperor Agricola had conquered the known universe.

As the procession moved along the main corridor of each starship in succession, the centurions and other officers keeping pace with the fast-moving tabellarius, the news was read aloud:

"Salve! Greetings from dominus et deus, Augustus Quintus Julius Agricola Cosmi Victrix, with news from Terra!" To some of the officers, the "master and God" comment was a little over the top, but they ignored the over-exuberance and listened for what the tabellarius would say next.

"Tribunus Marcus Avitus and Immune Antoninus Commodus have safely returned from their mission to Terra. While we have been without them for over ten long years from our point of view; from their perspective and planetary time-frame on Terra, they were there for forty-eight. In that time they have learned wondrous technologia, and have brought this and great quantities of tactical information to the emperor. Emperor Agricola and Queen Laelie are reviewing and discussing this information with their senior advisors and officers, and will soon provide orders for battle preparations. We are going to war, but not until we master the languages and the technologia of earth! Make ready, we are going to school. *Porro glorior!* – forward to glory!"

"Going to school, Tabellarius? What does that mean?"

"Centurion, begin reading this template-binding, it is called a *tableta electronicum,* workbook," the tabellarius said, handing out a folding tablet with an attached stylus pen. "Your task is to teach your officers these words in Angalesi, *English*, and for the Irish and any others to also learn these same words also in Spanish. You should also review the Latin-Spanish workbook to understand what has changed, as what we spoke in Hispania has changed somewhat in the two millennia since we departed Terra. After completing a lesson, you shall proceed to learn the next one. When you reach the end of these lessons, you will be given special training in some of the amazing technologia of Terra, academic studies in geography, history, culture, and of course, military studies."

Taking the thin stack of tabletae from a milite who accompanied the tabellarius, the praefectus navisium had the opportunity to ask just one last question.

"What of Rome? Who is the Emperor?"

The tabellarius paused, unsure how to answer. He looked at the scrap of paper onto which his speaking notes had been printed, by Immune Commodus, but the tabellarius found no direction or comments that would answer the question.

Centurion Tappulus, however, knew the larger situation very well, and understood what the lead centurion of each starship would need to hear. He spoke solemnly as the tabellarius and the milites exited the portal, bound for the next ship in sequence.

"Rome is no longer as we knew it. We are all that is left of the Roman Empire. Imperatus Agricola is thus confirmed as truly the Emperor for all Romans, for the entire cosmos. The number of inhabitants on Terra has grown beyond the counting."

"What can we do?"

"The emperor and his war cabinet are deliberating, however it is clear to me that we are going to take action to restore Roman power and order to this troubled planeta. We are going to war. *Porro glorior*, forward to victory! So get on with the schooling, and I will keep you all informed of plans as they are to be revealed."

Satisfied for the time being, the praefectus navisium bid farewell to his friend, envious about Centurion Tappulus's advanced access to the vital information. But then, as the more junior centurion turned to face his own immunes and other junior officers on his starship, he realized he held much more information than they needed to know. *I will give it to them slowly*, he thought, correctly understanding that the hardest part would be to keep them focused on going to school before they would be given any information about the ultimate plans for going to war.

Our time will come. Porro glorior, let the lessons begin.

Over the next week, more information was gradually disseminated downward through the chain of command. Romans and Hibernians used the tabletae to walk through two millennia of history, using this mind-numbing advance in technologia, their paper-thin tabletae guided them through unbelievable social, political, economic, technological, and cultural changes. The people of Rome, Éire, and Planeta Metallorum engaged in a multi-disciplinary university campus in space, *academia cosumicus*, studying a curriculum that provided the essential information to enable their transition to life on Terra. Languages were of prime import, with additional studies in history, geopolitics, economics, geography and technology. They had experienced things that those on Terra could only imagine, and had developed a strong sense of curiosity. They pursued their studies with an unwavering desire to learn all that they could.

Meanwhile, in the command pod, Agricola and his advisors were getting into far more strategic studies, having stayed ahead of the rest of their people by being the first to progress through each stage of the lesson plans developed by Professor-Tribune Marcus Avitus.

Understanding the seriousness of what was to come, the Irish and Roman leaders did not spend much time watching humorous videos, and they were forbidden completely from playing video games – however the miles gregarius, common foot-soldiers, were encouraged to become familiar with first-person shooter games and other combat-oriented games as, according to Commodus, these would help the men understand the extremely fast-paced, technology-driven, battle-sphere mentality that the greatest powers on earth had developed. He did not emphasize that the games were not reality, as he thought it best for the men to be allowed to fear and respect the opposition that they would soon face on Terra.

"Antoninus, with all that we have seen in the history lessons, the war and present-day documentaries, I am confused about something."

"What is it, Fabius?"

"Are you really telling us that every person, whether elite or plebian, has access to all of this information-technologia?"

"Yes, Fabius, they do."

"And they have the capability to form these on-line groups, like that amusing NovaRoma group of battle re-enactors? They can seek each other out, from within any nation and communicate across great distances.

"Yes, that is generally true. And when you speak of the on-line Romaphiles, be careful. Tribune Avitus has friends within their ranks. As you will see when the battle plans are released by the war cabinet, these and others of Tribune Avitus's friends on earth constitute an 'Eleventh Cohort', who are now seeing to preparations.

"But that has to wait for now. My point here is that yes, people have the ability to promote their causes, to rally themselves around issues, leaders, and philosophies that are as numerous as the stars in the night sky. However they can have no expectation of privacy. The nation-states have the ability to spy on every word they type, every image they exchange, and to whom they are communicating. But yes, in the more wealthy nations, everyone has access to all the technology you have seen. And in many nations, they also have access to weapons, like guns and those powerful crossbows we saw in that motion picture yesterday. They have missiles, that are large projectiles with an explosive capability, that can be hurled over distances that would take months to traverse even on horseback – spanning the full breadth of the Roman Empire, in our time, from Greece to Britannia, in mere minutes."

"What I cannot understand is why the leaders of these nation-states permit it? Why do they allow plebeians to have the ability to organize themselves so freely? What is it that I do not understand here?" asked Fabius Quintilianus, the least flexible thinker of the two philosophers in Agricola's retinue.

"I can answer that," interjected Marcus Avitus.

"Please do, Marcus, we are all confused by this excess of freedom. Why does it exist?"

"It all goes to philosophy and ethics. Keeping our focus on the six great powers, there is a wide divergence in characteristics owing to their different histories. However, in the past few decades a great shift has begun to take place, a shift toward the abrogation of these freedoms, as if the great nation-states have finally understood that such freedom can no longer be tolerated. But we must discuss the past, over a century ago, to see how this situation came to exist.

"Before all of this advanced technology was invented, the world was considered 'much bigger'. That is to say that the flow of information, of people, of goods, and of ideas was much slower. As you can imagine, when people had to travel by sailing vessel, horse, and foot – as we did in our time – it would take weeks, months, and years for information to spread across great distances. And as it spread, the message content would change, would become distorted, and would become less powerful and less important. Nations and governments themselves could therefore control the flow of information, allowing nations to be more homogeneous, to have people all share the same opinions, beliefs, traditions, and religion.

"But as the world 'got smaller', as ships became faster, mechanical printing-presses allowed printed ideas to be conveyed without being distorted, and the great philosophical ideas of antiquity – from the Greeks and Romans – were read by more and more well-educated leaders of the nation-sates, the flow of people and information increased. Ideas, like Republicanism and Patriota – ideas of the American Revolution – almost two hundred and fifty years ago – spread fast enough for people to organize themselves. In the case of America, they revolted, refusing to continue to pay taxes to Britannia without representation in the governing body of that once great empire.

"The revolutionary ideas of the successful American Revolution were written into their Declaration of Independence, where they stated that: "We hold these truths to be self-evident, that all men are created equal, that they are endowed by their Creator with certain unalienable rights, that among these are Life, Liberty, and the pursuit of Happiness."

"This one sentence is perhaps the most important sentence ever written over the last two hundred and fifty years, as this sentiment is the source of so many revolutions to this day. For example, the nation-state known as France – which we know as the Gallic *Provincia Romana,* was rocked by a revolution because the ideals of the Declaration of Independence infected the people of France. The French plebes searched for answers to their great plight by embracing right to Life, Liberty, and the Pursuit of Happiness."

"This also sounds similar to the teachings of Jesus Christ," observed Vibius Metellus.

"Certainly there is a connection there. Christianity had been adopted in America and in France as the predominant religion, and may be the well-spring of these ideals.

"In any case, the French people revolted in mass uprisings, and ultimately replaced the monarchy, rule by a sovereign king with a republican system based on rule by the people."

"And this republican system was based on Rome?"

"To an extent. However, the key point here was the people demanding what they perceived as their 'rights'..

"Their inspiration was from the ideas of the American Revolution. And to thank America for these ideas, the people of France made a colossus, the Statue of Liberty, and sent this in pieces aboard ships. Here is a picture of the Statue of Liberty. It stands on a small island at the entrance to one of the great cities of the world, New York City. Can you see these tiny people?" Marcus showed Agricola a picture of the Statue of Liberty on his tableta.

"Yes, I have seen the image of this colossus. She is beautiful, and so enormous! So she represents, or commemorates, these ideas: Life, Liberty, and the Pursuit of Happiness?"

"Yes, Emperor. But that was a very long time ago. Now the rate of change, and the capabilities of technologia, are far more advanced. Now ideas like these can spread at an instant, and people can organize themselves instantly into 'flash-mobs', suddenly congregating at a time and place of their choosing. For a nation-state, this is impossible to control. In the past few decades there have been numerous plebeian uprisings, where tyrants and other decadent and corrupt rulers have been replaced by plebeian revolutionaries. And these revolutions make use of these tablets and other forms of instantaneous electronic communications to organize their uprisings.

"Now, unlike Spartacus, the plebeians tend to be successful in overthrowing their tyrants. In large part, it is due to the freedoms they enjoy. Free people are, simply put, impossible to control, unless they believe that they are free and in control, hence, the façade of democracy."

"All very interesting philosophically, Marcus, but let's return to our original question, about how these people got the impression that they have these rights. Is it accurate to say that this Christian religion played a role in their having a popular expectation of freedom, in the form of 'God-given rights'? And that technologia has given the masses the power to take over their nation-states at any time they choose?"

"That, and the rise of liberalism in general, yes, Fabius."

"Liberalism?"

"Liberalism is a political philosophy or world-wide view that basically says that everybody has the right to equality and liberty."

"Again those words from the American Declaration"

"Precisely. And liberalism now also includes notions of democracy and multiculturalism."

"Democracy? I understand that term, from the Greeks. So they hold elections, and choose plebeian representatives?"

"Yes. In general, all great powers pretend to hold elections."

"Pretend?"

"Yes, the hidden tradition is for the elites to determine who the two or three candidates will be. The rich determine which of them gets more money, and the money and powerful supporters behind the scenes determine who will be elected. The plebeians are led to believe that they are actually determining who will be selected as their candidates, and that their votes are actually counted."

"But this is not true?"

"No, Imperator. It may be true in some of the smaller jurisdictions, however for the largest nation-states, the outcome is decided long before the ballots are cast. It is important, however, to convince the plebeians that this is the most suitable mechanism for them to express their discontent. Mass uprisings have to be avoided at all costs, of course, or the elites would lose control and be replaced by true plebeian-power structures, actual democracy in the classical sense."

"Are there any nations run by true democrats?"

"No, Imperator, there are none. Any that try, such as the result of a plebeian revolution, are soon converted to a form of tyranny of the minority, in one way or another. It is like two wolves and a sheep agreeing upon what shall be for dinner. Those in power always seek ways to maintain power. For some humans, it is in their nature."

"With all of this in mind, then, are not all of these great powers identical, or are there enough differences between them?"

"They all have differences, but power is power. The middling nations are always on the verge of plebeian uprisings, and perhaps this is part of the reason for their voluminous consumption. By trying to keep the plebeians at bay – giving each and every citizen what they demand – they forestall the next revolution. They keep them happy with bread and circuses, or, in this day and age, with sporting events, unhealthy yet tasty food, pornography, and instant gratification of their most base instincts. However, this puts their economies into perilous danger of collapse, and requires the nation-states to rely more and more on propaganda, trickery, and deceit so as to keep the population from knowing just how bad things truly are."

"And that takes us to the next topic in our preparations. The strategic picture and our strategic planning." Marcus now seemed deeply focussed.

"Proceed, Tribune. We have worked hard as your *discipuli*, students, and now I believe we need to turn this into a military planning, *occursus bellum*, war meeting."

"Dominus. At this point we should be a much smaller group. I recommend we limit the occursus bellum to just tribunes and above – and of course, Praefectus Tappulus, our two philosophers, Queen Laelie, and her top captains, myself and Antoninus."

"Agreed. All others, you will now leave us."

Nestor was dismissed to serve as an intermediary and to provide any assistance to the personnel in operating their tabletae and proceeding through their academic studies. This gave him a good chance to track down Ruth Daley, to see how she was doing with her interviews of the Hibernian women.

Nestor knew the lecture on the tenets of power that Marcus was about to begin, and was not going to miss anything he die not already know. *I have to be back in time to hear his decision*, Nestor thought, even though he believed that the decision was a foregone conclusion.

Over the next three hours, without a break, Marcus presented a series of slide-shows that gave Agricola and his war cabinet an overview of the military weapons, orders of battle, tactics and political structure of the six great nation-states: China, Russia, America, Europe, India and the South American Union.

The Romans were impressed with the pictures of warships, transport aircraft, armor, and self-propelled artillery, but they were surprised to learn that the science of engineered defenses had been abandoned altogether.

"Why are there no pictures of defensive fortifications?"

"Because, Kaeso, that is not the form that warfare takes. When there is war, there are typically only three or four ways they are fought. One way is when a great power occupies a weak nation, and the weak nation fights back with anything they can use. They call this 'terrorism' or guerilla warfare, as the form of opposition is usually seen as repugnant to the citizens of the greater power. For example, a great power will drop bombs on a village and later occupy it with armored vehicles. The opposition will use bombs, set to explode when the armored vehicle travels over it. The retaliatory bombing of a village from the air is somehow seen as more pure, more civilized, than blowing up the armored vehicle with an improvised bomb. The next form of warfare is bluster, where one side shows that it is more ready to go to war than the other, like two ridiculous birds puffing their feathers up, in competition for the hen. They do not actually come to blows, and the prize goes to the one with the greatest bluster. This is demonstrated when a show of military force is assembled, but not put into combat. The diplomacy that follows, sometimes referred to as gun-boat diplomacy, usually advantages the side that had demonstrated superior forces. The third form of warfare is economic warfare, where you are in a trading relationship with your enemy, but by insidious practices such as making them dependent on your cheap products, you undermine their economic might and wield disproportionate influence on them. In that way, a clever nation can force a superior power to bow to them, by virtue of controlling their economy through debt and inexpensive products. The fourth, final form of warfare, not seen in a very long time, is the one we are all familiar with – total war. That is when you use every influence, every political maneuver, every form of spying, skullduggery, trickery, and all possible weapons great and small to totally annihilate your enemy. It is the form of warfare the Tuathii applied to the Quadrupedii, and that Agricola the Elder applied to the Ordovicians in Britannia Minor."

"So which form of warfare do they use most, these six great powers of Terra?" Cerialis asked, contemplating potential adversaries to come.

"Between themselves they seem to mutually agree on economic warfare, while three of the greatest powers are constantly prepared for total war, yet prefer to use bluster to bully the lesser nations. They form grand alliances and have incessant discussions at a global venue called the United Nations, however this august assembly is largely ineffective as each of the greatest powers has the right to veto any important decision."

"So these great powers have unresolved issues, and there is no clear greatest power?"

"There was once, the United States, however in recent years their subservience to China, due to indebtedness and a complex consumer-producer relationship, has these two enemies deeply co-dependent on each other. The third great power, Russia, is expanding its influence on neighbor states, and becoming increasingly aggressive. Of course, all three of these greatest powers possess enough nuclear weapons to annihilate each other several times over, and have maintained a delicate balance based on a doctrine of 'mutually-assured destruction', whereby none can use their nuclear weapons without risk of being utterly destroyed in the retaliation that would surely follow.

A great deal of time was spent discussing why nuclear weapons had not been used, but the Romans understood from their familiarity with Equanimity drives and thorium reactors that awesome power can be unleashed from subatomic particles. What was of more interest to the Romans was the political structures, how power was sustained and managed in the great nations of the world.

At one point in the presentation, while Antonius was affording Marcus a break, by giving a 30-minute presentation on which modern-day weapons systems and command and control systems he felt could be easily integrated into Dupli-Tri starships. He included a replay of the video he had saved from the scoutship's encounter with the couple on the winding road near Cervantes. During this, Antoninus had shown the men what a laser-pointer was.

He also them to play with it, to get some hands-on experience with the amazing – yet now ubiquitous – modern day technology.

At one point, while Cerialis had been playing with the pointer, Antoninus's cat, Grigio, had jumped out of Neasa's hands and pounced on the moving dot of the laser pointer, as it was directed bouncingly across the floor by Tappulus.

The cat jumped and pounced wildly, chasing after the dot while Antoninus continued the presentation. Cerialis eventually gave the pointer back and Antoninus continued his presentation without using the pointer any further, as it was too distracting for everybody.

Tappulus picked the cat up, and it purred contentedly in his large hands. As Tappulus stroked Grigio under his nose, the cat pushed its toothy smile into Tappulus's fingers to get a better rub.

Looking at the skin under the cat's fur, Tappulus saw disgusting little creatures crawling around. "You've got fleas," he whispered to the cat, while continuing to pet it. "Good thing they're not going to tear you apart and eat you, like the Siphonaperistii monstrom do to the sheep they fed on," Tappulus said, his imagination wandering from the boring lecture.

And then it hit him. The behavior of the cat chasing the dot, pouncing on its prey, reminded him of the behaviour of the Siphonaperistii monstrom on Planeta Metallorum...

He immediately interrupted Antoninus, walked over to him and whispered briefly. After listening for a few seconds, Antoninus smiled broadly and gave his laser pointer to Aulus Tappulus, after showing him how to turn it on and off.

Tappulus left the pod, urgently seeking Primus Pilus Spurius Crispus to share his discovery.

While Tappulus was away, Antoninus and Marcus concluded their discussion on the great powers by introducing their analysis and conclusions, but they took care in how they presented their argument, as the conclusions that would be drawn would set the course for the entire military campaign to follow. After calling for a short break, when the men and women enjoyed some refreshments and had a chance to talk amongst themselves, Antoninus prepared the final presentation, which consisted of only twenty slides, the first of which was the scene of a plebeian uprising.

In the picture, the security forces were clearly evident by the matching uniforms, helmets, strange metal shields, and other accoutrements of police forces.

On the street in front of the lines of security forces, was a melee in progress. There were civilians scattered about, many with bloody injuries, some helping others retreat, while others were advancing on the security forces, with signs and sticks, and fabric covering their faces. The air all around was filled with smoke, which seemed to be emanating from small canisters, on the ground, presumably a crowd-control weapon used by the security forces.

Marcus resumed the lecture, with Antoninus operating the slides.

"So. What do you see here, in this picture?"

"Rebellion being put down by the state."

"Absolutely right, Kaeso. But do you suppose that the state was successful in doing so, or not?"

"They look to be winning the battle, so yes, they were successful."

"Actually, they were unsuccessful. This was a typical plebeian uprising just a few years ago in a nation-state of over fifty million citizens. They were unhappy with the continuously eroding economic conditions, high taxes, debased currency, and greed of their government. They demanded reforms, but the state refused to deliver, and only accelerated the pilfering of the nation's treasury. Sound familiar?"

"It is just as we have seen in Rome, when money rightly belonging to the territories, *aerarium*, is excessively transferred to enrich the senators, by being allocated to the imperial treasuries under senatorial control, the *fiscus*. Whenever this balance is tilted too far to the greedy senators, the territories rebel and attempt to cast off the empire. Of course this never ends well for the rebels, as the state responds with overwhelming force to restore order. That is so familiar, and what we see in that pictorial image," declared Kaeso.

"But Kaeso, you forget, I told you that in this case, the state lost the war. Why do you suppose that is, if as you argue, the state should respond with overwhelming force to put down the rebellion?"

Kaeso had no response, and none of the others wanted to try to reply, so Marcus continued.

"It is the ever-present worry that a state will be seen as having used excessive force and the risk to political leaders and heads of state of being held personally accountable for committing so-called 'crimes against humanity', that even when facing loss of control of their citizenry, these modern nation-states are unwilling to use the overwhelming force that Kaeso spoke of."

"Crimes against humanity? By what law?"

"A collection of human rights laws generally agreed upon by the great powers, at least, officially. Unofficially these great powers violate these laws whenever it suits them, but yet they have a terrible fear of being cast as not respecting human rights, as they assume that the world would condemn them for it, and condemn them personally for being responsible."

"I see. So they give up, and let the plebes raid the treasury? To redistribute it amongst the wretched poor?"

"No, Fabius, the treasury is at this point already bare. These revolutions change little, as the next regime that attempts to manage the nation face the same unresolved, and the cycle continues. No. The point here is that because of these ideals of liberal democracy, and predominantly Christian values, none of the great nation-states are willing to do what must be done to curb the head-long rush towards catastrophe that collectively, the human race has put itself into."

"And what do you propose? Perhaps we could use that strategy of bluster, demonstrate our superior power and force them to act, to change course and avert the coming catastrophe before it is too late?" suggested Fabius Quintilianus.

"I am afraid that that would be imprudent, Fabius. History has shown that the form of consensus required to restore order and implement the necessary changes is unattainable. There are too many vested interests and, as I discussed earlier, they may be fearful of losing their own hold on power. My conclusions is that we must either turn our backs on our homeworld, or we must conquer it completely. With the weaponry at our disposal, we have the means to restore a Roman republic that has the will and the means to change the planet, to preserve it and to restore the glory and order of Rome," Marcus said.

Agricola looked at Marcus, and at Antoninus, and saw determination and, clearly, agreement.

"Presuming for the moment that I am right in my belief that our people, the Romans and the Hibernians, would not forgive themselves if we turned our backs on our homeworld, and that your proposition is the direction we choose to take, then lay it out for me. How can we, with no more than nine major starships and a few puller-ships and scout-ships, and with not much more than one legion – even with the Dupli-Tri technologia, how can we hope to conquer such a populous and chaotic world?" Agricola asked, already knowing the answer.

"We do what Rome has always done. We conquer one strong enemy and use their forces, their resources, and their network of alliances to achieve our goals."

Seeing no opposition to his premise, Marcus continued.

"What I propose is that we compare and contrast these great powers, and look at each in terms of the tenets of power. We need to determine which great power has just the right balance of characteristics that would make it the most amenable to Roman rule. Rather than attempt to conquer the entire planeta, we conquer only the organs of power, of just one great power. Then we do as Dictator Julius Caesar did, and use the resources of that conquered nation to expand our empire."

"And in the process, this first-to-conquer state becomes Rome?" asked Fabius.

"Not in my conception, Fabius. This can only work if we have Emperor Agricola in full control, at the top, as dictator. Doing what has to be done without compunction. There can be no sharing of power. But we will come to that later. For now, let us begin our analysis."

"Proceed,"

"Dominus," and Marcus clicked to the next slide, and then began the well-rehearsed lecture he had prepared at his home near Lexington, Massachusetts.

"We will look at each of the great powers, China, America, Russia, Europe, India and the South American Union, in reference to ten characteristics, and we will then provide a balanced scorecard by which to demonstrate our conclusion that one of these nations, above all others, has the correct tenets of power for our purpose.

These ten characteristics are:

1. Military Power: the ability to project power around the globe, to transport large forces to battle and to sustain them for extended periods. In addition to quantity and capability of their weapons systems, many of which we have already looked at today, we will also consider the quality of their training. Much as the effectiveness of the Roman legion lay in the ability of our generals to order units to change their tactics, to re-organize into differing formations, and to seamlessly pivot from one direction to another. The quality of education and training of a military is relevant.

2. Military and Economic Integration: The degree to which the requirements of the military can be met by the factories and industry of a nation. Without this, opposing nations can cut off supplies through embargo and sanctions, making the military vulnerable to external economic factors. The greater the organic production of military requirements, the better. This also entails the co-dependency of the nation's economy to military funding, as this, controlled by the state, provides greater control over the economic life of the citizenry and therefore, citizenry dependency on military spending. We consider this in the context of a requirement for the construction of military equipment that combines the best of modern-day earth military technology with that of the Dupli-Tri.

3. Authoritarian State. This includes an obsession on internal security and the ability of the state to suppress dissent; the effectiveness of national and local police forces and the surveillance of the activities of the population. What you may not have understood about these wonderful tablets and other personal electronic devices is that they rely on systems which can be monitored by the state, and this allows

the state to know what is being sent through these devices. They can even cause these devices to turn on and send data, location, conversations, even pictures, of whatever is taking place around them. Through algorithms, they have the capacity to read into one's personal and unspoken thoughts based on their communications activities and can predict with great accuracy their future actions. However, if a state is not sufficiently authoritarian, they will not have these capabilities in place and the population will not have been habituated, through years of such practices, to this as being 'normal'.

4.   Nationalism. A coherent "us vs. them" perspective, whereby everything other than the self-perception of how the population sees their nation, is cast as 'evil'. Ideally, this is reflected in an exaggeration of the threat posed by the traditional enemy of the state. There should be an overwhelming atmosphere of xenophobia, fear of the alien, external, and not-understood outsiders.

5.   Religiosity. This feature is a double-edged sword. Overly strong religious beliefs can tie the hands of a state, however religious beliefs can also support the greater power of the state by virtue of the role religiosity can play in keeping the population in line. This also requires a unity of the state and religion, if not openly, then at least in the hearts and minds of those in control. Which particular religion a person subscribes to is irrelevant. They are all generally monotheist, believing that there is one singular god, in the image of mankind, that favors one set of followers over those of other religions. This attribute can be very useful in enticing the population to embrace the objectives of the state, as long as there is cooperation between church and state, so that the issues are framed correctly.

6.   Propaganda. Closely tied to the previous point, the effectiveness of propaganda, which requires the suppression or duplicity of the media – the people who tell the populace

what is happening and what is going on in their world. Do you recall those news-casts we showed? Where there is a man and a woman seated at a desk, and they tell you what happened today in your city? That is propaganda. People 'tune in' and watch these 'news-casts' to become informed, to hear about sporting and entertainment events, and to learn about the expected weather for the next few days. Propaganda is less effective if the media are free to report accurately and honestly. In what they call a 'free and open democracy', the media are supposed to be objective and to report accurately, even if it contradicts the interests of the state. In a climate like that, propaganda is less effective as people may have access to truthful accounts, thereby making the 'official' message less believable. However, when propaganda is well used, it can mobilize entire nations in support of the national objective.

7.   Elitism. Rule by an elite ruling class who choose their membership on their own. This also applies to professional spheres, whereby access within various trades, much like the guilds of our time, is controlled by those at the top. This is in contrast to meritocracy, where those with skill and enterprise are free to rise to the top. Elitism protects the few from having to share power and prestige with the many. A political class whereby, even if there are so-called democratic elections, only those who are blessed by the elites have any chance of success. Another aspect of elitism is that the elite must not be held accountable in the same manner as the population at large. We have discussed this earlier, if you recall. There must be stiffer consequences for minor offenses of the lower classes, and the elite must be exempted one way or another from consequences. In many cases, this is accomplished by a legal system whereby the elite can afford to hire better lawyers, and the poor, while given the fantasy of equality before the law, are hamstrung by having inferior legal representation. One other aspect of elitism is that there may be another stratosphere of rulers behind the official rulers,

who support and assist the ruling class – who are in turn beholden to these invisible ultra-class of benefactors and sponsors.

8. <u>Interventionism.</u> To have great power is nothing if it is not habitually used to intervene in the affairs of others. Here again habituation is a factor. If a state is habitually interfering with others, that is a 'normal' state of affairs, and therefore desirable for our purposes.

9. <u>Tradition.</u> Evoking past glories and drawing inspiration from past leaders. We should be particularly interested in nations that reach all the way back to what they call antiquity – to our time – ancient Rome. This can be seen in the symbology in their money, their most prominent national architecture and in the institutions such as legal system and political infrastructure.

10. <u>Technology.</u> The extent to which new technologies are created and developed in a nation are important factors. Not only due to vulnerability if the source of innovation is not their own, but also because having superior weapons systems gives a nation great advantage in all forms of warfare, from bluster and diplomacy all the way to total war.

After having presented the ten characteristics of great power, Marcus and Antoninus then evaluated each of the six great powers against the ten characteristics, and assigned a score to each one. In the end, they presented a simple six-by-ten matrix which resembled the layout of a standard legion: ten cohorts, six rows deep.

"What we see here is called a balanced scorecard. Each of the ten characteristics has been scored, as we evaluated each nation against the characteristic. We can go back and look at this in more detail."

"Please, no, Marcus! We have seen sufficient detail. Do I understand these scores correctly? One nation has the highest number, therefore it is rated the most suitable great power for our purposes? And many of these characteristics, it seems, come with a negative stigma, from the point of view of the liberal democratic traditions that the world pretends to subscribe to?" asked Agricola.

"Yes, Dominus."

"In some of those war videos, particularly those that describe the attempted conquests by the Germanic peoples under Hitaler..."

"Hitler, Dominus," interrupted Marcus, who then visibly regretted having been so impertinent.

"Quite right. Adolf Hitler. He is universally hated. A brutal tyrant. That condemnation that you say everybody is afraid of having aimed at them, for violating so many human rights?"

"Yes he is seen as evil, the epitome of a monster."

"And his system is described as fascist? Referring to our Roman word, fasces, the bundle of sticks that is stronger than an individual stick. This term, 'fascism', is used to describe regimes which would score highest on these ten characteristics of great power?"

"Yes, Dominus."

"So in fact, what we are attempting to do here today is to determine which of the six great powers of present day Terra is currently the most fascist? So that when we succeed in taking over that nation-state, it will allow for the best transition to our aims in totality?

"Dominus, as always, your comprehension is superb," said Marcus, sincerely impressed that Emperor Agricola, a man displaced from the 1st Century and then given a mere four weeks to be brought up-to-speed on two millennia of history, technological, social, and political change, and yet the man was able to follow a complicated ten-criteria by six-variable comparison, and extract the relevant conclusions:

The United States of America scored the highest.

After two weeks serving her like a slave, Tappulus was getting very frustrated. It was not that he could not simply have taken her, she seemed more than willing, but for some strange reason, Aulus wanted her to give herself to him willingly.

He had spent as much time as possible with the young academic, Ruth Daley, but with all of the military meetings and training sessions that he and the other senior officers were required to attend, and with the subsequent sessions he was required to conduct with his own subordinates in the Eighth Cohort, Aulus had not found the way to bed the beautiful woman.

That was very much lout of the ordinary for the man, who considered himself to be the gods' gift to women, by his own observation and the accounts of some of his past lovers.

And then it happened.

After taking some time out to watch a battle in the ludus on the lower deck, between three original Romans and five Metallorians fighting in the ancient Celtic style, Aulus had not at first noticed that Ruth was standing next to him.

Soon he became aware of an interesting aroma, one he had never smelled before. He looked around, and soon found the source.

"Ruth! You smell like grass," had been Tappulus's opening line. *Dumb, Tribune Tappulus, dumb! You know hundreds of better lines than that!* he chided himself.

"It's the henna," said Ruth, matter-of-factly.

"Henna?"

"Is that *lawsonia inermis*? From Egypt?"

"It has many names, but yes, that is another name for it."

"Why do you smell of the body art ink?"

"It is in my hair," Ruth replied, holding a handful up to his nose.

Eager at the chance to be closer to his quarry, Aulus took a deep inhale of her hair. "Aaaahh! Yes, that smells like a fresh-cut field on my brother's farm."

"Do you like the smell?"

"Oh yes, very much so. But why is it in your hair, as perfume?"

"Aulus, do you really think that this is my natural hair color?" Ruth asked, coyly.

"I assumed…"

"What little you know. My natural color is orange. I am a carrot-top."

"Orange? But it looks like red vinum. You color it, to make it more red, why?"

"I like the look of it, and I don't really like my orange hair."

"I am sure I would like it, your orange hair." Aulus offered.

"Would you like to see some of it?" Ruth said, putting one hand on his shoulder, seductively?"

"Why? Do you have a lock of your orange hair?"

"You are thick."

Confused by some of her expressions, Aulus kept silent. Then, as he reflected on his personal theory that when a woman touches a man for no reason, she is open to being touched by him. Her hand on his shoulder was an intimate opening. Thinking that he had a chance to finally taste her forbidden fruits, he suddenly understood her invitation to see her natural hair color. *There is one place on her body where she probably has not dyed her hair*, he realized.

Without another word, Aulus took small her hand in his and led her away toward his pod.

Even before the pod closed behind them, she was in his arms. After two weeks of waiting for him to make a move, Ruth had begun to worry that he would give up, and with so little time left before she would have to return to Earth with Marcus, she was starting to worry.

That added a degree of urgency to her undressing him, peeling off his tunic to get to his muscular body.

After some very eager kissing and fondling, she lay back on Tappulus's bed while he performed the Roman version of oral sex. After giving him a chance to figure it out, she soon found his approach tedious and ineffective.

"Is that how Romans do it?" Ruth asked.

"What is wrong with the way I am lapping?"

"That's the problem, you are doing it like a dog drinks water. That is not how it is done." Ruth said, switching positions so that she could perform oral sex on Aulus.

Tappulus lay back and experienced his first ever twenty-first century blow-job. However, before he was close to coming, Ruth stopped, smiled, with his cock in her hand, and then used the tip of his penis as a prop while she explained the finer points of cunnilingus.

Ever the attentive student when it comes to sex, Aulus was surprised to learn that there was so much more that a woman could experience, that required a more focused approach than his dog-lapping technique.

Ruth soon had him demonstrating his newfound mastery of the technique, which, when combined with the novelty of begin made love to by a muscular original Roman tribune from the first century, brought Ruth to an orgasm the likes of which she had not experienced for a very long time.

After recognizing that his lover's orgasm had subsided, Aulus moved up as if to enter her.

"Hold off, cowboy," she said.

"What?"

"If you think I am going to have unprotected sex with the likes of you, sated satyr, you have another thought coming," Ruth said, rolling away from him as if to reach for her garments.

"What are you talking about? What protection? You are safe with me."

"We need a Trojan."

"A Trojan? They are all gone. What was left of their kind after the Achilles and his Greeks defeated them, the Trojan diaspora, found their way to Italy and founded Rome! So if you need a Trojan, my lady, you have one right here!" Said Aulus, trying to save his sexual adventure from what seemed to be an unexpected turn of events. She wants another man here? A Trojan? Had been the conclusion he was struggling with.

Smiling broadly as she rolled back onto his bed, Ruth showed Aulus a Trojan condom. One of the few she had left after handing them out to the women, along with perfume, switches of fabric, a variety of feminine products to make their lives more comfortable, and hours and hours of discussions with Laelie and the other influential women. The Trojans had been well received, and even put to use in many of the couples, but apparently Tappulus had not gotten the memo.

"Relax. You are all the man I need right now. And I mean RIGHT NOW," she said, as she tore open the condom and removed the prophylactic.

Five days later, Aulus and Ruth got into a great deal of trouble. They had been having something of a party with a few of Tappulus's immunes from the Eight Cohort, when they had bragged about how well they could fly scout-ships now, what with the training flights they had conducted around the armada, directed by Antoninus Commodus and others.

Tappulus had also acquired the last bottle of tequila, and the four of them had proceeded to get completely drunk.

But when the booze ran out before the party was over, one of the immunes got a great idea.

Not all great ideas are good ideas, and what seems like a good idea when drunk, does not necessarily appear as such when looked back upon when in a sober state. These were truths that Tappulus would later learn.

Acting in their inebriated state, the four headed to the aft end of their colonist-ship, to where the scout-ships were housed. The fourth, the immune most expert with scout-ships, had already been to the bridge to arrange for one of his friends to help them out.

The four of them got into a scout ship, and headed out into space.

Their destination was in Ruth's hands, as she promised Aulus that she knew where they could get some more booze.

With the scout-ships quite easy to pilot, and navigating mostly on visual cues, they were soon closing in on Terra. Boston, Massachusetts to be precise.

The immune at the controls knew that there would be no impact when he piloted the scout-ship through the roof of the liquor store, but they all cringed.

The brilliant flash of yellow light as the roof exploded into Equanimity soon drew the attention people walking and driving about in the suburban Boston neighborhood. Soon calls had been put through to 911, and high quality pictures were being uploaded.

As the craft settled, the immune shut down the Equanimity-Drive, and Tappulus confirmed with him that the door could be opened.

Inside the liquor store, the men could not believe their eyes. The vast quantities and colorful assortment of boxes, bottles and advertising was a shock. They had never seen anything in their lives.

"Have we landed in the right place, Ruth?" Aulus asked, looking at the colorful boxes.

"Oh yea. This is booze. Those dark bottles, and boxes, over there – they are all vinum. Those, on that far wall, that is 'hard-stuff' – like tequila. And those boxes, along that long wall, that is beer. Over there, behind the door. That's the refrigerator. If you want cold beer, take it from there," Ruth said.

As they became aware of the sound of police sirens and fire trucks, the Romans became concerned.

"Relax, boys. We've got a few minutes. Quick, grab as many boxes as you can. I'll point out the good stuff."

Five minutes later, after loading a staggering quantity of booze into their scout-ship, they had made a good dent in the inventory of the bottle shop, and closed up the portal.

As their scout-ship rose out through the ceiling, the dash-camera of one of the police cars parked outside recorded their departure, as did a half-dozen civilians with their smart-phones.

Within an hour, after the joy-riders had returned to their starship, Aulus Tappulus was being yelled at by Legatus Crispus and Emperor Agricola was discussing the fate of Ruth Daley with Queen Laelie.

In the end, they decided that the best punishment would be the most natural one.

Tappulus had to distribute the alcohol throughout the ship, without receiving a drop of it himself. Ruth, on the other hand, was to returned to Terra the next day, with Marcus, Neasa, Connal and two immunes.

Tappulus had not been told that Ruth had to leave, and he had been quite busy delivering booze to the soldiers and citizens alike, that he had not known of Ruth's imminent departure.

When he finally caught up with her, she was dressed and packed, loitering in the main corridor with the Avitus's and the other Terra-bound Romans. "What do you mean you won't stay?" Tappulus said, incredulously.

"I have to go, because of what we the other day. And even if I did not have to go now, I would have eventually said goodbye to you," Ruth said, being harsh, as if that would make it easier.

"Why? I thought we were great together," said Aulus.

"This *has* great. Believe me, it has been an experience too precious even for my diary. But come on, Aulus, do you really expect me, a grown woman with an entire lifetime ahead of me, to stick with a man like you?"

"What do you mean? What complaint do you have? Was I not attentive? Did I not learn how to please you well? Am I not a great lover?"

"Sure. Perhaps the best I have ever had, physically. But a woman needs more than that. Would you stick around and raise kids with me, for example?"

Tappulus looked suddenly uncomfortable. "Well, maybe one day..."

"That's just what I mean, you idiot. You're a sexy, strong, mysterious man and I'm sure I'll dream about you for years to come. But I don't see this as anything long-term and you aren't looking for anything long term. You are merely a dream. to be remembered, but not pursued seriously," Ruth said, before kissing the shocked tribune on his forehead, and turning her back on him.

As she walked along the main corridor to joining Marcus, Neasa and the, Ruth did not look back.

And Aulus Tappulus did not take his eyes off of her, until she was well and truly gone.

Nunc scio quid sit amor, Tappulus thought to himself, *Now I know what love is.*

XXVI

COMMONITORIA INCIPENTES
{ Initiating Directive }

Unlike the dread that most academics feel when they return from vacation to find a mountain of term papers and other assignments piled in their cramped little offices, the eighteen-inch tall pile of documents was a welcome bonanza for Professor Horatio Avitus.

He knew that it would be the last time he would have an opportunity to work with his current cadre of students, which brought him a measure of remorse, but it was also a last opportunity to make his final selections.

He had recently returned from his rendezvous with Agricola's fleet, this time burrowing a slightly larger scout-ship into a remote area in the Townsend State Forest, an hour's drive from his home in Lexington, Massachusetts. He had made his preparations in the preceding week, and, with the help of a Dupli-Tri communications device that Antoninus Commodus had determined the use of – portable tachyon communications link – had received a simple voice signal from Agricola. It was the agreed upon *Epistula Initium*, Initiating Directive: *'iacta alea est,'* 'the die is cast.' This was his order to set his part of the plan in motion.

As a professor of Classical Studies at Boston University, Professor Avitus had developed close friendships with many of his students, acting more as a mentor than as a professor or graduate school advisor.

Over the years, Professor Avitus had cultivated deep and lasting friendships with several of his former students, and maintained contact with those he deemed most promising. With the exception of Ruth Daley and the Cuervo Twins, however, he had not formed close personal bonds. As much as he trusted Ruth and the Cuervos, however, he did not disclose his true identity as a Roman even to them.

In his nearly forty years as a professor at Boston University, Dr. Avitus had taught a wide range of undergraduate and post-graduate courses to over fifteen thousand students. These programs included Latin studies, rhetoric, logic, and some very specific masters and doctoral topics.

Marcus was always concerned that his unusual Italian accent, or his extreme familiarity with what it might have been like to be alive in the first century A.D. would give away his secret. However, he remained undetected.

In order to check on the status of the scout-ship, buried in the mountains of central Spain, Marcus and two other professors conducted an annual field study in antiquities, taking two dozen students on a Grand Tour of Europe. Each trip would include visits to art galleries, museums, holy sites and ancient ruins.

The students were required to complete term papers, give presentations and listen to the lectures that an Art History professor, a Philosophy professor, and Marcus gave at each of the sites.

Always commencing or ending in Paris or London, the 'European Field Tour' itinerary gave Marcus two opportunities to pass through the Lugo – Cervantes region. While in Lugo, the students would visit the Roman Wall and local museums, and if the weather cooperated, those art history students so inclined would make sketches and other artistic renderings of the World Heritage site, the most intact "Roman" city in Europe.

With the art history and philosophy professors in charge, herding kittens as it were, Marcus would take a vacation day and sneak into the scrublands to check on the scout-ship. He had purchased the land years ago, and left it in a wild, undeveloped state. Even so, there was always the risk of detection, so he had planted thickets of drought-hardy bushes to completely hide the area where the scout-ship was buried in the sandy soil.

On occasion, particularly when his arthritis was acting up, Marcus would crawl under the thicket, uncover the upper portal and enter the scout-ship,

Once inside, he would insert a thorium rod into the power-center, and activate the ship's electrical, communications and propulsion systems. He could always tell when Antoninus had been there, as there would be empty water bottles and snack food wrappers left behind. *He's such a slob*, Marcus would remark to himself, but he also felt more secure knowing that he still had at least one *amicissimus*, friend, alive in the universe.

After a few hours letting the Equanimity effects give his T-cells a boost, he would remove the fuel rod and exit the scout-ship, taking Antoninus's litter with him, and leaving him a riddle or two, in archaic Latin.

With a few years of physical aging repaired, he would rejoin the students in Lugo, and resume the Field Tour, giving the students a first class – and first century – tour of the sacred sites of antiquity. Some students would express surprise at the professor's apparent rejuvenation when he returned.

Some of his students found their professor to be deeply emotional at some of the Roman sites. He had nearly broken down in grief on one of his visits to Ostia, the ancient site of Rome, when he had given a speech on 'Horatius at the bridge' in the old amphitheater.

As Marcus gave voice to the story of Horatius, Herminius, and Spurius Lartius, his students became enthralled. In his mind's eye, Marcus saw ancient Rome in its glory, as it was on a boyhood trip he had taken with his father, traveling several weeks on horseback from Lugo, Hispania to Ostia, and Rome. He could still smell the bread in the air, hear the din of commerce and people in the streets and sense the long lost comfort of being *home*. As he concluded the story of three gallant Romans holding off the champions of the Tuscan Army of Lars Porcena long enough for five hundred Romans to dismantle the bridge over the flood-raging Tiber river, Marcus would always be overcome with emotions.

Sitting in the highest row of seats in the ruins of the small and acoustically perfect amphitheater in Ostia, the Cuervo brothers and other students over the years of these visits, heard perfectly his deeply felt sadness even though he spoke in a very quiet voice.

Many students attributed the emotional performance to his legendary oratory skills. A few thought that there was something more to it, but respected the old man's privacy too much to ask. But Eduardo Cuervo, an unusually perceptive young man, never forgot.

To Eduardo, it was as if the old prof was homesick, yearning to be with family and friends. He had that air about him, like a man displaced.

So when Professor Avitus contacted Eduardo to see how he was doing, the now forty-eight year old New York college teacher, he paid close attention to his old mentor, the man who had been so encouraging when the twins completed their post-graduate studies – Nestor in classical studies, Eduardo in Latin. The brothers had always believed that Professor Avitus had an ulterior motive for putting so much effort into their education and yet, until today, he had never asked anything of them – other than to cover his lectures and grade his papers during his annual trips to Europe.

"Eduardo, this is Horatio Avitus. Do you remember me?"

"Yes I do, Dr. Avitus. How are you doing, old soldier?"

Marcus froze for a moment. *Does Eduardo know?*

"Eduardo, call me Marcus, please."

"Surely, Marcus. So is it Marcus Horatio Avitus, then?"

"Actually, it is Marcus Horatius Avitus, but I have gone by Horatio during my academic career. Now then, what would you say if I asked you if you and your brother, Nestor, would like to meet some friends of mine?"

"*Old* friends?"

"Yes, old friends."

"Marcus, I have waited almost thirty years to hear you say that. This has something to do with our trip to Rome, doesn't it?"

"Can we meet to discuss it? Or do you have too many commitments?"

"I have no commitments. Bret died three years ago, and my son was killed in that stupid war in eastern Europe. Are you still at Boston U?"

"Yes. Would it be too much of an imposition if I asked you and Nestor to come here to join Ruth and I? It is rather important," Marcus said, nervously. That Marcus's new PhD student, Ruth Daley, was involved was a tantalizing fact for Eduardo, who found the smart young academic to be the perfect combination of sexy and smart. That she was involved in whatever it was that Marcus was up to meant that it would be interesting, at the very least.

"Marcus, I have nothing better to do. I'm on sabbatical for another two months anyhow. I could be there tomorrow. I'm pretty sure that Nestor can call in sick and come along. It's not that long of a drive."

"So you'll drive?"

"Yes."

"What kind of car do you drive?"

"A minivan. Why do you ask?"

"Would you and Nestor be willing to pick up a few packages along the way?"

"Sure. What and where?"

"Well, one of them is a bit out of the way, in Ottawa."

"Ottawa. You mean in Canada?"

"yes. There are four large boxes of....uniforms waiting there for me. They'll fit into your minivan, if you fold down your seats."

"I am intrigued, Marcus. Of course I will make the run to Ottawa for you. But why did you not simply ship them?"

"Because they are a military secret, Eduardo," Marcus said, putting it all on the line.

"Military? But I am not in the military."

"Well, Eduardo, I am. And you and your brother soon will be as well," said Marcus.

The hair on the back of Eduardo's neck stood up, and he held his breath. He could feel, and hear, his heart racing.

"Marcus, what type of military unit are these uniforms for?"

"For the Praetorian Guard, Eduardo."

That had been six months ago. Now, after having made the trip to rendezvous with emperor Agricola's armada, Marcus, Ruth, Nestor and Eduardo had completed a wide range of preparatory activities. The day had come for the arrival a large number of other past students that Marcus thought suitable candidates for recruitment.

Uncertain as to how well he would be received, Marcus decided to have the Cuervos and Ruth pretend to arrive just like the other ex-students, to act as spies within the audience, or at least, to remain anonymous at least for the start of the planned activities. He had them pack up their rooms in his large, country home, and drive out, to return at the appointed time, just like the others.

Later that morning, Marcus had welcomed a steady stream of current and former grad students into his large, dusty old home on a remote, forested property near Lexington, Massachusetts, a half hour drive from the campus of Boston University.

He surprised his guests by greeting them in full battle dress. Even as an old man, he looked imposing and comfortable in the leather, polished brass and steel uniform of a tribune.

Many of the students had been in Marcus's house over the years, and a few had remarked at how it seemed excessively large for the bachelor-professor, but he had always smiled wryly at them and said that it suited his needs just fine. It was a small hobby farm, where he grew heirloom fruits and vegetables, and the country air was fresher than in the congested cities. He raised free-ranging chickens and drew milk from cows he knew personally, which supported his longevity-focused lifestyle.

Inside the farmhouse, the sofas and bookcases had been removed from the large living room, replaced by a tight formation of folding wooden chairs, six rows deep and nine columns across, and a doubled-column on the left of the 'formation', five rows deep. More than a few students recognized the symbolism. It was laid out exactly like the 59 centuria of a legion: nine rows of 80-man centuria and one double-row of 160-man centuria. However, unlike a legion of over 5240 men, plus officers, the layout in Marcus's living room would only seat 59.

Hanging on the wall was something none of the students had never seen, an authentic-looking battle-standard, with the familiar looking MONVMENTAL Roman lettering and Roman numerals, indicating a particular Cohort, 'COH', and the number. What was unusual about this particular battle-standard was the number. In gold lettering was the Roman numeral 'XI', the Eleventh Cohort.

While they waited for others to take their seats, the Cuervo brothers chatted with the other passengers they had picked up on the drive from New York to Lexington.

"Have you ever heard of an Eleventh Cohort?" asked one of their passengers.

"Nope. Maybe it was from the early empire period."

"No way. The structure of the Legions was standardized long before that. Even during all the experimentation under Constantine II, the experimentation with different structures was always smaller, more specialized formations like *comitatenses* and *pseudocomitatenses*, higher-mobility units. I have *never* heard of an Eleventh Cohort in any Roman period," said Nestor.

"Maybe it's a joke, or something like a '5th Column', a subversive group," said Eduardo.

Laughing, Paul, the thirty-eight year old captain of a fire department in rural New York state, observed: "If that were true, this Eleventh Cohort would be acting in the interests of Rome, to undermine who, America?" he laughed.

The hubbub of small-talk ended when Marcus strode to the front of the room.

As cramped as the large room was, there was just enough space for a corridor running down each side of the cohort of chairs, but the assembled guests had their legs and arms up against each other, seated as though they were in a crowded subway.

"Friends, I have a proposition for you," Marcus began.

As the assembled scholars and students of Classical Studies listened intently, none of them noticed as two large men moved into position at the back of the room, blocking the only other exit.

Marcus stood in front, seeming to have somehow lost twenty years on his recent six-month sabbatical. He now looked no more than fifty years old. The tell-tale signs of a facelift or collagen treatment were not evident. His skin was supple and healthy and he stood straight and strong.

Robyn Innis, a current grad student having nearly completed her thesis on the legal status of women during the late republican period, thought that her prof must have gained twenty pounds on his recent vacation. *What had he said, 'to visit some old friends'?*

The room was rather dark, with the window shades drawn. A few candles burned on their wall-mounted sconces and the wood burning in the fireplace added a warm and seemingly ancient glow that reflected off of a red and yellow painted *scutum*, a shield, that was leaning against the wall behind Marcus, flickering as if from fires on some ancient battlefield.

"I am sure that all of you remember our class discussions on the tactical role that *betrayal* plays in siege warfare?"

A few nods.

"And the emphasis I always placed on examples such as Scipio Africanus's victory at the Battle of Llipa, and the Battle of Mediolanum, when Maximus Thrax defeated his successor, Gordian the Second?

"Well, I am about to make our discussions less theoretical, and more concrete, as it were. I am putting you into the sandals of the Alamanni king, Suebianus, the leader of the Germanic horde bearing down the River Po and onto Rome, and asking you if you will betray your people, as Suebianus betrayed the Alamanni just as Ballienus arrived at the River Po. On that day, given the betrayal of Suebianus and the mischief he created by giving contradictory orders to the Alamanni commanders, the defeat of the Alamanni force was total, with 300,000 Germanics slaughtered, and Rome was saved."

Most of the students smiled, enjoying what they thought was some kind of amusing prank by the lonely professor.

"Lisa, Ben, and David. This is not for the purpose of amusement."

He spoke in a stern tone, one that none of the students had ever heard before. "How will we betr - "

"Silentium!" commanded Marcus.

The room fell silent.

"I am going to tell you how it is and then ask you to make a decision," he continued, again in the quite tone he used when lecturing a large audience, a clear whisper that required absolute, attentive silence to hear. It was the professor's best crowd-control technique. With the room silent, he continued, somewhat louder with each word.

"My name is Marcus Horatius Avitus. Tribune and third in command of Legio Twenty-Seven, Hibernicus Domitianus. I was born in Lugo, Hispania in the first year of the reign of Nero Claudius Caesar Augustus Germanicus. Jules! What year is that Anno Domini?"

Put on the spot, Jules, now a Washington DC area police officer, quickly calculated. "That would be AD 44, no, AD 54."

"Tribune! You will address me by my title."

"Yes, *Tribune* Avitus!" Jules complied, his former USMC instincts taking over. "That would be the year 54 Anno Domini, Tribune!"

"Very good. And what Roman province was Lugo in, when I was born? – Ronald!"

"Er, Hispania Tarraconesis, Tribune!"

"Good."

"I then went on to serve in Britannia. Governor Agricola was the general in command of my Legio. What Legio was it? Anybody?"

"XX Valeria Victrix!" called out a few students, eager to enter the discussion, to exhibit their historical knowledge and to please their professor.

"Good. Now I am going to tell you something you will not believe...."

After Marcus had recounted the abduction of the Roman and Irish warriors from the Battle of Dubh Linn, he paused before moving on.

At the clap of his hands, a younger but plain, rather rugged-looking woman came out from the kitchen pushing a refreshment trolley. She walked along one side of the Eleventh Cohort of students, passing out cold cans of beer.

When one of the students asked her, "Do you have anything other than beer?" the unfamiliar woman stood up straight, smiled as if she knew something that the trouble-maker did not, and then suddenly threw a can of beer at the young woman's head.

She scored a direct hit.

The woman fell to the floor with blood flowing from her forehead.

At first the students around her moved towards her, as if coming to her aid, but when the violent women began brandishing another beer can, cocked and ready to throw – and motioned for them to remain seated, they complied. Fearful of being on the receiving end of a well-thrown beverage, even the cop turned his back on the victim.

With nobody coming to her aid, she felt embarrassed and isolated, but still found the self-respect to compose herself. She wiped the tears from her face and got back up into her chair, trying desperately to choke back the tears.

For her part, Princess Neasa had not understood the *Angleisii* words, but had taken the girl's interruption as an unacceptable degree of rudeness while her husband had been speaking. *Take what you are given and dry your baby tears* was her first thought.

But as a mentor of female warriors, Neasa saw some strength of character in the terrified young woman. It was not her fault that she was suddenly faced by an impossible situation that ran contrary to everything she thought she knew about the universe. Having handed out cold beer to whoever wanted one, Neasa returned to the kitchen. Moments later she re-appeared from the rear of the room and approached the young girl, handing her a wet tea-towel to wipe her face with, and gave her a glass of ice water.

The crowd having been suitably refreshed – and kept in line – Neasa returned to the kitchen and stayed out of sight while her husband resumed his lecture. She took out a glass for herself, and went to the refrigerator. Forgetting her warrior-queen behavior for a moment, she allowed herself a moment of thrill, pressing the glass against the tabs built into the refrigerator door. Neasa loved the ice dispenser. Like the gift of fabrics and sewing notions that Marcus had brought back to her on the starship, there were so many wonderful things to discover on present-day earth. While she listened from the kitchen, Neasa continued to poke around in 'her' kitchen, content to be house-bound, confined as she was to Marcus's home, at least until after the rest of their people arrived.

"So in six weeks' time, everything is going to change when Emperor Agricola and the Twenty-Seventh Legion arrive. Before that happens, all of you must prove where your loyalty lies."

He paused, assessing the group of men and women that he thought were most likely to embrace the opportunity to join the Romans before the battle began, to act as the Eleventh Cohort.

He believed that each of them would have different reasons to be inclined to embrace the Roman way of life. Some he considered to be egotistical and vain, the type who seek power for self-aggrandizement. Typically, those were the students who had gone on to become lawyers and bankers. Then there were those with what Marcus thought of as an expeditionary mindset, the type of people who want to know what is beyond the next horizon. There were also a number who had simply fallen in love with the legends and stories of life in antiquity. Those who wanted to experience an altogether different way of life – one more visceral and basic than the materialistic and self-absorbed life of the modern era. And finally there were those who had become misanthropes, who Marcus had the highest hopes for as they had come to hate what human kind had become, and what they were doing to their planet. These were the men and women he could shape into hard core eco-fascists.

"At this time, before I go into the details of what I expect from you, I will give any of you who are not ready and willing to pledge an oath of allegiance to Emperor Agricola, an opportunity to leave. I want you to understand, this is not a pledge you can make lightly. This is not a game, or a hobby, like a Romaphile group, with those battle re-enactments, festivals, and so on. And some of you may know that I am still active in that community, such as organizing the convention taking place in Washington next month. By the way, how many of you are planning to attend – I have not seen the latest list of confirmed participants," Marcus said, lying through his teeth.

Seeing the show of hands, every person in the room having signed on for the event, confirmed that his careful selection process, and favorable funding formula, had put the right people in the right place at the right time. It was also the first stage in building a collective, team, environment which Marcus intended to take to a much higher level in short order.

"That even will be the experience of a lifetime, trust me. But putting those plans aside for the moment, I want you to be sure that you understand that you are now dealing with the real thing. Life or death. Do you understand me?

"If you make the pledge, from that moment on *we own you.* We can ask you to throw your life away, and you will gladly do so in the manner we say. If you serve Rome competently, you may earn citizenship. Some of you may go on to great heights of success," Marcus looked at the Curevos in particular, and then at Ruth.

"You do have a few advantages over the rest of the world: you read and speak Latin, you have a comprehensive understanding and appreciation for classical history – my time –

and you have had the benefit of my mentorship in the crucial arts of philosophy, rhetoric, and Roman law. It was no accident that you are among those whose thesis topics, post-graduate work and even undergraduate papers delved into the topics that they did. It was all to prepare you for this day.

"If you accept, and make this *sacramentum*, oath, there will be no turning back.

"Who among you is not ready to make such a commitment at this time? If so, now is the time to get up and leave."

"I am!" said Nestor Curevo from his bac-row seat, slightly too quickly. Marcus ignored him for the moment, and looked at a man in the front row, who seemed visibly uncomfortable.

In the awkward silence that ensued, the man in the front row got up and began moving to the back of the room.

"I don't know what's gotten into you, man, but you've lost it," the young man said. "You're not a Roman. All of this is bullshit, or worse – some kind of sick game. I'm not going to sit around here and listen to this any longer, Doc. You need help," he said, over his shoulder as he headed to the front door.

Two others followed.

As Marcus's young son helped them find their jackets, much to their relief, they were about to depart.

"Anybody else?"

Two women seated near the back looked at the first three, who were just buttoning up their coats to leave, and got up to join them.

"Ok. Now I want five volunteers," said Marcus.

Within seconds more than half of the fifty-four remaining guests sprang to their feet, knowing what Professor Avitus had always said: When asked for volunteers, Roman soldiers never ask 'for what?', they simply stand to or step forward, ready to do whatever they are assigned.

"You, you, you, you, and you." Marcus said, indicating three men and two women.

"Kill the cowards," he ordered.

The five volunteers moved slowly at first, having trouble believing what had just happened, but also certain that it was real.

As the guards blocked their exit, one of the five who had decided not to pledge their lives had a change of heart.

"No. I want to take the pledge, Marcus. Tribune, please…"

Another who had declined tried to rush to the back door only to be confronted by another guard who had been lurking in the back hallway. The student's momentum carried him into the soldier, but he did not make contact with the soldier. He burst into a bright yellow flame, filling the corridor with a sudden, intense light that left those who had watched momentarily flash-blinded and completely shocked.

"That is an example of the alien technology I spoke of. It is a force-field that converts matter into energy. Best not to get too close to a legionary unless you are similarly protected by an Equanimity field."

One of the five who Marcus had selected moved in on her female counterpart. Understanding that her task was to kill one of the women who wanted out, the young woman with the gash on her face, Julie, whom Neasa Avitus had given the napkin to, lunged at the fearful woman. She got her hands around the other woman's neck, and began to choke the life out of her.

The other woman assigned to murder, and the three men, stood back and watched. They were not ready to engage yet, but they did block the paths of the other woman and two remaining men, who they would ultimately have to kill. All seven watched as the two women fought.

From some place deep inside her, the targeted woman began to fight back against her attacker, who moments earlier had wept after being struck with a beer-can. One moment earlier, terrified and ready to flee, she was now fighting for her life even as the choking grip around her neck sapped her strength. She clawed at her attacker, gouging her nails into Julie's forehead, re-opening the slash that Neasa Avitus had given her and adding a few more scratches down her cheeks.

But Julie had the upper hand, and continued to squeeze.

"That's it, keep squeezing. She'll stop resisting soon enough," Marcus encouraged. "What's the matter with the rest of you? Get on with it!" he ordered.

But it was too late. Tricia had reached a level of desperation she had never experienced, becoming an enraged animal, tearing at Julie's face and pressing her nails into her attacker's eyes.

Julie loosened her grip on her victim's neck, as she tried to move her head away from the fingers that were poking into her eyes.

With fresh oxygen coming into her lungs, the desperate woman threw Julie onto the floor, and climbed on top of her.

Now the tables were reversed, and it was the attacker who was in peril, blood pouring from the open gash on her forehead and her eye sockets as her erstwhile victim resumed pressing her fingers deeper and deeper.

As the blood changed from bright red to a darker fluid, and Julie stopped fighting back, it was clear to everybody that prey had become predator, and one of their former classmates, Julie, the beer-can girl, now lay dead on the floor.

"Well done, Tricia! You will live to fight another day. Now come back here and take your place, unless you still want to leave?"

Tricia, confused by the range of emotions and adrenalin rush of surviving her near-death experience, got off of her opponent and slowly moved back toward her seat.

All of the others in the room remained motionless, not believing their eyes yet unable to turn away as the impossible circumstances continued to unfold.

The three men and one woman designated as attackers now began to move in on the three remaining victims, no longer a fair fight given that one of the victims had been dispatched by the sentry. With the attackers moving in on them, the four took up defensive stances, standing together but not yet working together as a unit.

The ensuing fight took three minutes. Before it was over it was hard to tell who was who. At one point, one of the ones who had wanted to leave was trying to rip the flesh off of his attacker's face with his thumb hooked fiercely into the other man's mouth, attempting to pull his face off. But the other man swung his face and bit down hard until he had bitten the first man's thumb off. He spat the digitus out, and yelled "I'm with you, asshole! I just want to get the fuck out of here!"

When it was over, the second woman and the two men, all those remaining who had tried to depart, were dead. The four victorious attackers picked themselves up from the pile of bodies, and resumed their seats, panting. They looked at Tricia with a new respect, not seeing her as a victim or coward, but rather as one of a very small club. A club of every-day people whose lives had just been changed forever – a group of people who had just killed with their bare hands.

Laughing, Marcus and the Roman guards had enjoyed watching the life-or-death struggle. Such entertainment was not unusual for the Romans. However, many in the audience were inspired in a way that they had never before felt.

"In all of that, I am confused about who were our cowards and who were our volunteer attackers. But it matters not. What matters is that those of you who have succeeded in this have bloodied your hands. You have killed. And that was my point – in addition to ensuring security, of course.

"So then. Have you ever felt more alive than you do at this moment?" asked Marcus, rhetorically.

While the three miles gregarius, foot soldiers, disposed of the four corpses, making bright flashes as the bodies were converted to energy with the alien technology, Marcus and his son carried out a solemn ceremony at the opposite end of the room, that of having each new milite, recruit, repeat the *sacramentum militare*, military oath of allegiance, in Latin or English, depending on their capabilities.

They swore, repeating after Marcus: "I swear to the King of the Gods, Zeus. To Terra and Sol, and all the goddesses and gods, and to Agricola Augustus himself. I will be loyal to Emperor Agricola and his progeny for the rest of my pitiful life. My friends shall be his servants; his enemies my enemies. I will face any peril to defend him, and I will do so with my life and the lives of my family, to protect him against any conspiracy, threat, or other harm. If I fail to live by this oath, I shall be a traitor, cast out of society; my life cursed and forfeited, my family and property forfeited, and my bloodline cast into an inferno to suffer agony for eternity."

As Avitus Connal rolled a mobile smart-board to the front of the room, Marcus and Neasa began handing out large black plastic bags, each about the size of a pillow.

"Do not open these yet, as space is tight here. You are now officially milites, serving within the Eleventh Cohort of the Twenty-Seventh Legion. You will soon meet your centurion, a man from your time, in fact. And I am your tribune.

You, and I, together, are members of the Twenty-Seventh Legion. We serve the glory of Rome under Dominus et Deus, Imperator Quintus Julius Agricola. Accordingly, you have been issued the uniform of a milite, raw recruit, with the insignia of our unit – the Eleventh Cohort. A few of you will be assigned to protect the emperor, assisting the finest warriors in the legion, the Praetorian Guard. Those of you worthy of this task will be assigned to Centurion Eduardo Cuervo," said Marcus nodded and extended his arm in the direction of Eduardo, who was not at all surprised.

Eduardo, Nestor, Ruth and Marcus had gone over the plan for weeks. They even carried out some training, in full Praetorian Guard uniform, in the grounds of Marcus' remote acreage., the uniforms arriving with the Cuervos, who had picked them up at the leather artisan's shop in Ottawa, which specialized in making authentic Roman costumes for Hollywood.

"Just as you know that Immune Nestor Cuervo is the administrative coordinator for the convention and activities in Washington, Centurion Eduardo Cuervo will coordinate three contubernia of Praetorian Guards, with the assistance of some original Romans from my time, and will be known by their gold-on-black uniforms and the leones, lions, emblazoned on their chests," Marcus pointed to the chest-armor, neatly arranged along one wall.

"And by the way, some of your weapons were used by the cohort I commanded at the Battle of Dublinensis, in Ireland, nearly two thousand years ago. We will never know who would have won, of course, as our contest was interrupted by fate. However I am sure that my charming wife has her own opinion on that." Marcus smiled at Neasa, who understood that this was when she was to be formally introduced.

She made her way to her husband's side, now dressed in a long green dress with interwoven snakes embroidered around the neck and shoulders. The only jewelry she wore was a silver Tara broach, holding her outfit together pinned as it was through the coarse fabric over her shoulder.

"Cohort Eleven of the Twenty-Seventh Legion of Rome, it is my great honor to introduce you to Princess Neasa, of Cathair mac Cassan, Hibernia."

There were smiles and confused looks around the room.

"That is right, my wife is from the first century, but not from the Roman Empire. She was the commander of a maniple – that is two centuries – of woman warriors from *Clann Dalaigh* – now known as the Daley family, by the way – and *Clann mac Cassan*. The ancient gods must have decided that Princess Neasa and I were destined to kill each other. To my great surprise, and good fortune, we are to kill each other slowly over millennia, together forever, or as long as we can extend our lives anyhow, and not on the sacred battlefield of Dubh Linn!"

The audience erupted in applause, honoring the Celtic princess, who took her cue from Marcus and withdrew to the kitchen.

Marcus turned his attention to the map.

"You will have an opportunity to examine these diagrams when I have completed my briefing, Milites," he started. "Now then, tomorrow most of us will make your way to Washington, to check into the hotels and participate in the convention as though it were the simple, fun-lowing event that the First Lady has so graciously lent her support to. From the event website, you are aware of the detailed arrangements that have been made to acquire the necessary permits and security passes for the events scheduled for 21 April, the birthday of Rome, of course – our sacred day of Parilia – but also the day of the President's State of the Union Address. You should know that my vigorous support for your hobby has always had a deeper purpose.

Several of you will check in, collect your event and National Mall access passes for the convention, but rather than participate in the events, you shall to other places in Washington, but I will get to that later. In shortl, the mission of the Eleventh Cohort is to act as a vanguard, placing yourselves at your assigned locations at the specified times.

"You will not communicate with anyone about what has transpired here today. You will not make any notes or mark any maps. Your assignments are very simple, and we will take all the time we need tonight to go over your individual assignments in great detail. Recognize that from this moment on, your singular purpose in life is to carry out your mission as if your life, and the fate of the world, depended on it."

Marcus paused to look at his troops. They were eagerly attentive.

"First, the general overview…"

Hours later, after Marcus had laid out the plan in great detail, he stood back to watch his vanguard of traitors break into smaller groups of three or four, organizing carpool travel arrangements and sharing local knowledge. It was clear to Marcus that even if a few of his new protégées proved to be disappointments, a sufficient number should be in place to ensure the success of the mission.

It was the first time Marcus had the honor of commanding troops in many, many years.

XXVII

ADVENTVS VEHEMENS
{ Violent Arrival }

President Ross took his time as he entered the Joint Session of Congress, stopping to grasp outstretched hands reaching down from the highest row of seats in the back, and then glad-handing his way down the long left aisle towards the front of the House of Representatives.

Normally home to the 435 voting members plus 6 non-voting members of the Congress, seating in the House of Representatives was much tighter than usual, in order to accommodate 100 Senators, the Justices of the Supreme Court, members of the Cabinet, a variety of senior military and civilian leaders, and other notables.

In the galleries above were other important guests. As he took his place at the podium, with the speaker of the house and the vice president behind him, President Russell Ross took a few moments to savor the applause, much of it genuine, before nodding in acknowledgement, motioning his hands for all to be seated, so that he could begin his State of The Union address.

He had barely begun when he was rudely interrupted.

No less than five burly men he recognized from the Secret Service swarmed him, shielding him with their bodies as they collectively moved together, protecting their president as they made their way to the chamber's west exit.

Before they could reach the exit, a series of soundless explosions ahead of them filled the exit corridor with an intermittent series of blindingly bright yellow flashes punctuated by gunfire and the shouts of security personnel engaged in a desperate but losing battle. The sounds coming from the House indicated panicked chaos.

They tried moving up the ramp towards the southwest exit, only to see more yellow flashes ahead and hear a similar chaos.

Inside the elevator, the President waited with his security detail, one of whom repeatedly pressed the down button, but the elevator did not move.

Marcus's Eleventh Cohort agents had led the first of Agricola's shock-troops to the main electrical load center and shorted out the main and auxiliary power supply for the elevators with a jab of an Equanimity staff, cutting the power. They were careful not to destroy the panel that provided power to the main House Chamber, however. This was just one of the small details that the Eleventh Cohort were on hand to offer assistance, facilitating the rapid tactical action by the legionaries, who would have otherwise become lost in the complicated layout of the massive Capitol building.

All of them had taken tours of the complex over the years, whether during their university days with Professor Avitus, or in the years after out of curiosity – piqued by what they had learned of the neo-classical architecture and symbolism that had been introduced to them by their favorite professor.

In the days leading up to the State of the Union speech, those assigned with specific missions had poured over floor plans provided by Marcus, and confirmed their understanding of the layout by going to the visitor's center beneath the Capitol building, taking group tours that had been coordinated by Marcus Avitus.

Teams of Marcus's Eleventh Cohort had each escorted other shock-troops to their individual assignments, communicating in Spanish and naming objectives that had been briefed and rehearsed.

In this way, from the moment that the first of Agricola's ships had settled on the roadways on the east and west sides of the Capitol Building, and began to disgorge legionaries immediately as the ramps were lowered, it had taken less than three minutes to seize control of all exits from the South

Chamber, trapping the assembly. It had taken another five minutes to cut off internal passages and to nullify the small teams of security personnel.

With Equanimity fields making the legionaries invulnerable to small-arms fire, and the shock-and-awe effects that resulted from legionaries simply obliterating and passing through oval-shaped orifices in walls, the Romans were quite literally unstoppable.

Meanwhile, there was a fierce yet one-sided, battle taking place in the skies over Washington.

The four F-15 eagles and two F-135 fighter jets from 94th Fighter Squadron, on routine combat air patrol over the Washington area, along with several batteries of Patriot air defense missiles positioned at various sites in and around Washington, did their best to attack the alien vessels that had suddenly and unexpectedly appeared from the sky.

The egg-shaped craft were identical to the ones that had recently been all over the news, from what many believed to be hoax-videos, of the small craft captured on video by a couple in Spain several months before, and the witness reports of a similar vessel robbing a liquor store in upstate Massachusetts.

The ordinance had no effect on the egg-shaped vessels. Each missile strike was instantly converted by Equanimity fields into bright flashes of yellow light.

While starships settled over Constitution Avenue on the north and Independence Avenue to the south, two of the larger colonist-ships landed on the edge of the lawn area to the west, on either side of the massive staircases leading down from the Capitol Building. A series of warships and scout-ships took up positions all around an oval perimeter centered on the Washington Monument, encircling the entire NationalNational mall from the White House to the Jefferson Memorial, and from the Lincoln Memorial to the Capitol Building. As the starships settled into position, they immediately began projecting a protective energy-wall entirely around their perimeter, and across the top of it.

Those of Marcus's Eleventh Cohort who had not been within the security perimeter when the starships first appeared had simply used Equanimity staffs, to protect themselves while passing through the curtain as well as any steel fences that would have hindered them as they made their way to their assigned objectives, or to lead the path for the legionaries. Just as in ancient times, the use of unit signum poles and vexillum flags, held aloft by immunes and team leaders from the Eleventh Cohort, to indicate their positions. These battle standards gave the legionaries exiting the starships an immediate visual frame of reference to rally around and to follow into battle.

As the hovering starships had deployed their Equanimity-field energy curtains, linking with protective segments generated from adjacent starships, another wave of bright yellow flashes appeared as a wave of missiles were fired at the alien vessels and were destroyed.

While the furious series of explosions generated a great deal of noise and light, there was no effect on Agricola's fleet.

Even an atomic blast would have had no effect on the force-fields generated by the starships' powerful thorium reactors, the Nesslessness-Thing generators and the Equanimity effects they created.

The legionaries assigned with rushing into the Capitol Building, with smaller Equanimity fields protecting them, had ignored the security personnel they encountered as they made a rapid dash from their ships. They passed through the underground entrance at the Capitol Visitor Center and other entry points, following their contacts from Marcus's Eleventh Cohort of turncoats who betrayed their nation and were now the vanguard of the Roman invasion.

The heroic attempts of the Capitol security forces to slow down the intruders, and the bright yellow Equanimity flashes as their existence was converted into Nesslessness and Thing, lasted no more than five minutes.

After that, things quieted quickly as confusion and terror took hold.

And then the terrorist himself made his way from his command ship to the Capitol Building, ascending the grand staircase at a measured pace while Legion XXVII and the Eleventh Cohort stood by, ready to quell any type of resistance.

Emperor Agricola took his time entering the building, the future seat of Roman power.

Marcus had prepared Agricola well, providing him and the officers with schematics, photographs, and videos of the building. But even with foreknowledge of every detail of the building's layout, architecture, artwork, and history, Emperor Agricola was in awe.

He had never seen a more impressive building.

Of course, he understood the concept of neo-classical architecture, and recognized the elements borrowed from the Greek and Roman architecture from his time, but it was the way it was all brought together in the Capitol Building that impressed him most.

Even in a culture that had such amazing technologies as self-propelled horseless chariots, the knowledge web, sight-capturing devices,and video cameras, Agricola was impressed that the Americans still had a respect for art.

As he entered the Rotunda, he gazed through the Oculus to the Apotheosis of Washington fresco high above.

Marcus was right; it does remind one of the Pantheon, only on a much grander scale! thought Agricola.

As he noticed that he was about to tread on the star set in the marble floor in the middle of the rotunda, he recalled the first time he had seen the Golden Milestone

Mille viae ducunt homines per saecula Romam, a thousand roads lead men forever to Rome. Thinking of how that milestone had anchored everything to Senatus Populusque Romanus, SPQR, Emperor Agricola decided then and there that this would be the new anchor. He would have Marcus add this to the long list of decrees, for the transformation of the global power structures, to be anchored to this spot - the center of power for the Senate and People of the Roman Cosmos, *Senatus populusque Vniversitatis Romanae*, SPQVR. For the administration of what was known as the United States, the administrative authority and center of power would be known as *Senatus populusque Americanus Romanus*, SPQAR – the Senate and people of Roman America.

From this day forward, a golden milestone would be placed at the foot of these stairs, as *all roads lead to Vniversitas Romana, the center of the Roman Empire of the Cosmos.*

He would have liked to explore the hallways of the Capitol, look at the many frescoes that depicted great moments in the history of the United States and the many other great works of art incorporated in the seat of power of his new home, but he had more urgent matters that required his attention.

A dual line of Praetorian Guards lined the way to his left, for his entrance into what had up until this moment been called the House of Representatives.

From the Cogito Copiae he and his closest advisors had gone through, based on the intelligence that Marcus had provided, he knew the names, titles, and characteristics of the president and some of the more influential people he was about to meet.

He strode into the den of vipers without the slightest bit of fear.

He had expected to hear at least some noise. After all, with the most influential politicians and distinguished guests present, there should be some talking, or at least some whimpering.

But as he passed through the entrance to the chamber and walked down the carpeted decline, the only sound he heard was his own footsteps.

As he strode to the podium, he understood why the chamber was so silent.

Marcus was there, along with General Cerialis and a number of Praetorian Guards. The guards had just finished herding the President back to his place by the podium.

President Ross was about to see his term in office come to an abrupt end.

Seeing the President back off a few paces from the podium, where he had been placed by Agricola's men after the president's security detail had been Equanimized and POTUS dragged back into the Chamber, Emperor Agricola decided to punctuate his entrance, with the help of his personal Equanimity field.

Walking in a J-shaped arc so that he would be facing the assembly of noble hostages, Agricola rushed the last few paces right into the podium. He struck it with his Equanimity staff, converting it into a flash of yellowy Equanimity, momentarily blinding the crowd, all of whom had their eyes riveted upon him.

Well, I've made my entrance. Now it's time to make friends and influence people, he thought as he turned to the bewildered President Russell Carnegie Ross.

"Audi, vide, tace, si tu vis vivere!" said Agricola, glancing at Marcus, indicating that ti was time for him to begin to translate.

"Hear, see, be silent – if you hope to live!" shouted Marcus, his voice booming through the House Chamber.

Cameras originally set up to transmit President Ross's State of the Union address now continued to send live images to the communications relay vans parked in the north lot. Even those producers who could have shut off their networks did not, spellbound as they were by what they were seeing. Government representatives at major media broadcast centres were equally dumbfounded, and were too overcome by events to cease transmission of what was to follow.

Some of the House Chamber audience, and many watching on television, understood enough Latin to get the gist of his speech, even without the English translation provided by Marcus Avitus.

International television viewers were equally enthralled by the events, particularly those in Rome, Italy, where a great many were fluent in Latin, whether due to their association with the Vatican or as scholars of antiquity.

It was obvious to most that the man speaking was an authentic Roman.

As Marcus translated, Agricola continued.

"Who is in charge here?" he asked.

"I am," said President Ross, hesitantly, standing close to where the podium had been before it was Equanimitized.

Agricola took out his gladius and cleaved off the man's head in one fell swoop. As the head fell to the floor, Agricola was once again surprised at the buttery feeling his sword had as it sliced through the President's neck. He knew it was due to the Equanimity field around his sword, having removed all forms of resistance to his blade. The shock on the faces of the audience was indicative that his actions were producing the desired effects.

He turned his attention to the man he recognized as Vice President Rodriguez.

"Once again, I ask, who is in charge here?"

Knowing that there was only one correct answer, Vice President Rodriguez gave the only answer he could.

"You are. But who are you?"

"That is correct. I am in charge. But to make it easy for you to comprehend, I will lay it all out for you.

"This august chamber, the traditions and laws upon which your republic was founded, stand on the shoulders of the great Republic of Rome.

"As I entered this magnificent Capitol Building, I was deeply moved by the respectful acknowledgement that your architects and builders have made to the legacy of classical Rome.

"Your forefathers have done a wonderful job in laying the foundation for the Republic, and you have yourselves participated as Senators and Plebeian representatives. However, you have been unwise and foolish in what you have done with the power that has been concentrated in your hands.

"It is just as it was in the time of Aulus Vitellius Germanicus Augustus, at the end of the year of Four Emperors. How long did he last? Eight months? But I guess he was outdone by the fifteen months of your departed president."

Agricola glanced at the headless corpse at his feet, and then continued, with Marcus`s translations keeping pace.

"All of this pointless squabbling and in-fighting, with no thought to the good of your people, only how to enrich yourselves and reward those to whom you are beholden.

"Nothing has changed in two millennia, politicians think only of themselves.

"And that is why Titus Flavius Vespasian had to step in as emperor, to deal with the existential threat to the Republic.

"As I am sure your scholars know very well, Vespasian reluctantly accepted the burden of serving as emperor.

"In his ten years as emperor, he unified the armies and ended the chaos of in-fighting. He carried out the necessary financial reforms. He commenced great engineering works to benefit the people of Rome, including the Flavian Amphitheatre – the Coliseum – and many great aqueducts. And he brought the greedy, self-concerned senators back into a more reasonable and sustainable, yet suitably noble and comfortable level of wealth and entitlement.

"At that time the rich had so far over-reached what the good people of Rome could sustain. They forgot the meaning of SPQR, Senatus Populusque Romanus – the Senate and the People of Rome. That was yet another factor in the downward spiral under Vitellius Germanicus.

"And now, here we are, two millennia later, and Rome, as it is embodied by the Republic of the United States of America – the global power on this planet – faces new and as yet unaddressed existential threats.

"So it is with some reluctance that I, Quintus Julius Agricola, son of Gnaeus Julius Agricola, hereby suspend the Constitution of the Republic of the United States of America and declare myself Emperor of what shall be called *Senatus populusque Vniversitatis Romanae*, SPQVR – the Senate and People of the Roman Cosmos. And, for the administration of what was until now known as the United States of America, the administrative authority and center of power is hereby established as *Senatus populusque Americanus Romanus*, SPQAR – the Senate and People of Roman America."

If that was not already shocking enough, Agricola then dropped an even more shocking bombshell.

"At the end of this day only two hundred and fifty out of the five hundred and forty one of you senators and plebeian representatives shall remain. The rest of you will be dead.

"Fear not, those of you in the audience," Agricola gestured to the stunned audience in the gallery above. "You shall be allowed to live, to report what you saw. You are bearing witness to the rebirth of a once great nation.

"Those of you, the political elite, who survive the day, will be permitted to serve SPQVR – Universitas Romana – the Galactic Roman Empire. And you will have purpose. You will throw your lives into facing the terrible fates that comprise not one, but two existential threats to planet Earth – and to all of humanity.

"The first of these threats is the imminent destruction of the surface of the planet and all who live on it. While many of you doubt what science and observation tells you, it is with the greatest certainty that I tell you that planet Earth cannot support sixty billion human beings." Agricola paused, looking at the confused faces in the room.

"That is right. I said *sixty billion*. That will be the population of humans on this planet in one hundred years if your present course of population growth is not altered. I have seen it with my own eyes, on Planeta Caedum. There we saw a race, much like our own, that gradually converted the entire food-producing capacity of their planet, once much like Planet Earth, into producing the maximum quantity of food to feed the maximum quantity of inhabitants.

"They reached a slightly higher number, eighty billion, before total catastrophe. By that time they were eating food-products made from the processed remains of their own kind, along with any other form of nutrients that their great industry could wring from their exhausted planet.

"There was no art, no recreation, and no entertainment. There was no variety, nor were there any wild, untouched natural places. In the end there was not even enough air to breathe as their entire civilization ground to a halt. There was only the repugnant, inevitable outcome of population growth outstripping the planeta's finite resources.

"That is the fact of the climate and earth sciences: technology can continue to extend the productivity of a planet only so far. But in the end, logarithmic growth will overpower even the greatest genius of industry and toil.

"Unless this trend is stopped now, all of your progeny will be robbed of any meaningful life.

"But there is more. We have learned, and the fact of our presence before you is proof, that travel in the cosmos can cause a man to age very little while those he has left on earth continue to age quickly.

"We left Earth in the year 835 *Ab urbe condita,* since the founding of Rome, on this very day – 21 April. Your Christian calendar counts that as the year 82 Anno Domini, the year of your lord, Jesus Christ. Count the years as you wish, but we are of that ancient time, and yet here we are before you, conquering you.

"We could have left you to your fate, and found another planet – we control other planets in our galactic empire – where water is clean, land and earth are unspoiled, and air is fresh. But Earth is home.

"We are now a space-faring people, and in the life of a single individual, in proportion to the time spent travelling through space, one may return home to earth many times. But in this way of living – available to some of you – a life may extend to several hundreds of years of personal time, reckoned in the days and weeks you experience – and yet at the same time many millennia will have passed here on earth.

"In that context, those of us alive have need for the Earth to be habitable for what we would have once considered an impossibly long time.

"But the way you live, the foolish squandering of this sacred home planet for all of us, is a doomed path. It is a threat to the existence of my homeworld.

"And I, as Emperor of Rome of Earth and of the known universe, have been empowered by the Senate and the people to act as Dictator – to be a single unifying origin of guidance and authority – to lead our path away from catastrophe.

"And you have no choice but to follow my dictate."

Agricola paused, watching as Marcus Avitus completed his translation.

Silence befell the House Chamber.

"And there is yet another, even greater threat.

"The alien beings who abducted the Hibernians and Romans from the Battlefield of Dubh Linn during the second year of the consulship of Domitianus and Sabinus have decided that humankind are too dangerous a species as to be permitted to exist. We betrayed them and stole many of their starships. No doubt we have incurred their hatred. They are a simpleminded species that have totally exterminated two other species – laid waste to two entire worlds – for lesser crimes.

"And now they will be coming after us. Whether we stay and save humanity from itself, or whether we continue our odyssey in the cosmos, they are surely coming to exterminate you.

"These alien beings, we call Tuathii, have awesome power and the resources of countless worlds to supply their terrible armies like these three monsters standing before you," Agricola exaggerated, indicating the three Siphonapteristii lined up on the left. Centurion Tappulus and two immunes were watching them closely. Despite being in a massive chamber filled with tasty, warm-blooded creatures, the monsters remained quiescent, due to the harnesses that kept their primary feeler-antenna strapped down. Tappulus had installed a quick-release mechanism on one of the Siphonapterist's harnesses. All it would take would be a sharp tug on the leather lanyard he held in one hand, and the monster would be free to attack. If the brute attacked a Roman, protected by an Equanimity field, of course, the monster would be obliterated into the light and energy of the Equanimity effect. But the other humans, ripe with the smell of fear, would be entirely defenseless against the Siphonapteristii if their Roman handlers decided that it would be feeding time...

The audience saw the hungry look in the eyes of the monsters, and their ugliness only added to the terrifying effect that they had on the politicians and guests.

"This is just one of the alien races we have encountered. The Tuathii have a large number of other beings under their control, both great and small, and likely many more we have never encountered. We have no more than twenty years before the Tuathii force will arrive," he lied. "We must see to the defenses of our planet, or we will without doubt be completely annihilated.

"So that is the state affairs regarding humanity, and the looming threats you face. Threats from within, and threats from without. This great nation, until today known as the United States of America, will become the seat of great power. It shall from this moment on be called *America Romana*, Roman America. It shall be governed by the most courageous of your political elites, from this very chamber, forming the singular and highest administrative echelon of this nation. It shall be controlled from here in Washington, just as it was before, but all edicts and direction shall come from this group of elites – some of you here today shall constitute, as I said before, *Senatus populusque Americanus Romanus*, SPQAR – the Senate and people of Roman America, according to the principles and traditions of the Senate of Rome.

"There are written works on Roman history that provide you with enough information to understand how this is to be done. You will receive guidance from me, your Imperator, should you stray too far from what is required of you.

"That other chamber, which was until today your senate chamber, shall now become *Senatus populusque Universitatis Romanae*, SPQVR – the Senate and People of the Roman Cosmos. It shall be the supreme governing body for all nations on Earth and for all planets in the Roman Empire of the Cosmos. So in this one building there will now be two senates, with many of you in the Universal Senate, and others in the Americana Senate.

"From time to time, we will also convene the Senatus Juncturam, where both the Senatus Universitatis and the Senatus Americanus will be combined, for a joint session just as we are doing today, and in the tradition of your great nation.

"I am leader, dictator and emperor. When I have saved us from these two existential threats, there will no longer be need for a dictator. At that time all of the powers delegated to me as dictator shall be relinquished. If I do not relinquish these powers when a dictator is no longer required, then I shall be declared Tyrant and, as per Roman law, I shall be murdered – hopefully by those who love me most.

"Is that not true, Proconsul Americanae Cerialis?"

"Dominus et Deus, Imperator, it is true. I myself will be the first to reward your short-lived moment of Tyranny with my pugio."

"And I, with my gladius will be right behind!" added Tribunus Laticlavius Tappulus."

"As will I," added Tribune Marcus Avitus.

"It is settled, then. Now as for what is to be done. First of all, rest assured, you will have good leadership. I have designated my trusted friend Kaeso Petillius Cerialis as your Pro-Consul of Senatus Americanae. Of course, as dictator, I am the perpetual Consul Primus of both Senatus Cosmi and Senatus Americanae.

"Under our leadership but your own effort, you – the elite of this great nation – are the most qualified to affect what must be done. Those of you in attendance who are members of the judiciary – the Supreme Court – shall draft laws and decrees that establish the primacy of Roman law, and of my edicts, as the ultimate source of law and authority in America and in the known universe. Failure to satisfy me in your execution of this task will result in your execution, and that of your family and closest friends. Another jurist can no doubt be found.

"Those of you who were part of the military, surveillance and policing agencies – you members of the so-called 'Joint Chiefs of Staff', you shall continue to serve your nation as supporting adviser to the *concilia*, military council, of the Senatus Americanus. You will soon learn that your Pentagon and other key installations, have been isolated, locked down you would say, by my forces. Soon you will be permitted to communicate with them, to inform them that while there has been a change of command here in Washington, the military structure and chain of command will be preserved.

"Some of your installations, however, particularly those who continue to annoy my forces with their futile attacks, will be destroyed. Therefore if you love the men under your command as any good general or admiral must, you will issue orders for them to stand down and await further instructions.

"For the rest of you, and for those of you watching and hearing me on your televisions, be warned. All of your laws, your economic systems, how you organize your agricultural production and supply of energy for your transportation – all of this shall be radically changed. Effective immediately, you must cease to use carbon-based fuels. You must shutter your polluting factories. All of your industrial activities and methods of travel that choke our air and poison our water, and the many other ways you produce toxins which harm biological life on this planet, all of this must come to an end immediately.

"There will be a great deal of violence, harsh treatment and sacrifice in the days ahead. And it is with no remorse that I, as Dictator, shall preside over the necessary destruction of your old ways. I am responsible for the suffering ahead.

"And now, so that you may begin the gargantuan task ahead of you, we must conduct a swift form of senatorial selection and confirmation." Agricola smiled, as if contemplating an inside joke that only he was privy to.

"After the *selectio fieri*, selection process, your senators shall begin to implement the long list of my *Senatus consulta*, decrees. Based upon my *consulta*, the advice I give to your senators – advice which must be followed – your very own Senatus Americanae shall determine the details and instructions to pass on to your current system, what we would call magistrates, who will put these decrees into effect.

"And now to the selection process. First Consul of Romanus Americanae, Senator Cerialis and I will now begin to cull the herd.

"We will start with the power here, in the American Province of RomaNova. Senatus Americanus. There shall be three senators for each of your fifty states, therefore one hundred and fifty senators. From this number, one senator out of every three, therefore fifty senators, shall accompany elements of the Twenty-Seventh Legion in an exploration and, if necessary, conquest of nearby planetae that may be of use to Roma Universitatis, the Roman Empire of the known universe.

"Of the remaining two Senators for each Americanae Province, what you called 'state', one shall be in command of a new form of army, which shall be equipped with alien technology. You will be given roles in various committees and you shall be supported by the consilio – your Joint Chiefs of Staff.'" Agricola looked at the joint chiefs, and was pleased to see that some were taking notes. Whether they were plotting a revolt or taking notes on their role in the new system was irrelevant, *they are paying attention.*

"The other Terrestrial Senator shall be assigned various magistrates taken from you existing political and bureaucratic administrations to transform the provinces assigned to them. You will, together with other senators, determine how many functionaries, magistrates, and other personnel resources you shall control, and this you shall share with the two other senators you are tripled with. You will be given a range of powers you did not have in the past, however you will also have prohibitions that you may find difficult to adjust to.

"If you prove unequal to the task, I shall execute you and find a more competent replacement. Your replacement shall, by Roman law, be entitled to ownership of your entire family, all of your wealth, and other holdings and your entire family will be forfeited. If your replacement so wishes, he may kill all of your progeny, or accept some or all into his family, and make them his personal responsibility. In other words, we treat the senator as the head of the family, and if the head is to be cut off, the entire body invariably dies.

"However, if you do your job and transform your territory in the manner I direct, then you will enjoy great power, freedom, and perhaps most importantly, a form of near-immortality.

"That is right, for among the many treasures I have liberated from the Tuathii, there are unexpected benefits.

"And this takes me to the *senatus enim conversionem*, the senatorial rotation. From time to time as I direct, or as you may be permitted to suggest in the senate, the extra-terrestrial senator shall return to Terra and replace the political senator, seeing to the administration of the State. The former political senator shall assume command of the provincial army, ensuring continuity with plans and objectives that the provincial army is being applied to. And then the military senator takes a suitable portion of that military and as many citizens and slaves as is suitable, and with them be sent on an expedition to some extra-terrestrial location, into battle, colonization, or some other adventure to expand the glory and reach of the Romanus Cosmi civilization.

"And here is the good news. It is when you travel with the fleet, operated by Legio Two, that you receive the benefit of the rejuvenating effects of astrum navis, starship, travel. It is not the fountain of youth, as it cannot be conveyed by elixir or medicine, however those who spend time intus astrum navis, some of the effects of age and illness are partly reversed and wellness is restored.

"I hold out to you the example of my good friend, Commander of Cohort Eight of the Second Legion during the Battle of Dublinensis, Ireland, from the year you call Anno Domini 82. Now just look at this man!"

Agricola gestured at Marcus.

"He has stood on Earth for seventy-five years, plus another few months travelling in the cosmos and visiting Planeta Metallorum. Yet to look at him, he appears to you as a very healthy pentagenarian, fifty-year old. But it is a known fact that he is actually seventy-five years old from his perspective. On the other hand, the span of time from his birth to the present day is nearly two millennia. This is living proof that travel in the heavens is not something that waits for you after your death, when you may have hoped to be taken to heaven, to your ancestors, or whatever your faith promises to you. The wondrous possibilities of the cosmos are available to you now, as routinely as air-travel has been in your time.

"These and other benefits will be shared with those who best serve Roma Cosmi, to our satisfaction. But now we turn to the necessary homicidium, the culling of your number. This will be the first of many culls so it is your opportunity to show that you are worthy of being leaders of your people, that you are noble and courageous.

"All of you who were counted as Senators and Plebeian representatives of your great nation, you 'Congressmen and senators,' you shall assemble at the designated area on the grassy field just outside to the west of this chamber. We have citizens of your nation, who are already serving as the Eleventh Cohort of the Twenty-Seventh Legion on sentry duty. These milites and my officers leading them will guide you to where you are required to assemble. The former senators among you shall gather in the designated area to the north, the former plebeian representatives to the south.

"When I give the order you will engage in battle, plebeians against senators, until only two hundred and fifty of your number remain. There shall be no plebeians from this assembly when I declare the battle over. This means that two hundred and ninety one of you shall perish today.

"Here is how it shall be done. Senators shall be given a medallion, of which two hundred and fifty have been produced." Agricola held one up, feeling the roughness under his thumb, the lion and SPQVR on the face, arbor rosea on the obverse, with the number 2776 below it – indicating years since the foundation of Rome. Fittingly, one millennia after the American Revolution.

"One of these will be distributed, to each of you former senators, along with a variety of traditional Roman weapons. plebeians shall be given nothing; however your greater number and desperation should give you a fighting chance. Additional weapons will be nearby.

"In order to come out of this alive, you need to remove the medallion from the neck of a senator, and place it around your own neck. If you can keep the medallion until only twoe hundred and fifty of you are finally left alive, then you shall be a senator, with all of the benefits, power and responsibility that it conveys. For now, the current senators must fight to the death to retain their positions. The additional one hundred and fifty medallions we are offering, will be distributed into the arena, for any of you to fight for.

"I am confident that many great men and women will not survive the day, and I regret this; however, each and every one of you has demonstrated that you have the political acumen, resources and supportive families necessary to be capable politicians in the Americae Romanus, the new Roman state of America. I require your services as members of Senatus Populusque Americanus Romanus, SPQAR."

Looking up to the gallery above, for the first time becoming aware of the vision-capture machines and the terrified nobility in the viewing gallery, Agricola continued.

"And for the rest of you watching today's events through your vision boxes all around Terra, your fate also will be decided on another day. How you serve the restoration of the atmosphere, adapt to the de-industrialization and reduction in the impact of your manner of living, and how you organize yourselves into large, extended families under the Roman patriarchal system, will form one pillar of the basis for permitting you, and those under your protection, to serve and thereby become citizens of Universitatis Romanae.

"For those of you who oppose my cictatorship or the prompt execution of the decrees that this and other Territorial Senates will be charged with carrying out, for those who physically or by stealth interfere with censors, tax collectors, magistrates, and other administrators of Universitatis Romanae, I promise, death is coming for you.

"You are welcome to take your own lives if you know that you have no hope, or perhaps you will choose to make yourself available to the new armies that are to be raised. Your life is in your own hands, for a while at least.

"Take the lessons of history, of science, and the guidance provided in cecrees and other instructions that will now begin to flow from this, the Capitol of Romanus Cosmi, to transform your own nations in advance of conquest and imminent self-destruction. You may in that way earn a role in the future of your territory as it takes its place as a new province of Universitatis Romanae, with you as governor of a nation of Terra or of an entire planeta.

"The final two points I have for you to consider are matters of discourse and commerce.

"As for discourse, your provincial language may continue to be used for plebeian matters and private life, however I decree that the language of intercourse between provinces in Romani Americae, and of the future legions of the provinces of Americae, shall be Latin for the officers and Hispanic, Spanish, for the legionaries. Angalisii shall not be spoken in our military," Agricola said, revealing a hint of his bias against pale skinned men, and his favoritism toward olive skinned people – other than the lightly-shaded descendants of the Hibernian-Roman families – his people, of course. "Latin shall be the language at the highest levels of the ruling class, and for the recording and transmission of all laws and edicts from any Senate or other governing body. And now, as for commerce. Gold and silver shall be the commerce, any other form, as of now, has no value whatsoever.

"Legio Twenty-Seven is now in the process of making safe the largest hordes of gold that the nations of Terra have secreted away in vaults around the globe, and the more capable of your coin-makers shall be permitted to serve Universitatis Romanae by making new gold and silver coins, with the faces to match these medallions – the leo to symbolize the great species we have caused to become extinct, the arbor rosea, truly the tree of knowledge and the will to undo what we have done – and the year of minting, *abe urbe condita.*"

"It will take time for the new coins to work their way into the economic blood of Universitatis Romanae , so you will have to find ways to cooperate and to share what you need to sustain yourselves, but these shocks have taken place many times before when a false currency – like your fiat paper dollars – fails, and is replaced with real money – silver and gold. The only real money in Roma Cosmi shall be official coins of the Empire. Fraudulent transactions, substitutions, counterfeiting, tampering, and imitation of Roma Cosmi coinage shall result in execution.

"While I am dictator, you have no rights other than those I permit. You have no freedom, other than to serve. And you have no future, other than extinction, if you do not throw yourself into the service of humankind under my rule – to serve the glory and perpetuity of humankind in this harsh and unforgiving universe.

"It is a fact, as you see with your very eyes," indicating the Siphonapteristii, "that we are not alone in this universe. To the cosmos itself, we do not matter at all. So we must unite, as a bundle of sticks are stronger than an individual stick on its own.

"And that is why it will be the *plurale tantum*, the fasces, the ancient symbol of the bundle that represents the power and authority of the people of Rome, the symbol of our magistrates' power and legal jurisdiction, that shall be the symbol of a restored Roman Empire. The fasces is a symbol that was known to the architects who built the many great buildings that stand in this city. It is inside the oval office at the White House – my future residence. It is on the wall behind me, and on either side of the flag of the United States," he pointed to the flag displayed behind the rostrum, with a golden fasces on either side.

"It is at the feet of your Lincoln Memorial, and it is on the frieze of the Supreme Court building, in the hands of a centurion, representing order.

"It is a symbol that will long outlast my short reign as Imperator Augustus Maximus. It shall be the symbol of Senatus Populusque Universitatis Romanae, SPQVR, the interplanetary

Senate, for senatorial representatives of all territorial senates of Universitatis Romanae – just as it has been for your American republic. Because at its core, a republic has strength only from its people. I hereby conclude my opening remarks and place the two Senates into a short recess, so that you may relocate to the grasslands and assemble as directed into the line of Senators and the line of Plebeian Representatives.

"Once the task of reducing your number to two hundred and fifty has been accomplished, you shall be divided into two groups. One hundred and fifty , the inaugural Senatus Americanus Romanus shall be re-assembled into the smaller Senate Chamber. The additional one hundred inaugural senators of and Senatus Universitatis Romanae shall assemble in this very chamber, the larger of the two."

"You will then begin to work through the decrees and edicts and begin the reshaping of your nation.

"Orationis est fabula! That concludes this speech!"

With that, Emperor Agricola turned and slowly and deliberately walked up the left aisle, where he had not yet been, and looked into each of the faces of the stunned congressmen and senators, his steely gaze making personal contact with the strangers he would soon rely on to carry out his will.

Agricola then proceeded to explore the rest of the Capitol building, his Praetorian Guard fanning out much like the Secret Service of old.

For the next fifteen minutes, Emperor Agricola enjoyed a walk around the exterior of the new seat of his Imperial Power while his officers motivated the occupants of the House Chamber to disgorge through the west front of the Capitol Building.

Guided by soldiers in strange-looking Roman uniforms, Agricola realized that he was being escorted by heroic traitors of Marcus's Eleventh Cohort, taking him to the small stage and tent that they had erected for their Emperor.

He could see the excitement and determination in their faces. *They want to impress, and to serve. Marcus has done well cultivating these men and women.*

From the far side of the lawn east of the Capitol Building, with his Pretorian Guard and his senior officers assembled around him, he sat on the Tuatha-wood throne that had been placed on the platform by men from the command ship.

There would be a great many other observers, as Marcus's teams were escorting guests from the upper gallery of the House of Representatives to a designated area adjacent to the lawn area, while small teams of media were setting up camera positions under the direction of others from the Eleventh Cohort.

Kaeso Cerialis and Fabius Quintilianus were busy making preparations in the two senate chambers for when the surviving battle-hardened new senators would return.

That left only Vibius Metellus as the closest of Agricola's advisors to be on hand with Agricola and the rest of the officers. Emperor Agricola thought with satisfaction about the sequence of events that would take place when the two senates reconvened. The first order of business would be the two senates swearing the Roman oath of fidelity to the Senate and people of the Roman Cosmos and Emperor Agricola.

But Agricola derived the greatest satisfaction from the knowledge that his lifelong friend Kaeso Cerialis had embraced his invitation to act as First Consul for Senatus Populusque Romani Americae, SPQRA, the Senate and People of America Romanus.

As he thought about the historical importance of what was taking place on this, their first day back on Terra, Emperor Agricola was happy to see Vibius Metellus furiously scribbling notes and taking photographs with one of those amazing digital cameras. *Too bad Vibius Metellus's old student in Britannia, Publius Cornelius Tacitus, is not here to scribe the day's events. Tacitus was such a great scribe of history,* thought Agricola.

Inside the chamber, there had been some resistance to the order for the representatives and senators to relocate outdoors. It was as if the collection of great American leaders preferred the relative safety of the House Chamber, rather than finding out whether what the Roman leader said was truly going to take place.

One of them spoke out louder than the others:

"Patriots! Americans! Do not go out there! As long as we stick together, and refuse to leave, they will have no choice but to negotiate with us. They can't kill us all – that would defeat the purpose of coming here in the first place. They need us, so be strong, and don't cooperate. Stay here and be strong," said Senator Olsen.

Tribune Tappulus had been waiting for just such a hero. He promptly trained a penlight laser on the man, while another Roman yanked a lanyard, releasing one of the Siphonapteristii.

Trained that when released from the painful harness the monster was free to eat whatever warm-blooded creature was being illuminated by the salivation-triggering light, the giant flea leapt into the air and landed on top of Senator Olsen with all six legs grasping the man firmly, tearing him to shreds and devouring him in seconds.

The only people more terrified than Senator Olsen had been in the last second of his life, as his arms were ripped from his body before his very eyes, were the dozen or more senators and congressmen standing closest to him. As warm blood and guts sprayed onto their faces from the furious disassembly of Senator Olsen, the crowd rushed for the exits. Centurion. Tappulus began sweeping the laser-illuminator across the few who were not yet moving, agitating the two brutes who were still held still by their restraints, hoping to be released at any moment by the legionaries charged with handling them.

Tappulus had been saving the two hungry Siphonaperistii to be used on the lawn, however, and had the immunes lead them out of the building. Even in their more domesticated state, the fleas continued to be effective motivation for the terrified crowds.

Agricola watched with interest as the congressmen and senators issued from the impressive building like ants. For some reason Agricola did not know, they scrambled out of the chamber as if the last one out would be eaten alive. *Tappulus has unleashed his trained Siphonapteristii,* he realized, as they frantically made their way to the lawn between Agricola's podium and the Capitol building.

The 441 Plebeian Representatives and the 100 Senators were directed to the large rectangular areas that had been staked out and surrounded by milites of the Eleventh Cohort

Despite being somewhat taken aback by the impressive Capitol building and the strangeness of the unfamiliar territory they found themselves on, Cohort Four quickly oriented themselves and moved to their assigned locations, taking up positions every five yards around the perimeter. A separate squad from the more highly trained Cohort I, originally of Legio Two, took up their two-man-abreast formation down the centre of the two rectangles.

The troops knew that when all was said and done they would have to build relationships with the survivors of the day   the future senators – however they showed no sign of respect for their future political elites. They treated them like so many cattle, their Equanimity-staffs set on shock rather than obliterate.

There seemed to be three types of people in the herd. The smallest number had begun to come to terms with the terrible new reality they faced and made their way towards the front of the crowd with a view to reaching the starting line first – to gain an advantage over their rivals.

The second group moved along reluctantly, trying to avoid the danger posed by the legionaries with their strange weapons and the terrifying aliens coming behind them. They had by this time learned that *promoveo!* meant "move along!"

The third group gave the sentries the most difficulty, as they were essentially rendered incompetent by their fear. Some froze, unable to move despite being shocked and threatened by the legionaries. Others were moving, but so terrified that they were unpredictable and therefore difficult to manage individually. Every so often, one of these panic-stricken people would attempt to sneak between the sentries, to flee, or they simply lay on the ground and covered their eyes with their hands as if they could burrow into the ground and disappear.

Whenever one became a problem, a centurion commanding a team of legionaries would look to General Crispus or Tribunus Tappulus for direction. It quickly became necessary that when shock-prodding was ineffective, the stragglers were to be Equanimitized.

The occasional burst of intense yellow light that accompanied the transformation of human flesh and bone into Nesslessness and Equanimity was so shocking a sight that even the most fear-stricken people found a way to keep moving so as to stay alive.

Within ten minutes of commencing the herding operation, the remaining congressmen and senators were assembled in their respective rectangles.

With everyone in place, Emperor Agricola gave a nod to General Crispus, who then ordered a squad from the Eleventh Cohort into action. Marcu's one-time students of Roman history, who had never seen Ancient Rome, performed impressively, bringing a little bit of the pomp and ceremony of ancient Rome to the National Mall. To Agricola, their parade as the procession marched past his podium, was close enough to what he considered 'the real thing.'

At the front of the squad was an aquilifer, an Aquila-bearer, proudly holding a long staff topped with the outstretched wings of the golden eagle – the *aquila* – clutching the fasces, the bundles of sticks that represented the collectives strength of Rome.

Below the aquila were the letters SPQVR – Senatus Populusque Universitatis Romanae – The Senate and People of Roman Cosmos, surrounded by two laurel wreaths.

Next came the signum of Cohort Eleven, with three disks stacked one on top of another. Followed by battle standards of the various cohorts involved in the day's action, and then the penultimate battle standard, that of LEG XXVII itself.

Next came what the senators had been nervously awaiting, and which the congressmen dreaded even more. Five pairs of men, each carrying the ends of two long poles on their shoulders, marched toward them. Between the poles was suspended a large wooden box.

In each of the boxes was a collection of short swords, pugio daggers, knives, battle-axes, clubs and spears.

As the procession marched along one side of the rectangle, each of the five pairs of soldiers stopped, so that by the time the lead element of the procession reached the end of the rectangle the five boxes of weapons were evenly spaced along the rectangle, suspended on the poles held by the legionaries.

A third man in each of the five parties separated himself from the pair he had marched behind. These men were not dressed in the splendidly coloured brass and leather battle-armor of the legionaries but rather in simpler leather and burlap coverings that seemed to indicate a much lower status.

The politicians soon learned that these men were from contemporary times, and spoke perfect English.

As they made their way into the throngs of senators, they bumped into a few of them, despite the skittish politicians' efforts to avoid being disintegrated or shocked as they had seen happen to some of their colleagues who had gotten too close to the Roman soldiers.

"Senators, here are your medallions. You will note that they are numbered, one through two hundred and fifty. The first one hundred are being distributed to the one hundred of you former US Senators. The remaining one hundred and fifty will be up for grabs for four hundred and forty or so plebeian representatives. Clearly, almost three hundred of them will find themselves without a medallion, and they are free to take yours – and your life – from you. Therefore, if you can keep your medallion, then you shall live," said each of the five of Marcus's milites as they handed out medallions to the senators nearest them.

When all of the senators had medallions, some of them tried to hide them under their shirts. Others tried to hide them in their pockets.

Marcus's students had been told that this would happen, and what to do about it.

"There is no point hiding your medallion. First of all, your colleagues from the House of Representatives know who you are. But also, how you handle yourself in this battle will go a long way to which state – which province actually – you will be permitted to represent and which other high offices you will be assigned. So your best bet is to wear these visibly on your chest and show some courage," was the standard speaking point, repeated down the line to the mob of senators.

"Hey, you speak English perfectly. You're not like those Romans. Who the fuck are you?" asked one of the senators.

"I am a milite, Senator, a common foot-soldier, hopefully earning my citizenship by competent service to Rome," was the standard reply.

After a surprise signal from Tribune Tappulus, the final fifty medallions were then thrown high into the air. As they rained down on the throng of men and women about to die, a few outstretched hands reached up. One hand made an outfielder's catch and quickly withdrew, disappearing into the melee that immediately ensued.

As hoped, the chance to grab hold of one of the unclaimed medallions was the first sign of hope for the bewildered representatives, as if having hold of a medallion would somehow let them wake up and the horrible nightmare they found themselves inside would be over.

To General Crispus, watching from the sidelines and much closer than Agricola's podium, the hand had looked like that of a woman. He had noticed that there were many women amongst the two groups of politicians, something that had not been discussed when they had planned the selection process.

General Crispus made his way back to the podium, making a quick hand-gesture at a centurion standing at the central point of the nearest edge of each battle-box.

On some silent cue from their centurion, the re-enactors-turned-legionaries of the Eleventh Cohort tilted the wooden crates, spilling the weapons onto the grass, and then moved back to rejoin the line of soldiers forming the outer perimeter.

Emperor Agricola nodded at General Crispus for the fine job he was doing in orchestrating the event, encouraging the general to sit beside him.

"Emperor, those are not my men. Those are the milites recruited by Tribune Avitus, here in America, the 'Eleventh Cohort.'"

"Impressive. See to it that they are counted amongst us with the same rights and privileges as the new soldiers from Metallorum. In fact, we may find that many are worthy of being immunes and higher, given how much they know about present-day America. They have proven their loyalty to Rome, now let's ensure that they are given suitable positions. Perhaps assign one to each of the 50 trios of Senators, in some sort of liaison and surveillance capacity?"

"Very wise, Imperator. That would leave us with nine of Marcus' milites. I can find places for them within our formation. I will pass this on to Tribune Avitus. Imperator, look, it begins!"

After a moment of inactivity, a few politicians suddenly dashed for the nearest pile of weapons. Immediately after, there was a mad rush from both groups, like the start of a dodge-ball game, only this was no game.

Fortunately for the senators not only had the weapons been dumped on their side of the battlefield, but the congressmen had been clustered on the far side of their rectangle, so in the race for weapons, the congressmen had that much farther to travel.

A few dozen congressmen were fast enough to make it to the weapons in time to snatch one or two, even as senators were grabbing weapons from the same pile. Those who had been fast but not fast enough were quickly cut or stabbed by the more aggressive senators.

With blood starting to be spilled, and the senators organizing themselves defensively, as they all had medallions and were therefore on the defense, the focus on the fighting became the small clusters of representatives who had caught, or who had picked up, one of the additional fifty medallions.

They immediately regretted it, however, as they suddenly realized that they were surrounded by colleagues without medallions, many of whom were now closing in on them, to take their medallions – and their lives.

After one congressman was killed, a voice rang out: "One down, plenty to go around!" Senator Randle, the youthful yet experienced Senior Senator from Texas had been among the first to accept the new reality that Roman rule represented – and the opportunities it created for him personally.

He made good use of the five minutes that he and the other senators has spent milling about in their rectangle on the west lawn of the Capitol Building, and had quietly organized several of them into something of a collective force.

Some of Senator Randle's men were like himself, former military men, and took instinctively to his commanding personality.

After grabbing as many weapons as they could get their hands on, and grabbing a few extra medallions wherever they could, the twenty or so senators moved as a group toward the northeast corner of their rectangle. Senator Randle had them form themselves into a wide arc. With the north and east perimeter behind them, thereby covering their left and right flanks, and with six of their group held back within the center of their cheese-wedge formation as a reserve, they fought off their attackers with Roma-type effectivenss. Their quick thinking impressed all the Roman soldiers.

"Remember, guys, shout out when you get tired and we'll rotate in fresh people, like the Romans used to....like the Romans do!" said Senator Randle, as he took his place at the center of the arc. "Bring it on you mutherfuckers!" he shouted.

Meanwhile the bloodbath that had begun in the representatives' rectangle had now spread to the senate rectangle. With blood being spilled all around them, and holding tightly to whatever weapon they had been able to acquire, the politicians were brought to that most basic of human instincts – kill or be killed.

Those senators who were not part of Senator Randle's group had backed away as far as they could from the line between the two rectangles. A few, those who were old, out of shape, or otherwise appeared to be easy prey, were attacked and killed by small groups of representatives who seized the opportunity.

Whenever this happened, nobody would come to the aid of the besieged. Soon, however, a number of the combatants emulated Senator Randle's tactic, and formed a defensive arc on the north-west corner but had not considered the creation of a reserve force. They lasted longer than most of the others, many of whom were massacred by the desperate mass of humanity that rushed at them in packs of five or six, overwhelming the lightly armed who had not organized themselves into any type of formation at all.

As each was killed, those who remained struggled for both the medallion and the weapon that had been in the hand of the fallen.

Each medallion became the focal point for a heap of sliced, desperate and profusely bleeding human beings.

What surprised many of the participants was the powerful surge of adrenalin and courage that some of them felt when, for the first time in their lives, they had found themselves fighting for their continuing existence.

Not unfamiliar to the Romans surrounding them or watching from farther back, the battle-lust feeling took hold of the congressmen and senators like a forest fire in a hot wind.

And it was all being broadcast on live television to an utterly shocked and incredulous world.

Some of Marcus's Eleventh Cohort had strategically infiltrated or attached themselves to TV crews who had been set up to interview politicians after the State of the Union. These crews had been told, as the incredible events of the day had unfolded, that their service as journalists for "Senatus Populusque Universitatis Romanae, SPQVR" was a golden opportunity for their careers – and their continued lives.

All of the reporters and their crews had chosen life, only a few had even considered sacrificing their lives in the name of professional ethics, human rights or the pledge of allegiance to the Constitution of the United States of America.

Many of the talking heads back in the studios had even fallen into giving an ad-hoc play-by-play, commenting on the heroic efforts, courage and terrible outcomes that the well-known political elites were experiencing live on television.

The battle seemed to last far longer for the participants than for the observers, but was finished in less than twenty minutes.

As the number of intact people became fewer, and those holding medallions but suffering from mortal or serious wounds were hunted down by the less wounded, it became clear that the membership of the inaugural Senates of Universitatis Romanae and Americanus Romanus had been largely determined.

On a signal from Tribune Tappulus, a number of soldiers moved in to provide mercy for the wounded politicians.

Mercy came in the form of a gladius through the back of the neck, into the spine, or any number of other fatal blows – depending on how the mortally-wounded politician was postured on the blood-soaked grass.

Those legionaries sent to kill the wounded and dying did so without equanimity fields, so rather than vaporizing their bodies as would happen with Equanimity fields, the fallen bodies remained largely intact. They were patriots and martyrs to the new nation, and they had earned that much respect.

When the immunes counted 250 remaining "new" senators possessing medallions, they signalled that the cull was sufficiently completed. milites from the Eleventh Cohort then rushed onto the field to halt all further combat.

"Stop fighting, it is over. You shall live!"

The politicians had for the most part, already stopped fighting. Most of them panting heavily after the sustained combat, the adrenalin still pumping through their arteries, their fine clothes bloodied.

"Emperor, we have two hundred and forty, however ten or more of them may not survive the day. Can we transfer the more serious casualties to a starship, and see if we can save them?"

"By all means," said Agricola. "How did that tall man who organized the arc formation over on the far side do? I lost sight of him in all the excitement."

"He did very well. Most of his band made it. And that leads me to the problem."

"Problem? I like problems! What is it?"

"The women."

"Women? I did not expect any of the women to survive. Were there some there from Hibernia or something?" joked the Emperor.

"Yes, Imperatus. Two had fought with Senator Randle's band, and did surprisingly well. One of them is injured, but will recover. Two others wound up with medallions that changed hands several times – very crafty those two, they spent most of the battle protecting each other and letting the battle grind along without them, and then moved in on their quarry towards the end to obtain medallions – very shrewd."

"And the other?" the emperor demanded, starting to be annoyed by the piece-meal way that Tribune Tappulus was giving up the information.

"She is very special, Dominus. I want her for myself."

"Have you gotten over that Hibernian scholar so quickly, Aulus?" Agricola teased, referring the fling that Tappulus had had with Marcus Avitus's young PhD student, Ruth Daley. "Who is she, Aulus?"

"She is that one the medical immunes are giving so much attention to. I call her 'Lupa'."

"The she-wolf? Why?"

"Because, Imperator, at the very start, I watched her catch a medallion we threw into the crowd of plebeian representatives.

Even surrounded by large men she somehow survived. I watched her in battle, Dominus. She was amazing. Your wife would have had no problem admitting her into her Hibernian ranks."

"How badly is she injured?"

"Unbelievably badly. Most men would not have survived with the same wounds, yet she lives."

"Well don't just stand there, Tappulus, get her into a starship."

"But I need a decision first, Imperatus."

"On what?"

"Women cannot be senators, can they?"

"I have never thought about it," said Agricola. "Certainly they could not, back in the Rome of our time. But this is a different time, and these are a different people," he began. "And given the fact that Vibius Metellus has already had me elevate so many of the Hibernian women to high offices that would normally only go to men, perhaps we should allow women to serve in Senatus Romani Americae," he mused out loud.

"Imperator, if I may, that would be a good decision," interjected Vibius Metellus, who had been listening and had heard his name used, taking that as an invitation to join the discussion.

"Why is that Vibius?"

"Because you already told these people that if they earned a medallion, then they earn a place in one of the two senates. That speaks to your credibility as a man of honour, and…"

"Very well. Make it so. Vibius, make sure you pass this on to Marcus and Fabius, and ensure that Consul Cerialis adds this to the Inaugural Decrees."

"And Lupa?" asked Tappulus, showing concern as he watched her being carried toward a starship.

"Get on with it, Tribune. Save the female so that she can serve us in the Senatus Universitatis. Take your lady to the command ship. We'll have one of Marcus's milites find out if there is a husband to murder. Be as Romulus and kidnap your Sabine maiden – just be sure to be a better husband to her than you were to your last wife!" Agricola said, referring to the

Hibernian woman Tappulus had been paired with, but whom had refused to accompany him to Terra. Leaving her behind on Planeta Metallorum had made Tappulus the butt of some very cruel jokes, which he had reveled in for the joy of being freed from the woman that, even with Tuathii help, simply was incompatible with him.

Tribune Tappulus did not have to be told twice.

As he watched the Tribune rush off after the women he was so desperate to save, Emperor Agricola was happy to see the powerful bachelor finally in love again. Agricola hoped she would live, and be the first ever woman to serve on any Roman Senate.

Of course, a woman will never be emperor.

XXVIII

TYRANNI DELENDI SUNT
{ DEATH TO ALL TYRANTS }

Walking along the National mall to visit *sepulchrum tyranny,* the grave of the tyrant, Kaeso Cerialis was brought back to his happy childhood days with Julius Agricola and sweet sister, Julia, in Ostia, the ancient site of Rome. Perhaps his memory had been triggered by the sweet, cake-like aroma of the nearby *arbor roseaus,* Judas Trees. No longer required for the starships, the Tuathii had been settled on Earth and on the scores of new planetae that had been discovered and settled by the Roman Empire of the Cosmos, Universitatis Romanae.

As he walked along the row of Judas Trees that stood sentinel over the sacred Field of Patriots, he took stock of all that had transpired since Emperor Agricola had seized the organs of power of the United States, and, ultimately, Planet Earth.

In addition to the two parallel rows of Judas Trees, there was the ever-present Honor Guard of the SPQAR Marines, stationed at the four corners of the lawn area below the *Universitatis* and *Americanus* Senate Chambers. The lawn itself, the scene of the bloody massacre four decades earlier, was now a sacred site for all of RomaCosmi. Known as *agri patriota*, Field of Patriots, the lawn area was a constant reminder that the first senate of RomaCosmi, and that of Romani Americae, had been borne out of the sacrifice of the Plebian Representatives and Senators of the United States. The two hundred and forty-five survivors of that day had gone on to serve Rome as senators administering to the details of Emperor Agricola's *actum horibilis*, the brutal agenda that transformed the earth.

It had all started on the Sunday, two days after the events which took place at the Field of Patriots. Those who had been tricked by Agricola's direction to take refuge in the larger cities were obliterated by a storm of comets. Agricola had lied about where best to find sanctuary, but he had told a partial truth about the storm being a Tuathii storm. It had been puller-ships operated by Tuathii-led crews that had been dispatched to the asteroid belt in the months before the invasion, with orders to tug, nudge, and steer wave after wave of moderate sized asteroids into a collision-course with planet Earth.

With their experience at Planetae Caedum and Bellorum, the Tuathii were adept at calculating the forces required, and at coordinating their Octopodii crewmembers to achieve highly accurate placements toward the targeted cities. The target list had been carefully prepared by Antoninus, to ensure that the right mass, with the right trajectory, would obliterate the designated city, and avoid damaging the nuclear reactors and other toxic facilities that were found on one extremity or another, so as to allow for these to be safely powered down by and cleaned up afterwards.

Gravity and kinetic energy did the rest.

Agricola had ordered that the one hundred largest cities on earth were to be hit nearly simultaneously on that *diem infāmis*, day of infamy, in a brutal show of force that was designed to put every nation on earth into complete social collapse.

The Tyrant had a number of objectives which were all achieved on that day. First and foremost, he wanted to give the world such a brutal show of force that would leave no doubt as to the power within his command. He could destroy an entire nation at will, and the threat of more asteroids was held over the heads of any and all nations that resisted his rule. As it was, he had the Tuathii park hundreds of small asteroids in earth orbit, ready to be directed toward any designated target as required.

Second, and the reason for his having tricked untold millions of people to congregate in the largest cities, was that he had come to the conclusion that the populations of the largest cities were entirely surplus and expendable. In his cold, calculating mind, vaporizing the largest cities would make a sizable dent in what he saw as an obscenely overpopulated world. Taking their industry and other polluting infrastructure out of existence at the same time was simple efficiency.

But not all of the Romans had agreed. There had been heated debate on the issue. Agricola's officers and advisors had been split into three camps. The first group, led by Cerialis himself, argued that after a show of force, humanity could be forced to come to terms with the need to control population growth, reduce excessive pollution, to voluntarily de-industrialize their economies, and to use technologia and inventiveness to find ways to be less harmful to the air, soil, and water.

The second group, led by Fabius Quintilianus, believed that the fate of the Quadrupedii, with the collapse of their ecological system, was so far off into the future that no immediate action needed to be taken, that the science of climactic change was not proven and therefore did not provide a sufficient rationale for taking such drastic action. Furthermore, he felt that, given the incredible technological creativity of manking, a concerted effort to resolve the problems of the earth could have been found if humankind had the will – which would be enforced by a Roman dictatorship.

A third group, led by Marcus Avitus, wanted Agricola to go much further, to wage war on the population centers until the largest 1,000 were destroyed, along with nearly two billion inhabitants, in order to completely clear the largest cities – the sources of pollution and consumption – off of the surface of the planet.

The tyrant Agricola had listened to their arguments without revealing his personal views, and had then made the decree: We will simultaneously destroy their 100 largest cities. According to the calculations we have seen, this will remove eight hundred million out of eight billion, decimation, one in ten.

Obedient to their emperor more than to their own opinions, the officers then set about with the necessary preparations.

In the immediate aftermath of the *diem infāmis*, it had become apparent that scholars of antiquity, lovers of Rome, had avoided the cities, just as Agricola had intended with his hidden message. Whether they had heard it in the newscasts, or by word spread within their social groups or over the internet, many had understood that as Domitian was the brother, not son, of Emperor Titus, then what Agricola had said was an obvious lie. Therefore rather than *safety*, the cities would be the *worst place to be* on that day.

In a similar way, the comment about the shelter of a tent, for a contubernium, eight-man tent group, the fundamental building-block of the Roman legion, told Romaphiles and even some intuitive lay-persons that the guidance meant: *go camping with just what you need to be as a common foot soldier.*

With many of their cities destroyed, and the entire world in turmoil, groups formed, and began to organize themselves as supplicants to the inevitable arrival of representatives of the Universal Roman Senate, to embrace the rule of the Romans.

Following Marcus Avitus's strategic and political plans, Agricola had decreed that educated Romaphiles from the regions would be given elevated status, linked politically to the

RomaCosmi senate, in order to build up a new hierarchy of loyal forces to rule and to administer the territories.

All borders were to be redrawn along social, cultural, and linguistic lines, resulting in new nations being formed, and negotiating their place in the new RomaCosmi order.

With carbon-based fuel systems having been outlawed, other than for Roman-authorized uses, and with international air travel permanently shut down, the world suddenly became much larger.

Rather than a global society, and with the destruction of their national governments and larger cities, the new nations had to reorganize themselves on a more localized, smaller scale.

Over the ensuring years, as the Roman Americae dominance of the gradually reshaped world expanded, new factories were constructed, manufacturing thorium-powered locomotives and ships, so that cargoes could be moved across oceans and continents, albeit much more slowly.

The order of the way was sustainability, and great effort was expended to modify agricultural practices to be more locally-based, not requiring the vast amounts of fertilizers, mechanization, and scale of the abandoned ways. Large, mechanized corporate farms that relied on machines collapsed, and were taken over by the small farmer. America had been forced, by necessity, to return to its rural roots.

The resulting dislocations, however, had disastrous effects. Some regions fared reasonably well; some had excesses in one commodity and shortages in another; but a great many regions suffered hardships that they had not experienced for centuries.

Famine, pestilence, and death walked the planet for a decade, killing millions.

And there were wars. Not massive wars between nation-states, but small-scale wars between small city-states and principalities. This was particularly so in Europe and some parts of Asia, where feudalism was a natural fit for the small villages which, with the larger cities having been erased from the surface of the earth, became small bastions of power, until Roman control extended its reach farther into the hinterland.

It had taken a great deal of time for the de-industrialization and re-organization of the economies of the world to be able to sustain their reduced populations, to support collective effort, and to ensure that people did not starve in winter.

All of this had been as expected by Agricola and his officers, as it had been predicted by the expected sequence of events – first planned and then executed by the Romans – that had so altered the course of human history.

But there had been another, parallel, sequence of events that had not been forecast. A second group of people, versed in Latin and the study of antiquity, had also taken heed of Agricola's hidden message.

Some of the Christians and other well-organized people of faith had not been so easily fooled. Rabbis, Priests, Imams, and scholars within their communities had pointed out Agricola's lie, and had understood that they were being led like sheep to a slaughter, along with the rest of the urban populations of Terra.

Considerable numbers had organized themselves, stayed away from the cities, and been saved by their faith.

Among them, in Romani Americanae, was the first man to find a way to kill a Roman.

A former Colonel in the United States Marine Corp, Colonel Benjamin Davis had seen what Tribune Tappulus had done, using the laser-pointer to bring the trained monster-flea down on the vocal senator who had tried to stir up resolve inside the House Chamber.

Davis had made a mental note of it, and laid low like so many other Christians and devout believers of other faiths. Davis understood that the war against the Romans was just beginning. He hid his true allegiance to God, and had gone along with what he was required to do as a soldier under Roman command, always knowing that the time would come when his beliefs would force him to act.. When the time had come to lead his force of conscripts and proto-citizens to attack a hold-out group of Christians, ordered as he had been to clear the pocket of resistance in a hilly region of what has once been called 'North

Carolina', Colonel – turned – Centurion, Davis, had decided to make a stand.

The moment had been quite fortuitous. If it had not been for the arrival of some original Romans, a tribune from Davis's legion, with a cadre of harnessed Siphonapteristii, Davis would have been forced to fight fellow Christians. But thanks to the tribune's desire to rape a young woman that had been taken into custody, Davis saw an opportunity. He communicated his intent to some of his fellow Christian patriots with no more than meaningful eye-contact. They understood what he was about to do, and acted accordingly.

As Davis and his co-conspirators pretended to supervise the monstrous fleas, the tribune turned off his personal Equanimity-field generator so that he could grasp the shirt of the docile young woman. His intent was to drag her into a nearby building, rape her, and either kill her or throw her back into holding with the other prisoners. So intent was he on what he was going to do to the girl, he did not see all of the eyes that watched, spellbound and hopeful, as a laser-pointer was focused on his back.

By the time he sensed that something was wrong, and turned to look back over his shoulder, one of Davis's compatriots had released the giant flea's harness.

The tribune saw a shadow coming toward him and frantically reached for the control to activate his Equanimity-field, but he was too slow. His right hand was still clasped to the control when his entire arm was ripped out of his his shoulder by the monster.

They can be killed, was a thought shared by Colonel Davis and his fellow Christians. *We have done this before, and we can do it again*, he resolved.

Details of that incident and others like it had spread like wildfire through the underground pockets of patriots and Christians hidden within the slaves, conscripts, and probationary citizens of Romani Americanae, and had been the start of *Proelium Americanum*, the battle for America.

That struggle had begun only a few years ago, Cerialis reflected, when the Christians among the Senate Populusque

Americanus Romanus, SPQAR, had revealed their true loyalty and demanded that the outlaw status of Christianity be lifted.

They had not gone so far as demanding that Christianity should be the official religion of Americanus Romanus, but that day would surely come, he knew.

For Kaeso, they would never know if the tyrant had been right or wrong in his course of action, but it was no longer an important question. The issue had seemed important at the time, when they had debated it hotly before the conquest of America.

Perhaps it was all Vibius Metellus's fault, for comparing belief in climate change to reductio ad absurdum, the agnostic paradox, Kaeso reflected. Vibius had stated that for a non-believer in a singular God, such as the God of the Christians, Muslims, or Jews, it is necessary to become a believer out of the logic that, if the premise of a singular God is true, then believing in it is prudent. However, if there is not a singular God, then belief in this construct would do no harm – a harmless folly. However, to *not* believe in the one God – if He truly exists – would be unwise, as God might take vengeance on the unbeliever and punish him in some way. Therefore, the logic, if taken to an absurdity, is that one must believe in God because to not do so would entail an unacceptable and completely unnecessary risk.

Quintilianus had gone on to say that it was the same with climate science. To believe that humankind is the cause of the drastic imbalances in the climate, were it true, would be prudent. To believe it even if the science were not truth would do no harm. However, to *not* believe the science of climate change, and have it turn out to be true, would be an unacceptable risk as the consequences of not doing anything about man's impact on the earth would be to invite dire consequences, an unacceptable and unnecessary risk.

At the time, Agricola had not revealed his spiritual beliefs. He did not express his view about whether there were many Gods – as the Romans believed, a singular God – as the Christians and other monotheists believed, or that the Godhead was merely the Equanimity that is in all things, and is not aware – as the Tuathii believed. For all Kaeso knew, Agricola could have even ecome an atheist.

Agricola also did not reveal whether he believed climactic change was caused by human activity, or whether it was simply part of the natural cycle, as many citizens of Romani Americanae believed. One thing that was certain was that when they had been on their odyssey through the Tuathii star systems, Agricola had been repulsed by what had taken place at Planeta Caedum. He had said that he would destroy all of Rome before he would permit the number of inhabitants to become so excessive and unsupportable so as to result in people resorting to eating food that was made from, well, *people*.

Throughout the forty years of his reign on Earth, Agricola had held fast to whatever his beliefs were. He was determined to transform the way of living into one that could sustain humanity for millennia without sacrificing nature. And he was hated for it.

He was the biggest mass-murderer in the history of mankind. He destroyed the cities of the world and took away all of the comforts and amusements of the early twenty-first century. But, it was his taking away their freedoms that made him the most hated tyrant in history.

Whether in the form of the Charter of Rights and Freedoms, the principles of the Declaration of Independence, or any other source, the people of the world had once had something that bestowed upon them the essential notion of *freedom*. Under the tyrant, Agricola, they had none. Each and every day involved toil, want, struggle, and sacrifice. Life was contingent upon pleasing their Roman masters, or having scraped together enough food and other essentials to sustain themselves and their loved ones through winter, and they had to do it without gasoline or other combustible fossil fuels.

The little bit of electricity to which most were entitled was barely enough to provide lighting and refrigeration for their food supplies. There was no television, computer, or other distractions in the homes of slaves and proto-citizens. Only full citizens, limited to one in ten of the population, were permitted these pleasures. And even for the citizens, there were very few amenities in comparison to their past ways.

The hatred of the slaves and lowest ranked citizens was a constant threat in the early years of Agricola's tyranny.

In order to take their minds off of their discontent, Agricola first attempted to distract them, by instituting reforms that would create a pathway toward citizenship for an increased proportion of the population, but that did not satisfy the masses.

He then tried to revive the thrilling sport and entertainment of past Emperors of Rome, to distract the population by bringing back the tradition of gladiators, and various forms of sporting competitions, but that was met with mixed success.

In Americana Romana, small-town football stadiums became popular again, as playing a Roman form of professional football was declared a path to citizenship – bestowing all the benefits that came with becoming part of the ruling class. There was a catch, however, decreed by the Tyrant himself, that at the end of the season all teams within a net losing record, regardless of which region or territory they played in, would be lined up – coaching staff and all players alike – and would be ceremoniously decimated. The survivors would be provided proto-citizenship, and a modestly comfortable lifestyle. Citizenship was only for the victorious teams.

Yet even in America Romana, with the stronger economy that came with being the center of Universitas Romana power, and with better opportunities to become part of a colonist venture, there was a long memory to life before the Romans.

Forced to comply with the harsh rules dictated to them, the people hated the tyrant who occasionally rewarded their contempt with ruthlessness, ordering the slaughter of entire communities if an original Roman or a highly placed Romani Americae citizen was murdered.

Eventually, however, after decades had passed, people became habituated to the new way of life. They had made new traditions based on a much more localized way of living, and were far more involved with each other than in the former, largely suburban way of living. Because of the de-industrialized way of life, people had to work together more, cooperate, and interact. For some, this was somehow more fulfilling than their old way of life, despite the austerity of it. Homes were small, spartan, and full of life. People found ways to be content. In many cases, this was also accompanied by turning to religion, a variety of which had spread in different forms across the Universal Roman Empire. Unlike the Roman Empire of the first millennium, however, there was no singular 'official' religion, and in this, people had that one thing that had been taken away from them by the Tyrant – freedom to choose. At least, freedom to choose what they believed.

For the first time in human history, the promise of the original Rome was fulfilled – an empire that spanned the entire world and had vanquished all enemies, terrestrial or extraterrestrial.

And then the final days of the reign of Agricola the Tyrant had come. Forty years after the conquest of America, all of the 'original' Romans had gathered once again on Terra, having returned to Washington at the appointed time from their landholdings in the provinces of Earth or from nearby habitable planetae. The elderly Emperor Agricola was to address the Senatus Juncturam, the combined session of the Senates of Universitatis Romanae and of Americanus Romanus, in the very chamber where President Ross had been Equanimitized by Emperor Agricola.

Unlike all the other original Romans, Agricola and Laelie had chosen to never again travel to the stars. Many believed it was because the Tyrant was so obsessed with his project of de-industrializing the earth that he would not trust it to another person. Others believed that he simply was addicted to power, and enjoyed sitting in on the Roma-Cosmi Senate, jumping in whenever he liked with his occasional decree, or to personally sever the head of an excessively corrupt senator or other traitor to the Tyrant's principles of moderation, honesty, and prudence.

Whatever his reasons, the consequence was that he aged at a normal pace. For the other originals and highest level of modern-era senators and other nobles, with their frequent trips to the nearest planetae, the beneficial effects of space travel and exposure to Equanimity effects kept them young and vigorous.

But even to the end of his time, the Tyrant remained in control of his people.

In his address to the Senatus Juncturam, no others were given a speaking role – not even the pro-consul, Kaeso Cerialis. The disclosure of the many discoveries of rich, habitable planetae that the returned originals had explored, was made by the Tyrant. But for the first time in his reign on earth, Agricola seemed to exhibit a kinder, warmer side than anybody had seen of the Tyrant.

Rather than be jealous, Kaeso was sincerely happy to see his friend delivering good news, and generating excitement about a new wave of colonies.

However, as Emperor Agricola continued with his speech, summarizing the great progress that had been made in balancing the needs of the inhabitants of Earth with the limited capacity of the planet, and fully implementing Roman rule over every community on the planet, Kaeso began to sense a problem.

In preparing for the grand gathering of originals, and discussing the way forward, the two men had agreed that Universitas Romana, had reached the intended level of stability. There was a sufficiently strong military, with an ever-increasing fleet of thorium-powered spacecraft to continue the expansion and settlement of a growing list of habitable colonies, expanding the Roman Empire farther into uncharted space. There was effective policing and administrative control across the entire planet. There had been no hint of aggressive threats from beyond, not even the dreaded Tuathii – which Kaeso suspected never really was a threat.

More importantly, with a stable population of just three billion inhabitants who were living in a much more sustainable manner, the ecology of the Earth seemed to have come a long way to restoring itself – weather patterns had become moderated and predictable, soil, air and water quality had improved, and the long list of species under threat of extinction seemed to be returning. Certainly much of that was due to the outlawing of poaching endangered species, and other ecology-stabilizing benefits of a well-policed planet. Kaeso believed there had been some truth to the theory that excessive pollution and strain on the environment had been abated by the ruthless actions taken by Emperor Agricola. The tyrant's decrees that had forced slaves to replant massive forests and to rehabilitate formerly fouled streams may also have helped. But most significant was the fact that people no longer drove automobiles, and extensive networks of paved roads no longer had to be maintained. Travel was now by thorium-powered trains, boat, bicycle, horseback, and on foot.

People also no longer travelled great distances, or only rarely and by slower, less pollution-intensive means. With the bigger cities largely destroyed, life was now centered around the village where one lived and worked. Those changes were now the status quo, and were working very well. The yearning of the slaves and citizens to have large families was no longer a problem, what with the need for millions of colonists to serve as settler-citizens in the new colonies, seemingly departing on a daily basis.

So when Agricola put down the final page of the prepared speech, and began to speak extemporaneously from his head and heart and not from the written text, Kaeso felt the hairs on his neck begin to stand up.

Quintus, what in the name of the Gods are you doing?

"So despite all that we have accomplished here on Terra, and despite the peace and prosperity we are enjoying, it is not yet the time for me to retire," Agricola continued, drawing shocked silence and consternation from the senators and guests, most notably from the originals who knew him best.

"After touring the planet one more time, perhaps with some of you, my old friends, Laelie and I, along with our two children, will go away on a journey to investigate reports of an entirely new race that we believe is expanding into our portion of the cosmos. They may be hostile, or they may be amenable to negotiation. I must speak for all of you, for all of RomaCosmi, when I encounter them. Therefore I shall continue as Emperor until that, and any subsequent tasks, have been achieved."

Silence befell the chamber.

There has been no such report, thought Kaeso, alarmed.

Everybody knew that this was not what was supposed to happen. The historians, the original Romans, and even the priests of the multitude of religions now tolerated in RomaCosmi – all had expected the emperor to keep to his word and to retire, and to restore the Republic by returning all of his powers to the Universal Roman Senate.

In the still air of the chamber, it was as if an entire planet held its breath.

Emperor Agricola and Proconsul Cerialis locked eyes for an intense moment. In that exchange, as the elderly man looked into the impossibly young face of this friend, Kaeso Cerialis, the old Tyrant gave a tired, loving look.

Kaeso suddenly understood what was going on, and what he was really being asked to do.

Upon the subtle nod from Quintus Gnaeus Julius Agricola, *Dominus et Deus*, Imperatus Augustus Victrix Cosmi, master of the known universe, Kaeso sprang up and ran to his lifelong friend, drawing his pugio dagger from his belt.

Raising his hands defensively out of pure instinct, the Emperor was able to hold off his attacker for only a moment. As other originals joined in, some shouting *"sic semper tyrannis!* death to the tyrant!"* the old man could not hold them off.

The three closest attackers sensed the moment that the Tyrant was defeated, and all thrust their blades in rapid succession. Kaeso's pugio was the first, penetrating Agricola's stomach, drawing a painful cry.

An instant later, Tribune Tappulus drove his gladius in through Agricola's left side, striking bone that halted the short sword's progress. Finally Marcus Avitus shoved his pugio into the Emperor's other side, penetrating his right lung.

Held up for the moment by the three men standing around him, with many others surrounding them, knives drawn, but holding back as they watched the three originals hold their leader between them, Agricola watched as his blood poured onto their guilty hands.

Looking up from his mortal wounds, Agricola smiled at each in turn, and then stared at Kaeso as his life left him.

Suddenly life returned to his eyes, as if he had returned for some forgotten thing, and he looked urgently at Kaeso, and whispered: *"Gaudeo te hoc fecisse,* I'm glad that you did it..."*

ACTA EST FABVLA, PLAVDITE!

{ THE END - ACCOLADES! }

EPILOGUE

You have just completed the *Return of the Romans* odyssey. As you reflect on what you have read, a Tuatha root has just made contact with your leg. You suddenly have an overwhelming urge to go to www.amazon.com and post a book review. Somehow, it has been infused into your consciousness that posting a detailed, honest review, going into detail with lots of words about the good points and bad, is the only way to satisfy this urgent need to share the experience with others.

ABOUT THE AUTHOR

Gene Skellig is a former military pilot planning to retiring in the Ottawa reagion to take up writing full-time. With four young children to raise and a few lifetimes of dreams yet to fulfil, Gene's retirement will be very busy.

With an eclectic range of interests and a curious mind, there is no telling what new challenge he will take up next. One thing is certain, however, and that is that Gene Skellig loves to write! Much of his writing draws on the wide variety of experiences he has had in his life so far. The people he encounters each and every day provide the inspiration for his novels. To have a reader actually buy one of his book, let alone to to post a review or provide some other form of feedback, this is one of the small rewards that Gene appreciates most. It is a constant reminder that without readers it would be pointless to write.

To Gene, that moment between the desire to have achieved something and fact of having achieved it is the precise moment of equanimity. This moment of equanimity is addictive and profoundly satisfying.

Check out these other Gene Skellig books:

$3.50 off *Winter Kill – War With China Has Already Begun:* www.createspace.com/3537111 enter code PAC6SETA

$2.50 off *Homestay – A Japanese Girl's Romantic ESL Adventure In Vancouver,* **Canada**: www.createspace.com/ 3715916 enter code 9JGPMV3B

Lost Child (Volume One) - Anguish in the Nantahala http://www.amazon.com/dp/B007IK2MBA

Lost Child (Volume Two) - Retribution in the Nantahala http://www.amazon.com/dp/B0089Y0PEA